HAPPY
Ever
AFTER

Nora Roberts

HOT ICE
SACRED SINS
BRAZEN VIRTUE
SWEET REVENGE
PUBLIC SECRETS
GENUINE LIES
CARNAL INNOCENCE
DIVINE EVIL
HONEST ILLUSIONS
PRIVATE SCANDALS
HIDDEN RICHES
TRUE BETRAYALS
MONTANA SKY
SANCTUARY
HOMEPORT

THE REEF
RIVER'S END
CAROLINA MOON
THE VILLA
MIDNIGHT BAYOU
THREE FATES
BIRTHRIGHT
NORTHERN LIGHTS
BLUE SMOKE
ANGELS FALL
HIGH NOON
TRIBUTE
BLACK HILLS
THE SEARCH

Series

Irish Born Trilogy

BORN IN FIRE
BORN IN ICE
BORN IN SHAME

Key Trilogy

KEY OF LIGHT
KEY OF KNOWLEDGE
KEY OF VALOR

Dream Trilogy

DARING TO DREAM
HOLDING THE DREAM
FINDING THE DREAM

In the Garden Trilogy

BLUE DAHLIA
BLACK ROSE
RED LILY

Chesapeake Bay Saga

SEA SWEPT
RISING TIDES
INNER HARBOR
CHESAPEAKE BLUE

Circle Trilogy

MORRIGAN'S CROSS
DANCE OF THE GODS
VALLEY OF SILENCE

Gallaghers of Ardmore Trilogy

JEWELS OF THE SUN
TEARS OF THE MOON
HEART OF THE SEA

Sign of Seven Trilogy

BLOOD BROTHERS
THE HOLLOW
THE PAGAN STONE

Three Sisters Island Trilogy

DANCE UPON THE AIR
HEAVEN AND EARTH
FACE THE FIRE

Bride Quartet

VISION IN WHITE
BED OF ROSES
SAVOR THE MOMENT
HAPPY EVER AFTER

Nora Roberts & J. D. Robb

REMEMBER WHEN

J. D. Robb

Anthologies

FROM THE HEART
A LITTLE MAGIC
A LITTLE FATE

MOON SHADOWS
(with Jill Gregory, Ruth Ryan Langan, and Marianne Willman)

The Once Upon Series
(with Jill Gregory, Ruth Ryan Langan, and Marianne Willman)
ONCE UPON A CASTLE
ONCE UPON A STAR
ONCE UPON A DREAM
ONCE UPON A ROSE
ONCE UPON A KISS
ONCE UPON A MIDNIGHT

* * *

SILENT NIGHT
(with Susan Plunkett, Dee Holmes, and Claire Cross)

OUT OF THIS WORLD
(with Laurell K. Hamilton, Susan Krinard, and Maggie Shayne)

BUMP IN THE NIGHT
(with Mary Blayney, Ruth Ryan Langan, and Mary Kay McComas)

DEAD OF NIGHT
(with Mary Blayney, Ruth Ryan Langan, and Mary Kay McComas)

THREE IN DEATH

SUITE 606
(with Mary Blayney, Ruth Ryan Langan, and Mary Kay McComas)

THE LOST
(with Patricia Gaffney, Mary Blayney, and Ruth Ryan Langan)

Also available . . .

THE OFFICIAL NORA ROBERTS COMPANION
(edited by Denise Little and Laura Hayden)

NORA ROBERTS

HAPPY
Ever
AFTER

BERKLEY BOOKS, NEW YORK

THE BERKLEY PUBLISHING GROUP
Published by the Penguin Group
Penguin Group (USA) Inc.
375 Hudson Street, New York, New York 10014, USA
Penguin Group (Canada), 90 Eglinton Avenue East, Suite 700, Toronto, Ontario M4P 2Y3, Canada
(a division of Pearson Penguin Canada Inc.)
Penguin Books Ltd., 80 Strand, London WC2R 0RL, England
Penguin Group Ireland, 25 St. Stephen's Green, Dublin 2, Ireland (a division of Penguin Books Ltd.)
Penguin Group (Australia), 250 Camberwell Road, Camberwell, Victoria 3124, Australia
(a division of Pearson Australia Group Pty. Ltd.)
Penguin Books India Pvt. Ltd., 11 Community Centre, Panchsheel Park, New Delhi—110 017, India
Penguin Group (NZ), 67 Apollo Drive, Rosedale, North Shore 0632, New Zealand
(a division of Pearson New Zealand Ltd.)
Penguin Books (South Africa) (Pty.) Ltd., 24 Sturdee Avenue, Rosebank, Johannesburg 2196,
South Africa

Penguin Books Ltd., Registered Offices: 80 Strand, London WC2R 0RL, England

This book is an original publication of The Berkley Publishing Group.

This is a work of fiction. Names, characters, places, and incidents either are the product of the author's imagination or are used fictitiously, and any resemblance to actual persons, living or dead, business establishments, events, or locales is entirely coincidental. The publisher does not have any control over and does not assume responsibility for author or third-party websites or their content.

ISBN 978-1-61129-019-6

PRINTED IN THE UNITED STATES OF AMERICA

To my guys,
Bruce, Dan, Jason, and Logan

Love sought is good, but given
unsought is better.

—WILLIAM SHAKESPEARE

Beauty from order springs.

—WILLIAM KING

PROLOGUE

GRIEF CAME IN WAVES, HARD AND CHOPPY, BUFFETING AND BREAK-
ing the heart. Other days the waves were slow and swamping,
threatening to drown the soul.

People—good, caring people—claimed time would heal.
Parker hoped they were right, but as she stood on her bedroom
terrace in the late-summer sun, months after the sudden, shocking
deaths of her parents, those capricious waves continued to roll.

She had so much, she reminded herself. Her brother—and she
didn't know if she'd have survived this grieving time without
Del—had been a rock to cling to in that wide, wide ocean of
shock and sorrow. Her friends Mac, Emma, Laurel, a part of her
life, a part of *her*, since childhood. They'd been the glue mending
and holding all the shattered pieces of her world. She had the
constant, unshakable support of their longtime housekeeper, Mrs.
Grady, her island of comfort.

She had her home. The beauty and elegance of the Brown

Estate seemed deeper, sharper to her somehow, knowing she wouldn't see her parents strolling through the gardens. She'd never again run downstairs and find her mother laughing in the kitchen with Mrs. G, or hear her father wheeling a deal in his home office.

Instead of learning to ride those waves, she'd felt herself being swept deeper and deeper down into the dark.

Time, she'd determined, needed to be used and pushed and *moved*.

She thought—hoped—she'd found a way, not only to use that time, but to celebrate what her parents had given her, to unite those gifts with family and friendships.

To be productive, she mused as the first spicy scents of coming autumn stirred the air. The Browns *worked*. They built and they produced and they never, never sat back to laze on accomplishments.

Her parents would have expected her to do no less than those who'd come before her.

Her friends might think she'd lost her mind, but she'd researched, calculated, and outlined a solid business plan, a sturdy model. And with Del's help, a fair and reasonable legal contract.

Time to swim, she told herself.

She simply wouldn't sink.

She walked back into the bedroom, picked up the four thick packets she'd set on her dresser. One for each of them for the meeting—though she hadn't told her friends they were coming to a meeting.

She paused, took a moment to tie back her glossy brown hair in a tail, then simply stared into her own eyes, willing a spark to light in the deep blue.

She could make this work. No, no, *they* could make this work.

She just had to convince them first.

Downstairs, she found Mrs. Grady putting the finishing touches on the meal.

The sturdy woman turned from the stove, gave her a wink. "Ready?"

"Prepared anyway. I'm nervous. Is it silly to be nervous? They're my closest friends in the world."

"It's a big step you're looking to take, a big one you'll ask them to take. You'd be foolish if you weren't a bit nervous." She stepped over, took Parker's face in her hands. "My money's on you. Go on out. I've gone a little fancy, so you'll have hors d'oeuvres and wine on the terrace. My girls are all grown up."

She wanted to be, but God, there was a child inside her who wanted her mom and dad, the comfort, the love, the security.

Outside, she set the packets on a table, then crossed over to take the wine out of its cooler, pour herself a glass.

Then simply stood, holding the glass, looking out in the softening light over the gardens to the pretty little pond and the reflection of the willows mirrored on its surface.

"God! Do I want some of that."

Laurel bolted out, her sunny blond hair brutally short—a new look her friend already regretted. She hadn't changed out of her uniform from her position as dessert chef at an upscale local restaurant.

Her eyes, bright and blue, rolled as she poured her wine. "Who knew when I changed my schedule to make our Girl Night we'd get a last-minute lunch reservation for twenty? The kitchen was a madhouse all afternoon. Mrs. G's kitchen now . . ." She let out a huge groan as she dropped down to sit after hours on her feet. "It's an oasis of calm that smells like heaven. What's for dinner?"

"I didn't ask."

"Doesn't matter." Laurel waved it away. "But if Emma and Mac are late, I'm starting without them." She spotted the stack of packets. "What's all that?"

"Something that can't start without them. Laurel, do you want to go back to New York?"

Laurel eyed her over the rim of her glass. "Are you kicking me out?"

"I guess I want to know what you want. If you're satisfied with how things are. You moved back for me, after the accident, and—"

"I'm taking it a day at a time, and figure I'll figure it out. Right now, not having a plan's working for me. Okay?"

"Well . . ."

She broke off as Mac and Emma came out together, laughing.

Emma, she thought, so beautiful with her mass of hair curling madly, her dark, exotic eyes bright with fun. Mac, her bold red hair choppy in tufts, green eyes wickedly amused, lean and long in her jeans and black shirt.

"What's the joke?" Laurel demanded.

"Men." Mac set down the plates of brie *en croute* and spinach tartlets Mrs. Grady had shoved into her hands on the way through the kitchen. "The two of them who thought they could arm wrestle for Emma."

"It was kind of sweet," Emma insisted. "They were brothers and came into the shop for flowers for their mother's birthday. One thing led to the other."

"Guys come into the studio all the time." Mac popped a sugared red grape into her mouth from the bowl already on the table. "None of them ever arm wrestle each other for a date with me."

"Some things never change," Laurel said, raising her glass to Emma.

"Some things do," Parker spoke out. She had to start, had to move. "That's why I asked you all to come tonight."

Emma paused as she reached for the brie. "Is something wrong?"

"No. But I wanted to talk to you all, at once." Determined, Parker poured wine for Mac and Emma. "Let's sit down."

"Uh-oh," Mac warned.

"No uh-ohs," Parker insisted. "I want to say first, I love you all so much, and have forever. And will forever. We've shared so much, good and bad. And when things were at their worst, I knew you'd be there."

"We're all there for each other." Emma leaned over and laid a hand on Parker's. "That's what friends do."

"Yes, it is. I want you to know how much you mean to me, and want you to know that if any of you don't want to try what I'm about to propose, for any reason at all, it changes nothing between us."

She held up a hand before anyone could speak. "Let me start this way. Emma, you want your own florist business one day, right?"

"It's always been the dream. I mean I'm happy working in the shop, and the boss gives me a lot of leeway, but I hope, down the road, to have my own. But—"

"No buts yet. Mac, you've got too much talent, too much creativity to spend every day taking passport photos and posed kid shots."

"My talent knows no bounds," Mac said lightly, "but a girl's got to eat."

"You'd rather have your own photography studio."

"I'd rather have Justin Timberlake arm wrestling Ashton Kutcher for me, too—and it's just as likely."

"Laurel, you studied in New York and Paris with the aim of becoming a pastry chef."

"An international sensation of a pastry chef."

"And you've settled for working at the Willows."

She swallowed a bite of her spinach tart. "Well, hey—"

"Part of that settling was to be here for me after we lost Mom and Dad. I studied," Parker continued, "with the goal of starting my own business. I always had an idea of what it would be, but it seemed like a pipe dream. One I never shared with any of you. But over these last months, it's begun to feel more reachable, more right."

"For Christ's sake, Parker, what is it?" Laurel demanded.

"I want us to go into business together. The four of us, with each of us running our own end of it—according to our field of interest and expertise, while merging them together under one umbrella, so to speak."

"Go into business?" Emma echoed.

"You remember how we used to play Wedding Day? How we'd all take turns playing parts, and wearing costumes, planning the themes."

"I liked marrying Harold best." Mac smiled over the memory of the long-departed Brown family dog. "He was so handsome and loyal."

"We could do it for real, make a business out of Wedding Day."

"Providing costumes and cupcakes, and very patient dogs for little girls?" Laurel suggested.

"No, by providing a unique and amazing venue—this house, these grounds; spectacular cakes and pastries; heartbreaking bouquets and flowers; beautiful, creative photographs. And for my part—someone who'll oversee every detail to make a wedding, or other important event, the most perfect day of the clients' lives."

She barely took a breath. "I already have countless contacts through my parents. Caterers, wine merchants, limo services, salons—everything. And what I don't have, I'll get. A full-service wedding and event business, the four of us as equal partners."

"A wedding business." Emma's eyes went dreamy. "It sounds wonderful, but how could we—"

"I have a business model. I have figures and charts and answers to legal questions if you've got them. Del helped me work it out."

"He's okay with it?" Laurel asked. "Delaney's okay with you turning the estate, your home, into a business?"

"He's completely behind me on this. And his friend Jack's willing to help by redesigning the pool house into a photographer's studio, with living quarters above it, and the guest house into a flower shop with an apartment. We can turn the auxiliary kitchen here into your work space, Laurel."

"We'd live here, on the estate?"

"You'd have that option," Parker told Mac. "It's going to be a lot of work, and it would be more efficient for all of us to be on-site. I'll show you the figures, the model, the projection charts, the works. But there's no point if any of you just don't like the basic concept. And if you don't, well, I'll try to talk you into it," Parker added with a laugh. "Then if you hate it, I'll let it go."

"The hell you will." Laurel scooped a hand through her short cap of hair. "How long have you been working this out?"

"Seriously? Actively? About three months. I had to talk to Del, and Mrs. G, because without their support, it would never fly. But I wanted to put it all together before springing it on you. It's business," Parker said. "It would be our business, so it needs to be formed that way from the ground up."

"Our business," Emma repeated. "Weddings. What's happier than a wedding?"

"Or crazier," Laurel put in.

"The four of us can handle crazy. Parks?" Mac's dimples winked as she held out a hand. "I'm so in."

"You can't commit until you've seen the model, the figures."

"Yes, I can," Mac corrected. "I want this."

"Me, too." Emma laid her hand on theirs.

Laurel took a breath, held it. Released. "I guess that makes it unanimous." And she put her hand on theirs. "We'll kick wedding ass."

CHAPTER ONE

CRAZY BRIDE CALLED AT FIVE TWENTY-EIGHT A.M.

"I had a dream," she announced while Parker lay in the dark with her BlackBerry.

"A dream?"

"An amazing dream. So real, so *urgent*, so full of color and life! I'm sure it means something. I'm going to call my psychic but I wanted to talk it over with you, first."

"Okay." With the grace of experience, Parker reached over, turned her bedside lamp on low. "What was the dream about, Sabina?" she asked as she picked up the pad and pen beside the lamp.

"Alice in Wonderland."

"You dreamed about Alice in Wonderland?"

"Specifically the Mad Hatter's tea party."

"Disney or Tim Burton?"

"What?"

"Nothing." Parker shook back her hair, noted key words. "Go on."

"Well, there was music and a banquet of food. I was Alice, but I wore my wedding dress, and Chase looked absolutely amazing in a morning coat. The flowers, oh, they were spectacular. And all of them singing and dancing. Everyone was so happy, toasting us, clapping. Angelica was dressed as the Red Queen and playing a flute."

Parker noted down MOH for Angelica, the maid of honor, then continued to record other members of the wedding party. The best man as the White Rabbit, the mother of the groom as the Cheshire Cat, father of the bride, the March Hare.

She wondered what Sabina had eaten, drunk, or smoked before going to bed.

"Isn't it fascinating, Parker?"

"Absolutely." As had been the pattern of tea leaves that had determined Sabina's bridal colors, the tarot reading that had forecast her honeymoon destination, the numerology that had pointed to the only possible date for her wedding.

"I think maybe my subconscious and the fates are telling me I need to do an Alice theme for the wedding. With costumes."

Parker closed her eyes. While she'd have said—and would say now—that the Mad Hatter's Tea Party suited Sabina to the ground, the event was less than two weeks away. The decor, the flowers, the cake and desserts, the menu—the works—already chosen.

"Hmm," Parker said to give herself a moment to think. "That's an interesting idea."

"The dream—"

"Says to me," Parker interjected, "the celebrational, magical, fairy-tale atmosphere you've already chosen. It tells me you were absolutely right."

"Really?"

"Completely. It tells me you're excited and happy, and can't wait for your day. Remember, the Mad Hatter held his tea party every day. It's telling you that your life with Chase will be a daily celebration."

"Oh! Of course!"

"And, Sabina, when you stand in front of the looking glass in the Bride's Suite on your wedding day, you'll be looking at yourself with Alice's young, adventurous, happy heart."

Damn, I'm good, Parker thought as the crazy bride sighed.

"You're right, you're right. You're absolutely right. I'm so glad I called you. I knew you'd *know*."

"That's what we're here for. It's going to be a beautiful wedding, Sabina. Your perfect day."

After she hung up, Parker lay back a moment, but when she closed her eyes, the Mad Hatter's Tea Party—Disney version—ran manically in her head.

Resigned, she rose, crossed over to the French doors to the terrace of the room that had once been her parents'. She opened them to the morning air, took a deep breath of dawn as the sun took its first peek over the horizon.

The last stars winked out in a world perfectly, wonderfully still—like a breath held.

The upside of crazy brides and those of that ilk was wakefulness just before dawn when it seemed nothing and no one but she stirred, nothing and no one but she had this moment when night passed its torch to day, and the silvery light sheened to pearl that would shimmer—when that breath released—to pale, lustrous gold.

She left the doors open when she walked back into the bedroom. Taking a band from the hammered silver box on her dresser, she pulled her hair back into a tail. She shed her nightshirt for cropped yoga pants and a support tank, chose a pair of running shoes off the shelf in the casual section of her ruthlessly organized closet.

She hooked her BlackBerry to her waistband, plugged in her headphones, then headed out of her room toward her home gym.

She hit the lights, flipped on the news on the flat screen, listening with half an ear as she took a few moments to stretch.

She set the elliptical for her usual three-mile program.

Halfway through the first mile, she smiled.

God, she loved her work. Loved the crazy brides, the sentimental brides, the persnickety brides, even the monster brides.

She loved the details and demands, the hopes and dreams, the constant affirmation of love and commitment she helped to personalize for every couple.

Nobody, she determined, did it better than Vows.

What she, Mac, Emma, and Laurel had taken head-on one late summer evening was now everything and more than they'd imagined.

And now, she thought as her smile widened, they were planning weddings for Mac in December, Emma in April, Laurel in June.

Her friends were the brides now, and she couldn't wait to dig deeper into those fine details.

Mac and Carter—traditional with artistic twists. Emma and Jack—romance, romance, romance. Laurel and Del (God, her brother was marrying her best friend!)—elegant yet streamlined.

Oh, she had ideas.

She'd hit mile two when Laurel came in.

"Fairy lights. Acres and miles and rivers of tiny white fairy lights, all through the gardens, in the willows, on the arbors, the pergola."

Laurel blinked, yawned. "Huh?"

"Your wedding. Romantic, elegant, abundance without fuss."

"Huh." Laurel, her swing of blond hair clipped up, stepped on the machine next to Parker's. "I'm just getting used to being engaged."

"I know what you like. I've worked up a basic overview."

"Of course you have." But Laurel smiled. "Where are you?" She craned her head, scanned the readout on Parker's machine. "Shit! Who called and when?"

"Crazy Bride. Just shy of five thirty. She had a dream."

"If you tell me she dreamed a new design for the cake, I'm going to—"

"Not to worry. I fixed it."

"How could I have doubted you?" She eased through her warm-up, then kicked in. "Del's going to put his house on the market."

"What? When?"

"Well, after he talks to you about it, but I'm here, you're here, so I'm talking to you first. We talked about it last night. He'll be back from Chicago tonight, by the way. So . . . he'd move back in here, if that's okay with you."

"First, it's his house as much as mine. Second, you're staying." Her eyes stung, shined. "You're staying," Parker repeated. "I didn't want to push, and I know Del's got a great house, but— Oh God, Laurel, I didn't want you to move out. Now you won't."

"I love him so much I may be the next Crazy Bride, but I didn't want to move out either. My wing's more than big enough, it practically *is* a house. And he loves this place as much as you, as much as all of us."

"Del's coming home," Parker murmured.

Her family, she thought, everyone she loved and cherished, would soon be together. And that, she knew, was what made a home.

By eight fifty-nine, Parker was dressed in a sharply tailored suit the color of ripe eggplants with a hint of frill on her crisp white shirt. She spent precisely fifty-five minutes answering e-mails, texts, and phone calls, refreshing notes in various client files, checking and confirming deliveries with subcontractors on upcoming events.

At the stroke of ten she walked down from her third-floor office for her first on-site appointment of the day.

She'd already researched the potential client. Bride, Deeanne Hagar, local artist whose dreamy fantasy work had been reproduced in posters and greeting cards. Groom, Wyatt Culpepper, landscape designer. Both came from old money—banking and real estate, respectively—and both were the youngest child of twice-divorced parents.

Minimal digging had netted her the data that the newly engaged couple had met at a greenfest, shared a fondness for bluegrass music, and loved to travel.

She had mined other nuggets from websites, Facebook, magazine and newspaper interviews, and friends of friends of friends, and had already decided on the overall approach of the initial tour, which would include the mothers of both.

She scanned areas as she did a quick pass-through on the main level, pleased with Emma's romantic flower displays.

She popped into the family kitchen where, as expected, Mrs. Grady was putting the finishing touches on the coffee tray, the iced sun tea Parker had requested, and a platter of fresh fruit highlighted with Laurel's tissue-thin butter cookies.

"Looks perfect, Mrs. G."

"It's ready when you are."

"Let's go ahead and set it up in the main parlor. If they want the tour straight off, maybe we'll move it outside. It's beautiful out."

Parker moved in to help, but Mrs. Grady waved her off. "I've got it. I just put it together that I know the bride's first step-mother."

"Really?"

"Didn't last long, did she?" Movements brisk, Mrs. Grady transferred the trays to a tea cart. "Never made the second wedding anniversary, if I remember right. Pretty woman, and sweet enough. Dim as a five-watt bulb, but good-hearted." Mrs. Grady flicked her fingertips over the skirt of her bib apron. "She married again—some Spaniard—and moved to Barcelona."

"I don't know why I spend any time on the Internet, when I can just plug in to you."

"If you had, I'd've told you Mac's mother had a flirt with the bride's daddy between wives two and three."

"Linda? Not a surprise."

"Well, we can all be grateful it didn't take. I like the girl's pictures," she added as they rolled the cart toward the parlor.

"You've seen them?"

Mrs. Grady winked. "You're not the only one who knows how to use the Internet. There's the bell. Go on. Snag us another client."

"That's the plan."

Parker's first thought was the bride looked like the Hollywood version of a fantasy artist with her waist-length tumble of gilded red hair and almond-shaped green eyes. Her second was what a beautiful bride Deeanne would make, and on the heels of it, just how much she wanted a part of that.

"Good morning. Welcome to Vows. I'm Parker."

"Brown, right?" Wyatt shot out a hand. "I just want to say I don't know who designed your landscape, but they're a genius. And I wish it had been me."

"Thank you so much. Please come in."

"My mother, Patricia Ferrell. Deeanne's mom, Karen Bliss."

"It's lovely to meet all of you." Parker took stock quickly. Wyatt took charge, but genially—and all three women let him. "Why don't we have a seat in the parlor for a few minutes and get acquainted."

But Deeanne was already wandering the spacious foyer, scanning the elegant staircase. "I thought it would be stuffy. I thought it would *feel* stuffy." She turned back, her pretty summer skirt swaying. "I studied your website. Everything looked perfect, looked beautiful. But I thought, no, *too* perfect. I'm still not convinced it's not too perfect, but it's not stuffy. Not in the least."

"What my daughter might've said in many fewer words, Ms. Brown, is you have a lovely home."

"Parker," she said, "and thank you, Mrs. Bliss. Coffee?" she invited. "Or iced sun tea?"

"Could we just look around first?" Deeanne asked her. "Especially outside, as Wyatt and I want an outdoor wedding."

"Why don't we start outside, then circle back through. You're looking at next September," Parker continued as she moved to the door leading to the side terrace.

"A year from now. That's why we're looking at this time, so we can see how the landscape, the gardens, the light all work."

"We have several areas that can be utilized for outdoor weddings. The most popular, especially for larger events is the west terrace and pergola. But . . ."

"But?" Wyatt echoed as they strolled around the house.

"When I see the two of you, I picture something a little different. Something we do now and then. The pond," she said as they rounded to the back. "The willows, the roll of the lawns. I see a flower-strewn arbor and white runners flowing like a river between the rows of chairs—white again, strung with flowers. All of that reflected in the water of the pond. Banquets of flowers everywhere—but not formal, more natural arrangements. Cottage garden flowers, but in mad abundance. My partner and our floral designer Emmaline is an artist."

Deeanne's eyes took on a gleam. "I loved what I saw of her work on the website."

"You can speak with her directly if you decide to have your wedding with us, or even if you're just considering it. I also see fairy lights glittering, candles flickering. Everything natural, organic—but sumptuous, sparkling. Titania's bower. You'll wear something flowing," she said to Deeanne. "Something fairylike, with your hair down. No veil, but flowers in your hair."

"Yes. You're very good, aren't you?"

"It's what we do here. Tailor the day to reflect what you want most, what you are, individually and to each other. You don't want formal, but soft and dreamy. Neither contemporary nor old-fashioned. You want *you*, and a bluegrass trio playing you down the aisle."

"'Never Ending Love,'" Wyatt supplied with a grin. "We've already picked it. Will your artist of a florist work with us, not only on the wedding landscape, but the bouquets and all that?"

"Every step of the way. It's entirely about you, and creating the perfect—even too-perfect—day for you," she said with a smile for Deeanne.

"I love the pond," Deeanne murmured as they stood on the terrace looking out. "I love the image you've just painted in my head."

"Because the image is you, baby." Karen Bliss took her daughter's hand. "It's absolutely you."

"Dancing on the lawn?" Wyatt's mother glanced over. "I checked out the website, too, and I know you have a gorgeous ballroom. But maybe they could have dancing out here."

"Absolutely. Either, both, however you want it done. If you're interested we can set up a full consult, with my partners, discuss those areas, and more details."

"What do you say we take a look at the rest." Wyatt leaned down to kiss Deeanne's temple.

$\mathcal{A}$T FOUR THIRTY, PARKER WAS BACK AT HER DESK REFINING SPREAD-sheets, charts, schedules. In concession to the end of the day's appointments, her suit jacket hung on the back of her chair, and her shoes sat under the desk.

She calculated another hour's paperwork, and considered the day a blissfully light one. The rest of the week promised to be insanely jammed, but with any luck, by six she'd be able to change into casual clothes and treat herself to a glass of wine and actually sit down to a meal.

She went *hmm?* at the rap on her doorjamb.

"Got a minute?" Mac asked.

"I happen to have several on me. You can have one." Parker swiveled in her chair as Mac hauled in two shopping bags. "I missed you in the gym this morning, but I see you've continued your weight lifting."

Grinning, Mac flexed. "Pretty good, huh?"

"You're ripped, Elliot. You'll have showstopping arms on Wedding Day."

Mac dropped into a chair. "I have to do justice to the dress you found me. Listen, I've sworn not to become Mad Bride or Weepy Bride or other various aspects of Annoying Bride, but it's getting close and I just need assurances from the goddess of all wedding planners."

"It's going to be perfect, and exactly right."

"I changed my mind on the first dance again."

"It doesn't matter. You can change it up until the countdown."

"But it's symptomatic, Parks. I can't seem to stick to a basic item like a damn song."

"It's an important song."

"Is Carter taking dance lessons?"

Parker widened her eyes. "Why would you ask me?"

"I *knew* it! God, that's so sweet. You got Carter to take dance lessons so he won't step on my feet during our first dance."

"Carter asked me to arrange it—as a surprise. So don't spoil it."

"It makes me gooey." Her shoulders lifted and fell with her happy sigh. "Maybe I can't stick because I keep going gooey. Anyway, I had that off-site engagement shoot this afternoon."

"How'd it go?"

"Aces. They're so damn cute I wanted to marry both of them. Then I did something stupid on the way home. I stopped by the shoe department at Nordstrom."

"Which I have already cleverly deduced by the shopping bags."

"I bought ten pair. I'm taking most of them back, but—"

"Why?"

Mac narrowed her green eyes. "Don't encourage the lunatic. I couldn't stick, again. I already bought my wedding shoes, right? Didn't we all agree they're perfect?"

"Stunning and perfect."

"Exactly, so why did I buy four alternate pair?"

"I thought you said ten."

"The other six are for the honeymoon—well, four of them, then I really needed a new pair of work shoes and they were so cute I got one pair in copper and another in this wild green. But that's not important."

"Let me see them."

"The wedding shoes first, and don't say anything until I line them all up." Mac held up both hands. "Total poker face. No expression, no sound."

"I'll turn around, work on this spreadsheet."

"Better you than me," Mac muttered, then got to work.

Parker ignored the rustling, the sighs, until Mac gave her the go-ahead.

Turning, Parker scanned the shoes lined up on a work counter. Rose, crossed over, scanned again. She kept her face blank, said nothing as she picked up a shoe, examined it, set it back, moved to the next.

"You're killing me," Mac told her.

"Quiet." She walked away to take out a folder, slipping out the photo taken of Mac in her wedding dress. She took it back to the selection of shoes, nodded.

"Yes. Definitely." She picked up a pair. "You'd be a lunatic not to wear these."

"Really!" Mac slapped her hands together. "*Really?* Because those were the ones. The. Ones. But I kept waffling back and forth and sideways. Oooh, look at them. The heels, they're all sparkly, and the ankle strap's so sexy—but not too sexy. Right?"

"The perfect blend of sparkly, sexy, and sophisticated. I'll take the others back."

"But—"

"I'll return them because you've found the ultimate wedding shoe and need to stick. You have to remove the others from your sight and stay out of the shoe department until after the wedding."

"You're so wise."

Parker inclined her head. "I am indeed wise. And as such, I do believe this pair may very well be Emma's wedding shoe. I'll exchange it for her size, and we'll see."

"Oh, oh, again, wise points." Mac picked up the pair Parker

indicated. "More romantic, more princessy. This is great. I'm exhausted."

"Leave the wedding shoes—all of them—with me. Take the others. Oh, and check your calendar when you get home. I added in consults."

"How many?"

"Out of the five tours I did today, we have three full consults, one need to talk it over with Daddy—who's footing the bill—and one who's still shopping around."

"Three out of five?" Mac did a double fist pump. "Woo-hoo."

"I'm betting four out of five, because Daddy's girl wants us, and wants us bad. The fifth? The bride just isn't ready to decide. Her mother wants us, which my instincts tell me is a strike against us in this case. We'll see."

"Well, I'm psyched. Three fulls and I've bagged the perfect wedding shoes. I'm going home to give my guy a big wet kiss, and he won't know it's because he's taking dance lessons. Thanks, Parks. See you later."

Parker sat, studied the shoes on the counter. She thought of Mac rushing home to Carter. Thought of Laurel greeting Del when he came home after a two-day business conference in Chicago. And Emma maybe sitting out on her little patio having wine with Jack and dreaming of her own wedding flowers.

She swiveled around to stare at the spreadsheet on the screen. She had her work, she reminded herself. Work she loved. And that's what mattered right now.

Her BlackBerry signaled, and a glance at the readout told her another bride needed to talk.

"I've always got you," she murmured, then answered. "Hi, Brenna. What can I do for you?"

CHAPTER TWO

$\mathscr{P}$ARKER DEALT WITH THE SHOES, AND BECAUSE SHE WAS ON A tight schedule, she only indulged in one pair for herself. She met a bride, the bride's favorite aunt—who would give her away—and the bride's maid of honor for lunch to discuss wedding favors, music, and—coincidentally—shoes.

She swung by the bridal boutique where, at the request of another bride, she assisted in the finalization of the gowns for the wedding party, gave her input on underpinnings and head-dresses, met yet another bride and entourage to pore over linen choices. Then she dashed to Coffee Talk for a quick meeting with Sherry Maguire, Carter's delightful sister, whose wedding was imminent.

"Diane's being a poop," Sherry announced and pouted with her chin on her fist.

"The wedding's not about your sister."

"I know, I know, but she's still being a poop. A total downer. A kill-all-the-joy bitchfestia."

"Sherry, in less than two weeks you're marrying the man you love. Correct?"

The light sparked in Sherry's summer blue eyes. "Oh yeah."

"Everything about the day has been designed to make you happy, to celebrate that love. Correct?"

"God. God. It really has. You, all of you, have been amazing."

"Then be happy. Celebrate. And if your sister's cranky about it, I have to say that's her problem."

"That's exactly what Nick says." Sherry tossed up her hands, then shoved them through her sunny blond hair. "And my mother. But . . . she says she's not coming to the rehearsal or the rehearsal dinner."

The poop, Parker thought, but showed only light sympathy. "I'm sorry. Why not?"

"She's not in the wedding, she says. Well, she didn't *want* to be. I asked her to be the matron of honor, but she didn't want that. Didn't see why she should have to go through all that fuss, why I wanted a matron *and* a maid of honor."

"Your sister and your oldest, closest friend."

"Exactly." Sherry thumped a fist on the table, then jabbed a spoon in the whipped cream on her fancy coffee. "So now, she doesn't see why she should get a sitter and come to the dinner. I said the kids were invited, too, but then it's how she's not going to ride herd on them all night at a rehearsal dinner, then turn around and ride herd on them at the wedding. Too much stimulation for them, she says, too exhausting for her. So I said we'd pay for the damn sitter then so she and Sam could have the night out. And she got huffy about *that*. I can't win."

"Stop trying to."

"But she's my sister, Parker. It's my wedding." Tears sparkled as emotion trembled in Sherry's voice.

And this, Parker thought, had been throughout the entire process, the most cheerful, delightful, and flexible of brides.

Damn if she'd see a moment of it spoiled for her.

"I'll speak with her."

"But—"

"Sherry." Parker laid a hand over hers. "Trust me."

"Okay." Sherry sucked in a breath, blew it out as she blinked back the tears. "Sorry. I'm an idiot."

"You're not." To emphasize it, Parker gave Sherry's hand a quick, firm squeeze. "Let me say, because I know a lot of idiots, you just don't make the cut. So, do me a favor and put this out of your mind for now. Just put it aside and concentrate on how good things are, and how wonderful they will be."

"You're right. I knew you'd make me feel better."

"That's what I'm here for." Under the table, Parker turned her wrist to check the time. She could spare another ten minutes.

"So, you're all set on your spa and salon dates, your final fittings?"

The ten eked to nearly fifteen, but she'd built time in to cushion the trip back home for the early-evening consult. Even the rain that splattered as she walked back to the car didn't worry her.

She had plenty of time to drive home, freshen up, grab the files, check on the refreshments, and run through the client data with her partners. But to save time, she plugged in her phone and used the voice controls to contact Laurel.

"Icing at Vows."

"Hey, I'm on my way in. Are we set?"

"Coffee, tea, champagne, simple yet fabulous hors d'oeuvres, chocolates. Emma's already switched the flowers. We all have—or will have—our sample albums. Wow, is that thunder?"

"Yeah, it just opened up." Parker shot a glance to the angry boil of clouds. "I'll be home in about twenty. Bye."

The storm roared through, wild and vicious, and she thought just how much she'd have enjoyed it if she'd been inside. Soon would be, she thought, but adjusted her speed cautiously as rain hurled against the windshield.

She rolled along the road toward home, going over details about the new clients in her head.

It happened fast, all in a rain-washed blur.

The dog—deer?—raced across the road. The oncoming car swerved to avoid it, fishtailed. Parker eased off the gas, tapped her brakes, even as her heart leveled again when the animal cleared the road.

But the oncoming car fishtailed again, straight at her.

Once again her heart flipped. With no choice, she cut the wheel hard to avoid the collision. Her car skidded, bucked onto the shoulder of the road. Her rear end shimmied around while the car jolted side to side. The oncoming car nipped by her.

And just kept going.

She sat, her hands glued to the wheel, her knees shaking, and her heart a drumbeat in her ears.

"Okay," she breathed. "I'm okay. Not hurt. I'm not hurt."

Since she wanted to stay that way, she ordered herself to steer the car fully onto the shoulder until the shaking stopped. Someone else could come along and broadside her.

The best she could manage was a thumping limp.

Flat tire, she thought and closed her eyes. Perfect.

Grabbing her fold-up umbrella from the glove box, she got out to survey the damage.

"Oh, not a flat," she muttered. "A flat's just not good enough. *Two*. Two goddamn shredded tires." She rolled her eyes to the heavens, which, she noted bitterly, were already clearing.

She found the faint shimmer of a rainbow arching in a miserly glint of sun personally insulting under the circumstances.

She would, almost certainly, be late for the consult, but she wouldn't arrive soaking wet.

Bright side.

She climbed back in, called for roadside assistance. Because her hands still shook, she opted to wait another few minutes before calling home.

She'd just say she had a flat, she decided, and was waiting for the guy to come change it. She could damn well have changed a flat tire if she'd had to, she mused. But she only had one spare.

Pressing a hand on her jumpy belly, she thumbed a Tums out of the roll in her purse.

Probably thirty minutes for the tow truck, if she was lucky, then she'd have to ask the driver to take her home, or call a cab. She wasn't going to call home and ask one of her partners to come get her and let them see the car.

Not before a consult.

A cab, she decided. If she called a cab it would be on its way here along with the tow truck. More efficient that way. If she'd just stop shaking, she could get everything in order again. Deal with the situation.

She heard the roar of an engine, and her gaze flew to the rear-view mirror. Already slowing down, she realized as she let air out again. A motorcycle, which certainly had more than enough room to get around her.

Instead, it pulled up behind.

Good Samaritan, she thought. Not everyone was a negligent ass like the other driver had been. She pushed her door open to tell the biker she'd already called for help, and stepped out.

And saw Malcolm Kavanaugh pull off the black helmet.

It just got better and better, she thought. Now she was being "rescued" by her brother's friend, their current mechanic, a man who irritated her more often than not.

She watched him survey the situation while the thinning rain dampened his black, unkempt hair. His jeans were ripped at the knee, stained with oil on the thighs. The black shirt and leather jacket added to the image of sexy bad boy with a build for sin.

And eyes, she thought as they met hers, that challenged a woman to commit one. More than one.

"Are you hurt?"

"No."

He gave her a long look as if deciding for himself. "Your airbag didn't deploy."

"I wasn't going that fast. I didn't hit anything. I *avoided* getting hit by a moron who swerved to avoid a dog, then kept coming at me. I had to cut toward the shoulder and—"

"Where is he? The other driver?"

"He just kept going. Who does that? How can anyone do that?"

Saying nothing, he reached by her, pulled her bottle of water out of the cup holder. "Sit down. Drink some water."

"I'm okay. I'm just angry. I'm really, really angry."

He gave her a little poke, and she sat sideways on the front seat. "How's your spare?"

"It's never been used. It's new. I got all new tires last winter. Damn it."

"You're going to need a couple new ones now." He crouched for a moment so those sharp green eyes were level with hers.

It took her a moment to realize the movement, and the matter-of-fact tone of his voice, were probably designed to keep her calm. Since it seemed to be working, she had to appreciate it.

"We'll match them with what you've got," he continued. "I want to check the car out while I'm at it."

"Yes, fine, okay." She drank, realizing her throat was raw. "Thanks. I'm just—"

"Really, really angry," he finished as he straightened. "I don't blame you."

"And I'm going to be late. I hate being late. I've got a consult at home in, oh hell, twenty minutes. I need to call a cab."

"No, you don't." He looked back down the road at the approaching tow truck.

"That was fast, you were fast. I didn't expect . . ." She paused as her brain started to function again. "Were you out this way, on your bike?"

"I am out this way, on my bike," he corrected. "Since you called in for service due to being run off the road. You didn't call the cops?"

"I didn't get the plate, or even the kind of car." And that galled her. Just *galled*. "It happened so fast, and it was raining, and—"

"And it would be a waste of time. Still, Bill's going to take pictures and report it for you."

She pressed the heel of her hand to her forehead. "Okay. Thanks. Really, thank you. I guess I'm a little rattled."

"First time I've seen you that way. Hold on."

He walked to the truck, and while he spoke with his driver she sipped the water and ordered herself to settle down. Everything was fine, just fine. The driver would give her a ride home, and she wouldn't even be late. Ten minutes home, five minutes to freshen up. She'd give the simple flat tire story after the consult.

Everything was just fine.

She looked up as Malcolm walked back and handed her a fire-engine red helmet. "You'll need this."

"Why?"

"Safety first, Legs." He put it on her head himself and his grin edged ever so slightly toward smirk. "Cute."

"What?" Her eyes popped wide. "If you think I'm getting on that motorcycle—"

"You want to make your meeting? Keep your rep as Ms. Prompt and Efficient? Rain's stopped. You won't even get wet." Again he reached past her, but this time their bodies bumped. He pulled out again holding her purse. "You'll want this. Let's go."

"Can't the driver—can't he just drop me off?"

Mal strapped her purse to the bike, swung a leg over. "You're not afraid to ride a bike, are you? And for what, about six miles?"

"Of course I'm not afraid."

He put on his helmet, turned on the bike, gave the engine a couple of muscular revs. "Clock's ticking."

"Oh for God's—" She bit off the words, clipped her way to the bike in her heels, and, keeping her teeth gritted, managed to get a leg over the bike behind him. Her skirt hiked up high on her thighs.

"Nice."

"Just shut up."

She felt rather than heard his laugh. "You ever ride a Harley, Legs?"

"No. Why would I?"

"Then you're in for a treat. You're going to want to hold on. To me," he added after a beat.

She put her hands lightly on either side of his waist.

But when he revved the engine again—she knew damn well he did it on purpose—she swallowed pride and wrapped her arms around him.

Why, she wondered, anyone would want to drive something so noisy, so dangerous, so—

Then they were flying down the road, and the wind blew cool and balmy and *gorgeous* over every inch of her.

Okay, a thrill, she admitted, and her heart skipped as he leaned into a turn. A terrifying sort of thrill. Like a roller coaster, which was another thing she could admit was exciting without being a necessary experience in a well-rounded life.

The landscape whizzed by. She smelled the rain, the grass, the leather of his jacket, felt the throb of the bike between her legs.

Sexual, she admitted. Add arousing to that terrifying thrill. Which was surely the reason people rode bikes.

When he swung onto her drive, she had to resist flinging her arms up in the air to feel the wind give her palms a slapping high five.

As he stopped in front of the house, Del came out.

"Mal."

"Del."

"Parker, where's your car?"

"Oh, I had a flat just down the road. Mal came by. His tow truck driver's fixing it. I have a consult."

Her brother cocked his head, and she saw the corner of his mouth twitch. "Parker. You rode on a motorcycle."

"So what?" She tried to ease off gracefully, but the heels and skirt added challenge.

Mal simply swung off, then plucked her off like a package for delivery.

"Thank you. Very much. I have to run or—"

"You'll be late." He unstrapped her purse. "You probably don't want to wear this."

He unclipped the helmet, took it off for her.

"Thank you."

"You said that already. A few times."

"Well . . ." Uncharacteristically blank, she turned and hurried toward the house.

She heard Del say, "Come on in and have a beer."

And tried not to wince when Mal drawled out a "Don't mind if I do."

Mal followed Del inside, and caught a glimpse of Parker charging up the stairs. The woman had legs, what he thought of as Hollywood legs.

The rest of her partners—the cool blonde, the raven-haired beauty, the willowy redhead—stood in the doorway of what he supposed they called a parlor, all talking at once.

They made a hell of a picture.

"Flat tire," Del said and kept walking.

The Brown mansion had style, Mal thought, had class, had *weight*, and still managed to feel like a home instead of a museum. He figured that clicked on credit for those who lived there, and had lived there.

Warm colors, art that drew the eye rather than baffled it, comfortable chairs, glossy tables, and flowers, flowers, and more flowers mixed together with that style, that class and weight.

But he never felt as if he should keep his hands in his pockets for fear of getting a fingerprint on something.

He'd been through most of the place—excluding Parker's private wing (and wouldn't it be interesting to change that?), and always felt comfortable. Still, the easiest and most welcoming area of the house remained Mrs. Grady's kitchen.

The woman herself turned from the stove where she stirred something that turned the air to heaven.

"So, it's Malcolm."

"How're you doing, Mrs. Grady?"

"Well enough." She cocked a brow as Del took a couple beers from the refrigerator. "Take those outside. I don't want you underfoot."

"Yes, ma'am," both men said together.

"I suppose you'll be staying for dinner," she said to Malcolm.

"Are you asking?"

"I will if Delaney's forgotten his manners."

"He just got here," Del muttered.

"As the other boys have wheedled a meal after the consult, I can stretch things to one more. If he's not picky."

"If you're cooking it, Mrs. Grady, I'll be grateful for even a single bite."

"You've a clever tongue, don't you, boy?"

"All the girls say so."

She let out a quick bark of a laugh, and tapped her spoon on the edge of a pot. "Outside, the pair of you."

Del opened the fridge, grabbed two more beers. He shoved three of the four on Mal, then flipped out his phone as they walked outside. "Jack. Mal's here. Got beer. Get Carter." He snapped the phone closed again.

He still wore his suit, Mal noted, and though he'd taken off his tie, loosened his collar, he looked every inch the Yale-educated lawyer. He shared his sister's coloring—thick, dense brown hair, misty blue eyes. Her features were smoother, softer, but anyone with working eyes would make them as siblings.

Del sat, stretched out his legs. His manner tended to be more casual and a hell of a lot less prickly than his sister's, which might have been why they'd become poker buddies, then friends.

They popped the bottles, and as Malcolm took the first cold sip, his body relaxed for the first time since he'd picked up his tools twelve hours earlier.

"What happened?" Del asked.

"About?"

"Don't play me, Mal. Flat tire, my ass. If Parker'd had a flat, you'd have changed it—or she would have—and she wouldn't have ridden home on your bike."

"She had a flat." Malcolm took another pull on his beer. "In fact, she had two. They're toast." He shrugged. He wouldn't lie to a friend. "From what she said, and how it looked when I got there, some asshole swerved to avoid a dog. Parker had to cut it hard to the shoulder to avoid getting creamed. Wet road, maybe a little overcompensating, she had herself a little spin, shot out the two left tires. Looked to me from the skid marks, the other driver was booking—she wasn't. And he kept right on going."

"He left her there?" Outrage colored Del's voice, blew across his face in a storm. "Son of a bitch. Did she get the plate, the make?"

"She got nothing, and I can't blame her. It must've happened at the peak of that quick squall, and she was busy trying to get control of her car. I'd say she did pretty well. Didn't hit anything, didn't even pop the airbag. She was shaken up, and she was pissed. And she was extra pissed thinking she'd be late for her meeting."

"But not hurt," Del said, mostly to himself. "Okay. Where?"

"About six miles out."

"Were you out this way, on your bike?"

"No." Damn third degree. "Look, Ma got the call, and she came out to tell me somebody ran Parker off the road, and she was stuck, so I rode out to check on her while Ma dispatched Bill."

"I appreciate that, Mal." He glanced over as Mrs. Grady walked out, then set a bowl of pub mix and a plate of olives on the table. "Sop up some of that beer. Here come your boyfriends," she added, nodding across the lawn as the dusk light flickered on.

"You." She poked Malcolm in the shoulder. "You can have one more beer, as we won't be sitting down to dinner for another hour or more, then that's it until you park that monster machine back at your own place."

"You and me could go out dancing first."

"Careful." She twinkled at him. "I've got plenty of moves left in me."

She strolled back into the house, leaving Malcolm grinning. "Bet she does." He tipped his beer toward Jack and Carter in greeting.

"Here's what the doctor ordered." Jack Cooke, the golden-boy architect and Del's college pal, opened a beer. The sturdy boots and jeans told Mal Jack had focused on site work rather than office work that day.

He made a contrast with Carter's oxford shirt and khakis. Carter's reading glasses poked out of his shirt pocket and had Malcolm imagining him sitting up in his new study grading papers with his Professor Maguire tweed jacket neatly hung in the closet.

He figured they made a motley crew—if he had the meaning right—with Del in his slick Italian suit, Jack and his work boots, Carter in his teacher's khakis, and himself . . .

Well, hell, if he'd known he'd get invited to dinner, he'd have changed his pants.

Probably.

Jack grabbed a handful of pub mix. "What's up?"

"Somebody ran Parker off the road. Mal came to the rescue."

"Is she okay?" Carter set his beer down quickly without drinking. "Is she hurt?"

"She's fine," Malcolm said. "Couple shredded tires. No big. And I get a couple of beers and dinner out of it. Pretty good deal."

"He talked Parker onto the bike."

Jack snorted, glanced from Del to Mal. "You're not kidding?"

"Lesser of two evils." Amused now, Malcolm popped an olive. "My bike or being late for her meeting. Anyway . . ." He popped another olive. "I think she liked it. I'll have to take her on a real ride."

"Right." Del let out a half laugh. "Good luck with that."

"You don't think I can get her back on the bike?"

"Parker's not what you'd call your Motorcycle Mama."

"Careful what you say about my ma." Mal considered as he sipped his beer. "I've got a hundred that says I can get her back on within two weeks for a solid hour."

"If you throw away your money like that, I'll have to keep buying your beer."

"I'll take your money," Jack said, and dug into the pub mix. "I have no scruples about taking your money."

"Bet." Malcolm shook on it with Jack. "Still open to you," he told Del.

"Fine." As they shook, Del glanced at Carter. "Do you want in?"

"No, I don't think . . . Well, actually, I guess I'll put mine on Malcolm."

Malcolm gave Carter a considering stare. "Maybe you are as smart as you look."

CHAPTER THREE

IN MALCOLM'S EXPERIENCE, MOST PEOPLE DIDN'T SIT DOWN TO A meal of honey-glazed ham, roasted potatoes and baby carrots, and delicately grilled asparagus on your typical Tuesday. And they probably didn't chow down with candlelight, flowers, and wine sparkling in crystal glasses.

Then again, the Brown household wasn't most people.

He'd have skipped the fancy French wine even without Mrs. Grady's baleful eye. He'd long ago grown out of the stage where he'd knock them back before climbing on his bike.

He'd had vague plans to go home, sweat off the long day with a workout, grab a shower, slap something between a couple slices of bread, pop a brew, and zone awhile in front of the tube.

He'd've been fine with that.

But he had to admit this was better.

Not just the food—though, Jesus, Mrs. Grady could cook—

but the place, the whole ball of wax. Pretty women, men he liked, the amazing Mrs. Grady.

And, particularly, the always intriguing Parker Brown.

She had a face for candlelight, he supposed. Elegant but not cold, unless she wanted it to be. Sexy, but subtle, like a hint of lace under a starched shirt.

Then there was that voice—low register, a wisp of smoke, but changeable as the weather from brisk to prim from warm to ice. She got things done with those tones. Knew, he decided, just how to use them.

She'd had to relate the full story of her near miss, and used the casual notes with hints of temper. If he hadn't seen her himself directly after the incident, he might have bought her pretense that she'd never been in any real danger, and was only annoyed with her own overreaction and the other driver's carelessness.

Even with the act, the others smothered her with concern, peppered her with more questions, slung outrage at the other driver. And dumped gratitude on him until he felt buried in it.

He figured he and Parker hit about the same level of relief when the topic shifted.

He liked listening to them, all of them. Group—or he supposed more like family—dinner ran long, ran loud, and involved a whole hell of a lot of cross talk. That was fine with Mal. It meant he didn't have to say much himself, and to his way of thinking you learned more about people when you let them take the wheel.

"What are you going to do with your pool table?" Jack asked Del.

"I haven't decided."

It stirred Malcolm enough to ask. "What's wrong with the pool table?"

"Nothing."

"Del's selling his house and moving in here," Carter told Mal.

"Selling it? When did that happen?"

"A very recent development." Del arched his eyebrows at Mal as he buttered one of Mrs. Grady's fancy crescent rolls. "You want to buy it?"

"What the hell would I do with it? It's big enough for a family of ten and their grandparents from Iowa." He considered as he cut another bite of ham. "Any way to just buy the game room?"

"Afraid not. But I've got a couple ideas on all that."

"Let me know when you're ready to sell the pinball machines."

"Where are you going to put them?" Jack demanded. "You've barely got room to turn around in that place over your mother's garage."

"For the classics I'll toss out my bed and sleep on the floor."

"Boys and their toys." Laurel rolled her eyes toward Del. "You can't put yours in our bedroom. Line in the sand, Delaney. Indelible line."

"I had a different location in mind." Del glanced at Parker. "We'll talk about it."

"All right. I thought you might want to convert one of the attics," Parker began, "but I took a look myself, and I don't know that they'd safely hold all that weight. At least not if you wanted to keep the slate pool table."

"I wasn't thinking up. I was thinking down."

"Down?" Parker repeated. "Where . . . Oh God, Del, not one of the basements."

"How many attics and basements are in this place?" Mal whispered to Emma.

"Three attics, two—no, three basements if you count the scary boiler room where the demons who eat the flesh of young girls live."

"Cool."

"Sure, if you're a young boy like Del was." Emma narrowed her dark eyes as she glared across the table. "But if you're a young girl playing Treasure Hunt, you could be scarred for life by a certain mean boy with a flashlight with a red bulb, a shambling walk, and a low, maniacal laugh."

She picked up her wine, shuddered a little. "I still can't go down there."

He tuned back in while Parker and Del batted basements around, Laurel sat smiling into her wine, Jack grabbed another roll, and Mac whispered something in Carter's ear that made the tip of that ear flush pink.

Interesting.

"Look," Del said, "you use the west wing basement to store event supplies—extra tables, chairs, whatever."

"We're buying more. Investing in our own," Parker pointed out. "So we snag the rental rather than subbing it out."

"Which is good business. I've been down there too many times to count when I've pitched in with events. You have enough space for a showroom."

"It's not the space, Del, you can have the space." Obviously weighing options, Parker frowned at her water glass, then at Del. "We could move the storage to the east side, but even then—"

"No, no!" Emma waved both hands. "It's too close to the Hellmouth."

"And he's still there," Del said darkly, "waiting for you."

"I hate you, Delaney. Beat him up, Jack," Emma demanded. "A whole lot."

"Okay. Can I finish this roll first?"

"East, west," Parker interrupted, "it's still a *basement*. There's next to no natural lighting, the ceilings are barely seven feet, concrete floors, parged walls, pipes everywhere."

"All the better for a Man Cave. Besides, why do you think I

keep him around?" he gestured at Jack. "He's more than a pretty face."

"Take a cavernous basement and remodel it into a MEA? That's Manly Entertainment Area, to you civilians," Jack explained as interest lit in his smoky eyes. "I can do that."

"The walls are a foot thick," Del went on, "so the space could be used even during events and nobody'd hear a thing." He lifted his wineglass, swirled the last half inch of wine while he aimed his gaze at Emma. "Just like nobody hears the pitiful screams of girls being eaten alive by the demon with a single red eye."

"You bastard." Emma hunched her shoulders.

"Let's go take a look."

Parker stared at Del. "Now?"

"Sure."

"I'm not going down there," Emma muttered.

"Aw, baby." Jack leaned over to wrap an arm around Emma. "I'll protect you."

She shook her head at Jack. "You say that now."

"You guys go ahead." Mac waved her wineglass. "Carter and I are just going to finish our wine, then we have . . . some things to do at home."

"There's peach pie yet," Mrs. Grady announced.

"Well . . ." Mac smiled. "We have dessert at home, don't we, Carter?"

His ears blushed again. "Apparently."

"Come on, Mal," Del invited. "We'll give you a tour of the depths, work up an appetite for pie."

"Sure." He rose after they did, reached for his plate to clear it.

"Leave that for now." Mrs. Grady wagged a finger at him. "Go on and explore first."

"Okay. Best ham I ever ate."

"I'll wrap some up for you to take home."

He bent down as he passed her. "I owe you a dance," he whispered in her ear and made her laugh.

"What was that about?" Parker asked him.

"Private conversation."

He tagged along, taking back stairs he imagined had once seen the scurry of servants and wondering why Parker still wore those skinny heels.

As Del hit switches, hard fluorescent lights flickered on to reveal a massive labyrinth.

He noted the low ceilings, unfinished walls, exposed pipes, and, as they turned into an open area, the utilitarian shelving, stacks of tables, chairs, stools.

A basement, no doubt, with just a pleasing edge of creepy and as ruthlessly clean as the kitchen of a five-star restaurant.

"What, do you have basement gnomes that come out and scrub at night?"

"Just because it's storage and utility doesn't mean it shouldn't be clean," Parker answered. "Del, it's depressing down here."

"Now."

He moved into a passageway, ducked under more pipes with what Mal assumed was the grace of experience, and kept winding.

"Old boiler room." Del jerked a thumb at a locked wooden door. "Where demons drool and sharpen their fangs on the bones of—"

"I didn't fall for that when I was eight," Laurel reminded him.

"It's a damn shame." He slung his arm around her shoulders; she wound hers around his waist.

Malcolm adjusted his stride so he walked beside Parker. "It's a lot of space."

"It's had a few incarnations and various uses. Storage and utility, just as now. And my great-grandfather had a workshop down here. He liked to build things, and so it's told he liked to have a quiet space to retreat when my great-grandmother was on a tear. They stored preserves and root vegetables, whatever else they canned during harvests. My father said his parents outfitted it as an air-raid shelter during the fifties."

As the space widened again, she stopped, put her hands on her hips. "God, Del, it's *creepy*. It's like a catacomb."

"I like it." Jack circled, eyes narrowed. "Take out that wall, widen the opening. Beams, columns. That brings in one more window, a little more light."

"You call that sliver a window?" Laurel asked.

"Lighting's a priority, and we have ways." Jack looked up. "We'd have to reroute some of the pipes, give you more headroom. Space isn't an issue, so I'd fir out the walls, run the electric, more plumbing. Put a nice john over there, balance that with a closet over here. Me, I'd put in a gas fireplace. Heat and ambiance, maybe do some stone or brick on that wall. Tile the floor, put heat elements under the tile.

"You've got your storm cellar doors out there. I want to think about that, take measurements, but it's doable. Oh yeah, it's doable."

Del glanced at Parker, cocked an eyebrow.

"If it's what you want, of course, I'm fine with it."

"There's your green light, Cooke."

Jack rubbed his hands together. "Yeah, baby."

"They're going to start talking about bearing walls and rough plumbing." Laurel shook her head. "I'm going up. I've barely cleared the brain haze from the construction of my auxiliary kitchen. Which is the work of genius," she added to Jack.

"We do no less."

"I'll go with you." Parker started out with Laurel, stopped. "Jack, can we do heated floors in the storage area?"

"All that, my lovely, and more."

She smiled. "Maybe we'll talk."

By the time Malcolm came back up—and damn if Jack hadn't made him see a space as slick, maybe even slicker, than the testosterone paradise in Del's current house—Mrs. Grady, Emma, Laurel, and Parker had made a serious dent in the clearing up.

He took Mrs. Grady's hand, shaking his head. "Uh-uh. You sit." He gestured to the bench in the breakfast nook. "The one who cooks doesn't clean up. That's the Law of Kavanaugh."

"I always liked your mother."

"I'm pretty fond of her myself. Want some more wine?"

"I've had my share, but I wouldn't mind a cup of tea."

"You got it."

He walked back to the stove, shook the kettle, then bumped Parker out of the way to fill it from the tap. He answered her stare with one of his own.

"Problem?"

"No."

"Your hair smells like this white flower that bloomed all over this bush I had under my bedroom window when we were stationed in Florida. It gets its hooks right in me."

He set the kettle on the burner, turned it on. The other men walked in as he took a stack of dishes from Emma.

"Damn," Del complained. "We didn't stay down there long enough."

"You can grab what's left on the table," Laurel told them. "We're shorthanded as Mac and Carter ducked out to have dessert at home. Which is spelled s-e-x."

"If they'd waited an hour, they could've had pie and sex." Malcolm found a cup and saucer in a cupboard. "It doesn't get any better than that."

And, he discovered in short order, it was damn good pie.

He gauged his timing before he pushed back from the table.

Del and Jack huddled over designs Jack sketched on a legal pad someone had dug up, and Laurel talked recipes with Mrs. Grady.

"I've got to take off. Thanks, Mrs. Grady."

"Poker night," Del said, glancing up. "Bring cash."

"Sure, since I'll be leaving with yours."

"You give my best to your mother. Parker." Mrs. Grady tapped a finger on the table. "Get Malcolm the leftovers I put aside for him."

Even better, Malcolm thought, and flashed Mrs. Grady a grin when she winked at him. He trailed Parker into the kitchen.

"Looks like I'll be eating like a king tomorrow, too." He tucked the container under his arm.

"Mrs. G has a weakness for strays. I didn't mean it like that," she said quickly.

"I didn't take it like that."

"I'm really grateful for your help tonight. You saved me a lot of time and aggravation. I'll walk you out."

She'd pulled out that formal tone, he noted. The one that clearly ordered a man to take a step back. He moved deliberately closer as they walked through the house.

"Can you give me an estimate on when I can pick up my car?"

All business now, Malcolm mused. "Ma'll call you about the tires in the morning, and work that out with you. Since I've got it in, I can give it a once-over."

"I was going to schedule a general maintenance next month, but yes, since it's already there."

"You been having any problems with it?"

"No. None."

"That should make it easy."

She reached for the door. He beat her to it.

"Thanks again. I'll expect your mother's call tomorrow."

Brisk and dry as a handshake, he thought. He set the container down on a table holding a vase of fat orange roses. Sometimes, he thought, you moved fast; sometimes you moved slow.

He moved fast, giving her a quick yank that had her body colliding with his. The way she said *excuse me*, like a veteran school-teacher to an unruly student made him grin before he took her mouth with his.

It was even better than the pie.

Soft, tasty, ripe, with just a hint of shock to cut the sweet. He felt her fingers dig into his shoulders, and the light tremble might have been outrage, might have been pleasure.

He'd tasted her before. Once when she'd grabbed him and planted one on him to take a slap at Del, and again when he'd followed his own instincts on a visit to their place in the Hamptons.

And every taste made him want more.

A lot more.

He didn't bother to be gentle. He imagined she'd had plenty of the smooth type, the polite type, and he wasn't inclined to be either. So he pleased himself, letting his hands run up that truly exceptional body of hers, then down again, enjoying her slow melt against him.

When he heard the low purr in her throat, when he tasted it on his tongue, he let her go. He stepped back, picked up the container of leftovers.

He smiled at her. It was the first time he'd seen her stunned and speechless.

"See you later, Legs."

He strolled out, strapped the container onto his bike. When he swung on, revved the engine, he glanced back to see her standing in the open doorway.

She made a hell of a picture, he thought, framed there in her power suit, just a little bit mussed, with the big, gorgeous house around her.

He tapped his helmet in salute, then roared away with that picture as clear in his head as the taste of her on his tongue.

Parker stepped back, shut the door, then turned and jumped when she saw Laurel in the hallway.

"Can I just say *wow*?"

Parker shook her head, wished she had something to do with her hands. "He just . . . grabbed me."

"I'll say. And let's have one more *wow*."

"He's grabby and pushy and—"

"Really, really hot. And I say that as a woman madly in love with your brother. I might also add," she continued as she walked to Parker, "that as I didn't politely avert my eyes and go away, I happened to observe you weren't exactly fighting him off."

"He caught me by surprise. Besides, I wouldn't give him the satisfaction."

"Sorry, but he looked pretty satisfied. And Parker?" She gave her friend's arm a pat. "You look flustered, glowy, and dazzled."

"I am *not* glowy."

Laurel simply turned Parker by the shoulders to the big foyer mirror. "You were saying?"

Maybe color did glow in her cheeks, and maybe her eyes were a little dazzled, but . . . "That's irritation."

"I won't say 'liar, liar,' but, Parks, under that skirt, your pants are on fire."

"All right, fine. *Fine*. He's a good kisser, if you like the rough, arrogant style."

"You seemed good with it."

"That was only because he ambushed me. And this is a stupid conversation about nothing. I'm going up."

"Me, too, which is why I got an eyeful of the nothing."

They started up together, but before they separated Parker stopped on the landing. "I was wearing the Back-Off Cloak."

"What?"

"I'm not stupid. He made a little move in the kitchen. Actually, he makes little moves every time I run into him, which is disconcerting, but I can handle it. So when I walked him to the door, I thought he might get ideas."

Laurel's eyes widened. "You swirled on the Back-Off Cloak? The famed shield that repels men of all ages, creeds, and political affiliations?"

"Yes."

"Yet he was not repelled. He's immune." She gave Parker a slap on the arm. "He may be the only creature of his kind."

"It's not funny."

"Sure it is. Also sexy."

"I'm not interested in funny and sexy with Malcolm Kavanaugh."

"Parker, if you weren't interested, on some level, you'd have flicked him off like lint on a lapel. He . . ." Laurel searched for the right word. "He intrigues you."

"No, he . . . Maybe."

"As your friend, let me say it's nice to see you intrigued by a man, especially since I like the man, and have noted he is also intrigued by you."

Parker jerked a shoulder. "He just wants to get me in bed."

"Well, of course he wants to get you in bed. But I'm not at all convinced it's 'just.'"

"I'm not going to have sex with him. We have a business relationship."

"Because he's your mechanic?"

"He's Vows' mechanic now, and he's Del's friend."

"Parks, your excuses are so lame they're limping, which makes me think you're worried you want to have sex with him."

"It's not about sex. Everything's not always about sex."

"You brought it up."

Caught, Parker admitted. "Now I'm bringing it down. I've got too much on my mind to think about this anyway. We're jammed tomorrow. We're jammed for the next five days straight."

"We are. Do you want me to come up, hang out awhile?"

The fact that she did, really did, only confirmed to Parker she was making too much out of nothing. "No, thanks, I'm good. And I've got a little work I want to get in before bed. I'll see you in the morning."

She walked up alone, and switched on the TV for company. After slipping out of her shoes, she checked them for any dings, scrapes, or scratches. Satisfied, she set them in their proper place on the shoe wall of her closet. She dropped her suit in the dry cleaning bag, replaced her jewelry in the slots designed for them in the thin drawers.

She slipped on a nightshirt, a robe, tucked her phone in the robe pocket. She considered a long, hot bath, but exed it out since long, hot baths encouraged thinking and dreaming. She didn't care to do either.

Instead, she fixed her mind on the next day's schedule while she cleansed, toned, moisturized her face.

Glowy, she thought, giving her reflection a cool stare. What a silly word. It wasn't even a word in the first place, and totally inaccurate.

Laurel had romance fever. Nearly all brides caught it, and due to its side effects they saw everything and everyone through a pretty haze of love.

Nice for them, she admitted as she took the band from her hair. Good business for Vows.

And speaking of business, she'd take an hour now to input all the new data from the evening consult and the initial choices made by the clients.

An estimated 225 on the guest list, she thought as she wandered back into the bedroom with the intention of going to work on her laptop in her sitting room. A bridal party of six, including a flower girl who'd be five by the June wedding.

The bride's favorite flower was peony, her color choices—for now anyway—pink and green. Soft tones.

Soft, Parker thought again, and changed direction to open her terrace doors and step out. She'd just get a little air first, just take in a little of the night air.

The bride wanted soft and delicate. She'd asked Parker to meet her at the salon to view the gown she'd chosen, which proved she was a bride who understood that the wedding dress created the center of whatever tone or theme or mood the wedding took.

All those lovely, floaty layers, Parker recalled, the subtle gleam of seed pearls and tender touches of lace.

Pastels and peonies, shimmering tulle, and whispered promises.

She could see it. She would see to it. She excelled at seeing to things.

There was no reason, no good reason to feel so restless, so unsettled, so addled.

No reason to stand here looking out at night-drenched gardens remembering the unexpected thrill of a motorcycle ride that had lasted only minutes.

And had been fast and dangerous and foolishly exciting.

Like, very like, the hard, rough kiss of a brash man in her own foyer.

She wasn't interested in those things. Absolutely not. Intrigued, maybe, but intrigued was a different matter. She found sharks intriguing when they swam their eerily silent way in the tank at an aquarium, but that didn't mean she had any interest in taking a dip with them.

Which wasn't a fair comparison, she admitted with a sigh. Not fair at all.

Malcolm might be cocky, he might be brash, but he wasn't a shark. He'd been so natural with Mrs. G, and even a bit sweet in that area. She had unerring radar for phonies when it came to their behavior with those she loved, and there hadn't been a phony note in Malcolm's.

Then there was his friendship with Del. Del might tolerate professional relationships with phonies and sharks, but never a personal one.

So the problem, if there was a problem, was obviously with her. She'd just have to correct it. Correcting, solving, and eliminating problems was her stock-in-trade.

She'd just figure out the solution to this one, implement it, then move on. She needed to ascertain and identify said problem first, but she had a pretty good idea of its root.

At some level of the intrigue—not interest, but intrigue—at some level of *that* level, she was attracted.

In an elemental, strictly chemical way.

She was human, she was healthy, and Laurel was right. Malcolm was hot. In his primal, rough-edged manner.

Motorcycles and leather, torn denim and cocky grins. Hard hands, a hungry mouth.

Parker pressed a hand to her belly. Yes, definitely an aspect of attraction. Now that she'd admitted it, she could work out the best way to defuse it.

Like a bomb.

Like the bomb that had gone off inside her when he'd yanked her . . . Yanked her, she thought again. She didn't like being yanked.

Did she?

"Doesn't matter," she mumbled. You fixed problems with answers, not more questions.

She wished she didn't have so many damn questions.

In her pocket, her phone rang. She plucked it out like a woman reaching for a float in a stormy sea.

"Thank God." She breathed out relief. Crazy Bride would absolutely, no question, give her a problem she could efficiently solve. And keep her mind off her own.

"Hi, Sabina! What can I do for you?"

CHAPTER FOUR

$\mathcal{P}$ARKER PREPPED FOR THE MORNING STAFF MEETING WITH BLACK-Berry and laptop. She sat at the large round table in what had been the library of her home and now served as Vows' conference room.

The walls of books and the rich scent of leather remained, and on brisk fall or cold winter mornings a fire would snap away in the hearth as it had for as long as she could remember. Lamps that warmed cozy seating arrangements had belonged to her grandmother. The rugs, a bit faded and frayed with time and use, came down from a generation before that. Framed articles on Vows and the women behind it were displayed artfully on the walls between cabinets.

On the long table nearby, her mother's silver coffee service gleamed, and under it, tucked behind the antique doors, sat an office-sized refrigerator stocked with water and soft drinks.

To her mind the room epitomized the blending of tradition and enterprise essential to her goals for herself and her business.

She checked the day's agenda, including the morning appointments, the afternoon's bridal shower, and the rehearsal for Friday evening's event. Her phone signaled as Mac came in with a basket of muffins.

"Laurel's on her way. Emma says she's not late."

Parker nodded. "Friday night's bride. Good morning, Cecily! Ready for the big day?"

She nodded again as Mac held the coffeepot over Parker's cup. "Um-hmm. That's so sweet. Yes, we can do that. Oh, absolutely." She listened, winced only a little.

"I think that's incredibly generous of you and Marcus. I know you must be," she responded. "Listen, I'm just thinking, just throwing this out there. I wonder if considering the wedding cake and the groom's cake, another might be overkill. Not quite as special as you'd like. What about a cupcake? Heart-shaped, elaborately frosted with their names on it. It would fit right on the head table in front of them. Be exclusively theirs."

Listening again, Parker began to key in data one-handed on her laptop. "Leave it to me. You know Laurel will make it beautiful, and very special."

Parker just beamed out a smile as Laurel came in and narrowed her eyes at the statement.

"What's your sister's favorite flower?" Parker asked. "Dahlias. Lovely. Oh, of course he can if he wants to. I'll be available for that if he can get here just a few minutes early tonight. Yes, we're excited, too. Not a word, I promise. See you tonight."

"What am I making beautiful and special?" Laurel demanded.

"A cupcake. One single cupcake." Parker held up one finger. "Heart-shaped, maybe a little oversized just for impact. Maybe iced with dahlias as the design and with the names Griff and Jaci—Friday night's groom's brother and the bride's sister, also the BM and MOH. They've been dating about six months now. He's going to propose at the wedding, as a crescendo to his toast to the bride and groom."

"Why would he want to do that?" Mac demanded.

"I don't know, because he's crazy from love, because he wants to tie the way he feels about her to the way his brother feels about his sister. He asked his brother and the bride first, and they *love* it. They're weeping with joy. And," she added with a steely look at Laurel, "she wanted another cake. I talked her down to cupcake, so you owe me."

"What'd I miss?" Emma rushed in. "I'm not late."

"You're late," Mac corrected, "and love is in the air is what you missed."

"Oh, well, that's all over the place around here anyway."

"New business, just so Emma's up-to-date." Parker ran through the phone call and resulting additions. As she expected, Emma went dewy-eyed.

"That's adorable."

"It won't be if she says hell no," Laurel pointed out.

"She won't." But Emma looked stricken. "Oh God, what if?"

"Let's take a good look at the two of them tonight," Parker suggested. "See what sense we get. If we think oops, we'll come up with a plan to cover. Next? Today's afternoon event. Bridal shower with guests arriving at two."

"Champagne Elegance," Laurel said. "That's the name of the cake as that's what the very snooty MOH and bridal shower hostess demanded as ambiance. We have a small-scale wedding cake with champagne accents, a variety of cookies, mini pastries, chocolates. The caterer's providing the girly food, the champagne, and the coffee and tea. Party favors include chocolates in glossy white boxes, with monogrammed silver ribbons accented with a sparkly hair clip."

"I've done white roses, as requested." Emma gulped coffee. "Individual contemporary bouquets in black vases for each table.

Tink's finishing up the arbor and pergola as we speak. We'll do white rose displays in the portico urns, and on the terraces."

"The guests have been requested to wear white," Parker reminded her partners. "We're to wear black, as are all the subs and the string trio who'll play during the mingling and nibbling portions of the event. The forecast is for mostly sunny, light winds, and a high of seventy-one. So we should be able to hold the event outside as we hoped. Gift table will be under the pergola. At three, we'll set up the bride's chair, and at three fifteen, begin the opening of gifts. I'll be keeping the record of who gave what for the bride. By four fifteen, we should be able to transfer the gifts to the limo. By four forty-five, we wave good-bye. Mac?"

"The MOH wants candids, by which she actually means carefully posed shots where everyone, especially her, looks fabulous and happy and natural and ten pounds lighter. She wants a shot of the bride with every gift, and with every guest. No problem on my end."

"The Mason-Easterbay wedding party should arrive at five thirty for rehearsal. They have reservations at Carlotta's for seven thirty, so they need to be out and gone by seven. Any problem there?"

When she got negatives, Parker moved on. "Any questions, problems, comments, sarcastic remarks about their actual event?"

"If I'd known there was a sarcastic remark slot, I'd've had one ready," Laurel told her.

"Otherwise, today. I may need to have somebody drive me into the garage to get my car. Or I'll take a cab if everyone's busy. Mrs. Kavanaugh's calling me this morning, and hopefully can give me a time frame. I do have an appointment here at ten." She waited a bit. "With Carter's sister Diane."

"What about?" Mac wondered.

"About her being a bitch. Sorry, I shouldn't call your soon-to-be sister-in-law a bitch. To your face."

"No problem. She is kind of a bitch. The passive-aggressive type that makes me want to boot her in the ass. Often."

"The sky's never blue enough for Diane," Emma commented. Her family and the Maguires had been friends for years.

"What's she being a bitch about?" Laurel asked.

"She's upset Sherry. Didn't want to be in the wedding because it's too much fuss, too much trouble."

"She's been snarky about the wedding right along." Mac nodded, shrugged. "She's given me some nudges about it, and about mine. Who wants that in their wedding party? Sister or not."

"Now she's saying she won't come to the rehearsal dinner. Not in the wedding party, doesn't want to get a sitter, doesn't want to come with the kids and deal with them. Me, I'd say fine, don't, but Sherry wants her there." Parker's eyes glittered. "So she'll be there."

"Kick her ass, champ."

Parker smiled at Laurel. "Count on it. Once I've done that, I'll be available to pitch in with anything for anyone, until it's time to get my car."

"Maybe you'll get more smoochies."

"Laurel."

"What? Do you think I'm keeping that to myself?" She grinned as both Mac and Emma demanded details.

"Malcolm Kavanaugh, in the foyer, with a hot embrace."

"Well, well." Mac wiggled her eyebrows.

"There's no 'well, well' about it." Wanting to move on, Parker pulled out her casually dismissive tone. "He was just showing off."

"He's good at it," Laurel put in. "I got singed by the heat, and I was fifteen feet away."

"Are you going out?" Emma asked her.

"If you mean am I going out at some point to pick up my car, yes."

"Come on. Are you going to see him—a date," Emma qualified.

"No. It was just a . . . He was being a smart–ass, that's it."

"You kissed him first." Emma wagged her finger. "Fourth of July."

"I was mad at Del, and it was a mistake. And that doesn't mean—" She broke off and grabbed her ringing phone.

"Saved by the CrackBerry," Mac announced.

"Hi, Buffy." Taking advantage, Parker pushed up, walked out of the room as she spoke.

"They've got the hots, the mutual hots." Laurel folded her arms. "I am not mistaken on this."

"He looks at her. Don't give me that smirk." Emma pointed at Mac. "He looks at her, a lot, and she tries not to look at him. I say mutual hots a definite."

"He's got that whole James Dean thing going."

"The sausage guy?" Mac asked, frowning at Laurel.

"No, Jesus, Mackensie." Laurel aimed her gaze at the heavens. "That's Jimmy Dean. *James.* Bad boy, all attitude."

"I kind of like that he rattles her," Emma decided. "Our Parker isn't easily rattled, which is one of the aspects that makes her our Parker, but I kind of like seeing it."

"He's not slick, which earns him points from me." Laurel shrugged, rose. "We'll see where it goes, if anywhere. Meanwhile, duty calls." She paused at the doorway. "Hey, you know what Parker said after the smoking-hot kiss?"

"What?" Mac demanded.

"Absolutely nothing."

PARKER MIGHT NOT HAVE THOUGHT OF ANYTHING TO SAY THEN, but she had plenty to say to Carter's older sister.

She greeted Diane at the door herself, extending both hands and a beaming smile. "Di, it's so good to see you! Thanks so much for making time today. How are the kids?" she added as she drew Diane inside.

"They're fine."

"Mac tells me they got a puppy recently." Deliberately she draped an arm over Diane's shoulders, just a couple of girl pals catching up, to lead her into the parlor.

"My father managed to get around me there. Of course, he's not the one dealing with it."

"Isn't that always the way?" Parker said cheerfully. "I know an excellent trainer if you're interested in a little help. She's wonderful, and has kid-puppy classes, so the kids get involved in the work. How about some coffee?"

"I'm cutting back on caffeine."

"I drink far too much of it myself. We've got some lovely green tea. Carter says it's your favorite."

With a quick hitch in her stride, Diane stared, blinked. "Carter did?"

"It's surprising isn't it, what our brothers notice and remember? Let's sit down. You look just terrific, Diane. What *have* you been doing?"

Obviously flustered, Diane pushed back at her bob of brown hair. An attractive woman, she habitually marred her looks with a dissatisfied expression. "I joined a yoga class a couple months ago, but it's so full of nonsense that I—"

"Oh, I love yoga." All smiles, Parker poured the tea. It was no accident she used one of her grandmother's best Doulton tea services. Diane, she knew, noted and set store by such things. "Even a fifteen-minute session helps me release all the stress of the day. Good for you for taking a little me-time. With your work, your family, all those obligations, you have to fit twenty-five hours into every day. I honestly don't know how you do it, and here I've added to those hours by asking you to come talk to me."

"I assume it's about Sherry's wedding, and I don't really understand what that has to do with me."

"Can you believe it's almost here?" Undeterred, Parker sipped her tea. "And before we know it, it'll be Carter and Mac." She reached out to take Diane's hand again. "It makes us family. And that's what sparked this idea I have."

"What idea?"

"I should start at the beginning, and the credit for that goes to Mac. You know that Sherry's main wish for the wedding was fun. She wants it to be a fun day—friends and family—a celebration. I have to tell you, Di, so many brides are focused on the tiny details, the minutiae. And of course, that's what we do here. It's part of what we offer. But it's so refreshing to work with your sister, a woman who sees the big picture. She sees, well, your parents, and you."

"Me?"

"You and Sam and your children. What you've built—the life, the family, the continuity. It isn't an easy thing, that build—as you know—and she sees what you've accomplished. And all that starts with the wedding itself, the celebration of those first steps. You're her big sister. You took the steps before her, and you've helped show her the way. You've been a huge influence on her."

Diane sniffed. "Sherry never listens to anything I have to say."

"You know, I think those who have impact and influence over us are often unaware. Why just the other day . . ." She broke off, gave a little shake of her head. "I don't want to betray a confidence, but since it's family, Sherry told me just the other day how important you are to her, how much you mean to her. I guess it's easier to say that to someone just a little outside, isn't it?"

Again the stare, the blink. "She said that?"

"Yes, and it made me realize . . . I'm ahead of myself again." With an easy laugh, Parker waved a hand as if she'd scattered her thoughts. "Mac's idea. She's put together photographs of Sherry, of your family, Nick and his family. Old photos, recent ones. A kind of chronological retrospective. Mac's so talented. I know I'm biased, but I have to say the CD she created is wonderful. Sweet, funny, charming, poignant. The idea is to run it at the rehearsal dinner."

"Oh, I'm not going to—"

"What it's missing," Parker interrupted, "is a narrator. An emcee if you will. Someone who's been there from the beginning. Not your parents, as it's a surprise for them, too, and Mac added their wedding photo to kick the whole thing off. I thought Carter, as he's a teacher as well as her brother, so he's used to speaking in public, but when Sherry and I talked, I realized no. It's a sister thing. A big sister thing. After all, who has a more unique, clever, intimate perspective on Sherry, on your family, on Nick and his, than you? Please say you'll do it."

Again, Parker reached out a hand, making that contact, making it personal.

"I know it's a lot to ask, and it's such short notice, but it's all just coming together. We really need you."

"You want me to . . . to narrate pictures?"

"Not just want, but need. And not just pictures. It's a journey, Diane. Sherry and Nick's, yes, but also all of you. Family's so essential to both of them. I've gotten to know them and understand that over these past months. It's going to be the highlight of the evening. Carter's drafted out the script, and he's hoping you'll say yes and work with him on refining it."

"Carter wants me to—" She broke off, obviously stunned.

"Oh, I know you're incredibly busy already, and it's a lot to ask. But I'll help as much as I can, as much as you want or need. Frankly, I don't think you'll need any help. Anyone who can manage a family the way you do can, in my opinion, manage anything."

"I might be able to do it, but I'd have to see the CD and whatever Carter's written before I could commit."

Parker whisked a file off the table. "I happen to have a copy of both right here. The CD runs just about twelve minutes. Have you got time to watch it now?"

"I . . . I guess."

"Perfect. I'll just get my laptop."

Twenty-six minutes later, Parker wheeled the tea trolley back in the kitchen.

"I see by the canary feathers stuck to your lip that you pulled it off." Mrs. Grady set the basket of cherry tomatoes just harvested from her kitchen garden on the counter.

"I troweled it on pretty thick, then I shoveled on more. She'll not only attend the rehearsal and the rehearsal dinner, but she'll emcee Mac and Carter's CD. And bless Carter for being willing to step out as emcee, especially since it was as much his idea as Mac's."

"He's a good boy. And his older sister's always been a pain in the rear."

"Well, she's attractive, but she lacks Sherry's vivacity and easy confidence. She's smart, but not as innately bright as Carter, and not anywhere near as sweet. She's the firstborn but not, I think, often first otherwise. And it irks. All I had to do was make it as much about her as Sherry." Parker shrugged. "And tell her a few truths. Her family loves her. She's important to them. Some people just have to hear it, a lot."

"I bet it didn't hurt it came from you. 'Parker Brown needs my help.'"

Parker shrugged again. "Whatever works. The bride gets what she wants and deserves." She glanced at her watch. "And I'm on schedule."

She pitched in on decor for the event, checked on Laurel's

progress, spoke with the caterers on their arrival, the parking attendants at theirs.

She stepped out on the terrace for a last check as Mac took shots of the setup, and thought, Champagne Elegance all around.

Not her particular taste for a wedding shower—and since she had three in planning stages for her friends, she had plenty of ideas—but the scene had an appealingly stylish Deco feel, with just enough lush from Emma's stunning arrangements to soften it.

"Totally Gatsby," Mac said as she lowered her camera.

"I was just thinking that. I'd say the hostess, and the bride, will be very pleased."

"You've already scored today. Carter sent me a text. His sister wants to meet him after his classes today and talk about the script for the rehearsal dinner. Nice job."

"I think she'll do one, too. I really do. She was excited about the whole thing when she left."

"Diane? Excited? Did you spike her tea?"

"In a manner of speaking, but it was the CD itself that did it. She got misty a few times."

Mac's eyebrows winged up. "I underestimate my own power. Everything a go inside?"

"Emma was just finishing the public areas, and Laurel's done and with the caterer. I'm about to . . ." She laid a finger on her headset. "Be right there. Our hostess just arrived," she told Mac. "I'll go meet her, bring her through."

"I'll go around, get some unobtrusive shots of arrivals."

With a nod, Parker started inside. "Em, Laurel," she said into her headset, "we're green."

Within the hour, Parker watched women in stylish white suits, floaty white dresses, sharply tailored white pants mingle on the terrace. They sipped champagne, chatted, laughed, nibbled on pretty passed hors d'oeuvres.

Mac moved among them, capturing moments. The burst of delight as the bride-to-be threw back her head and laughed, the affectionate hug of greeting between friends, the sweetness of a granddaughter tapping flutes with her grandmother.

It pleased her, as it always did, to see happiness here, to feel it sparkling in the air like champagne, to know what had come to her could be a setting for joy.

Today it pleased her to be in the company of women, and to have played a part in creating this individualized vision of the female ritual.

At the appointed time, she moved forward to ask the guests to be seated for lunch, then again retreated to the background. Then braced when the hostess made her way over, her face set in harassed lines.

"Olivia asked about games. She wants shower games."

Which you expressly vetoed, Parker remembered, but smiled. "I can take care of that."

"She asked about games *and* prizes. Obviously I haven't prepared for—"

"It's not a problem. I'll see to it during lunch. How about three? I find that's just enough. Fun and simple games with pretty prizes for the winners."

"I don't want to hand out anything tacky or foolish. I'd want something in keeping with the ambiance."

And gee, Parker thought, I was going to get the glow-in-the-dark dildos. "Absolutely. Leave it to me. We'll have it all arranged for after lunch. Please, go enjoy yourself. Don't worry about a thing."

She waited until she'd slipped inside. "Laurel, I need you to take over outside," she said into her headset. "The BTB wants games and prizes. I need fifteen minutes to set it up."

"Got it."

"Emma, I need a small prize table set up."

"Oh, for God's sake—"

"I know, I know. Whatever you can do. You've got forty minutes."

She charged up the back steps, all the way to the gift room, a space designed for gift wrapping, present storage. Inside one of the cabinets she had labeled, prewrapped gifts. She scanned, debated, and after choosing three, slipped them into white embossed gift bags, tucked in black tissue. From another cabinet she grabbed a stack of notepads, pencils, pulled other supplies.

She dashed back down, set the bags and the box of supplies on the dining room table, then zipped through the kitchen and into the old butler's pantry to choose the proper tray for the display.

"What are you after?" Mrs. Grady asked from behind her.

"The BTB wants games, which the hostess vetoed during the planning stages. I don't think white bags on a white tray, and we don't have an appropriate black one. I think silver. Or glass. Maybe glass."

"Try both."

"Good idea. Can you come, give me an opinion?"

Mrs. Grady walked along with her. "Oh, your car's back."

"Back where?"

"Here."

Parker stopped, frowned. "My car's here?"

"Delivered about twenty minutes ago. Washed and waxed, too. I put the bill up on your desk."

"Oh. But I didn't ask him to deliver it. I was going to—"

"Saves you time, doesn't it?" Which, in Mrs. Grady's opinion, made Malcolm Kavanaugh a very shrewd customer.

Parker said nothing, only continued to frown as she arranged the bags on the silver tray. "I think the glass one's better. The silver makes too much of a statement, and Emma could sprinkle some white rose petals on the glass, and with the little black vases . . . Who delivered the car?"

Mrs. Grady smothered a smile. "Didn't catch his name. Well, theirs, as the one had another following him in a tow truck."

"Oh. Um . . . The glass?"

"I'd say. It's classy, but more subtle than the silver."

"Yes, that's what I'm after." She stepped back. "I'll leave this here, go see if I can help Emma set up the table."

She started out. "Really, I could've picked up the car."

"No doubt. What do you say when someone does you a favor?"

Parker heaved out a breath at the implied *tsk* in the tone. "You say thank you. I will. When I get a chance."

She didn't have one, or so she told herself. The event required her focus, and with the additional time for the unscheduled games ran about thirty minutes over. Which cut back on the time to prep for the evening's rehearsal.

"The games were a hit," Mac commented.

"They generally are."

"Nice prizes. I really liked the travel jewelry caddy, the green leather? Somebody who's going to Tuscany for her honeymoon could really use one of them."

"Maybe somebody'll get lucky." Parker chugged from a bottle of water. "We seriously pulled that off. And our hostess didn't bat an eye at the additional invoice for the prizes, especially since I gave her the extra half hour on the house."

She took a last scan of the terrace. They'd broken down all the tables, but had left the pergola and urns dressed. They had only to set up the refreshment table, and they were good to go.

She probably had five minutes now to call in her thanks, but really, she had to check the invoice first. For all she knew he'd gouged her on a delivery charge.

"I'm just going to—" Her phone rang. "God. Crazy Bride."

"Better you than me. Go ahead. We've got this."

Crazy Bride ate up her time. And gave her space to think.

S̸HE'D SEND A THANK-YOU *NOTE* WITH THE CHECK FOR THE SERVICE and tires. That was, Parker decided as she ran the rehearsal, appropriate.

"With five minutes to go," she said, "the groom's brother—and best man—will escort their mother to her seat, with her husband following. That's perfect. The best man will join the groom, standing to the groom's left. And at three minutes to go, the bride's brother will escort their mom to her seat. Brother moves up to the left of best man, right of George. Angle just a little, Sam. Exactly. Music change for the bridal procession. Wendy, Nikki, Addy—and I'll be there to cue you tomorrow. Remember to smile, ladies. Then Jaci, the maid of honor.

"Good. When she's halfway down, it's time for the ring bearer. That's the way, Kevin!"

The five-year-old strutted down to laughter and applause.

"And the flower girl. Really good, Jenny, and tomorrow there'll be real flowers in your basket. Kevin on the boys' side, Jenny on the girls'. You stand right there with your daddy, Kevin. Then . . ."

She trailed off, blank as she looked back and saw Malcolm leaning on one of the urns, a bouquet in his hand. She couldn't see his eyes, not with the sun slanting off the dark glasses he wore. But she could see his grin clearly enough.

"Then?" the groom prompted with a laugh. "Do I get married?"

"Almost. Music change, everyone stands. And the bride begins her walk escorted by her father. And," she said to the groom, "she's the most beautiful woman in the world. She's everything you've ever wanted. And she's about to be yours."

She waited. "Stop here. And as you requested, your mom will step over with you and your dad. The minister will ask who gives this woman, and your line, Mr. Falconi?"

"Her mother and I."

They kissed their daughter, then took her hand and placed it in the groom's.

"Lovely. Now . . ."

She ran them through the ceremony, hitting the highlights, outlining the timing and choreography.

"He'll say you may kiss your bride."

"I got that part." The groom spun his bride, dipped her while she laughed, and bent to give her a lavish kiss.

"Cecily, if you get cold feet tomorrow, I'm happy to stand in for you."

The bride laughed again, twinkling at Parker. "My feet are really, really warm, but thanks."

"I bet. At that point, you'll face your friends and family, the minister will introduce you for the first time as husband and wife, and those of us not still swooning over that kiss will applaud. Music changes to recessional, and you'll walk down the aisle. Mac will take you from there. From here, the rest of the wedding party recesses in reverse order. Flower girl and ring bearer first."

Good, she thought, very good. If everyone smiled and beamed like this tomorrow, they'd hardly need the sun.

"After the wedding party, the parents and grandparents of the bride, then the groom's. Mac will also need all of you for wedding pictures. The guests will be escorted inside the Solarium for canapes and drinks to keep them happy during the photo session."

She ignored the itch at the back of her neck. She *knew* he was staring at her, as she outlined the timing and procedure for introductions, dinner, toasts, the shift to the Ballroom, first dances, cake cutting, and so on.

"The Bride's and Groom's suites will be available to the wedding party from four until the end of the evening. We'll transfer the gifts from the gift table to the newlyweds' limo, as well as any flowers they want to take with them or give to others. I know it's a lot, but my partners and I will be here for all of you every step of the way. All you really have to do is enjoy and celebrate."

CHAPTER FIVE

$\mathscr{S}$HE RAN THE SHOW LIKE A VELVET-VOICED GENERAL, MALCOLM thought, striding around in her mile-high heels and severe black suit. A lot of smiles, though, he noted, and buckets of warmth.

Except when she looked in his direction.

He waited her out, smothered in the scent of roses that made the bouquet he carried seem a bit puny. Still, he'd wrangled it from the nose-ringed Goth girl who worked with Emma, so he'd kept it all in the family.

Emma breezed by him. "Mine?"

"Not anymore."

"Still very pretty. Parker's going to be a few more minutes."

"I've got time."

"Grab a drink if you want. There's plenty. Or you can wait inside."

"I'm good, but thanks."

"I've got to go. If you were over at my place, you saw we're neck deep."

"Wedding tomorrow?"

"No, actually, they had a conflict, so they rehearsed for their Friday wedding tonight. I've got an outside event tomorrow, and Parker's got a couple tours, plus we've got another full-staff consult. And a four-event weekend."

"Busy girls. I'm fine here. Go ahead."

"She won't be long," Emma assured him and hurried away.

When he waited another fifteen minutes, he figured she took her time. But she came out again, with that ground-eating stride she managed to make look both unhurried and graceful.

"I'm sorry to keep you waiting," she began. "If I'd known you'd planned to come by, I'd have told you we had a rehearsal."

"I didn't come to see you."

She opened her mouth, closed it again.

"I came by to see Mrs. Grady." He gestured with the flowers. "To thank her again for dinner and the ham sandwich I had for lunch today."

"Oh, well, she's not here."

"I got that."

"She went out with friends. Dinner and a movie. You brought her flowers."

"Coals to the place that has all the coals."

"She'll love them, and she'll be sorry she missed you. I'll put them in water for her."

"Okay."

But when she reached for them he turned and started to the house. He glanced back. "Coming?"

"I don't want to hold you up any more than I already have," she said as she walked with him.

"I've got nothing booked. You?"

"Actually, I was going to call you," she said, evading the question, "to thank you for having my car sent out. You didn't have to go to the trouble, but I appreciate it."

"We're both full of thank-yous."

"Apparently." She led the way in, through the kitchen and back into the butler's pantry.

He stopped, looked around. "Wow. This place just keeps on keeping on."

"My family's always liked to entertain, and often in a way that takes a lot of space." She chose a vase from a cabinet. "Del may be home if you want company."

"You know, it feels like you're trying to shake me off."

"Does it?" She added flower food and water to the vase. "That would be rude."

"And you wouldn't be."

"Oh, I can be, depending on the circumstances." She waited a beat. "But doing me a favor, two actually, and bringing one of my favorite people flowers aren't meriting circumstances."

"I can't say I thought of kissing you as doing you a favor."

He felt the temperature drop twenty degrees.

"That's not what I meant."

"I bet that usually works. The freeze," he added. "But me? I don't mind the cold."

"I'm sure that's handy for you, and I also think you've gotten the wrong impression."

When she turned, he shifted, and boxed her in. "No, I haven't."

Her eyes flashed, blue lightning cased in ice. "I don't like being maneuvered."

"No, you like doing the maneuvering, and you're damn good at it. I admire that. When I was doing gags—"

"Gags?"

"Stunts. Stunt work. Anyway, back then I liked to watch the

horse wranglers if I had a chance. You've got the same kind of skill with people. It's impressive."

"I'd say thank you, but we seem to have passed that phrase around plenty already."

"Don't mention it." He eased back. "I like your house. Who wouldn't, but I mean I like how it works. I like seeing and figuring out how things work."

"How the house works?"

"House, home, business. Canvas."

She paused at that, a flower in her hand, and just stared at him.

"You let people paint the picture they want on it. You guide a lot of the strokes, maybe influence them toward certain colors, but they get what they want at the end of it. It's good work."

"Th—" The phone saved her from another thank-you. "Excuse me. Hello, Bonnie, what can I do for you?" She wandered a few paces away.

Malcolm heard the hysteria through the phone even before Parker yanked it an inch from her ear. "I see. Yes, I . . ."

He listened—why the hell not—and began to stick flowers in the vase himself.

"Of course I understand. But I also think you're very stressed just now, again understandably. I bet Richie is, too. Well, Bonnie, your mother isn't marrying Richie, and though I know she loves him, she doesn't know him the way you do. I think, if Richie thought of it as anything other than a silly, blowing-off-steam male tradition, he'd never have told you. But he did, and the way he did tells me he thinks of it as a joke. His brother's just doing what brothers often do."

She closed her eyes a moment, listened as she thumbed out a Tums. "Yes, I do understand, but you're not marrying Richie's brother. I'm sure none of you, really, want something as unimportant as this to cause any sort of a family rift."

She listened again. "Yes. Mmm-hmm. Does Richie love you? Mmm-hmm. Has he given you any reason to doubt that, any reason not to trust him? What I think isn't important. It's what you think, and what you feel. But since you asked, I think I'd laugh it off, and I'd go have a wonderful time with my friends before I spent the next week getting ready to marry the man I'm just crazy about."

While she wound it up, he finished the arrangement, then stepped back, hands tucked in his back pockets to study the result.

"That's nicely done," Parker commented.

"It's not bad. So . . . problem?"

"Nothing major."

"The groom's brother's hired a stripper for the bachelor party. She projected," Malcolm added, "really well."

"I guess she did. Yes, and the bride hit flashpoint, aided by the fury and dire warnings of her mother—who really doesn't think anyone's good enough for her baby girl, and will, I predict, always find fault with Richie."

"She wanted you to back her up."

"Naturally."

"And you soothed and smoothed while managing to turn it back on her. Nice wrangling, Tex."

"If you're mature enough to marry, you ought to be mature enough to stop crying to Mommy every time something upsets you. And if she doesn't trust her perfectly affable, devoted, and honest-to-a-fault fiancé not to jump on a stripper a week before the wedding, she shouldn't marry him."

"That's not what you said to her."

"Because she's the client." She caught herself. "And I shouldn't be saying it to you."

"Hey, what's said in the— What is this room?"

"Butler's pantry."

"No shit?" He let out a half laugh as he scanned the space again. "Okay, what's said in the butler's pantry stays in the butler's pantry." That got a smile out of her, a faint one. "You calmed her down."

"For now anyway. They're moving to Atlanta—he's been transferred—in a couple months. The mother is supremely pissed over that, and it's the very best thing that could happen. They've got a good chance, I think, if she gets out from under Mommy's thumb."

"It tensed you up."

She shrugged and picked up the vase. "I'll get over it."

"I gotta ask you something."

She glanced back at him as they walked out. "What?"

"Do you own a pair of jeans?"

"Of course I own a pair of jeans."

"How about a leather jacket, with or without designer label."

"Your interest in my wardrobe is very strange." She set the vase on the counter, then handed Malcolm a notepad and pen. "You should write her a little note, so she'll see it with the flowers when she gets home."

"Okay, while I'm doing that, go put on the jeans and jacket."

"Excuse me?"

"I love the way you say that. You'll enjoy the ride more out of that suit."

"I like this suit, and I'm not going for a ride."

"I like how you look in the suit, but you'll be more comfortable on the bike in jeans." He tucked a thumb in his front pocket, leaned a hip against the counter. "It's a nice night. Neither of us have anything booked. So, we'll take a ride, clear your head. I'll buy you dinner."

"I'm not getting back on that motorcycle."

"You're not afraid of the bike, or of having dinner with me."

"It's not a matter of fear but preference."

He smiled. "Prove it. Here's the deal. You take the ride, have dinner—casual, public place—I bring you home. If you don't have fun, or at least enjoy the change of pace, I back off. All the way."

This time the look was regal, and just a little amused. "I don't need to negotiate to get you to back off, Malcolm."

"You're right about that." He waited a beat while their eyes stayed locked. "So why haven't you backed me off?"

Good question, she thought. She might as well figure out the answer. "A ride, a casual meal. That's it."

"That's the deal."

"I'll go change."

She did something for him, Malcolm thought as he scrawled *You still owe me a dance* on the notepad. He wasn't altogether sure what it was she did, but it was something.

He wanted his hands on her, no question, but Parker Brown wasn't the jump in, roll around, then roll off type. Added to that, he valued his friendship with her brother.

He walked out of the kitchen, wandered the first floor.

If he considered Parker an easy bang, and acted on it, he'd fully expect Del to kick his ass, or try to. Reverse positions, he'd do exactly the same. And that was one of the reasons he valued the friendship.

He poked into what he figured they called—due to the big-ass piano—the music room. The misty watercolors shimmering on the walls were undoubtedly originals, and nice enough. But the collection of instruments in a fancy glass case caught his interest.

Guitar, violin, various flutes—maybe a piccolo—a concertina, a drum, harmonica, what he thought was a dulcimer, a cowbell, bongos, and a few things he couldn't readily identify.

If it hadn't been locked, he doubted he'd have resisted the urge to open the cabinet and try out a couple of instruments, just to see how they sounded, to see how they worked.

And, he supposed, that was why he didn't consider Parker a casual bang. He had this urge to open her up, see how she worked.

Rich girl—wealthy woman, he corrected—with exceptional looks, the pedigree, the connections, the smarts. And she worked as hard, maybe harder, than anyone he knew. She could've coasted on her very fine ass, jetting off for drinks in Majorca, sailed the Aegean to sun those amazing legs, sipped wine in a Parisian cafe between shopping sprees.

Instead, she'd founded a business with childhood pals that kept her running around at other people's beck.

He wandered to the piano, improvised a few chords.

Not for the money, he decided. He didn't get the greed vibe from her. Money would be a result, a practicality of business, but not the essential ingredient. He knew what it was like when money was the essential.

Satisfaction played a role, but there had to be more.

He wanted to figure it out.

He sensed her—a little heat along the skin—and looked up to see her in the doorway.

And oh yeah, he wanted his hands on her.

She wore jeans as well as she wore her woman-in-charge suits. Her boots had short, skinny heels. She wore a bright red shirt under a thin leather jacket the color, like the boots, of dark chocolate. Silver hoops glinted on her ears.

Classy Biker Babe? he wondered.

No. Just classy.

"You play?"

"Me?" He shrugged. "No. I just mess around. That's some collection."

"Yes. My father's mostly. He had absolutely no musical talent, and so admired those who did."

"Del plays a mean piano, especially after a couple beers. How about you?"

"Piano, violin—with or without beer. The dulcimer."

"I thought that's what that was. What's this one?"

She walked to the case as he tapped the glass toward a small, key-shaped instrument.

"A trump or jaw harp. You hold it against the teeth, or the lips, and pluck. Simple, effective, and very old."

"Is that a piccolo?"

"No, that's a soprano flute. That's a piccolo. I can get the key for the case."

"No, that's okay." He wondered, idly, where people came up with names like piccolo or saxophone. "I just like knowing what I'm looking at. Plus, if you opened it, I'd just want to play with everything and we wouldn't get to that ride."

He shifted so instead of shoulder-to-shoulder they stood face-to-face. "Maybe by the end of it, I'll figure out what I'm looking at."

She stepped back. "It's not that complicated."

"You're not doing the looking. Ready?"

She nodded, led the way out. On the way she picked up a purse with a long strap, and slipped it on cross-body.

"One thing I know about you. You think things through." He tapped the bag with his finger. "Getting on a bike, need your supplies. So you put them in something you can hang on, instead of hang on to. Smart. I like smart."

He opened the door, holding it until she'd walked through.

"I like practical. That's not practical." She gestured toward the bike.

"Sure it is. It gets me where I'm going, gets good gas mileage, and can fit in small spaces for parking."

"I'll concede those points. I doubt it feels practical through a Connecticut winter."

"Depends." He walked down to unstrap a helmet. "Before you get on," he said as he handed it to her, "and in the interest of fair play, I've got a bet going."

"A bet?"

"With Del. Jack and Carter wanted in on it. I bet Del a hundred I'd get you back on the bike."

Her eyes, he noted, neither heated or frosted. They just narrowed a fraction.

"Is that so?"

"Yeah. Del figured no way in hell. Jack's with him on it, so I've got two on the line. Carter put his hundred on me."

She turned the helmet in her hands. "You're telling me this after I've agreed to take this ride, but before I actually take it. Meaning, I can toss this helmet in your face and tell you to go to hell."

"Yeah."

She nodded again. "Carter can keep his full winnings, but I want half of yours—Del's hundred specifically." She put the helmet on.

"Fair enough." Grinning, he swung onto the bike.

He didn't have to tell her to hold on this time, he noted, and with her arms wrapped around his waist, he roared off.

Maybe her heart thundered, especially on the curves, but Parker couldn't deny she enjoyed the sensation. Neither could she deny if she hadn't wanted to be there, she wouldn't be.

Curiosity, she thought. Now she'd satisfied the curiosity. Yes, streaking down the road, punching through the wind, was just as thrilling as it had been on her initial, brief ride.

It didn't mean she'd make a habit of it, but she appreciated being able to file the experience under Things Accomplished.

Almost as much as she appreciated winning the hundred from Del.

Served him right.

Since she was in the process of admissions, she had to admit it had been damn perceptive of Malcolm to calculate her reaction.

Then again, maybe he'd banked on his own dubious charm to persuade her to keep the deal. Though she couldn't see the point of that. Safer to have said nothing.

And wasn't *that* the point? she realized.

He wasn't the type to take the safe choice.

The hell with it, she decided. She'd enjoy the experience before filing it away.

That enjoyment climbed several levels when she realized he zigged and zagged his way toward the water. She caught the scent of it, damp and tinged with salt. She watched the sun flood its evening light over the sound, glint and glimmer over the bumps of Calf Island, catch in the rippling white sails of pleasure boats.

And all the while the machine growled under her, vibrating with power.

Obligations, schedules, duties shed from her mind, and blew away like feathers in the wind. The thunder of her heart throttled back to a steady, relaxed beat as she watched gulls soar and dip. If the phone in her bag rang, she didn't hear it, didn't give it a thought.

She lost track of the time, noting only the softening of the light and the air as he doubled back.

He slowed as they cruised into Old Greenwich. Tourists and locals mingled on the busy main street, drawn by the shops and restaurants, the easy distance to the shore. But the bustle didn't diminish the neighborhood feel.

He turned off the main, putting with traffic before swinging into a minuscule parking spot. He pulled his helmet off as he turned to look at her.

"Hungry?"

"I guess I am."

"I know a place here that serves the best pizza in Connecticut."

"Then you haven't tasted Mrs. G's."

"Maybe I'll get lucky there, but in the meantime . . . You can let go now."

"Oh." A little flustered she hadn't realized she still had her arms around him, she pulled back, climbed off.

He hooked the helmets on the bike. "It's not far. Just enough to stretch it out a little before we eat."

"I don't mind a walk," she began, then flipped open her purse at the signal. "Sorry, that's voice mail. I'd better check."

"How many?" he asked when she muttered a curse under her breath.

"Three."

"Do they ever give you the night off?"

"It happens. Rarely, but it happens. People planning a wedding, or a big event like an important anniversary, it becomes their world for a while. Every idea or problem or decision can take on enormous magnitude."

She started to slip the phone back into her bag, thinking she'd duck into the rest room first chance and handle whatever she could.

"Go ahead and do the callbacks."

"That's all right. It can wait for a bit."

"You'll be thinking about them, and thinking how to duck away to deal with them. Might as well just do it."

"I'll make it quick."

He slowed the pace to a saunter, listening while she spoke to someone named Gina about chiffon versus taffeta. They agreed Parker would meet her to check out both samples. Then she discussed a Cinderella coach with a Mrs. Seaman. Parker promised to arrange one as she pulled out a notepad and wrote down the specifications. Finally, she assured somebody named Michael that both he and his fiancé, Vince, still had time to learn to swing dance, and rattled off the name and number of a dance instructor.

"Sorry," she said to Malcolm as she slipped the phone back into its pocket. "And thanks."

"No problem. Okay, I don't care about chiffon or taffeta, or the difference in weight and sheen, but where the hell do you get a Cinderella coach outside of Disney?"

"You'd be surprised what you can get, especially if you have the right resources, and in this case a virtually unlimited budget. Mrs. Seaman—that's Seaman Furniture—wants her daughter to arrive and depart in a Cinderella coach, I'll make that happen. After I check with the bride to make sure that's what she wants."

"Got it. Now, why do Michael and Vince need to swing dance?"

"They're getting married in February, and finally decided on a Big Band–era theme. They're wearing zoot suits and spats."

He took a moment to absorb it. "You're not kidding."

"No, and I happen to think it'll be fun. So naturally, they want to swing, and particularly well for their first dance."

"Who leads? That's a serious question," he said when she gave him a bland stare. "Somebody has to."

"They can flip a coin, I suppose, or leave it to the instructor. I think Vinnie because Michael's the one who's worried about it, and Vinnie's pretty gung-ho."

"Then maybe . . . Wait a minute. February? Is it Vinnie Calerone?"

"Yes. Do you know him?"

"Yeah. Knew him when we were kids. My ma's friendly with his. When he heard I moved back, he came to see me. I service his Mercedes. He said he was getting married in February, said he'd get me an invite."

"Were you close?"

"Not especially." He glanced at her, then decided to finish it out. "He was getting the shit beat out of him back in the day. It looked to me like he'd have held his own one-on-one, but there were two of them. I evened the odds. And I was right. He held his own. Vinnie's wearing a zoot suit." His grin spread with easy humor. "I can actually see that."

"You got into a fight for him?"

"Not for him, especially. It was more the two-against-one deal. Beating somebody up because he's gay is ignorant. Ganging up to do it? That's cheap. Anyway, it only took a few minutes. This is the place."

She stared at him another moment, then turned to look at the restaurant. Despite its situation on the inlet, it was little more than a hole-in-the-wall with faded clapboard siding.

"It doesn't look like much, but—"

"It looks fine, and I'm in the mood for pizza."

"That makes two of us."

CHAPTER SIX

THEY KNEW HIM, PARKER NOTED, WHEN A COUPLE OF THE STAFF called him by name. The pizzeria may have been small and on the shabby side, but the scents circulating in the air from the open kitchen and the jammed tables told her Malcolm knew his pizza.

They squeezed into a table preset with paper placemats depicting Italian landmarks.

"You want to steer clear of the Chianti," Malcolm told her, "but you can get a pretty decent carafe of Cab."

"That'll work."

A waitress bopped over. She had improbable red spiky hair and a nose as perky as her breasts. She might have been just old enough to order the Cab for herself.

"Hey, Mal!"

"How's it going, Kaylee?"

"Oh, you know." She slid her gaze toward Parker, and away

again, but the glance lasted just long enough to show Parker the disappointment and miff. "Get you a drink?"

"The lady'll have the Cab. You can bring me a Coke. Luigi's tossing tonight?"

"You got it. You want your usual?"

"We'll think about it."

"Okay. I'll get your drinks."

Parker cocked an eyebrow as the girl walked off. "She's got a crush on you."

He leaned back, leather jacket open, a day's scruff on his face, green eyes lit with cocky humor. "What can I say? Women flock to me."

"She'd like to break the carafe of Cab over my head."

"Maybe." He leaned forward again. "She's seventeen, just started her first year at community college. She wants to be a fashion designer. Or a songwriter. Or."

"There should always be ors at seventeen. And crushes on older men."

"Did you have one?"

She shook her head, not in denial but amusement. "No wine for you?"

"I made a deal with my mother, back when I was about a year younger than Kaylee. For every beer or its like I drank, I had to wait an hour once I finished it before I got behind the wheel."

"You drank beer at sixteen?"

"If I could get it, sure. And knowing there was the possibility, she laid down the law. If I wanted the wheels, I had to make the deal."

"A lot of teenagers make deals they don't keep, or intend to keep."

"In my world if you make a deal, you keep the deal."

She believed him, and appreciated it, as that had been true

in her world as well. "And now that you provide your own wheels?"

"Doesn't apply. A deal's a deal for the duration."

"Did you decide what you want to order?" Kaylee set the Coke in front of Malcolm, and managed to place the carafe and wineglass in front of Parker without making eye contact.

"Not yet." He started to pull one of the laminated menus out of its holder.

"What's your usual?" Parker asked.

"Pepperoni, black olives, hot peppers."

"Sounds good."

"Okay. Have Luigi toss us a large, will you, Kaylee?"

"Sure, Mal. We've got those zucchini fritters you like tonight, if you want a starter."

"That'd be great. We'll share an order."

Parker waited until the girl walked away. "Does she get her heart broken every time you come in here with a woman?"

"I don't generally bring women here. I tend to go for something a little more on the quiet side on a date."

"This isn't a date," she reminded him. "It's a deal."

"Right." He reached over for the carafe, poured her a glass.

She sipped the wine, nodded approval. "It's good, and hopefully contains no arsenic. So. Your father was military."

"Yeah. I was an army brat until I was eight, and he was killed in El Salvador."

"It's hard to lose a parent, and so young."

His eyes met hers in a moment of shared loss. "Hard anytime, I'd say."

"Yes, anytime. Your mother moved back here, to Greenwich."

"You get a pension, a flag, and some medals. They do what they can do, but she had to work. Her brother has a restaurant. You probably know that."

"Some. I don't know your uncle or his wife particularly well."

"You're not missing much, from my point of view. He worked her like a dog, and she was supposed to be grateful for the roof he put over our heads. And she was. She . . ."

When he trailed off, Parker gave him a moment of silence. "How's your mother doing on the computer?"

"Coming along. Thanks, Kaylee," he added when the girl set the appetizer and two small plates on the table.

"Luigi says to say hi before you go."

"Will do."

"The first time I met your mother," Parker continued, "she was cursing the computer, and not very happy with you for making her use one."

"That was before she figured out how to play computer Scrabble. She just bought a laptop so she can play at home."

Parker sampled the zucchini. "These are good." She took another bite. "Excellent, in fact."

"It's a little low-market for your clients," Malcolm commented when she scanned the restaurant.

"Not necessarily. It could be a fun, casual location for a smaller, more laid-back rehearsal dinner. Also a nice suggestion for out-of-town wedding guests looking for local flavor and good, casual food. Family owned is always a nice touch."

"How do you know it's family owned?"

"It has that feel, plus it says so right on the front of the menu."

"Talk to Luigi. He owns the place."

"I might do that. So, how did you go from doing stunt work in LA to owning a garage in Greenwich?"

"Is this small talk, or are you interested?"

"It can be both."

"Okay. A gag went south, messed me up. Some bean counter cut corners, and the equipment was faulty, so they paid me off."

"How messed up?"

"Broke a lot of bones, bruised a few organs, sliced some skin." He shrugged, but Parker didn't buy it had been that simple, that casual.

"It sounds serious. How long were you in the hospital?"

"Put me out for a while," he continued in that same careless tone. "By the time I got back on my feet, the lawyers had duked it out. I had a nice chunk of change, and decided I'd had enough of jumping off buildings and crashing into walls. I had enough for my own place, and that was always the goal anyway."

"And you don't miss it? Hollywood, the movie business?"

He gestured with a zucchini before eating it. "It ain't what it looks like in your neighborhood cineplex, Legs."

"No, I don't suppose it is. And I wish you wouldn't call me that."

"Can't help it. Got planted in my head that day you and Emma played soccer at her parents' big bash."

"Cinco de Mayo. I have a perfectly good name."

"It's Spider-Man's name."

She smothered a laugh. "His name's Peter."

"Stranger that it's Spider-Man's last name. I worked on those movies."

"You worked with Tobey Maguire on the Spider-Man movies? What was . . ." She narrowed her eyes. "I bet you use that sort of connection to score with women all the time."

"It's an angle." He smiled as Kaylee set the pizza on its holder.

"Anything else I can get you?"

"We're good, Kaylee. Thanks."

"The zucchini was wonderful," Parker told her and got a quick shoulder jerk.

"I'll let them know you liked it."

"She'll always hate me." Parker sighed. "So the pizza better be worth the harsh thoughts that must be clouding my aura."

"The hot peppers'll clear that aura right out."

"We'll see about that. Have you always been interested in cars and mechanics?"

"Like I said, I like knowing how things work. The next step is keeping them working. Have you always been interested in weddings?"

"Yes. I liked everything about them. So the next step is helping create them."

"Which involves being on call pretty much around the clock."

"It can. And you don't want to talk about weddings."

"You don't want to talk about cars." He lifted a slice, slid it onto her plate.

"No, but I'm always interested in business. Let's try something else. You mentioned you lived in Florida. Where else?"

"Japan, Germany, Colorado."

"Really?"

"I don't remember Japan, and I'm fuzzy on Germany." He took a slice for himself. "The first place I really remember is Colorado Springs. The mountains, the snow. We were there for a couple of years, but I always remember the snow. The way I always remember the smell of that bush outside my window in Florida."

He took a bite of pizza, angled his head. "Are you going to try it or not?"

Judging it cool enough not to singe the roof of her mouth, she sampled. Nodded. "It's fabulous. Really." She took another testing bite. "But I have to give Mrs. G's the edge, and consider this the second-best pizza in Connecticut."

"Looks like I have to talk Mrs. Grady out of a slice of pie to see if you're being honest or stubborn."

"I can be both, depending on mood and circumstances."

"Let's try out the mood and circumstances on honest. Why'd you come out with me?"

"We made a deal."

He shook his head, studying her over his slice. "Might be a factor, but it's not why."

She considered, took a sip of wine. "You irritated me."

"And you go out with guys who irritate you?"

"I did this time. And you made it a kind of dare, which pushed the next button. Lastly, I was curious. Those are the various factors that make up the whole, and the reason why I'm sitting here enjoying this very superior pizza instead of— Oh hell." She yanked out her ringing phone.

"Go ahead. We can get back to it."

"I hate people who talk on cell phones in restaurants. I'll be right back." She scooted out, snaked her way through the door. "Hi, Justine, give me one minute."

He didn't mind watching her walk away, he decided as he topped off her wine. The jeans were a damn good fit.

Kaylee set another Coke in front of him, whisked the other away. "You looked like you needed a refill."

"Good timing. How are you liking college?"

"It's okay. I really like my art class. Anyway, who's your friend?"

"Her name's Parker."

"Is she a doctor or a cop?"

"No. Where'd that come from?"

"My dad says the only people who should answer cell phones in a restaurant are doctors and cops."

He glanced at the cell phone peeking out of her apron pocket. "How many texts have you sent on that tonight?"

Kaylee flashed a smile. "Who counts? I guess she's pretty."

"You'd guess right. Any more trouble with your carburetor?"

"No. Whatever you did worked. It's running great. But it's still a million years old and puke green."

"It's five years old," he corrected. "But it is puke green. If you can talk your dad into it, I know a guy who'll give you a good deal on a paint job."

"Yeah?" She brightened. "I'll start working on him. Maybe you could—" She broke off, lost her glow. "Your friend's coming back in."

Kaylee turned back toward the kitchen. Not quite a stalk, Malcolm noted, but close. Amused, he gave his attention to Parker as she sat back down. "Chiffon? A tango emergency? Somebody want to ride into the wedding on a camel?"

"I talked a groom out of a chariot once, and it wasn't easy. I could deflect a camel. Actually, one of our October brides just learned her father's in Vegas, where he eloped with the gold-digging bimbo bitch—her phrase—he left her mother for."

"Happens."

"Yes. The divorce became final just this week, so he didn't waste any time. Which also happens. The new bride is twenty-four, two years younger than the daughter."

"Adds an ouch to the equation."

"It certainly does, and it also happens," Parker put in. "But add up all those 'it happens,' and it's tough to swallow."

"Sure. And still probably tougher on the first wife than the daughter." Though she hadn't finished the first slice, he slid a second onto Parker's plate. "What did she want you to do about it?"

"She doesn't want either of them at the wedding, doesn't want him giving her away, as planned. She'd been prepared to tolerate the aforementioned gold-digging bimbo bitch as her father's guest, but she'll be damned if she'll have her there as his wife, her—too bad a word to say in public—stepmother, or lording her new status over the bride's still-devastated mama."

"I've got to give her points on all of that."

"Yes, she's perfectly justified, and if that's the way she really wants it to be, that's the way we'll make it be." She washed down pizza with wine. "The problem is, she loves her father. Despite his questionable judgment and the distinct possibility he's suffering from male midlife insanity—"

"Hey, we're not the only ones who get it."

"You get it more often and generally with more severe symptoms. Despite," she repeated, "she loves him, and I'm afraid not having him walk her down the aisle will mar the day for her more than the GBB, and when she forgives him, and she will, down the road she'll always regret the decision."

"Is that what you told her?"

"I told her the day is hers, hers and David's, and whatever she wants or doesn't want, we'll work it out. And I asked her to take a day or two to be sure."

"You think she'll opt for Dad."

"I do, and if I'm right, I'll follow up with a private and very pointed chat with the GBB regarding protocol and behavior at a Vows event."

"You'll scare the shit out of her."

"I'll do no such thing," Parker said, with a small smile.

"And you'll enjoy it."

She took a deliberately delicate bite of pizza. "That would be petty, and unattractive."

"Every minute of it."

She laughed. "Yes, I will."

"It gives us a little more common ground."

"How's that?"

"I figure if you've got to take someone down or set them straight, you might as well enjoy it on some level. I heard you took Mac's weird mother down a while back."

"And I don't consider feeling a lot of satisfaction from it petty or unattractive. She had it coming. How did you hear about that?"

"Guys talk, too. Del's got a sweet spot for his Macadamia, and having her screwed with by her mother burned his ass. Plus, I'd handled her not that long before, so I knew some of the score."

"That's right, when Mac had her car towed." She sighed happily. "Good times. So, I imagine Linda was very annoyed when she came into your garage to get it back."

"That's one way to put it."

She nibbled more pizza, eyeing him. Then shook her head. "Okay, dish it out. All I heard was you told her she couldn't have the car until she paid the towing and storage fee, and she went on one of her rants."

"That's about it. She's got a hell of a rant. She tried to dump it all on Mac, but that didn't play for me, especially since I had some of the background from Ma."

"Your mother knows Linda?"

"Knew plenty about her, and my mother's a solid data source. Even without it, I'd've gotten the picture pretty quick. Still, bottom line, I towed the car, I get paid." He gestured with his Coke. "She moved from rant to wheedle. You know, couldn't I please help her out, do her this little favor. But the best part of the show was when she offered to pay the charges with personal services."

"She . . . Oh God."

"First time I've been offered a blow job for a towing fee."

Stunned speechless, Parker only stared at him.

"You asked."

"Yeah, I did. Even if Mac ever does, don't tell her that part."

"She already asked, and I didn't. Why would I? Her mother embarrassed herself. That's got nothing to do with Mac."

"No, it doesn't, but a lot of people don't see it that clearly."

He did, she realized. For whatever reason, he saw it with absolute clarity. "She's taken a lot of hits over the years for Linda's actions. Linda will ruin or at least take some shine off Mac's wedding if she can."

"She won't." He shrugged and ate. "What Mac doesn't handle, Carter will. What they don't, you will."

"I'm going to remember that the next time I wake up from a Linda nightmare. Did you tell Del about . . . Linda's offer?"

"Sure. A guy gets that kind of offer, he's got a right to brag about it to his friends."

"You're a very strange species."

"Back at you, Legs."

The entire experience—the word helped her put the evening in perspective—turned out to be a great deal easier and more enjoyable than she'd expected. But then, she admitted, her expectations had been dead low.

It would, certainly, be more pleasant having a friendly relationship with him, as a friend of Del's. Like she had with Jack.

Then again, she didn't have this underlying and stubborn spark of attraction to Jack.

Still, a spark could be managed until it flickered out. Especially since the spark was very likely a reflexive response to a very attractive man who clearly showed interest, when she hadn't had the time or inclination for male company in quite a while.

She worked out the practicalities in her head as they walked back to his bike.

She strapped on the helmet and straddled the bike behind him.

And discovered, the moment they'd woven their way out of town, riding at night was a whole different thrill.

A whole new sense of freedom washed over her. The single headlight slicing down the dark road, the canopy of stars and moon overhead, and the sparkle of them on the black plate of water.

Side by side with the thrill rode a sense of ease, of clearing out all those details that crowded her mind. She liked the crowd, she thought, even fed off it. But it had been too long since she'd just emptied out and recharged.

Who knew that an evening with Malcolm would push that lever?

Reality waited, and she valued her reality, but he'd given her a respite, a little adventure, and a very pleasant break from routine.

When they zipped down the long, curving drive to her house, she felt refreshed, content, and very friendly toward Malcolm Kavanaugh.

And when he cut the engine, silence rushed in, another lovely sensation. She swung off, pleased with how natural the move had become, and unstrapped her helmet.

She handed it to him, then laughed. "I have to say, that's the easiest hundred I've ever won."

"Same goes." He walked her to the entrance portico. "So you enjoyed yourself."

"I did. Thank you for—"

With her back against the door and his mouth feasting on hers, the rest of the words tumbled out of her brain. That hard, compelling body pressed to hers as he took her hands, held them in his at her sides, as his teeth incited wild thrills with hungry nips and bites.

Trapped, she should have objected, refused, but the sensation of helplessness, a touch of panicked excitement, of being carried off, simply dropped the ground away from under her feet.

She fell, without any attempt to catch herself, and answered the assault with equal fervor and a reckless greed.

The kick of her own heart shocked her back—or nearly.

"Wait," she managed.

"Just give me another minute."

He wanted more; he took more. And so did she.

It was that simmering, smoldering heat inside the cool package that had caught him from the jump. Now, as it hit boil, he was happy to have it burn him down to the bone.

He held her hands to prevent his own from streaking over that gorgeous body, to make sure he didn't lose control and use them to pull off those classy clothes and get to skin.

When he felt that control begin to fray he lifted his head, but he didn't let her go, didn't step back.

"That ought to demonstrate I won't be backing off."

"I never said—"

"We made a deal."

"That doesn't mean you can . . ." She paused, and he watched her gather herself, steady herself.

Jesus, he admired that.

"That doesn't mean you can just grab me anytime you want, or put your hands all over me when the urge hits."

"Didn't grab you," he pointed out. "And didn't put my hands all over you." He gave the hands he still held a squeeze to remind her. "Thought about it though."

"Regardless, I'm not going to— Would you please give me some room?"

"Sure." Now he let go of her hands, stepped back.

"I'm not going to tolerate this kind of behavior. You can't just push yourself on me whenever you like."

"I might've pushed a little. So guilty." In the dark his eyes gleamed like a cat—one on the hunt. "But, honey, you were right in there with me, and I figure you've got the spine to admit it."

She said nothing for a moment. "All right, that part may be true. But just because I have a physical reaction to you doesn't mean . . . What are you smiling at?"

"You. I just really like the way you talk, especially when you're riding the high horse."

"Damn it, you're frustrating."

"I probably am. I was going to say I have some kind of thing for you, and want to figure out how it works. But we can go with physical reaction if you like that better."

"You better understand I take relationships seriously, so if you think I'm just going to jump into bed because—"

"I didn't ask you to bed."

He watched her eyes smolder and had to order himself not to press her right back against the door again.

"You're going to stand there and tell me that's not what you want, not what you intend?"

"Sure, I want you in bed—or any place that's handy—and I intend to have you. But I'm not in a hurry. You jump in? It takes off the edge, and I like the edge. Plus, it's hard to figure out how something works if you're busy just banging."

It was completely honest, and so damn logical she faltered. "This is a ridiculous conversation."

"It seems sensible and civilized to me. That's right up your alley. Do you want me to say I think about peeling you out of one of those fancy suits of yours, finding out what's under it? Getting my hands on what is? About feeling you move under me and over me, and being inside you, watching your face when you let go? When I make you let go?

"I do, Parker. But I'm not in a hurry."

"I'm not looking for this—you—this."

"Everybody looks for this. You're not looking, or you weren't looking for this with me. I get that loud and clear. But I'm not backing off. Because it's a solid fact we've got a thing, sorry, a physical reaction. And if you didn't want me to make any moves on it, you'd have shut me down, taken me down. Maybe even enjoyed doing it."

"You don't know me as well as you seem to think."

He shook his head. "Legs, I've only scratched the surface, and I'm coming back for more."

The argument was—not really an argument, she realized, and whatever it was, she was losing it. "I'm going in."

"Then I'll see you around."

She turned her back, half expecting him to move in again. But when she opened the door, he simply stood back in what she'd have called a gentlemanly manner if she hadn't known better, until she stepped inside, closed the door.

She stood there a moment, trying to regain the equilibrium he'd managed to shatter. She heard the engine kick on, rip through the quiet.

Which was, she realized, exactly what he'd done. He'd ripped through her quiet.

Everything he'd said was true.

More, he understood her pretty damn well with that scratch of the surface of his. That was . . . frightening and gratifying at the same time.

Nobody, she admitted as she started upstairs, nobody she didn't consider family knew her all the way through.

She wasn't at all sure how she felt about Malcolm getting all the way through, and wasn't at all sure she'd be able to stop him.

Mostly, she thought, she didn't know what the hell to do about him.

CHAPTER SEVEN

𝒜LTHOUGH IT HAD BECOME TRADITION, PARKER WOULD HAVE PRE-
ferred to skip the sexy breakfast story. But motorcycles had a
distinct sound, one Mac had heard clearly while she and Carter
had been enjoying some time on their new patio when Parker had
ridden off on Malcolm's bike.

Mac may have dragged herself into the home gym when
Parker was nearly finished and Laurel well on her way, but she had
more than her biceps on her mind.

And she'd dragged Emma along with her.

"I asked Mrs. G for pancakes," Mac announced. "I especially
like pancakes with a sexy breakfast story."

"Who's got one?" Laurel demanded.

"Parker."

"Wait a minute." Laurel whipped around to where Parker
stayed a bit longer than necessary in forward fold position. "You
have a SBS, and didn't tell me?"

"It's nothing. Plus we're jammed for the next several days."

"If it's nothing, where did you and Malcolm go on his bike last night for almost three hours? No, don't tell us now." Mac only smiled, gave an exaggerated wave when Parker straightened. "We need the pancakes."

"I don't monitor *your* comings and goings, Mackensie."

"Oh, don't pull *Mackensie* on me." Mac waved that off, too, and started biceps curls with the Bowflex. "Carter and I heard Mal drive in, and I saw you leave because I was outside. So yeah, I kept an ear out for you after. You'd have done exactly the same."

"Did you have a fight with him?" Emma asked. "Are you upset?"

"No, I'm not upset." After dabbing her damp face with a towel, Parker walked over to drop it in the hamper. "I just don't have time for pancakes and gossip."

"Unless it's one of us in the spotlight?" Laurel cocked her head. "We share, Parker. It's what we do. If you're pulling back from that about this, it tells me you've got concerns about where it's heading."

"It's not that at all." Yes, it was, she admitted. Yes, it was exactly that. "Fine. Fine. We'll have the pancakes and the rest, but I have a lot of work—we all do—so we'll keep it short."

When she walked out of the room, annoyance in every stride, Emma looked at the others. "Should I go talk to her?"

"You know she has to stew." Laurel grabbed a towel, swiped her face, her throat. "She's a little pissed, but she'll get over it."

"You're right about her being unsettled over this thing with Mal." Mac moved from biceps curls to triceps kickbacks. "If it was no big, she'd have told us, or laughed it off when I brought it up. When's the last time Parker was unsettled over a guy?"

"That would be over nobody back in never," Laurel stated.

"That would be the who and when. Good thing or bad?"

"Good, I think." Since she was there, Emma ordered herself onto the elliptical. "He's nothing like her usual, which would be part of the unsettled, and there's nothing that would have gotten her to go out with him if she didn't want to on some level. Plus, Mac said she was wearing jeans and that really cute chocolate brown leather jacket. So she changed her clothes to go with him."

"I wasn't spying," Mac said quickly. "I just saw. I mostly just saw."

"Who's saying otherwise?" Laurel flicked it away. "If I'd heard her go off with him, I'd have done the same. Jesus, it's a good thing Del doesn't know. And let's just keep it that way until we get a better sense of this. I don't want him getting worked up over Mal and Parker the way he did Emma and Jack. Now I've got to go shower, and praise Jesus, he had an early breakfast meeting. See you downstairs."

"I thought she'd get a kick out of it," Mac told Emma when they were alone. "I didn't want to upset her."

"It's not your fault. Laurel's right, it's what we do."

*I*T'S WHAT THEY DID, PARKER REMINDED HERSELF. BY THE TIME she'd showered and dressed for the day, annoyance had tipped over into guilt for snapping back at her friends.

She'd made too much of it all. And she'd internalized the entire business, something she admitted she tended to do too easily and too often.

So they'd have their tradition, just as they should. They'd have a few laughs, and that would be that.

When she walked into the kitchen, Mrs. Grady stood at the counter mixing the batter.

"Good morning, my girl Parker."

"'Morning, Mrs. G. I hear we're having pancakes."

"Mmm-hmm." Mrs. Grady waited until Parker poured a cup of coffee. "So, will you be getting a tattoo next?"

"What?"

"Seems like the next step after riding the roads on a Harley."

Parker didn't have to see Mrs. Grady's tongue to know it was firmly in her cheek. "I thought, given what I do, maybe a small heart in a discreet location. Maybe with HEA inside it, for Happy Ever After."

"Very pretty, and appropriate." She set the batter aside while she prepared a bowl of berries. "We may bump heads over the boy, as he's brought me flowers *and* asked me out to go dancing."

"You're enjoying this."

"Of course. He reminds me of someone."

"Oh?" Parker leaned on the counter. "Who?"

"I knew a boy with some rough edges, altogether cocksure of himself, and a gilded tongue when he wanted to use it. Handsome as sin and twice as sexy. When he set his eye and his intentions toward a woman, by God, she knew it. I was lucky. I married him."

"Oh, Mrs. G, he's not . . . Is he really like your Charlie?"

"He's of the type, which isn't a type at all. Pulled himself out of hard times, dealt with the scars from it, pushed himself to make a mark. A little bit of the wild side there, always. With my Charlie, I told myself, oh no, I won't get tangled up with this one. And I said it again, even when I was already tangled up."

The smile warmed her face and went deep into her eyes. "It's hard to resist a bad boy who's a good man. They'll knock the legs right out from under you. I'm grateful every day, however short our time together was, that I didn't resist very long."

"It's not like that with me and Mal. It's just . . ." And that, Parker admitted, was part of the problem. She didn't know what it was.

"Whatever it is, you deserve the attention, and to enjoy yourself more than you do. Aside from this." Mrs. Grady laid her hands on Parker's cheeks, patted them. "Which I know you enjoy every minute of. But aside from this."

"I don't want to enjoy myself into making a mistake."

"Oh, I wish you would." On that, she drew Parker closer and kissed her forehead. "I really wish you would. Go on, sit down and drink your coffee. What you need is a good breakfast and your friends."

Maybe she did, Parker admitted. But after she sat, she took a call from one of the weekend's nervous brides. Since it was second nature to handle someone else's worries or problems, dealing with it settled her.

"Emma and Mac'll be right down," Laurel announced as she came in. "Need any help, Mrs. G?"

"Under control."

"Hey, nice flowers."

"My boyfriend sent them to me." She added a wink. "The one Parker's trying to steal away from me."

"That slut." Amused, Laurel got her coffee and walked to the breakfast nook to sit. "After our initial business, we can shift to event mode. We could have the meeting here, as I know damn well you have everything to do with tonight's event on your BlackBerry. It'll save the time you're worried about."

"All right. I shouldn't have slapped at Mac."

"Knee jerk. I probably would've done the same, only more so."

"But we expect bitchiness from you."

"Nice hit." Laughing, she pointed at Parker. "I'm not going to say anything to Del for the moment, but—"

"There's nothing to tell. As you'll soon see once everyone's here."

"And here they come. Prepare to illuminate."

"I'm sorry," Parker said even as Mac sat down.

"Water. Bridge. Bygones."

"Eat some fruit," Mrs. Grady insisted, and set the bowl on the table.

"I made too big a deal about it." Obediently Parker spooned berries into the small clear dish at her plate. "With all of you, and with myself. It's just all so strange, and that's why. And still, pretty straightforward."

"Why don't you tell us, and we'll decide the strange," Laurel suggested. "Because by stalling, you're making that big deal."

"All right, all right. He came by to bring Mrs. G flowers."

"Awww" was Emma's instant reaction.

"Since she wasn't here, it seemed awkward not to ask him in while I arranged them, and he could leave her a note. Anyway, I wanted to make it clear I wasn't interested."

"You asked him in to tell him you didn't want to see him?" Mac put in.

"Yes. He's got this habit of . . . moving on me, and I wanted to make it clear—and all right again, I didn't end the move the other night when—"

"The hot kiss," Emma put in.

"It wasn't—" Yes, it was, Parker admitted. "After he had dinner here, and I walked him out, he caught me off guard, and I responded. That's all there is. I'm human. But, particularly since he's a good friend of Del's, I felt I had to make it clear I wasn't interested."

"Did he buy that? Mmm, thanks, Mrs. G." Mac dove for the platter of pancakes Mrs. Grady put on the table. "Because if he did, my opinion of his basic intelligence drops several levels."

"Apparently he didn't, because he proposed this deal. I'd go out for a ride, a casual dinner, and if I didn't enjoy myself, he'd back off."

"And you agreed?" Laurel grabbed the syrup. "You didn't

squash him like a bug or level him with the Parker Brown freeze ray?"

Parker lifted her coffee, took a slow sip. "Do you want me to tell this or not?"

"Proceed," Laurel said with a wave of her hand.

"I agreed because it seemed simple, and yes, because I was a little curious. He's Del's friend, and there's no point in having bad feelings. I'd go, then he'd back off. No hard feelings either way. Then when we got outside, he told me about the bet."

"What bet?" Emma demanded.

Parker filled them in.

"Carter bet?" Mac threw back her head and laughed. "And *on* Mal? I love it."

"I love it that he told you before you got on the bike." Emma shook her fork. "He had to know it gave you an excuse to flip him off."

"And I give him that. And he'll give me, at my insistence, half his winnings. Fair's fair."

"Where'd you go?" Emma wondered.

"Into Old Greenwich, some little pizza joint. Nice, actually. And I won't deny it's fun to ride the bike—it's great fun—or claim it was a painful experience to split a pizza with him. He's an interesting man."

"How many calls did you take while you were out?" Laurel asked her.

"Four."

"And how did he take that?"

"Like business is business and go ahead. And yes, points for him. But the thing is we had a perfectly pleasant evening, then the minute we're back and at the door, he . . ."

Emma wiggled in her seat. "Here comes the really sexy part."

"He just takes over. He has this way of cornering me, and my brain shuts off. He's good at it, and my brain just closes down. It's reflex," she claimed. "Or reaction."

"Is he all hot and fast, or slow and easy?" Mac asked.

"I'm unaware if he has a slow speed."

"Told you." Mac elbowed Emma.

"After my brain started working again, I told him I wasn't having it, that he couldn't just grab and go whenever he wanted. And he just looked amused. Pretty much like the three of you—and you, too, Mrs. G, because I see you over there—are looking now."

"Kissed him back, didn't you?" Mrs. Grady pointed out.

"Yes, but—"

"So even if he hadn't knocked your legs out from under you, you wouldn't have one to stand on."

She wanted to sulk, badly. So she shrugged instead. "It's just a physical reaction."

"I don't know about that," Laurel began, "but if it is, I have to say, so what?"

"I'm not going to get tangled . . ." She remembered Mrs. Grady's phrase, cut her eyes in that direction and saw the housekeeper raise her eyebrows. "I'm not going to get involved this way with someone when I feel it could be a mistake. Especially when he's a friend of Del's, of Jack's, of Carter's. Especially when I really don't know him well, or know that much about him."

"Isn't dating someone part of the process of finding out about him?" Emma reached over, laid a hand on Parker's. "You're interested, Parker. It's all over you. You're attracted. And you're nervous about it."

"You had fun with him, Parks." Mac lifted her hands. "Why not have some fun?"

"He's immune to your Back-Off Cloak, and your freeze ray.

He doesn't act or react in a way you can predict or control." Laurel gave Parker's leg a pat under the table. "So you want a reason to say no."

"I'm not that shallow."

"Not shallow. Nervous about letting him get too close because he could matter more than you bargained for. I think he already does."

"I just don't know. And I don't like not knowing."

"Then take a little time," Emma said, "and find out."

"I'll think about it. I will." How could she not, Parker admitted? "And that's all there is of this morning's sexy breakfast story. I appreciate everything, I really do, but we have to switch modes. We're already running behind with the meeting. We have an event to prep for."

$\mathcal{M}$AL INSTALLED NEW MOTOR MOUNTS ON A HONEY OF A '62 T-BIRD Sports Roadster. At the customer's directive, he'd all but rebuilt the engine, and when the job was done, all 390 cubic inches would growl down the road like a big sleek cat. He'd already replaced the brake pads, fixed the cooling system, and refined the three two-barrel Holley carburetors.

By his calculations, in a few hours he'd be taking this big bastard for a test drive.

"That's a beauty."

He pulled his head from under the hood to see Del, lawyer-suited-up, inside the cavern of the garage.

"She is that. Sixty-two, M-Code," Mal added, "bullet sleek. One of about two hundred sold back in the day."

"Really?"

"Bitch was pricey. Customer bought this at an auction, had it restored. Rangoon Red exterior, two-toned red and white in. White-

walls, wire wheels. He got a clue after he'd had the exterior and interiors restored that the reason it might be giving him some trouble
on the road was the hundred-twelve original miles on the engine."

"And that's where you came in."

"We fix. Take a look."

"Sure, as long as I'm not required to know what I'm looking
at, or half of what you're talking about."

"This baby has the chrome dress-up package."

Del looked in, saw a big engine, a lot of black, some gleaming
chrome, and various parts stamped with Thunderbird. Because he
knew his job, he nodded. "So, what'll she do?"

"When I'm finished? Just about anything you want her to
except kiss you good night." Mal pulled the bandanna out of his
back pocket, wiped his hands. "Are you having trouble with the
Mercedes?"

"No. I had a breakfast meeting in town, so I swung by after to
drop off the papers you asked me to draw up. I can give you about
ten minutes if you want to look over them now. Or I can leave
them in your office, and you can read them when you've got a
chance, call me with any questions."

"I've got my hands full here, so I'll read through them later. As
long as I'm not required to know what I'm looking at, or half of
what you're talking about."

"I'll walk you through it whenever." With a thoughtful frown,
Del looked under the hood again. "Maybe one of these days you'll
walk me through an engine."

Mal's office consisted of a cubbyhole off the garage outfitted
with a metal desk, a couple of filing cabinets, and a swivel chair.
Del stepped in, took the file out of his briefcase, and set it on top
of the inbox.

Mal stuck the rag back in his pocket. "We may want to take
that ten minutes to talk about some personal business."

"Sure. What's up?"

"I took Parker out last night."

After one slow take, Del shook his head. "You talked her back onto the bike? Did you have a gun?"

"We made a deal. We'd take a ride, grab some dinner, and when I dropped her back home, if she hadn't had a good time, I'd back off."

"So you—" A faster take this time. "Back off from what?"

"From her, and this thing we've got going."

"What thing would that be?"

They shared that, Mal thought, the instant Brown frost. "You really want me to spell that out for you?"

"And when did this *thing* start?"

"For me? About two minutes after she first opened her mouth to me, and it's been clicking up some levels since. For her? You'd have to ask her yourself. Since she did have a good time, and I won't be backing off, I'm being up-front with you."

"Just how far has this thing gone?"

Mal paused a moment. "You know, Del, I get how you are about Parker, about all of them. Switch the circumstances, I'd probably be the same, so I get it. But I'm not going there with you, not about Parker. If you want to ask her, that's between the two of you. But I'll say this, if you think I'm just after a quick score, you and me? We don't know each other as well as either of us thought."

"She's my sister, goddamn it."

"If she wasn't, we wouldn't be having this conversation. She's also a beautiful, smart, interesting woman. And she's nobody's push-over. If and when she wants to shake me off, that's what she'll do."

"And if she does?"

"I'll be sorry, because, like that car, she's a rare breed. Classy and powerful and fucking gorgeous. And worth a hell of a lot of time and trouble."

Frustration radiating like sunlight, Del shoved his hand in his pocket. "I don't know what I'm supposed to say about this."

"Can't tell you." Mal shrugged. "By the way, you can pay her my hundred. After we made the deal, I figured I should be up-front with her, so I told her about the bet in case she wanted to get pissed off and flip me off."

"Great. Perfect."

"She didn't get pissed. She just wanted a cut of the bet. Jesus, who wouldn't go for a woman who thinks like that? Anyway, it seems fair her take comes from you. I'll collect my share from Jack, and the two of you can settle it with Carter."

"I don't know if we're square on this. I have to get my head around it. But I know this: If you screw with her, if you hurt her, I'll kick your ass."

"Got that. How about this? If I screw with her, if I hurt her, I'll let you."

"Son of a bitch. Read the damn papers." Without another word, Del strode off.

Could've been worse, Mal considered. Del could've punched him in the face the way he had Jack over Emma. So, he figured he and Del were one up there.

He shrugged it off, then went back to work on the engine, on something he knew, absolutely, how to fix.

KNOWING HER SCHEDULE, DEL MADE IT A POINT TO GET HOME early enough to corner his sister. She had rehearsals, and an event, which might have equaled an overfull plate for anyone else. But he knew damn well Parker routinely built in time for emergencies.

This, to his way of thinking, qualified.

He timed it strategically, arriving at the end of the first rehearsal, while Laurel was busy in her kitchen, Emma and her team already dressing the house for the arrival of the evening's bridal party, and before the second rehearsal.

Mac, he knew, would be occupied with her camera.

He strolled up as Parker waved off the first clients and their party.

"You're home early."

"Yeah, I juggled some things so I could get back and give you all a hand."

"We can use it. The next rehearsal's in about fifteen minutes, and tonight's bride and party are due in about thirty for hair and makeup. We're on schedule, but—"

"Good, let's take that fifteen." He took her hand to stroll onto the lawn.

"Should I assume someone saw me with Malcolm last night, and reported to you?" She smoothed down the line of her suit jacket. "We know each other too well, Del."

"I'd have thought. But then I wouldn't have thought you'd be out doing an Easy Rider."

"What does that even mean?"

"Look it up."

"Fine. If you're going to try a lecture on the risks of motorcycles, you have to first provide me with an affidavit stating you haven't ridden on one or driven one within the last thirty-six months."

Okay, he'd bench that argument. To buy a little more time, he took out his wallet, pulled out a hundred, and passed it to her.

"Thanks." She folded it, tucked it into her pocket.

"Did you go out with him because of the bet?"

"I went out with him despite the bet."

"Since all bets are off, are you planning to go out with him again?"

"He hasn't asked me, and I haven't decided." She turned her head to give his face a long study. "Since you show no signs of being in a fight, and I imagine Malcolm can give as good as he gets, I have to assume no punches were thrown when he told you I knew about the bet."

"I don't make a habit of punching people. Jack was an exception," he qualified before she could speak. "And Mal avoided that by telling me about . . . all this straight off."

She paused. "He told you himself?"

"And you didn't."

Considering Malcolm's tact, she answered without thinking. "Del, are you really living with the illusion I tell you about every man I date?"

"So you and Mal are dating?"

"No. Maybe. I haven't decided. Do I give you a cross-examination over everyone you date, or dated before you and Laurel? And if you say that's different, I may punch *you*."

"I'm trying to find a phrase that merely alludes to 'that's different.'" Because it got a snicker out of her, he took her hand as they walked. "Let's back up to the point that none of the guys you've dated have been friends of mine. Good friends of mine."

"True. And did I get in the middle when things changed between you and Laurel? My brother and one of my closest friends? And, no, Del, it's still not different."

"I'm not getting in the middle. I'm just circling the outer perimeter, trying to get a gauge of the ground."

"I don't know the ground yet. We went for a ride, had pizza, and . . ."

"And?"

"And completed the standard hat trick of dating with a kiss good night."

"So you're interested in him."

"I'm not disinterested. It surprised me, but I'm not disinterested. I had a good time last night, and I didn't expect to. I relaxed and enjoyed myself, and it's been a long time since I've done that with a man. Just enjoyed myself. He might be your client, Del, or a casual acquaintance, but the fact that he's your friend says you not only like him, but you trust and respect him. Is there any reason I shouldn't?"

"No." He sucked in air and scowled into the distance. "Damn it."

"And the fact that he told you about this himself, it matters. I didn't tell Laurel or any of the others until this morning. And I'm not sure I'd have done it then if Mac hadn't heard the bike, and seen me ride off with Mal. That doesn't speak as well of me."

"You didn't want to put them in the middle, an awkward place between you and me."

"That was part of it—not the main, but part." She paused, turning so they stood face-to-face. "Don't put me in the middle, Del, between you and your friend. Please don't make me a point of contention."

"I won't. Unless he screws it up. Then I'll kick his ass. He already knows that. Actually, he agreed if he screwed it up, he'd let me kick his ass. And yeah," Del admitted, "that speaks well of him, too, because I know him, and he meant it."

She wrapped her arms around Del to hug. "I'm really good at taking care of myself, but it's awfully nice to have a big brother I know will do it for me, whenever I need it."

"Count on it."

"I do. Now." She drew back. "If you're here to help, go find

Emma. She'll be the one most in need of extra hands. And here comes the next group."

She left Del to cross toward the parking area to greet the first arrivals. It was odd, wasn't it, she thought, that she'd barely acknowledged to herself she had a genuine interest in Malcolm Kavanaugh, yet she'd spent a good deal of her day talking about him.

And more, she admitted, thinking about him.

CHAPTER EIGHT

$\mathcal{B}$EFORE HER PARTNERS JOINED HER FOR THE MORNING SUMMIT ON the day's events, Parker got in a solid workout, showered, dressed for the long day, and reviewed the files.

The Friday night wedding had run like silk, requiring no more than the expected racing around, heading off potential glitches, and quick decisions behind the scenes.

And fortunately for all involved, Jaci said yes to Griff.

Today, with two events scheduled, the work more than doubled. Timing, always an essential ingredient, became absolutely vital, and included all the setting up for the late morning wedding with seventy-five guests, breaking it down, then redressing the stage for the evening's job.

Emma and her team, Parker knew, had the bulk of the purely physical work, hauling flowers and material, dressing the exterior and the interior spaces—twice—with a complete breakdown between. Most of Laurel's work—the cakes, the pastries, the chocolates—

would be done before the first event, with only the setups needed. So she'd fill in where any holes widened, and work with the caterers.

Mac would have to be everywhere, before and during the events, and Mac and Parker would have the primary job of keeping the bride and groom happy and on schedule, reining in the wedding party, the parents.

She checked her own emergency kit: bandages, breath mints, aspirin, notepad and pencil, mini hairbrush, comb, nail file, wet naps, spot remover, lighter, eyeglass cleaner, and a Swiss Army knife that included a pair of scissors.

She had her second and last cup of coffee while reviewing her spreadsheet and highlighting any potential problem areas. And was set for the meeting when Laurel breezed in.

"I don't want to make another woodland violet for a decade, but, baby, is that Wildflower Wedding Cake a beauty. Go, me."

"Go, you. How's the White Lace?"

"It's—and I do say so myself—stunning." Laurel poured coffee from the pot, added a small muffin. "Emma's already dressing the entrance with her team. Our first event, the casual country deal, is going to be beautiful. She'll head up as soon as she's finished the front urns. She wants to do that herself."

She plopped down. "So, did Mal call?"

"Why would he?"

"To talk to his Bitchin' Biker Babe?"

"Aren't you the cutest thing?"

"I am." Laurel patted the hair she'd already scooped up and back for work. "I really am. Why don't you call him?"

"Why would I?"

Obviously amused, Laurel leaned her elbow on the table, braced her chin in her hands. "Del thinks it's weird, but he's not inclined—yet—to beat Malcolm up."

"Such restraint."

"It is for Del when it comes to you. I could tell Del to tell Mal to call."

"When do we graduate from high school again?"

"It's fun."

Parker shook her head. "It wasn't even a date. A nondate and a couple of kisses."

"Hot, steamy kisses."

"Regardless," Parker began, and Mac strolled in.

"'Morning, both. Did Mal call?"

"No. And could we all just—"

"You should call him. Maybe try the message machine conversations." As Laurel had, Mac hit the coffee setup. "Carter and I had the best message machine conversations. We still do sometimes. Or e-mails. Emma and Jack did the sexy e-mailing. Your CrackBerry's fused to your hand anyway, so it'd be easy."

"I'll keep that in mind for down the road to *never*. Now maybe we could, I don't know, discuss the two major events we're getting paid to orchestrate today?"

"You're so strict."

Emma raced in, a Diet Pepsi in one hand, her laptop in the other. "I feel like I've already run five miles this morning. Did—"

"No." Parker didn't snap it, but it was close. "Malcolm didn't call. No, I'm not going to call him, leave a message on his machine, or e-mail him. Does that cover it?"

"You could take your car in for service. No, he just did that. You could take the van in," Emma decided. "No, he did that a couple months ago, and boy, did I get a lecture. Maybe—"

"Maybe we could get to work."

"She's irritated he didn't call," Laurel said.

"I am not irritated he—"

"More irked." Mac pursed her lips, considered. "That's her irked tone."

"If I'm irked, it's with you."

Ignoring her, Laurel shifted to Mac. "He's probably one of those three-day-rule guys."

"That's such a stupid rule."

"I know!" Emma settled in. "Who comes up with that stuff?"

Mac popped some muffin in her mouth. "People like Parker."

Parker waved a hand. "Just let me know when you're all finished. No rush, no rush at all. We've just got a bride, her wedding party, the hair and makeup team arriving in sixty-five minutes. No worries."

"Remember when she was dating that guy? The guy with the thing and the . . ." Mac skimmed her thumb and forefinger over her chin.

"That guy?" Laurel sniffed. "We didn't like that guy."

"He never looked you in the eye." Emma gestured with her bottle.

"And he chortled." Mac nodded wisely. "He's the only guy I ever knew who actually chortled. I don't think you can trust a chortler."

In the way of forever friends, Parker knew exactly who they were talking about. She started to point out she'd only gone out with him a handful of times, then wisely—or stubbornly—said nothing.

"That's so true," Emma agreed. She gave Parker a smile. "And because we didn't like him or trust him, we didn't say much about him. To you."

"Since we like Mal, we have a lot to say."

As it made perfect sense to her, Parker only sighed. "Okay, but at this point there's nothing to talk about. And there may never be. If there is, you'll all be the first to know."

"That's fair." Laurel glanced at her friends, got their nods. "Agreed." She circled her hands in the air as if wiping a slate. "Open to work mode."

"Excellent, as is the weather forecast for today. Mostly sunny, minimal chance of rain, light breezes, seasonal temps. The Gregory-Mansfield event this morning has no known danger zones or specific problems or entanglements to watch for."

"Just the usuals then," Laurel put in.

"Exactly. I spoke with the bride this morning, and she's good. Reports that she and her mother had a good weepy chat last night, and got it out of their system."

"I like her." Emma sipped her soft drink. "We're not required to like our brides, so it's a bonus."

"She's been great to work with," Parker agreed. "For the timetable."

She ran through it, section by section, confirming her partners' readiness, needs.

"The flowers are all charm, heavy on the woodland violets."

"Don't mention woodland violets." Laurel rolled her shoulders. "I made over two hundred for the cake."

"It's woodland meadow all the way," Emma continued. "The portico, Bride and Groom suites are finished, as is the foyer, staircase, and nearly all the interiors. We're still on the rest of the exterior, and I need to get back to it soon. The flower carts we've designed are going to be awesome, and she's going to love the mini watering cans filled with the flower I can't mention on the tables at the reception."

"I'll get the arrival shots," Mac added, "then stick with the bride and her party until I'm alerted the groom's heading in. Get his arrival, and back to the bride for the candids during hair, makeup, dressing—shifting to the groom and party. I have some solid concepts for formal shots, exterior. Using Emma's awesome flower carts."

"The cake's complete. No further assembly on that one. Emma and I can dress the cake and dessert tables during the brunch."

"I think the breakdown, second setup will be today's major challenge." Parker skimmed the schedule. "It's all in the timing."

"Won't be the first or the last." Laurel shrugged. "The cake for the second event does need some on-site assembly, but we're good there. Groom's cake's finished, the desserts nearly so. I need about an hour there, and I can steal that before the first event."

"I've already talked to my team on the timing." Emma blew out a breath. "We'll work our asses off, but we'll get it done. We'll start on the Grand Hall as soon as the guests move to the Ballroom for dancing. All twelve bouquets are complete, as are the three— jeez, three—flower girls' pomanders and halos. I can use any available pair of hands and or backs and legs. Jack and Del are pitching in, and Carter, too, when Mac doesn't need him. We should be good."

"Problem areas," Parker began. "Henry, the FOG's brother, really likes his vodka, and when he really gets a lot of what he likes he tends to pat and pinch and otherwise inappropriately touch female asses. I'll be watching him, but can use more eyes throughout. MOB has a feud going with her own mother-in-law, one of long-standing. They have, I'm assured, issued a detente for today. But emotions and alcohol, as we know, often trump detentes. The SOB," she continued, referring to the bride's sister, "has been divorced for three years or so from the groom's good friend who is one of the ushers. They did not part amicably, so there's a second possible problem area.

"Okay," she added, "quick rundown on timing."

WITHIN THE HOUR, PARKER, IN A SUBDUED GRAY SUIT, STOOD ON the portico to greet the bride. While Mac scooted and shifted to get her shots, Parker offered a welcoming smile.

"Ready for your day, Marilee?"

"I'm so ready. Oh, oh, look at this." The bride, already radiant without makeup, with her hair yanked back in a messy tail, grabbed her mother's hand, and her best friend/maid of honor's. "It's . . . it's like a magical forest glade. A wild, secret forest."

"Emma will be so happy you like it. We all are. And this is just the beginning. Why don't I take you up to the Bride's Suite, or today maybe we should call it your bower."

Amid more pots of violets and wild roses, among trays of champagne and colorful fruit, Parker hung the bride's gown, the attendants' dresses, served refreshments, answered questions.

"Hair and makeup are heading up," she said when she got the alert through her earbud. "I'm going to leave you to Mac for now. I'll be checking back in. If you need me in the meantime, just push one-one-one on the phone."

She strolled out, then went into a dash to check on Emma's progress outside. Emma was right, she noted; the flower carts were wonderful. If the entrance was magic forest glade, here the guests would step into magic forest meadow.

More deep red wild roses and rich purple violets twined up the portico. Charming and generous arrangements of wildflowers spilled from carts and tubs. Even now members of Emma's team added small distressed copper holders with more flowers to the sides of the chairs they'd covered with pale green slips.

Pretty, she thought, as the pictures Mac would take.

She pitched in for the ten minutes she could spare, then hurried back to greet the groom.

"Groom's on-site," she told Mac through her headset.

She greeted, escorted, offered refreshments, hung tuxes.

And noticed the groom's father, a widower of five years, standing alone on the small terrace.

She slipped out with him.

"Mr. Mansfield, I wonder if you'd like to take a little walk with me, see the area we've dressed for the ceremony."

She hooked her arm through his. "It'll give the wedding party a little time to settle in," she added as she walked him out.

"It's going to be a beautiful day," he said.

"It really is."

He was, she thought, a handsome man. His hair, full, thick, and pewter gray, his face lightly tanned and strong-featured. But his eyes were full of sorrow.

She spoke gently. "It's hard, I think, to face the happy times, the important moments, without someone we love, someone who made those times and moments possible."

He reached up a hand to cover hers. "I don't want it to show. I don't want any cloud on Luke's day."

"It's all right. He misses her today, too. He thinks of her, as you do. But it's different for you. She was your partner. I think Luke's going to have what you and your wife had with Marilee. The love, the bond, the partnership."

"Kathy would have loved Marilee." He took a deep breath, then another when he saw the terrace, the pergola, the lawns. "She would have loved this, every moment of this. You're giving our boy a beautiful day."

"We just set the stage. You and your wife helped make him into a man, and now he and Marilee are giving each other a beautiful day."

She pulled out her tissues, quietly offered one as his eyes filled.

"Mr. Mansfield—"

"Under the circumstances, I think you should call me Larry."

"Larry, I know what it's like to face those happy times without the ones you most want to share them with."

He nodded as he composed himself. "I knew your parents."

"Yes, I remember you and your wife coming to parties here. Luke looks like her."

"He does. God, yes, he does."

"I think, when we have those times, those moments, all we can do is hold those who can't be here with us." She laid a hand on her heart. "Knowing they're proud and happy, too."

He nodded, and the hand over hers tightened briefly. "You're a good girl, Parker. A wise young woman."

"I think Marilee's a lucky one, with her husband and her father-in-law. Would you like to walk some more?"

"No, I think I should go back. Be with my boy." He smiled at Parker, laid a hand on his heart as she had. "We'll go be with our boy."

She took him back, pleased to be able to make him laugh on the way. Then she walked quickly into the happy chaos of the Bride's Suite.

Women were gowned, men suited. The ring bearer entertained, the flower girl pampered. On the dot of the designated schedule, Parker lined up attendants, helped adjust rose and violet halos, pass out bouquets, dab moist eyes to protect makeup.

"Groom's in place," Laurel said through her earbud.

"So are we. Cue music for parents." After sending the bride's grandparents down, she turned to Larry, who would escort his own mother down the aisle. "You're up." On impulse, she rose to her toes, kissed his cheek. "Good luck. You look beautiful, Mrs. Mansfield. Enjoy the wedding."

With the clock ticking in her head, she watched them go. "Mother of the bride and son, your turn. After seating your mom, Brent, move up on the left of the best man. And go!"

Lovely, she thought. It all looked lovely, and right on time. "Cue procession music. First attendant . . . Go. Smile! Head up. You look amazing. Second attendant . . . Go. Shoulders back, Rissa! Maid of honor, on the mark." She didn't have to remind this one to smile, she noted, as the MOH was already beaming. "And go. Perfect. Okay, Cody, remember your job." She winked at the little boy who carried a white pillow with mock wedding rings. "Batter up!"

He grinned and strutted out.

"Your turn, Ally. You look like a fairy princess. Sprinkle your petals, and smile. Have fun, then go right to Mommy up front. Good girl."

"Oh boy, oh boy," Marilee said with a breathless laugh.

"You're not only a beautiful bride, but one of the happiest I've ever sent down the aisle. Ready for the big moment, Mr. Gregory?"

"She's not nervous, so I'm nervous for both of us."

"It doesn't show. You just look incredibly handsome. Take a few breaths, easy in and out. Cue bride's music. Here you go. Take that one moment at the entrance to pause. Let everybody get a good view of how amazing you look. And go!"

Parker waited until all attention focused on the bride, until the angle changed so there was no chance she'd come into Mac's frame.

Then she moved out, and off to the side to be, like her partners, invisible, but ready to address the smallest glitch or biggest problem.

For the next twenty minutes, Parker was pleased not to be needed at all.

"So far, so good," she murmured into her headset. "And beautifully done. Are we set in the Solarium for guests during photos?"

"Set and double set," Emma assured her. "And the Grand Hall's on schedule. I say so far, so excellent."

"You'd be right. MOH didn't get all the weepies out. She's okay, but she's going to need a touch-up before photos."

"Makeup's in the kitchen," Laurel told her. "Grabbing some food during the break. I'll send someone out in five."

"Five works. We're at ring exchange."

When the happy couple danced down the aisle—literally, as the groom stopped halfway to lift his laughing bride and swing her in a circle—Parker applauded.

Then got back to work.

With Mac herding the bridal party in one direction, she herded guests in the other. Subcontractors scrambled to rearrange chairs, add tables to the terrace.

After the photo and cocktail break—and only six minutes off schedule—Parker invited the guests into the Grand Hall for brunch.

There were always details that needed attending, adjusting, but watching the dancing during reception, Parker felt everything, onstage and backstage, had run particularly smoothly.

"Parker." Larry stepped up to her. "I know you're busy, but I wonder if you could indulge me."

"Of course. What can I do for you?"

"I wonder if you'd give me a dance."

Not usual protocol, but she knew when a rule needed to be bent or broken. "I'd be delighted."

"It's been a very good day," he said as they stepped onto the floor. "A joyful one. You helped me get to the point where I could fully enjoy it."

"I think you'd have gotten there on your own."

"I hope so, but I didn't have to. I watched you today, something I'm sure I'd have missed if we hadn't talked."

"Oh?"

"You're very good at your work, and very good at not letting it show it's work. Your parents would be very proud of you, of what you've built here."

"Thank you."

"My mother was impressed, and believe me, she doesn't impress easily. She has a dear old friend whose granddaughter just got engaged. If my mother has her way, and she usually does, you'll have another client."

"There's nothing we like more than a satisfied referral."

She nearly missed a step as she caught a glimpse of Malcolm—where the hell did he come from?—leaning against the wall, talking to Jack.

And watching her.

He threw her off, she admitted as she ordered herself to tune back in to Larry for the remainder of the dance. That had to stop. But the bottom line was, at the moment, she couldn't allow herself to be thrown off. She had a schedule to keep, an event to follow through to the end, and another to begin.

When the music ended, she stepped back.

"Thanks for indulging me." Larry gave her hands a squeeze. "You and your partners put on a beautiful wedding."

"That's exactly what we love to hear, and I have to get back to it."

She signaled the DJ to start the next segment—bouquet toss, garter toss, both of which she organized and supervised. She helped a guest locate a left shoe—a very nice Jimmy Choo—kicked off in the enthusiasm of a dance, and helped another with a quick repair on a hem.

Since Laurel was busy helping the caterers serve cake and coffee, Emma and her team had sectional breakdowns and redressing already underway, and Mac would continue to rove and roam and document the reception, Parker grabbed Del.

"We need to start transferring the gifts."

"Sure. Emma shanghaied Jack on flower detail. They're doing something somewhere."

Parker knew precisely what and where. "They're changing over the Solarium and the Grand Hall for the next event."

"Okay."

She jogged down the back stairs. "Where's Malcolm?"

"Somewhere. Why?"

"I saw he was here, that's all."

"Is that a problem?"

"No." She felt her shoulders tense, willfully relaxed them. "I just wasn't expecting him. It's a busy day."

"So put him to work."

What she did was put him out of her mind and she, Del, the valets, and the drivers began to transfer wedding gifts from the display tables to the bridal limo.

By the time the task was completed, some of the early departures called for their cars. She guided some out, assisted those to whom the bride and groom had offered flowers.

Keeping to the timetable, she dashed back up to give the DJ the nod for announcing the last dance.

Laurel stepped up beside her. "I'll do the sweep if you take the herding. You're better at herding."

"Agreed."

"Take-away cake and desserts are all boxed up so I can give Emma a hand, at least until Mac and Carter are free, then I've got to hit my own stuff for the next event."

"She's on her way to box whatever flowers the bride wants to take or give away from this point."

"I'll stick with her until I have to move on. How'd you talk Mal into hauling flowers?"

"What? I didn't." Parker's eyes widened. "He is?"

"I ran into him when he was carrying a small forest into the Grand Hall. From woodland violets to a rain forest of exotic orchids and whatever else is in there. Gotta say, Emma's done the amazing again."

She didn't know what to think about Malcolm and orchids,

and didn't have time in any case. Herding included making certain the guests worked their way out of the house instead of wandering through it, and giving the bride and groom her attention until they were safely in their limo and driving away.

When they were gone, she let out one satisfied breath.

"Nice job."

And whirled around to see Malcolm in the doorway holding a plate.

"It was, but it's only half the job today."

"So I'm told. Here."

She frowned at the plate he held out. "I don't want that. I don't have time for that."

"I'm just the messenger. Mrs. Grady sent it, and according to the rules of Mrs. G, as messenger I'm required to tell you to sit down for five minutes, eat. She made me promise to report back to her either way." He cocked his head. "I don't know about you, but I'm not bucking her."

"Fine." She took the plate holding some sort of cold pasta and vegetable medley, sat on one of the portico benches, and ate.

Malcolm pulled a small bottle of water out of his pocket, offered it.

"Thanks. You picked a bad day to drop by and hook up with Del or Jack or Carter. Saturdays are routinely our busiest, and we've called all hands on deck."

"I didn't come by to hook up." He dropped onto the bench beside her. "I came to collect my hundred from Jack, and to see you."

"I'm too busy to be seen."

"I'm seeing you now."

"We appreciate you pitching in, but you don't have to—"

"No problem. I got food, beer, and some damn good cake out of it. Did you get any of that—the cake?"

"No, I haven't—"

"Had time," he finished and smiled at her. "I hear there's a big fancy dinner and more cake on tap later. Hauling flowers and chairs and whatever around for that seems like a good trade."

She stabbed more pasta. She noted he'd shaved that morning and his jeans were free of holes and grease stains. Despite the chill, he wore only a black tee.

"Your garage is open on Saturdays. Why aren't you working?"

"I worked till one." He leaned back, closed his eyes. "Put in a long one last night."

"What's a long one?"

"Till about two. Kid banged up the grill, cracked a headlight on his daddy's Jag, which I cleverly deduced he wasn't supposed to drive while said daddy was away with his girlfriend. The kid was desperate to get it fixed before the old man got back and before the household staff noticed and narced on him. Paid me to expedite the parts and labor."

"That's deceitful."

He opened his eyes. "He's not my kid, so that's not my business. If it were my business, I'd probably say if the old man paid as much attention to the kid as he does to the girlfriend, the kid wouldn't have taken the Jag out in the first place. Hell of a ride, anyway."

"He may be an exceptional father just taking a couple of days for himself."

"The kid's mother is on a year's sojourn—that's the word the kid used—in Tibet where she's exploring her spiritual self or whatever the fuck, to revisit her truth after divorce three. So he's dumped on the father who leaves him with a house full of paid staff while he pursues his work and his women. Being rich doesn't make you a selfish bastard," he added, "it just makes you a hell of a lot more comfortable when you already are."

Sympathy warmed her eyes, her voice. "You're talking about Chad Warwick."

"Yeah, that's the kid. You know him?"

"I know the family, though that's not an accurate term for the situation. I heard Bitsy was going to Tibet. Also heard that she's spent the last couple of months on her spiritual sojourn on the Côte d'Azur."

"Nice."

"No, it's really not. Poor boy." She rose, held out the plate. "You can report back to the general, and take proof that I followed orders."

He got to his feet, took the plate. Held her gaze as the light breeze ruffled his already ruffled hair. "I'll be staying for the next round."

"That's up to you."

Now he reached around, closed his hand over her ponytail. "I got my hundred, so the rest of it's about seeing you." He leaned down, took her mouth—hard, hot, fast. "So, I'll be seeing you."

When he strolled out of sight, Parker told herself she could spare thirty seconds to sit down, to get her legs back under her.

Since it took twice that, she had to sprint up the stairs to check on the suites, and stay on schedule.

CHAPTER NINE

As EXPECTED, THE EVENING EVENT ENTAILED PROBLEMS, MINI crises, and personal conflicts Parker outmaneuvered, solved, or tamped down.

She solved the potential combat between the feuding MOB and GMOB by taking each on separate tours of the facilities while the other got her face time with the bride.

And firmly played Switzerland when each woman listed the faults and failings of the other.

She managed to keep the groom's good friend occupied, and segregated from any areas his ex-wife, the bride's sister, might pass through.

While personalities and defusing human time bombs ate up most of her time and energies, she passed what she thought of as guard duty on to Mac or Laurel long enough to run personal checks on the setup.

Step-by-step, she glimpsed Emma transforming forest and meadow into an elegant and elaborate feast for the eyes while Laurel added finishing touches on a five-layer cake as spectacular as a white diamond.

In the Bride's Suite, Mac documented another transformation—one of woman to bride, capturing the moment of pride and pleasure when their client stood in her glimmering white gown, sparkling with silver beads on the strapless bodice.

Parker watched the bride sweep back her elaborate skirt so her mother—obviously too overcome to think of feuds—could fasten the icy fire of diamonds around her daughter's neck.

"Something old," the mother murmured.

Parker knew Mac would capture that iced fire, the lovely lines of the bride's shoulders, the sweep of the dress—but the moment and the photo would also illuminate the emotion between mother and daughter as they smiled into each other's damp eyes.

"Baby, you look like something out of a dream."

"I feel . . . God, I— Mom. I didn't expect to get all choked up."

Parker handed her a tissue.

"You were right, Parker," the bride added as she carefully dabbed the corners of her eyes. "About not wearing a veil." She touched a hand to the simple band sparkling in her dark, upswept hair. "About keeping the headpiece understated."

"You couldn't look more perfect, Alysa," Parker told her. "Unless . . ."

As Emma was still completing the Ballroom, Parker took the bridal bouquet from its box, offered it to the MOB. "One last lovely detail."

With the trail of silver-edged orchids accented by clear beads in her hand, the bride turned to the cheval glass once again. "Oh. Oh. Now I—I guess I feel like something out of a dream."

The MOB laid her hand on Parker's arm, sighed.

And that, Parker thought, was the best acknowledgment of a job—so far—well done.

She heard the squeal—young, happy, not distressed—but hurried to the other side of the room as Mal, his arms full of flower girl, opened the door.

"Excuse me, ladies, but I found this fairy princess. Is this the entrance to the castle?"

"It certainly is." Parker started to reach out for the girl when a woman called out, and headed toward them, the other two flower girls on each hip.

"Leah! I'm sorry, so sorry. She got away from me, and I couldn't catch up with her with the other two."

"No problem."

"They're ready for pictures," Parker said. "So you can take them right in to Mac. I'll give you a hand."

She took the unrepentant Leah. "Thanks," she said to Mal before carrying the little girl away.

"Bye, Mal! Bye!" Leah called over her shoulder, and Parker's lips twitched in amusement as the girl added noisy blown kisses to the farewell.

When she came back, she found Mal helping himself to the cheese tray.

"Good stuff," he commented.

"Protein helps keep the energy up."

"Okay." He spread some Port Salut on a cracker. "Have some energy."

It couldn't hurt, she decided, and accepted. "Where did you find Leah?"

"The kid? Right out in the hall, dancing. Doing, you know. . ." He twirled a finger in the air. "She's all about her getup. I'd just taken the—what is it, FOG?—or maybe it was the other, the

FOB—a shot of Jack Black, so she couldn't have been out there long."

"We appreciate the help."

He smiled. "Show me."

"I don't have time for this. I have to—" She held up a hand. "Red Alert. Solarium."

"What are you, Captain Kirk?"

But she was already streaking out of the room. "What's the— Well, damn it," she muttered into her headset. "I'm on my way."

"What's the deal?"

"One of the guests decided the B and G's specific directive of no children under twelve didn't apply to their four kids, who are now apparently wreaking havoc during the preceremony cocktails. Laurel's the only one down there, helping the servers, and she's about to blow."

"Do you often have to sprint through the acres of this house?"

"Yes."

"Then why do you do it on stilts?"

"These are exceptionally attractive Pradas, and I'm wearing them because I'm a professional."

She sure as hell could move in them, he thought. "It doesn't have anything to do with vanity."

"By-product."

She slowed from sprint to brisk as they entered the Solarium.

He heard the kids before he saw them. Easily enough, he mused, as they were yelling, squalling, crying at the top of their lungs. He saw, as he imagined Parker did, the varied reactions of the other guests who'd arrived early enough to enjoy a few belts and some fancy finger food before the I Dos. Amusement, annoyance, distress, disdain.

A hell of a mix, he thought. And when he noted one of the uniformed caterers sweeping up broken glassware, a hell of a mess.

As Parker wove through the crowd with the accuracy and focus of a heat-seeking missile, he noted the kids came by their manners naturally. Mama was shouting, too.

"Parker." Laurel, who wore a white chef's apron over her business suit, bared her teeth in what could only loosely be called a smile. "Mrs. Farrington."

"Parker Brown." Parker stuck out a hand, grabbed Farrington's before the woman could object, then kept hold of it. "So nice to meet you. Why don't you and the children come with me? Is their father with you?"

"He's at the bar, and we don't have any intention of going anywhere."

"Laurel, why don't you locate Mr. Farrington and ask him to join us? You have very handsome children," she told the woman. "I have to ask you to control them."

"Nobody tells me what to do with my own children."

Parker's smile remained; it simply turned fierce. "As this is my home, my property, and your children were specifically not invited to today's event, I'm doing just that."

"We're here as a family."

Parker caught her breath as one of the boys fighting on the floor hurled a toy car at his brother. Malcolm caught it one-handed an inch before it collided with a glass cylinder filled with orchids.

"And are you prepared to pay for damages? Today isn't about you and your family," she continued, and though her voice stayed low, the tone shifted to hard-nosed. "It's about Alysa and Bo. The invitation clearly expressed their wishes for no children under twelve."

As the din stopped, she glanced down to see Malcolm hunkered with the four boys, all of them wide-eyed and blissfully quiet.

"I think that's selfish and inconsiderate."

"I'm sure you do," Parker said equably. "But it remains their wish."

"I told her not to bring them." Mr. Farrington walked up, a low-ball glass in one hand. "I told you not to drag them along, Nancy."

"And I told *you* that I expect my own cousin to have more tolerance and affection for my children than to bar them from his own wedding."

"Would you like to continue to argue about it here?" Parker smiled grimly. "In front of those children and the other guests? Tell me, Mrs. Farrington, did you RSVP for six?"

The woman pressed her lips into a hard line, said nothing.

"As I don't believe you did so, we have no dining accommodations for your children, and as it's a plated meal, no dinner. However, we'll be happy to make arrangements for child care for them elsewhere in the house, with appropriate food and beverage during the wedding and reception. I can have two licensed child care providers here within twenty minutes, for a fee of fifty dollars an hour. Each."

"If you think I'm going to pay you to—"

"You'll either agree to the child care and the quoted fee, or you'll have to arrange for your own off-site. My job is to carry out Alysa and Bo's directives and wishes. And I'm going to do my job."

"Come on, Gary, we're leaving. Get the boys."

"You go." Gary shrugged. "Take the boys, or leave them and I'll pay the fee. I'm staying for the wedding. Remember, Nancy, Bo is *my* cousin."

"We're going. Boys, *now*! I said right now!"

The crying, yelling, arguing revved up again as she grabbed, dragged, and hauled four angry kids away. Parker and Laurel exchanged glances. Laurel nodded and followed Nancy Farrington out.

"I apologize," Gary said. "We've been going around about this for weeks, but I thought we'd settled it. Then she had the boys in the car when I came outside. I shouldn't have let it go. I suspect they broke that tray of glasses I saw one of the servers taking out. What do I owe you?"

"Accidents happen, Mr. Farrington. I hope you enjoy the wedding. Malcolm, would you come with me?"

"Sure." He dropped the toy car he still held in Gary's hand. "Classic," he said, and strolled out after Parker.

"What did you say to shut them off?" she demanded.

"I told them I was holding the 'Vette hostage. Really nice Matchbox edition of the '66. And that if they didn't knock it off, the lady talking to their mother was going to arrest them."

"Arrest them?"

"It worked. Then when they shut up, we talked about cars. They'd been playing cars when their mother came in and told Esme, the nanny, to get them dressed in their suits. They hate the suits, by the way, and just wanted to play cars. Who could blame them?"

"Well, you handled it very well."

"There might've been four of them, but you had the tougher job. They're brats, sure, but she's a stone bitch. So, how about a beer?"

"I don't have time for a beer. That ate up most of the arrival, mixer, photo time. Mac's nearly done with the groom's party."

"How do you know?"

She tapped her earpiece. "She told me. We're green to go," she said into her headset and made Malcolm grin. "Cue guest seating music, please, and close the bar. If we don't close the bar, a lot of people never get outside," she told Malcolm. "Ten minutes to groom's entrance. I've got to get upstairs. Thanks for your help."

"No problem. I'm going to get that beer before I'm shut out."

He liked watching her work. He didn't know what she was doing most of the time, but that didn't cut into the enjoyment. She covered ground, a lot of ground, or seemed to fade into the background. More than once he saw her produce something from a pocket, apparently she had a few hundred of them inside that all-business suit jacket, for a guest.

Kleenex, eyeglass cleaner, safety pins, tape, matches, a pen. She had a small department store on her from his point of view. Now and then he saw her lips moving, responding, he assumed, to something from her headset. Then she'd head off in a new direction, to some new duty or to avert some new crisis.

Occasionally she huddled with one or more of her partners, or one of the subcontractors, then they were all off and running.

But if you weren't paying attention, it looked as if the entire deal ran on its own, sort of organically.

All the hoopla of the wedding itself—fancy dresses and tuxes, a cargo ship of flowers, candles and rivers of that strange white gauze winding around stuff. Music, tears, a lot of twinkling lights coming on to the ahhs of the crowd.

Processions, recessions, then hot dog, the bar's open again and the horde's guided in for more food and drink to hold them off until it's time for the big elaborate dinner. More flowers, candles, twinkling lights, music, toasts, table-hopping. All timed, he saw, to the minute.

Then it's the exodus to the Ballroom for party time, and before the last guest's out the door, an entire hive of worker bees are clearing, cleaning, breaking down half the tables.

He knew this for a fact, as he somehow got drafted for the breakdown.

By the time he'd made it up to the Ballroom, the party was in full swing. More tables, more candles and twinkles, and a load of flowers. Hot music now to lure guests onto the dance floor, another bar, along with servers passing trays of champagne.

The centerpiece here, he noted, staggering among Emma's banquet of flowers, was Laurel's cake as artwork. Since he'd sampled her wares before, he expected it to taste as amazing as it looked.

Something to look forward to.

He caught sight of Mac, slipping and snaking through the crowd, circling in and around the dance floor and tables, getting her shots.

Malcolm treated himself to a beer before winding his way to stand with Carter.

"Some bash," he commented.

"One of the big ones. I can't believe my sister's going to be doing this next week."

"Yeah, that's right. I got an invite to that. I guess it'll be different to be on that side."

"For all of us. Mac and I decided it's a kind of practice run for our turn. Figuring out how to be part of the wedding and run it at the same time."

"Well, she won't be taking her own pictures, unless she's got a clone."

"No." Carter grinned. "She's still trying to figure out how to take some of it, but she's got a woman she likes and trusts to do the photography. And they're all holding regular summits to determine the best ways to make it run smoothly."

"If anybody can. Listen, while I've got you for a minute, do you ever do any tutoring? You know, a one-on-one kind of thing?"

"With my students?" Carter angled away from the crowd. "Sure."

"No, I mean outside that."

"Not really. I could."

"This kid's been working for me a few months. Good mechanic. He's got potential. I figured out a while back he can't read. I mean, he can, but barely. Enough to get by, enough to fake it."

"Illiteracy's a bigger problem than a lot of people realize. You want to help him learn to read."

"I'm no teacher, and hell, I wouldn't know where to start anyway. I thought about you."

"I could help with that, if he's willing."

"He'll be willing if he wants to keep his job, or I can make him think that if he balks."

"How old is he?"

"Seventeen. Nearly eighteen. He's got his high school diploma—mostly, from what I get—by paying other kids to get him through, or charming the girls to. I'll pay the freight for it."

"No freight, Mal. I'd like to do this."

"Thanks, but if you change your mind on the kid or the freight, no hard feelings. I'll tell him to call you, and set it up."

Malcolm took a swallow of beer, nodded to where Parker crossed from one end of the Ballroom to the other. "So, tell me something I don't know."

"Sorry?"

"Parker. Tell me something about her I don't know."

"Ah . . . Um."

"Jesus, Cart, not like dirty little secrets. But if she's got some, I'll get you drunk and work them out of you. I mean stuff like what does she do when she's not doing this?"

"She mostly always does this."

"For fun. Do I have to go get you a beer just for this?"

"No." Carter drew his eyebrows together in thought. "They

hang together, the four of them. I try not to speculate on what goes on when they do, because some of it probably involves me. Shopping. She likes to shop. They all do."

"That doesn't come as a surprise."

"Well . . . She's a big reader, one with very eclectic tastes."

"Okay, that's a good one."

"And . . ." Obviously warming to the task, Carter accepted the beer Malcolm snagged off a passing tray. "She and Laurel both like old movies. The classic black-and-whites. She goes to fund-raisers and charity events, some of the club functions. She and Del split those up. It's a Brown thing."

"Noblesse oblige."

"Exactly. Oh, and she's interested in doing a book."

"No shit?"

"None. A wedding book, with each of them doing a section on their particular areas, and her tying them together. Which is pretty much how Vows runs. And I have to assume you're not compiling this data on her out of idle curiosity."

"You'd be right about that."

"Then you should know, nobody compiles data outside of the NSA like Parker Brown. If she's interested in you, she's got a file on you." Carter tapped his temple. "Up here."

Malcolm shrugged. "I'm an open book."

"Nobody is, even if they think they are. Gotta go, that's Mac's signal. Ah . . ." He held the barely touched beer out to Malcolm.

At loose ends, Malcolm wandered downstairs, and found Mrs. Grady paging through a magazine with a cup of tea at the kitchen counter.

"Coffee's fresh if you're after it."

"Wouldn't mind, unless you want to go up to the party and give me that dance."

She laughed. "I'm not dressed for a party."

"Me, either." He took a mug, poured himself some coffee. "Hell of a party though."

"My girls know how it's done. Did you get your dinner?"

"Not yet."

"How do you feel about chicken pot pie?"

"Fondly."

She smiled. "It so happens I have some I'd be willing to share."

"That's lucky for me, as it so happens I was hoping to have dinner with the woman of my dreams."

"Parker's busy, so you'll have to settle for me."

"There's nothing about you that involves settling."

"You are a clever one, Malcolm." She gave him a wink and a poke. "Set the table."

She got up to put the casserole in the oven to heat and noted he hadn't corrected her about Parker being the woman of his dreams.

She enjoyed his company. It was true enough, she admitted, that there were qualities in him that reminded her of her own Charlie. The combination of easy charm and rough edges, the casual strength and the occasional glint in his eye that said he could be dangerous when he chose.

After they sat and he'd taken the first bite, he grinned over at her. "Okay, it tastes as good as it looks. I cook a little."

"Do you now?"

"Takeout and nuking get old, and I can't always hit on my mother for a meal. So I put something together a couple times a week anyway. Maybe you'll give me the recipe?"

"Maybe I will. How's your mother?"

"She's great. I bought her a Wii. Now she's addicted to Mario Kart and Bowling. She kicks my ass in Bowling, I kick hers on Mario Kart."

"You've always been a good son."

He shrugged it off. "Some times better than others. She likes her job. That's important, liking your work. You like yours."

"Always have."

"You've been with the Browns ever since I heard about the Browns, and I guess before that."

"It'll be forty years next spring."

"Forty?" It didn't hurt her vanity to see his genuine shock at the number. "So you were, what, eight? Aren't there laws about child labor?"

She laughed, pointed a finger at him. "I was twenty-one."

"How'd you start?"

"As a maid. Back then, Mrs. Brown, who'd be Parker's grand-mother, had a full staff, and was no easy woman to work for. Three housemaids, the butler, the housekeeper, cook and kitchen staff, gardeners, drivers. There were twenty-four of us as a rule. I was young and green, but needed the work, not just for my keep but to get through the loss of my husband in the war. The Vietnam War."

"How long were you married?"

"Almost three years, but my Charlie was gone for a soldier nearly half of that. Oh, I was so angry with him for signing up. But he said if he was going to be an American—he'd come over from Kerry, you see—then he had to fight for America. So he fought, and he died, like too many others. They gave him a medal for it. Well, you know what that is."

"Yeah."

"We'd been living in the city, and I didn't want the city when I knew Charlie wouldn't be in it with me again. I'd been doing for a friend of the Browns, and she remarried and was moving to Europe. She recommended me to Mrs. Brown, the one who was, and I started on as a maid. The young master, Parker's father, was near my age, a bit younger when I started on. I can tell you he didn't take after his mother."

"I've heard a few things that tell me we're all better off for that."

"He had a way of navigating the gap between his parents. He had a kindness to him, a shrewdness, yes, but a kindness. He fell for the young miss, and that was lovely to see. Like a romantic movie. She was so full of fun and light. I can tell you when the house came to them, it was full of fun and light—and that hadn't been the case before, not in my time. They kept the staff on who wanted to stay, retired those who wanted to retire. As the housekeeper at the time was ready to go, the young miss asked if I wanted the position. It was good work for good people in a happy home for a lot of years."

She let out a sigh. "It was my family who died on that day, too."

"I was in LA, and I heard about it, even before my mother told me. The Browns made a mark."

"They did. This house, this home is part of the mark."

"Now you run it pretty much solo."

"Oh, I have help with the cleaning. Parker leaves that for me to decide when I need it, what I need. We still have gardeners for the grounds, and Parker and Emma deal with them for the most part. And Parker?" She stopped, laughed. "It's the same now as ever. No one has to tidy up after that girl. You're lucky if she isn't organizing you to within an inch. I get my winters off in the island breezes, and any time I need between. And I have the great pleasure of watching two children I saw take their first steps leave their own marks."

She scooped another helping in his bowl. "You remind me of my Charlie."

"Really? Want to get married?"

She wagged the spoon at him. "That right there would've rolled just as quick off his tongue. He had a way with the ladies, regardless of their age. It gives me a soft spot for you, Malcolm. Don't disappoint me."

"I'll try not to."

"Are you after my girl, Malcolm?"

"Yes, ma'am."

"Good. Don't screw it up."

"I take that as a green light from your corner, so how about some tips on navigation?"

She shook her head. "I don't think you need them. I will say she's all too used to the men who go after her being predictable. You wouldn't be. The girl wants love, and with it the rest she grew up with. That kind of partnership, respect, friendship. She'll never settle for less, and shouldn't. She won't tolerate dishonesty."

"Lying's just lazy."

"Which you've never been. You've got a way of nudging people to tell you things about themselves without telling much of anything about you and yours. She'll need to know you."

He started to say there wasn't much to know, then remembered his open-book comment to Carter and the response. "Maybe."

She waited a beat, watching him. "Do you see much of your uncle and aunt?"

His face closed up. "We stay out of each other's way."

"Tell her why."

He shifted, obviously uncomfortable. "It's old business."

"So was all you wanted to hear from me over chicken pot pie. The old goes into making us what we are, or what we're hell-bent on not being. Now go on back to the party, see if she can make use of you. She appreciates useful."

"I'll help you clean up."

"Not tonight. Go on, get out of my kitchen. Get in her way for a while."

CHAPTER TEN

$\mathscr{H}$E GOT IN HER WAY. IT WAS HARD TO COMPLAIN WHEN HE MAN-
aged to get in her way and be useful at the same time, but still . . .
he got in her way.

By the end of the evening, she wasn't sure what to do with
him or about him. Enjoy it, and him—that was her friends' advice.
Yet how could she enjoy something, or someone, who made her
so uneasy?

She told herself to concentrate on the job, on her work, on the
details of the wedding, and managed to do so. Through most of it.
When she helped escort guests out at the end of the evening,
Parker congratulated herself on having avoided, patched over, or
negotiated around the many pitfalls inherent in tonight's particular event.

And Drunk Uncle Henry slipped past her radar.

"Beautiful! Beautiful wedding, beautiful girl."

"Thank you, Mister—"

"Beautiful!" He wrapped Parker in a boozy hug that included his busy hands on her ass.

Before she could break away, she spotted Malcolm striding up. Her first thought was *oh, no*. She didn't need a white knight who'd very likely punch first and ask questions later.

"Mister—"

"Hey, Pops." Malcolm's remarkably cheerful tone matched the quick grin on his face. "You're going to want to move those hands. How're you getting home?" Since the man was already unsteady, Malcolm easily peeled him off Parker. "Have you got a ride?"

"I can drive." Henry swayed, grinned, lifted a thumbs-up sign. "One hundred percent."

"I think that's a hundred proof." Malcolm maneuvered Henry so that the man's arm slung around his shoulders. "Hey, have you got your keys? I'll hold on to them for you."

"Ah . . ."

"Hey, Dad!" A man hurried down the steps, sent a quick, apologetic look toward Parker. "Sorry, he got away from me. Let's go on out, Dad. Mom and Anna are coming right down. My wife and I are taking him home," he explained to Malcolm.

"Okay. I've got him. I'll help you out with him."

"Beautiful wedding!" Henry exclaimed on the way out. "Got to kiss the bride."

"And any other female under a hundred and twenty he could get his hands on," Mac commented. "Sorry, I was just heading down, and didn't move as fast as Mal when you got the DUH treatment."

"I lived." Parker blew out a breath, tugged her jacket into proper lines.

"Em and Laurel are helping the stragglers find misplaced whatever. Jack and Del and Carter are doing the security sweep in cleared areas. We did good."

"We did great. I'll start sweeping this level if you want to take over here."

"Good enough."

Parker moved into the parlor, through to the Great Hall and the Solarium where the subs had already removed and transferred flowers, tulle, lights, candles.

Here, for the moment, it was quiet, shadowy, with the wistful scent of flowers still lingering in the air. They'd dress it all again in the morning for Sunday's more intimate event, but for now—

"Henry's poured into the backseat of his son's Lexus," Malcolm said from behind her.

She spun around, watched him move in through that shadowed light. Though he moved with hardly a sound, the room no longer seemed quiet. "That's good. Thanks for the assist."

"Easy enough. You thought I was going to clock some drunk old guy for wanting a squeeze of a very nicely toned ass."

"It was a momentary concern."

"For the future? Clocking happy drunks is a cheap shot. If I'm going to punch somebody, I like it to be worthwhile."

His voice remained easy, casual, so why, she wondered, did that wistful, flower-scented air suddenly seem electric, suddenly feel dangerous along her skin? "So noted."

"Plus, as it's a really great ass, it was hard to blame him."

"I thought you liked the legs."

"Baby, there isn't an inch of you that isn't prime, and you know it."

She tilted her head, doing her level best to match his easy tone. "That didn't sound like a compliment."

"It wasn't. It's just a fact." He started toward her in the shadowy light, and she had to fight the urge to step back. "What do you do after one of these to wind down?"

"It depends. Sometimes a group after-event debrief. Some-

times we all just limp off to our own corners to— Wait," she said
when his arms locked around her.

"I thought we'd try another kind of winding down."

He took her mouth in a flash of heat that was more threat than
promise. His hands slid down, slid skillfully over her until thrills—
yes, dangerous thrills—shot over her skin. Under her skin.

She told herself to break it off, then as that heat sizzled into her
bones, wondered why.

"I want my hands on you, Parker." Not casual now, not easy.
Here was the recklessness she'd sensed under the calm. He took
his mouth from hers, skimmed his teeth along her jaw. "You know
that, too."

"That doesn't mean—"

"Let me." He slipped a hand between them to flip open the
buttons of her jacket.

"I have to—"

"Let me," he repeated, and swept his thumbs over her breasts.

Her breath snagged as the sizzle shifted to ache, and the ache
to raw, stark need. "I can't do this now. I'm not going to bed with
you when—"

"I didn't ask you to bed. I just want to touch you." While he
did, he watched her face, watched her face until his mouth came
to hers again, all fire and demand.

"Come out with me tomorrow."

"I . . .Yes. No." Why couldn't she *think*? "I have an event."

"Next night you're free." He glided a hand down the outside of
her thigh, up again until the muscles went to water. "When is it?"

How was she supposed to form a rational response when he
was turning her body inside out? "I think . . .Tuesday."

"I'll pick you up at seven. Say yes."

"Yes. All right, yes."

"I'd better go."

"Yes."

He smiled, and when he jerked her back against him, she thought *oh God* before she went under again.

"Good night."

She nodded, said nothing else as he let himself out the Solarium door.

Then she did something she never did after an event. She sat alone in the dark composing herself while her partners handled the bulk of the work.

As part of her routine, Parker spent her postevent Sunday evening on paperwork, for Vows, for the house, for her personal business. She cleaned up her e-mails, her texts, voice mails, reviewed her calendars—personal and business—for the next two weeks, reviewed the schedules of her partners, made any necessary additions or changes.

She rechecked her list of errands to run the next morning.

She didn't consider it busywork. She made it a habit, a strict one, to start every Monday with a clean desk.

Satisfied, she opened the file on the book proposal she'd been toying with, did some tweaking. Almost ready, she thought, to show to her partners, get their input, have a serious discussion on moving forward.

By eleven, she was in bed with a book.

By eleven ten, she was staring at the ceiling thinking about an entry on her calendar.

Tues, 7:00: Malcolm.

Why had she said yes that way? Well, she knew exactly why she'd said yes, so it was ridiculous to ask herself the question. She'd been sexually flustered and aroused and *interested*. No point in pretending otherwise.

So flustered, aroused, and interested, she hadn't even asked where he planned to go, what he planned to do.

How was she supposed to dress, for God's sake? How was she supposed to prepare without the smallest detail to go on? Did he plan to take her to dinner, a movie, a play, straight to a motel?

And why would they go to a motel when they both had homes?

And why couldn't she stop *thinking* and just read her damn book?

She could just call him and find out. But she didn't want to call him. Any normal man would've said, *I'll pick you up at seven, we'll go to dinner.* Then she'd *know* what to expect.

She certainly wasn't going to dress up when he'd probably pick her up on his motorcycle. She didn't even know if he had a car.

Why didn't she know that?

She could ask Del. She'd feel stupid asking Del. She felt stupid thinking about asking Del.

She felt stupid.

She'd let him put his hands all over her, was unquestionably thinking about letting him do it again—and more—and she didn't even know if he owned a car. Or how he lived, or what he did with his free time, except play poker on poker night with her brother and his friends.

"I could drive," she murmured. "I could insist we take my car, then . . ."

When her phone rang, she snatched it off the night table, thrilled to get her mind off her own personal insanity and onto a bride.

"Hi, Emily. What can I do for you?"

★ ★ ★

$\mathcal{M}$ONDAY MORNING, DRESSED IN A RUSTY RED JACKET AND BLACK pants, with heels low enough to suit errands, stylish enough to handle appointments, Parker hauled her dry cleaning bag to the stairs.

"Here, I'll get that." Heading over from his wing, Del shifted his briefcase to take the bag. "Dry cleaning? If I take this down to your car, will you drop mine off, too?"

"Can do, but make it quick." She tapped her watch. "I'm on a schedule."

"There's breaking news." He set the bag and briefcase down. "Be there in two. Don't carry that down."

"You might as well get Laurel's while you're at it," she called after him.

"Make that five."

She started to pick up the bag again, shrugged, carried his briefcase down instead. Emma strolled out of the parlor.

"Hey. I copped coffee from Mrs. G, so I thought I'd check the house flowers while I was here. Heading out?"

"Monday morning errands, then a consult at the bridal shop, and so on."

"Dry cleaning." Emma waved her hands. "Can you take mine?"

"If you get it here fast."

"I'm practically back already," Emma claimed as she dashed out the door.

Parker checked her watch, then walked back to pick up the weekly cleaning from Mrs. Grady.

By the time she'd loaded that in her car, Del came out with two more bags. "I can pick this up when it's ready," he told her. "But maybe I need to rent a truck."

"Not done yet. Emma's getting hers."

He tossed the bags in. "You know, with the amount you have, they'd pick up and deliver."

"Yes, but I'm going right by there anyway." She took in a deep breath. "Fall's coming. You can smell it. The leaves are starting to turn already." Stupid, stupid, she thought, but couldn't stop herself. "I guess when the weather turns, Malcolm must have to stow his motorcycle."

"Mostly. He's got a 'Vette, some vintage deal he restored. Pretty slick. He won't let anybody else drive it. And he's got a truck." He shot her a look. "Worried about your transportation?"

"Not especially. That's a lot of vehicles for one person."

"It's his deal. He picks up vintage cars at auctions, restores them, flips them like houses. Seems there's a hell of a market for that kind of thing, done right." He reached around to tug her ponytail. "Maybe he'll teach you to rebuild an engine."

"A useful skill, I'm sure, but I don't think so." She glanced over to see both Emma and Carter carting laundry bags. "Maybe we could use that truck."

"Ran into Mac on my way." Emma puffed out a few breaths. "So we've got the whole haul."

"Are you sure you can manage all this?" Carter asked Parker.

Didn't she always? she thought but only pointed to the car. "Load it in." And she'd make sure it was labeled on the other end.

"I can pick it up—" Carter began.

"Del's on return detail. That'll be Thursday," Parker told her brother. "After two. Don't forget. Full consult on the Foster-Ginnero wedding," she said to Emma as she rounded the car. "Five sharp."

"All over it. Thanks, Parker."

She drove out, imagining both Del and Carter would be on their way close behind her. Jack, she knew, had already left for an early meeting on a job site. Emma would shortly begin processing the morning's flower deliveries while Mac worked through the morning on photos—and handled an afternoon studio shoot, and Laurel baked for an outside job for Wednesday evening.

A full day for all, she mused. Just the way she liked it.

She dropped off the dry cleaning first, personally tagging each bag.

Systematically, she worked down her list. Banking, stationery store, office supplies, stops to replace the supplies she'd been called on to use during the past week's events. She added to her in-house supply of emergency party favors, thank-you gifts, hostess gifts, loading all carefully in her car, in order.

And paused to take calls, answer texts from clients.

She got her weekly manicure and arrived at her consult fifteen minutes early.

She loved the bridal shop, the soft, female fragrance in the air, the sparkling displays, the flow and sheen of white gowns.

There were elegant or edgy offerings for attendants, lovely choices for mothers of brides or grooms all carefully arranged with pretty and plush seating areas throughout, with roomy and multimirrored dressing rooms.

"Parker." The owner herself moved around a counter. "We're all set for your client. First dressing room. Champagne, an assortment of cookies for the bride, her mother, and her two friends. We've got four gowns earmarked for the first round. You said ivory, elaborate, full skirted, lots of sparkle."

"That's our girl. She won't want anything sleek or simple, and she's got the build to carry a big dress. Monica, since I'm early, I want to look for something I think would work for Laurel."

Monica clapped her hands together. "I was hoping you would."

"More contemporary, but with just a touch of thirties glamour. Maybe a subtle sweep in the skirt. Fluid, but with a tucked waist." She gestured to the gown on the nearest display. "That's not quite it, but it's the idea."

"I've got a few minutes, too. So let's play."

There was nothing, to Parker's mind, quite like the pleasure of browsing through wedding gowns. Studying the lines, the tones, the details. Imagining it all. And since Monica had an eye and an efficiency Parker respected, she spent a satisfying ten minutes.

"This one's almost there." She held up a gown, studied it from bodice to hem. "But I'd want a little more interest in the bodice. Laurel's small-breasted. She's also wonderfully toned, so I think she'd like strapless or spaghetti straps, especially as it's going to be a summer wedding. And I'd want a touch of elegant fun in the back."

"Wait! I have one in the back we were holding. The client went in a different direction. Shouldn't have, if you ask me. I think it may be what you're after. Let's go back and take a look."

She stepped into the back with Monica where more lovely gowns waited for the future bride to embrace or decline.

She saw it before Monica reached for it. She saw Laurel.

"That's it! Oh, yes, that's exactly it." She studied it, top, bottom, front, back, eyeing every detail and embellishment. "Monica, this *is* Laurel. You've done it again."

"I think that's 'we.' This is a four."

"And so's Laurel. It's fate. Can I take it home for approval?"

"As if you had to ask. I'll have it bagged for you."

"Thanks so much. I'm going to make a quick call before our bride gets here."

"Take your time. If they come in, we'll get them settled first."

Parker took out her phone as Monica went out. "Mrs. G? I've found Laurel's wedding dress. Can you set things up for tonight? It is. It's absolutely perfect. I'll try to find the headpiece while I'm here. It'll have to be after the consult at five. Thanks, Mrs. G. I'll be home in a couple hours."

She pocketed the phone and, after giving the dress another sigh, went out to meet her client.

If browsing gowns was a pleasure, helping an eager bride find hers could be fraught with peril or full of joy.

She dealt with a little of both with Emily.

"I don't want to look like anyone else." Emily brushed her palms over the flouncing layers of tulle.

"No bride ever does," Parker told her.

The four earmarked gowns had been tried on and rejected, as had another half dozen.

And the second bottle of champagne opened.

The problem with selection by committee, Parker mused, was that often the committee couldn't agree on anything, almost on principle. What the bride liked, the mother didn't. What the mother liked, one of the friends dismissed.

"I tell you what. Why don't you all take a break? We'll have all these taken out, and you have a cookie, some more champagne. Clear your mind. Give me five minutes."

She thought she had it now, and went into a huddle outside the dressing room with Monica.

"An overskirt of tulle would work, as long as there's texture and sparkle under it. Let's keep the midriff snug, and continue the sparkle. She needs something other than strapless or a standard neckline. I saw something with a delicate tulle halter. It had a silver jewel accent between the breasts and I think a lace hem with a demi train."

"I know exactly the one." Lips pursed, Monica nodded. "You may be right. I'll have it brought in along with let's say two others that may suit. I have one with a pick-up skirt big enough to hide an army under."

"Excellent. One of the problems is the mother wants bride white."

"The mother's wrong. With her coloring Emily needs the warmth of the ivory. She'll see it when we hit the right gown."

Ten minutes later, Parker helped hook the back of the gown. "Nobody say a word." She smiled as she said it, but the order was firm. "No comments until Emily turns around and sees for herself. Let's get her thoughts and impressions first this time."

"It feels good. I love the skirt." She smiled nervously at Parker. "The lace and the tulle and the silk and the pattern of the flowers and beads. But I thought bigger, if you know what I mean."

"Let's see what you think when you see the full effect. There. The back's gorgeous, by the way. Now deep breath, and turn around to the mirrors."

"Okay, here we go."

Emily turned, and Parker thought: bull's-eye. She recognized the stunned, misty-eyed delight, the awareness, and the change of body language as Emily straightened, lifted her head.

"Oh, oh, look at me! Look at this." She traced her fingertips down the sparkling midriff. "I love the halter style, the way it's so delicate, not like straps."

"You wouldn't be able to wear a necklace," one of the friends commented.

"But think of the earrings this dress would handle," Parker said quickly. "Anything from subtle studs to long chandeliers. And with a headdress, a tiara to play off the gorgeous brooch-work on the bodice, you'll sparkle for miles."

From experience, Parker watched the mother's reaction, smiled to herself. "What do you think, Mrs. Kessler?"

"I think . . . It's just . . . Oh, Emmy."

Parker handed out tissues.

The headdress, the underpinnings, took a fraction of the time already spent. At the bride's request, Parker stayed to suggest gowns for the bridal party while the bride got her first fitting.

Parker adjusted her schedule, and pleased the two friends—

one-third of the bridal attendants, with her choice of stylish, off-the-shoulder gowns in the bride's choice of rose red.

She left her very happy client and carried what she hoped would be her friend's wedding gown out of the shop.

"Parker Brown."

She glanced over, faltered briefly. "Mrs. Kavanaugh. How are you?"

"Good enough." Kay Kavanaugh's wild orange hair blew in the light breeze as she tipped her green-framed glasses down her nose. "Buying a dress?"

"No, actually, taking one for approval for a friend. Laurel Mc-Bane. I think you've met Laurel."

"She brought her car in for Mal to fiddle with. Seems like a sensible girl. She's getting married to your brother, isn't she?"

"Yes, next summer."

"The other two you're working with, they're getting married, too."

"Yes, Mac this December, and Emma next spring."

"You're dating my boy, aren't you?"

The segue from weddings to Malcolm threw her off again. "We went out to dinner, but . . . Yes, I suppose I am."

"I want coffee. You can meet me in there." She pointed to one of the cafes along the main street.

"Oh, thank you, but I really need to—"

"You ought to be able to spare ten minutes for a cup of coffee when somebody asks you."

She knew when she'd been neatly put in her place. "Of course. I'll just put this in the car."

"Need a hand?"

"No, no thank you. I have it."

"Inside, then."

Good God, Parker thought, what was this about? And it was

ridiculous to be nervous about having a cup of coffee with a perfectly nice woman, just because that woman was the mother of a man she was . . .

Whatever she and Malcolm were.

She loaded the dress, locked the car, checked her watch. She had twenty minutes to spare. What could happen in twenty minutes over coffee?

Inside, she crossed to the booth where Mrs. Kavanaugh already consulted with the waitress. "They have good pie here. I'm having apple pie."

"Just coffee for me," Parker said as she slid in across from Malcolm's mother. "Is it your day off?"

"Afternoon off. I had some things to take care of." Kay sat back. "My boy has an eye for pretty women, but he's not stupid about it."

"That's . . . good to know."

"I saw he had one for you the first time you came into the garage. It took him long enough to get around to it—that's where he's not stupid. It's clear you're not stupid either."

Parker considered a moment. "I can't think of anything to say to that except no, I'm not."

"But you're a different kettle than what we're used to around our place."

"I'm not sure what you mean."

"If you don't, I'm going to think you are stupid. You're a Brown, with the Brown name, the Brown status, and the Brown fortune. Don't saddle up your high horse," Kay warned as the waitress brought the pie and coffee. "I'm not finished. You act like a Brown, and by that I mean you act like the ones who raised you to be one. Your parents were good people, people who didn't flaunt that name, status, and money. Didn't shove it in anybody's face. I worked some of the parties they threw back when you were a kid. To my mind you can tell what makes up a person by how they treat the hired help."

Stumped, Parker added some cream to her coffee.

"I like your brother, too, even if he and the others won't let me in on their poker nights because I don't have the right plumbing."

At Parker's laugh, Kay smiled, and Parker saw Malcolm. "If you're asking, both Del and I know and appreciate the privilege we were born into."

"I can see that for myself. You don't exactly sit around on your butts, do you? You know how to work and how to build something for yourself and who comes after. That's a thumbs-up to your parents, and to you."

"That's a lovely thing to say."

"Lovely or not, it's how I see it. If Mal's got his eye on you, it's dead on you. It's not on what comes with you—that name, status, or money." Kay cocked a brow at the flash in Parker's eyes. "And you just answered the only question I had about this. You already know what he's looking at, so I could've saved my breath. Now I can enjoy my pie."

"Mrs. Kavanaugh—"

"I think you can call me Kay after this. Or Ma Kavanaugh, if that suits you better."

"If I thought Malcolm had 'his eye' on the Brown assets, I'd—"

"Have already given him the heave-ho. I'm not stupid either."

"Do the two of you always interrupt people in midsentence?"

"Terrible habit." Kay smiled again. "Want some of this pie? It's damn good."

Parker started to refuse, then picked up the second fork the waitress had laid, took a small sample. "You're right. It's damn good."

"I hate to be wrong. Mal had a rough time as a boy," she

continued. "Some of that's on me, and maybe why I hate to be wrong. Some of it's just the way the cards got dealt. But it didn't ruin him. I think he used it to make something of himself, to prove something. He's got flaws, and I'm the first to point them out, but he's a good boy. I figure you could do worse, and I figure you couldn't do much better."

Parker couldn't stop the smile. "He loves you, too. In a way that shows. It's one of the things about him I find appealing."

"He's never let me down, I'll say that. Not once, not ever. We try to have a Sunday dinner at my house once a month. You come next time. I'll tell Mal to work it out with you."

"I . . . I'd like that."

"I'm no Maureen Grady in the kitchen, but I won't poison you. Have some more pie."

Parker picked up the fork again, and had some more pie.

CHAPTER ELEVEN

A̶FTER THE EVENING CONSULT, LAUREL TUCKED HER FEET UP, stretched her arms. "I think this one's in the running for Ditzy Bride status. Not only does she want her MOH to walk her two Siamese cats down the aisle rather than carry a bouquet, but wants to include them on the guest list."

"Which means us providing, and her paying for, a meal—they'll have the salmon—for each." Mac rolled her eyes.

"Plus collar boutonnieres." Emma only laughed. "And a cat sitter through the reception. Where are you going to get a cat sitter?" she asked Parker.

"I'll talk to her vet. At least she didn't insist on having them at the head table during dinner."

"But it was close. Well, that's a problem for another day," Laurel decided. "What I want now is a nice glass of wine before I see what I can mooch from Mrs. G for dinner since Del called and has a late meeting."

"Change of plans there," Parker announced. "We have something to do upstairs."

"Parker, I can't possibly do a summit. My brain's tired."

"It's not that kind of a summit." Parker got to her feet. "And I think your brain will wake up for it."

"I don't see . . ." Realization dawned, clearly, in Laurel's eyes. "You found a dress for me."

"Let's go see."

Grinning at her friends, Laurel bounced in her seat. "It's my turn! Is there champagne?"

"What do you think?" Mac demanded and hauled her up.

"Same rules as before," Parker said as they all started up together. "If it's not the one, it's not the one. No hurt feelings."

"I haven't even decided on the style I want yet. I keep circling around. But I'm pretty sure I don't want a veil, it's so medieval. Apologies," she said to Emma. "But maybe I'd just go for some sort of hair ornament or flowers, so I don't think the dress should be too traditional. I don't want to go ultracontemp either, so . . ."

"And so it begins." Mac wrapped an arm around Laurel's waist, hugged. "It's Bride Fever, honey. Been there, done that."

"I didn't think I'd be here doing that, but I surrender. This is why Del said he'd be home late?"

"I called him when I found the dress." Parker paused at the closed door of the Bride's Suite. "He's hanging out with Jack and Carter. Ready?"

Laurel pushed her swing of hair behind her ears, gave herself a quick shake. Laughed. "Absolutely ready."

As had been done for Mac, then Emma, Laurel's dress hung in full view. A bottle of champagne chilled in a silver bucket with a pretty tray of fruit and cheese beside it.

Mrs. Grady stood, pincushion and camera at the ready.

"It's beautiful, Parker." Eyes intent, Laurel stepped closer. "I haven't been sure about strapless, but I love the way the neckline curves a little—softer—and the ruching and beadwork on the bodice adds that texture and sparkle." Reaching out, she brushed the skirt—just fingertips. "I haven't been sure about sparkle."

"I like the way the material pulls in at the waist, soft gathers to that center silver work, then the drape down from there." Mac angled her head, circled, nodded. "It'll photograph beautifully."

"The way it flows and folds down at the center of the skirt," Emma added. "With the silver beadwork along the edges. More interest, but not fussy. And the way those lines and textures are mirrored in the back. It's really lovely, Parker. Good work."

"We'll see about that once the girl's in it." Mrs. Grady waved a hand. "Get her going. I'll pour the champagne."

"No peeking," Mac warned as she turned Laurel's back to the mirror.

"Luckily it's your size, so it shouldn't need much fitting. So I picked up the underpinning. Even if you don't like the dress, the underpinning will work with anything you end up with."

Mac grabbed her own camera once they had Laurel covered up again, caught moments of Parker and Emma smoothing skirts, buttoning the back.

Mac clicked her glass to Mrs. Grady's. "What do you think?"

"Lips zipped until the bride has her say." But her eyes were damp.

"Okay, you can turn around, take a look."

At Parker's directive, Laurel turned. Her face stayed neutral as she studied herself. "Well . . ." Somber, she turned one way, then the other, with a slight shake of her head that had Parker's heart dropping.

"It may not be what you had in mind," Parker began. "What you've imagined wearing. It's your day. It has to be exactly right."

"Yeah, it does. I'm not sure . . ." Laurel turned her body so she could see, then study, the back. "I just don't know . . . how you do it! Psych!" She laughed and threw her arms around Parker. "You should've seen your face. So damn stoic. I love you. I love you guys. Oh, it's gorgeous. It's so perfectly perfect. I have to look at me again."

As she broke away to spin in front of the mirror, eyes sparkling, Parker just said, "Whew."

"You're three for three." Emma tapped glasses. "And though I was going to make a pitch for one, you're right about the veil, Laurel."

"Thinking that, I picked these up." Parker crossed over to open a box holding two jeweled combs. "I had this idea. If you can stop admiring yourself for a couple minutes, I want to try something."

"Can't I admire myself while you try it? Look at me." Lifting her skirts, Laurel took another spin. "I'm a bride!"

"Then hold still. I was thinking if you swept your hair back from the temples with these, then we had the hairdresser do something fun in the back."

"And we'd add some flowers—she might have enough for a French braid," Emma calculated, "leaving the rest of her hair down. We have them wind some thin, beaded ribbon through the braid, and pin a small clip of flowers. Sweet peas, you said you wanted sweet peas and peonies primarily."

"I do love sweet peas," Laurel confirmed, then reached up to touch the sparkles in her hair. "I love the combs, Parker. It's just exactly the sort of thing I was trying to visualize. Oh, the dress. The dress. It's just a little bit thirties. Classic but not traditional. It's my wedding dress."

"All of you together now," Mrs. Grady ordered, "before you get too sloppy on joy and champagne. There's my girls," she murmured as they lined up for the photo.

★ ★ ★

$\mathscr{M}$AC SCANNED PARKER'S ENORMOUS AND TERRIFYINGLY ORGA-
nized closet. "Maybe if I had a closet this size, I could keep it all
neat and organized."

Parker rejected a red shirt and moved on. "No, you couldn't."

"That's cold. True, but cold."

"If you kept your closet organized, you wouldn't be able to
buy another white shirt just because it's cute, because you'd be
perfectly aware you already have a dozen white shirts."

"Also true, but there's something to be said about knowing
where your red patent leather belt is when you absolutely need
your red patent leather belt." Mac opened a drawer in one of the
many built-in cabinets that held Parker's collection of belts, neatly
coiled in color groups.

"Since you know where everything is, and keep a detailed list
on your computer of the entire contents and their specific location, why is it taking you so long to pick something out?"

"Because I don't know where we're going or how we're getting
there." Frustration shimmied in her voice as she rejected another
shirt. "And because it's important I don't make it look important."

Understanding perfectly, Mac nodded. "Cashmere sweater,
strong color. Vee or scoop with a white cami, black or gray pants.
Heeled booties, color depending on the color of the sweater. It's
going to be cool tonight, so wear that excellent leather topper, the
one that hits about midthigh and has the swoosh when you walk."

Parker turned to her friend. "You're absolutely right."

"Image is my business. Wear some great earrings, and leave
your hair down."

"Down?"

"It's sexier down, less studied. Go for some smoke on the eyes
and pale lips. I don't have to add, wear excellent underwear just in

case, because you only have excellent underwear. I'm often struck with underwear envy."

Parker considered Mac's overall vision. "I haven't decided if Malcolm's going to get a chance to see my underwear."

"Yes, you have."

"I haven't decided if he's going to get a chance to see it tonight."

"That just makes it sexier."

"It just makes me more nervous, and I don't like being nervous." She opened another drawer. Shook her head, opened another. "This? Good strong plum color, V-neck, but with the mandarin collar, there's a little interest."

"Excellent. If you have a softer plum-tone cami, and you will, go for that instead of white. And the gray pants, stone, straight leg. Then . . ." She crossed to the wall of shoes, ordered by type, subcategorized by color. "Then you've got these truly delicious heather booties in suede with this great tapered heel. The colors and fabrics are all soft and rich, but the combination's got a casual yet put-together Parker feel."

"It's good."

"Oh, and wear those big hammered-silver hoops. You hardly ever wear them, and they'll rock this outfit."

"They're so big."

Mac pointed a finger. "Trust me."

"Why do we go to all this trouble?" Parker asked. "Men don't notice anyway."

"Because what we wear affects how we feel, how we act, how we move. And that they do notice. Especially the move. Get dressed, smoke the eyes. You'll know you look good so you'll feel good. You'll have a better time."

"I'd have a better time if I knew what to expect."

"Parker?" Mac skimmed a hand down Parker's ponytail as

their eyes met in the mirror. "Most of the guys you go out with, you know what to expect from minute one. They don't make you nervous. I haven't known you to get beyond a solid like or maybe a nice, safe care about since college."

"Justin Blake." Parker smiled a little. "I really thought I was in love with him then . . ."

"The world caved in," Mac said, thinking of when the Browns had died. "He wasn't really there for you, didn't have it in him to be."

"And that was that."

"That stayed that, too. I really think Mal's the first risk you've taken with a guy since Justin Selfish Asshole Blake."

"And that turned out so well."

Mac turned, laid her hands on Parker's shoulders. "I love you, Parks. Take a chance."

"I love you, too." Parker let out a breath. "I'll wear the big silver hoops."

"You won't be sorry. I have to get going. Have fun tonight."

Of course she'd have fun. Why wouldn't she? Parker thought as she swung on the leather topper Mac had correctly recommended.

She knew how to have fun.

She wasn't all business all the time, as most, if not all, of her clients could attest. And all right, maybe having fun with clients *was* business, but it didn't negate the fun factor.

She knew she was overthinking the entire thing, which meant she started overthinking the overthinking until she wanted to smack herself.

Nothing relieved her more than the ring of the front door. At least now she could get started on whatever she was doing for the evening.

"Casual," she said to herself as she walked to the door. "Easy. No stress, no pressure."

When she opened the door, he stood there, leather jacket over an untucked shirt the blue of faded jeans, thumbs tucked in the pockets of dark pants.

Casual, she thought again. He certainly knew how to be.

"You look good."

She started to step out. "Thanks."

"Really good." He didn't move out of her way, but into her. A smooth move, she'd think later, that put his hands in her hair and his mouth on hers.

"You didn't say where we were going," she managed. "Or how . . ."

She spotted the car now, a low-slung beast in shining black. "That's quite a car."

"It's heading toward cold tonight. I didn't think you'd want the bike."

She walked off the portico and had to admire the lines. Del had been right. It was very slick. "It looks new, but it's not."

"Older than I am, but it's a nice ride." He opened the door for her.

She slid in. It smelled of leather and man, a combination that only made her more aware of being female. When he got in beside her, turned the ignition, the engine made her think of a fist, coiled and ready to strike.

"So, tell me about the car."

"Sixty-six Corvette."

"And?"

He glanced at her, then shot up the drive. "She moves."

"I can see that."

"Four-speed close-ratio trans, 427 CID with high-lift camshaft, dual side-mount exhausts."

"What's the reason for a close-ratio transmission? I assume that was transmission, and the close ratio means there's not much difference between the gears."

"You got it. It's for engines tuned for max power—sports cars—so the operating speeds have a narrow range. It puts the driver in charge."

"There wouldn't be any point having a car like this if you weren't."

"We're on the same page there."

"How long have you had it?"

"Altogether? About four years. I just finished restoring it a few months ago."

"It must be a lot of work, restoring cars."

He slanted a glance at her as his hand worked the gearshift. "I could point out the irony of you saying anything's a lot of work. Plus it's a driveable ad for the business. People notice a car like this, then they ask about it. Word gets around. Then maybe some trust fund baby who's got his granddaddy's Coupe de Ville garaged decides to have it restored, or some dude with a wad of cash wants to revisit his youth and hires me to find and restore a '72 Porshe 911 wherein he lost his virginity, which takes some doing in a 911."

"I'll take your word."

He grinned. "Where'd you lose yours?"

"In Cabo San Lucas."

His laugh was quick. "Now, how many people can say that?"

"A number of Cabo San Lucans, I imagine. But to return to the car, it's very smart. The idea of a driveable ad for your business."

It *did* move, she thought. Hugging the curves of the road like a lizard hugged a rock. And like the bike, it spoke of power in subtle roars, smooth hums.

Not practical, of course, not in the least. Her sedan was practical. But . . .

"I'd love to drive it myself."

"No."

She angled her head, challenged by the absolute denial. "I have an excellent driving record."

"Bet you do. Still no. What was your first car?"

"A little BMW convertible."

"The 328i?"

"If you say so. It was silver. I loved it. What was yours?"

"An '82 Camaro Z28, five speed, cross-fire fuel-injected V8. She moved, at least when I finished with her. She had seventy thousand hard miles on her when I got her off this guy in Stamford. Anyway." He parked across from a popular chophouse. "I thought we'd eat."

"All right."

He took her hand as they crossed the street, which gave her, she told herself, a ridiculous little thrill.

"How old were you when you got the car?"

"Fifteen."

"You weren't even old enough to drive it."

"Which is one of the many things my mother pointed out when she found out I'd blown a big chunk of the money I was supposed to be saving for college on a secondhand junker that looked ready for the crusher. She'd have kicked my ass and made me sell it again if Nappy hadn't talked her out of it."

"Nappy?"

He held up two fingers when they stood inside, got a nod and a wait-one-minute signal from the hostess. "He ran the garage back then, what's mine now. I worked for him weekends and summers, and whenever I could skip out of school. He convinced her restoring the car would be educational, how I was learning a trade, and that it would keep me out of trouble, which I guess it did. Sometimes."

As she walked with him in the hostess's wake, she thought of her own teenage summers. She'd worked in the Brown Foundation, learning along with Del how to handle the responsibility, respect the legacy—but the bulk of her holidays had been spent in the Hamptons, by the pool of her own estate, with friends, with a week or two in Europe to top it off.

He ordered a beer, she a glass of red.

"I doubt your mother would've approved of the skipping school."

"Not when she caught me, which was most of the time."

"I ran into her yesterday. We had coffee."

She saw what she'd seen rarely. Malcolm Kavanaugh completely taken by surprise. "You had . . . She didn't mention it."

"Oh, it was just one of those things." Casually, Parker opened the menu. "You're supposed to ask me to dinner."

"We're having dinner."

"Sunday dinner." She smiled. "Now who's scared?"

"Scared's a strong word. Consider yourself asked, and we'll figure out when it'll work. Have you eaten here before?"

"Mmm. They have baked potatoes the size of footballs. I think I'll have one." She set her menu aside. "Did you know your mother worked for mine occasionally—extra help at parties?"

"Yeah, I knew that." His eyes narrowed on her face. "Do you think that's a problem for me?"

"No. No, I don't. I think it might be a problem for some people, but you're not one of them. I didn't mean it that way. It just struck me . . ."

"What?"

"That there'd been a connection there, back when we were kids."

The waiter brought their drinks, took their order.

"I changed a tire for your mother once."

She felt a little clutch in her heart. "Really?"

"The spring before I took off. I guess she was driving home from some deal at the country club or wherever." Looking back, bringing it into his mind, he took a sip of his beer. "She had on this dress, the kind that floats and makes men hope winter never comes back. It had rosebuds, red rosebuds all over it."

"I remember that dress," Parker whispered. "I can see her in that dress."

"She'd had the top down, and her hair was all windblown, and she wore these big sunglasses. I thought, Jesus, she looks like a movie star. Anyway, she didn't have a blowout. She had a slow leak she didn't notice until she did, and pulled over, called for service.

"I'd never seen anybody who looked like her. Anybody that beautiful. Until you. She talked to me the whole time. Where did I go to school, what did I like to do. And when she got that I was Kay Kavanaugh's boy, she asked about her, how she was doing. She gave me ten dollars over the bill, and a pat on the cheek. And as I watched her drive away I thought, I remember thinking, that's what beautiful is. What it really is."

He lifted his beer again, caught the look on Parker's face.

"I didn't mean to make you sad."

"You didn't." Though her eyes stung. "You gave me a little piece of her I didn't have before. Sometimes I miss them so much, so painfully, it's comforting to have those pieces, those little pictures. Now I can see her in her spring rosebud dress, talking to the boy changing her tire, a boy who was marking time until he could go to California. And dazzling him."

She reached out, laid a hand over his on the table. "Tell me about California, about what you did when you got there."

"It took me six months to get there."

"Tell me about that."

She learned he'd lived in his car a good portion of the time, picking up odd jobs to pay for gas, for food, for the occasional motel.

He made it sound funny, adventurous, and as they ate, she thought it had been both. But she also imagined how hard, how scary it would have been all too often for a boy that age, away from home, living on his wits and whatever he could pocket from work on the road.

He'd pumped gas in Pittsburgh, picked up some maintenance work in West Virginia, moved on to Illinois where he'd worked as a mechanic outside of Peoria. And so had worked his way cross-country, seeing parts of it Parker knew she had never seen, and was unlikely ever to see.

"Did you ever consider coming back? Just turning around and heading home?"

"No. I had to get where I was going, do what I was going to do. When you're eighteen you can live off stubborn and pride for a long time. And I liked being on my own, without somebody watching and waiting to say I knew you wouldn't make it, knew you were no good."

"Your mother would never—"

"No, not Ma."

"Ah." His uncle, she thought, and said nothing more.

"That's a long, ugly story. Let's take a walk instead."

On the busy main street they ran into people she knew, or people he knew. On both sides there was enough puzzlement and curiosity to amuse him.

"People wonder what you're doing with me," he commented, "or what I'm doing with you."

"People should spend more time on their own business than speculating on other people's."

"In Greenwich everybody's going to speculate about the Browns. They're just going to be careful when it's you."

"Me?" Honestly surprised, Parker frowned at him. "Why?"

"In your business you get to know a lot of secrets. In mine, too."

"How's that?"

"People want their car detailed, for instance, and don't always make sure everything's out of it they don't want other people to see."

"Such as?"

"That would be telling."

She elbowed him. "Not if I don't know who left the what."

"We have a running contest at the garage. Whoever finds the most women's underwear in a month gets a six-pack."

"Oh. Hmmm."

"You asked."

She considered a moment. "I can beat that," she determined. "I can beat that."

"Okay."

"I once found a Chantelle demi-cut bra—black lace, thirty-six-C, hanging on a branch of a willow by the pond and the matching panties floating in the water."

"Chantelle who?"

"That's the lingerie designer. You know cars. I know fashion."

"Something about cars and weddings," he said as he opened the passenger door for her, "must make women want to take off their underwear." He grinned as she slid in. "So feel free."

"That's so sweet of you."

When she settled back in the car again, she considered it a successful evening. She'd enjoyed it, enjoyed him, learned a little more—even if she'd had to nudge, poke, and pry the more out of him.

And had only had to excuse herself twice to take calls from clients.

"Big wedding this weekend," he commented.

"Two big, two medium, and a coed wedding shower Thursday evening, right after rehearsal. Plus two off-site events."

"Busy. Why does a guy want to go to a wedding shower?"

She started to give him the diplomatic, professional response, then laughed. "Because their fiancee makes them. We set up a cigar bar on the terrace. It helps get them through."

"Morphine wouldn't do it for me. The wedding deal. I meant Carter's sister."

"Oh yeah. We're all looking forward to that. Sherry's been nothing but fun to work with. We don't get many like her. You're at table twelve. You'll have a good time."

"Planning on it."

When he turned into the drive, she was as sorry to see the evening ending as she'd been skittish to have it begin.

"Summer's done," she said as she got out of the car into the crisp. "I love fall, the color of it, the smells, the change of the light. But I'm always sorry to say good-bye to the green and the summer flowers. I guess you're sorry to say good-bye to your bike until next year."

"I'll get a few more runs in. Take a day off and we'll have one together."

"Tempting." And it was. "But we're packed for the next couple weeks."

"I can wait. I'd rather not." He stepped closer, and though he didn't touch her, she felt the spike of excitement. "Why don't you ask me in, Parker?"

She intended to say no, had intended to say no since she'd dressed for the evening. Too soon, too much, too risky.

She opened the door, held out her hand. "Come in, Malcolm."

He took her hand, shoved the door closed behind him. His

gaze stayed on hers, compelling, the only contact but palm to palm.

"Ask me upstairs. Ask me into your bed."

She felt her heart beat, rapid kicks at the base of her throat. Be sensible, she ordered herself. Be careful.

Instead she moved into him this time, took for herself this time by laying her lips on his.

"Come upstairs, Malcolm. I want you in my bed."

CHAPTER TWELVE

$\mathcal{I}$T WAS A LONG WAY UP, HE THOUGHT, LONG ENOUGH FOR HIM TO sense her nerves. She was skilled at hiding them, but he'd learned how to read her. Especially now when he was aware of her every move, her every breath.

They climbed the graceful stairs to her wing where the quiet was so absolute he swore he could hear his own heartbeat. And hers.

She stepped into the bedroom—big, filled with quiet colors, art, photographs, the soft gleam of furniture he imagined had served generations.

She locked the door, caught his raised brow.

"Ah . . . it's not usual, but Laurel or Del could . . . Anyway, I'll take your jacket."

"My jacket?"

"I'll hang up your jacket."

Of course she'd hang up his jacket. It was perfectly Parker. Quietly amused, he stripped it off and handed it to her. When she crossed to a door, went inside, curiosity had him following.

Closet wasn't a big enough or fancy enough term. None of the closets he'd ever owned or seen held curvy little chairs, lamps, or an entire wall of shoes. In an alcove—and closets didn't generally run to alcoves—a lighted mirror ranged above some sort of desk or kneehole cabinet where he assumed she fussed with her hair and face, but the only thing on it was a vase of little flowers.

"So is this everybody's closet?"

"Just mine." She tossed her hair as she glanced back. "I like clothes."

As with *closet*, he didn't think *like* was a big or fancy enough word for Parker Brown's relationship with clothes. "You've got them color coordinated." Fascinated, he skimmed a finger over a section of white tops. "Even, what do you call it, graduated, like a paint fan."

"It's more efficient. Don't you keep your tools in order?"

"I thought I did. There's a phone in here."

"It's a house phone." She took her own out of the purse she set on a drawer-filled counter.

"Need to make a call?"

"It needs to charge," she said, walked by him and out.

She could give tours in this closet, he thought, taking another moment. Have cocktail parties. Hold board meetings.

When he went out, she'd set the phone on the charger on the nightstand closest to the terrace doors. And to his continued fascination began to fold down the bedspread—comforter—whatever it was.

He just leaned on the wall and watched her. Brisk and graceful, he noted, as she smoothed out, folded, smoothed. Parker Brown would never just fall into bed.

No wonder he'd never felt about any other woman the way he felt about her. There was no other woman remotely like her.

"I don't make a habit of this." She set the folded cover on the bench at the foot of the bed.

"Folding down the bedspread?"

"Bringing men here. If and when I do—"

"I'm only interested in you and me. You're nervous."

She turned to walk to the dresser. Her gaze met his in the mirror as she unfastened her earrings. "You're not."

"I want you too much to be nervous. It doesn't leave any room." He walked to her now. "Are you finished?"

"What?"

"Overthinking, second-guessing."

"Nearly."

"Let me help you with that."

He took her shoulders, jerked her against him. The hard, hot demand of his mouth helped. Quite a bit.

Even as she lifted her arms to circle his neck, he tugged her sweater up and off in one quick, impatient move. He tossed it on a chair.

"You can hang it up later."

"You don't hang sweaters."

"Why not?"

"It—" Her breath sucked in when he skimmed his hands over the thin chemise, over her. "It ruins the shape."

"I like yours." He pulled off the chemise, tossed it on the sweater. "Nice." He trailed his fingers over the lacy cups of her plum-colored bra. "It's the kind of color coordination I can get behind."

Her laugh ended on a shaky gasp as his hands slid down, his lips roamed down. As he knelt down. "Malcolm."

"Better take off the shoes." He tugged the short, inside zipper on the boots. "Wouldn't want you to forget yourself and wear them to bed."

"Are you making fun of me or seducing me?"

"I can do both. You're not the only multitasker in the room."

Once he'd pulled off her boots, he ran his hands up her legs. "Now these are the Holy Grail."

"You've seen my legs before."

"Not like this." He unhooked her pants, slid the zipper down, then guided her pants down her legs with his hands. "No, not like this." He lifted them one at a time to free them from the pool around her feet.

He ran his hands up, calf to thigh to tease the edges of plum-colored lace.

Her phone rang.

He looked up, his eyes sharply green, almost feral. "Not this time."

She shook her head. "No, not this time."

He sprang. His movement so quick both her vision and her mind blurred. His mouth didn't merely take but possessed while those rough-palmed hands raced over her, setting off charges under her skin. The nerves that had ridden there exploded into pure, primitive need.

She tugged at the buttons of his shirt. Her hands wanted flesh, too. Wanted to take it, to own it. When she had it, the muscles, the ridges, the rough and the smooth, need leaped to craving.

She tried to satisfy it, her mouth on his throat where the blood beat hot, her teeth on his shoulder where muscles tensed like wires. But the claws of it only sharpened.

He could have taken her there and then, hard and fast. She wanted him to, heard herself tell him to, to feed and sate that craving before it ate her alive.

He swept her up. It wasn't like being carried to bed but like being dragged into a cave. And she reveled in it.

When she was under him, she arched up, pressed urgently against him.

"Now. Now, now, now."

He managed to shake his head. "You're killing me."

He couldn't want so much and end it almost as it had begun. But the whiplash of lust was brutal, and she was a storm raging, slashing under him, around him, over him. Her body, so firm, so arousing with that silky skin over disciplined muscle, eroded control. He needed more of it before he took all.

Not to savor, since he knew savoring would drive him mad, but to devour in great gulps of greed.

Those perfect breasts possessed at last by hands and mouth while her nails dug into his back, his hips. Those incredible legs, open for him, winding around him, the muscles of her long thighs quivering as he did what he liked. All he liked.

And that face, the cool, classic beauty, flushed now, fierce now, eyes deep and blue, lips hot and avid.

He drove her up once, his hands rough, ruthless, for her, for himself. He wanted to see her break for him, rise and shatter. She cried out, her nails digging deeper. And as she broke, he plunged into her.

She cried out again, a strangled sound that gasped out pleasure. That pleasure, wild and whippy, blew through her like a gale, again, again, until there was nothing else.

Lost in the speed, drowned in sensation, she drove as she was driven, with a kind of dark fury.

He thrust deep; she rose high, their bodies sheened with the sweat of effort and greed. She saw his face above her, the tumble of dark hair around it, those feral eyes fixed on hers.

She tried to speak, to tell him . . . something. But all that would form was his name.

When the phone rang, she only heard the frantic pounding of her own heart.

She lay stunned under him, breathless from the storm and from the full weight of him that had dropped on her like a stone.

They'd torn each other to bits, she thought, in every way but bloody. She'd always considered herself open and responsive in bed—with the right partner—but this had been like a pitched battle with one goal.

Give me all you've got, then give me more.

Which, she concluded, explained the sensation of mild shock and smug satisfaction.

She liked to think he felt the same, or he'd just dropped into a coma. Not a heart attack, at least, since she could feel that beat slamming against her.

When she lifted her hand to his hair, he grunted.

Not comatose then, but a . . .

"You're a flopper," she told him, and his head shot up.

"What?"

"You're a flopper, which is why . . ." The sheer insult on his face turned on the light in her brain. "Oh God, not *that* way." Laughter bubbled up, fought to get past the anvil on her chest. She gasped with it, waved her hands in the air, fought to get words out through the uncontrollable giggles. "After. You flop after."

"I'm a guy, which you should've figured out by—"

"Not *that* way either." More laughter, helpless, finally rolling free when he shifted. She sucked in air, had to sit up, hold her own ribs. "*After*-after. You just collapse." She slapped one hand on the other. "Dead weight. But it was all right because I'd stopped breathing anyway somewhere between the third and fourth orgasm."

"Oh. Sorry." He shoved the hair out of his face. "You count orgasms?"

"It's a hobby."

Now he laughed. "Happy to add to your collection."

She didn't cover herself, and he admitted he'd thought she'd be the type to grab for the sheets once the heat of sex cooled a little. But she sat there, rosily naked, smiling at him.

"You're full of surprises, Legs."

"I like sex."

"Really? I'd never have guessed."

"I often forget I like sex during extended periods when I'm not having sex. It was nice to be reminded."

She reached out, traced a finger over the cross-hashing scars over his hip and thigh. "That had to hurt."

"That's from the big one. Mangled me some."

"And this?" She brushed the thinner lines over his ribs.

"Yeah. There, the shoulder. A few others here and there."

"This?"

He glanced down at the sickle-shaped scar on his right thigh. "That's from another gag. A little miscalculation. You don't have any."

"Scars? Yes, I do."

"Baby, I've been over every inch."

"Here." She rubbed a fingertip a few inches above her hairline on the left side of her head.

He sat up, gave a rub himself. "I don't feel anything."

"Well, it's there." And seemed, ridiculously, a point of pride now. "Four stitches."

"That many?"

"Don't brag."

"How'd you get it?"

"We were in Provence, and it had been raining all day. When the sun came out, I ran out onto the terrace. I was seven. I slipped and went headfirst into the iron railing."

"Wounded in Provence."

"It hurt just as much. How about these?" She frowned at the thin, almost even grouping of horizontal scars on his left shoulder blade. And felt his body tense this time when she touched them.

"No big. I got knocked into a locker. Metal louvers."

She left her hand where it was. "Your uncle."

"It was a long time ago. Got any water handy?"

Ignoring the question, she leaned over, laid her lips on the scars. "I never liked him."

"Me, either."

"Now I like him less. I'll get the water."

She got up, walked into the closet. He was sorry to see she'd pulled on a robe when she came back with two little bottles.

Cold ones.

"You've got a fridge in there?"

"A small one built in. It's convenient. And . . ." She twisted the top on her bottle. "Efficient."

"Hard to argue." He saw her eyes slide over to her phone, had to smile. "Go ahead. No point in you being distracted."

"I promise our brides round-the-clock availability. And even if I didn't," she added as she walked over to pick up the phone, "some of them would call whenever they got an itch. A wedding can and does take over the world when it's yours. Clara Elder, both times," she said when she checked the display. She switched to voice mail.

He heard her sigh, watched her close her eyes as she sat on the bed.

"Bad news?"

"Hysterical, weeping brides are never good." When she listened to the second message, she opened the drawer of her nightstand, took out a roll of Tums, thumbed one off.

"What's the problem?"

"She had a fight with her sister, who's also her maid of honor, about the dress she wants her to wear. The MOH hates it, and according to Clara, the groom took the sister's side, resulting in another big fight with him walking out of their apartment. I have to return her call. It may take a while."

"Fine." He shrugged, glugged down some water. "I get to see how you fix it."

"Appreciate the confidence," she replied, then hit the key to return the call.

"Want something stronger than water?"

She shook her head. "Clara, it's Parker. I'm sorry I couldn't get to the phone quicker."

She lapsed into silence during which Malcolm could hear the hysterical bride's voice if not the words. High-pitched, full of angry tears.

So, he concluded, the strategy was to let her vent it out, pour out the anger and tears to a sympathetic ear. While Clara vented, Parker rose to open the terrace doors. Cool air blew in, lightly scented with the night. Malcolm appreciated the way it fluttered Parker's robe.

"Of course you're upset." Parker all but cooed it. Cool air, he thought again, over hot temper. "No one can really understand the stress of all the decisions and the details but you. Naturally you were hurt, Clara. Anyone would be. But I think . . . Um-hmm. Ah."

She continued to make soothing and agreeable noises as she closed the doors again, walked back to the bed to sit. And this time rested her head on updrawn knees.

"I understand exactly, and you're right, it's your wedding. It's your day. My sense is that Nathan wanted to help— Yes, I know that, but let's face it, Clara, men just don't get it, do they?"

She turned her face, offered Malcolm a smile and eye roll. "And sometimes they just step in it, then can't figure how to get out. I really think Nathan was trying to smooth things over with you and Margot because he hated for you to be upset. He just went about it clumsily."

She listened again, and Malcolm could hear the bride's tone clicking down several levels.

"It's not that the details aren't important to him, Clara, it's that you're more important. Anger and stress, Clara, on both your parts. You know he adores you, and he knows, too, how much you and Margot mean to each other. No." She cast her eyes to the ceiling. "I don't think you were wrong."

She mouthed: *Yes, I do.*

"I think emotions got the best of everyone. And, Clara, I know how much you'd regret it if your sister wasn't standing beside you on the most important day of your life. Yes, the dress is important. It's very important. I think I can help there. Why don't we all meet at the shop next week? You, Margot, and me. I'm sure I can find something that makes you both happy."

She listened another minute or two, adding soothing noises, directing the solution in easy tones.

"That's right. Why don't you call Nathan now? Yes, I know, but how happy are either of you going to be if you let this fester between you? The dress is important, but nothing's more important than you and Nathan starting your life together . . . I know you will." She laughed. "I bet. I'll see you and Margot Tuesday. That's what I'm here for. Good night."

"Good job."

Parker blew out a breath. "She wants her sister to wear celadon, which the sister hated. Said it makes her look sallow, and having met Margot, I'm sure it did."

"What the hell is celadon?"

"It's kind of a celery color. A good sister shouldn't want her MOH to look sallow, but a good MOH sucks it up and wears what the bride wants. It's basic wedding rules. So, huge fight, which continues via phone, drawing the MOB in, who wisely kept her mouth shut. Then the poor groom tries to defuse the situation, telling the furious bride that it's no big, just pick another dress. It's all about you and me, baby. To which the bride explodes, and so on and so forth."

"So it's all about celery."

She laughed. "The celery is the MacGuffin. It's about power, control, emotions, stress, and family dynamics."

"You got her to agree to a different dress and call the guy all without telling her she was stupid."

"That's the job. Plus she wasn't stupid so much as too focused on the minutiae, which she should leave to me."

"And the minutiae is why you keep Tums in the nightstand?"

"They help when furious, crying brides call at night." She pushed her hair back over her shoulders, studied his face. "I have to get up early."

"Do you want me to go?"

"No, I don't, but if you stay, you need to know I have to get up early."

"It's handy because so do I." He set the water down, then reached out to pull her hair back over her shoulders. "Why don't we take round two a little slower?"

She linked her arms around his neck. "Why don't we?"

*H*E HEARD THE BEEP, OPENING ONE EYE TO THE DARK. HE FELT Parker stir beside him then reach over to turn off the alarm.

"I should've asked you to define early," he mumbled.

"Full plate today, and I want to get my workout in before it starts."

He opened both eyes to read the clock. Five fifteen. Could be worse. "I wouldn't mind a workout. Next time I'll bring some gear."

"I've got extra gear if you want to use the gym."

"I don't think yours'll fit me."

She turned the light on low as she rose and, swinging on the robe, walked to an adjoining door. "Just a minute."

In just about that minute, while he contemplated catching another half hour of sleep, she came in carrying a gray T-shirt, gym shorts, and socks.

"Del's?"

"No. I keep a supply of various things for guests."

"You keep clothes for guests?"

"Yes." She dropped them on the bed. "And as you can see, it's a useful habit. Unless you were just making noises about a workout."

"Give me five minutes."

She took little more than that to change into a sexy red tank and pants that hit just above her knee. She pulled her hair back into a tail. And hooked her phone on her waistband.

"How many days a week do you put in on that body, Legs?"

"Seven."

"Well, from my perspective, it's worth it." He gave her ass a quick pat that had her blinking. "In memory of Uncle Henry."

Laughing, she guided him to her gym.

He stopped in the doorway. He'd seen their setup at their beach house in the Hamptons, but that was small change compared to this.

Two treadmills, an elliptical, a recumbent bike, Bowflex, free weights, a bench press—not to mention the huge flat-screen and the glass-fronted fridge holding bottles of water and juice. Towels, he noted, neatly folded, alcohol wipes, killer view.

"Convenient," he said, "and efficient."

"For years it's mostly been Laurel and me using it, with Emma and Mac making the occasional visit. But recently it's been getting a lot more traffic. I think we'll add another elliptical and bike, maybe a rower. So." She took a towel from the pile. "I catch up on the morning news while I do a couple miles, but there are a couple of iPods if you want music."

"Of course there are. I'll take a run with tunes."

Different world, he thought as he set himself up on a treadmill. It beat the hell out of the setup he had at home. Classy, sure, but it damn well was efficient. He had a fondness for efficiency.

Plus it wasn't a hardship to take his run while Parker took her strides beside him.

He put in a solid three miles before moving on to the free weights. While she used the Bowflex, they sweat in companionable silence.

He hit the fridge for water while she unrolled a mat and started some sort of yoga deal and seemed to flow from one tricky position to another.

"You'll have to show me how that works sometime."

She rose from basically bending herself in two and moved into some sort of long, fluid lunge. "I've got a really good instructional DVD for beginners."

"Of course you do, but I think I'll let you do the instructing. You're fucking beautiful, Parker. I'm going to grab a shower, okay?"

"I . . . Sure. I'm going to be about fifteen minutes."

"Take your time."

He walked out, his mind full of her, then spotted Del, dressed in sweats, heading toward the gym. Del stopped, an almost comical freezing of motion.

Here we go, Malcolm thought and kept walking. "Hey."

"Hey?" Del goggled at him. "That's all you have to say?"

"Nice gym. I slept with your sister, and you can take a swing at me like you did at Jack over Emma, but it's not going to change it. It's not going to stop me from sleeping with her again."

"For fuck's sake, Mal."

"I gave you fair warning, and I didn't push her. And I can tell you that part wasn't easy. She's the most amazing woman I've ever met, and that's on every level I can come up with. If you've got a problem with it, Del, I'm going to be sorry, but that's not going to change anything either."

"Just what the hell are your intentions?"

"Jesus." Malcolm dragged a hand through his hair. "That's a serious question? My intentions are to be with her as often as I can, in bed and out. She's beautiful and she's smart and she's funny even when she doesn't mean to be. And goddamn it, she's got me by the throat."

Del took a minute to pace back and forth. "If you screw this up, if you make her unhappy, I'll do more than take a swing at you."

"If I screw this up, you won't have to take a swing at me. Parker would already have flattened me."

He left Del muttering to himself and hit the shower.

He'd just finished dressing when Parker came in.

"Should I apologize for my brother?"

"No. If I had a sister I'd probably punch first, discuss later. It's cool."

"Our relationship's more complicated than most siblings'. When our parents died, he . . . Del feels he has to look out for me—for all of us, but especially me."

"I get it, Parker. I can't blame him. More, it's part of who he is, and who he is is a friend of mine. He give you some grief?"

She smiled now. "In his Del way, and I gave him back some in my way. We're fine. He's your friend, too, Malcolm."

"That's right, so I think we'll just get this one thing out there now, before we go wherever we're going. I don't care about the money."

Her eyes chilled. He thought no one did cold disdain quite like Parker Brown. "I never thought you did, nor did Del."

"The thought's going to jingle eventually, so let's just head it off. You've got a hell of a place here, and I don't just mean the house. Your place, Parker, around here. I've got to respect the time, the effort, the smarts that earned you, the Browns, that place. But I make my own, and that's how I like it. I take care of myself and my mother because that's my place. I don't see money or status or what's it—pedigree—when I look at you. I just see you, and you need to know that."

As she had the night before, she walked over to the terrace doors, opened them to the air. Then turned to him. "Do you think I'm slumming?"

He considered her a moment. Not just angry, but a little hurt. As he'd been with Del, he was sorry for it, but it didn't change anything. "No. That's beneath you. I'm clear on that. I want to make sure we're all clear, on both sides."

"Apparently we are."

"You're a little pissed." He moved to her. "You'll get over it. Want to catch a movie tonight? They're doing a Hitchcock deal. I think it's *Notorious* tonight."

"I really don't know if—"

"Well, I'll call you, see what's up."

"You're welcome to coffee and breakfast in the kitchen," she told him, absolutely, perfectly civil.

"Sounds good, but I've got to book." He grabbed her, just grabbed her and gave her a quick reminder of what they had between them. "See you later," he said as he headed for the door.

He glanced back to where she stood in the center of the open doors, the sky and trees at her back. "Lay off the Tums, Legs."

CHAPTER THIRTEEN

$\mathcal{T}$HIS ONE WAS PERSONAL. SHERRY MAGUIRE WAS A FRIEND, AND SHE was Carter's sister—that made her family. Adding to the impact and intimacy of the connection, Carter's subbing for Nick during the previous January's wedding planning meeting had brought him and Mac together.

This wedding, Parker determined, would not only go off without a hitch (one that showed, anyway), but would be one for the books. Vows would give Sherry and Nick the day, and the memories, of a lifetime.

And in a very real sense, Parker saw it as a prelude to Mac's wedding in December.

Many of the same people would attend, she thought as she did a full sweep of the event areas. Her goal was to give the clients, friends, family, perfection, while whetting the appetite for the wedding of her childhood friend and partner.

It wasn't the first time one or all of them had been guests as well as providers, and they had plenty of tricks up their sleeves to carry it off.

She noted Emma had mastered the quick change from business suit for the afternoon event and worked with her team to clear the formal roses and lily arrangements, the swags of white and burnt gold, the marble stands and urns. Emma wore running shoes, many-pocketed jeans, and a sweatshirt.

And would change yet again, Parker thought, in the family wing for the event.

Already the ambiance Sherry wanted came to life with the wide, cheerful faces of candy pink gerbera daisies, the saucer-size blooms of zinnias in bold, happy colors, the soft, almost sheer pinks of baby roses. Flowers crowded huge white baskets, spilled and tumbled out of enormous bowls in fanciful and fun groupings.

Nothing formal or studied, not for Sherry, Parker noted.

She lent a hand, carrying arrangements to the Bride's Suite, setting them as directed among the candles already in place. She took the main staircase down, delighted with the twining of pretty lace with a bright rainbow of more baby roses.

It was exactly Sherry, she thought—sweet, fun, and happy.

From there she dashed outside to where Jack and Carter helped Tink transform the pergola into a frame of cheerful flowers. Her nerves jingled at the sight of Carter on the ladder. The man wasn't known for his grace.

"It's going to be just beautiful. Carter, maybe you could come down and give me a hand."

"Nearly got this."

She held her breath, tried not to think of broken arms and ankles as Carter leaned out to twine a swag. He nearly missed a step on the way down, but managed to do no more than bang his elbow.

"It's looking pretty good, don't you think?" he asked Parker.

"It's looking great and just like Sherry."

"I'm nervous." He took off the glasses he'd put on for the close-up work, stuck them in a pocket. "I didn't think I would be. The rehearsal last night went so well, was so easy and fun. Big thanks again for getting Di involved. She actually enjoyed herself."

"Part of the job."

"I have to keep busy." His hands went in and out of his pockets. "If I don't, I remember my baby sister's getting married."

"Well, I can do you a favor. I'm swamped, and if you could take this checklist in, go over it with the caterer, it would free me up and help with your nerves."

And mine, she thought, as he wouldn't have to climb any more ladders.

"I can do that. Have you seen Mac?"

"She's helping with the changeover in the Solarium, but I'm going to have to break her away soon."

Before that, she added her hands to the ones adding nosegays to the white-covered chairs. They were lucky with the weather, she thought, so Sherry could have her outdoor wedding. When the sun went down, it would cool off considerably, but the outdoor heaters would keep the guests comfortable enough if they wandered onto the terraces.

And the trees, she thought with one last look, were as bright and colorful as Emma's flowers. After a glance at her watch, she hurried inside to check Laurel's progress. And, she thought, to grab a couple quick slugs of coffee.

The bride and her party were due in fifteen.

"Please tell me you've got fresh coffee, and that you're nearly . . . Oh, Malcolm."

"Hey, Legs." He paused from plating some of Laurel's gorgeous cookies to give Parker a once-over. "New look for you. Cute."

She wore a full white apron over the blue dress she'd chosen for the wedding. She wouldn't have time to change later. She had shed her heels for Uggs.

Far, she thought, from her best presentation, however efficient. He, on the other hand, wore a dark suit, a snowy white shirt, and a tie in subtle stripes.

"You, too." She'd never seen him in a suit, she realized. They'd been together nearly every night through the week, slept together, and she hadn't been entirely sure he even owned a suit.

"I put him to work." Laurel stood on a step stool, putting finishing touches on the five-tiered cake. "Del deserted me. Nice presentation," she added to Malcolm. "I may keep you."

"But you still don't trust me with the pastries."

"Baby steps."

"Laurel." Parker took a step closer. "That cake. It's so damn happy."

The square layers rose up, stacked like wicker boxes and drenched in color, with a combination of real and sugar-paste flowers blooming over it.

"It's a winner, inside and out, but I think my favorite touch is the topper—and that goes to you, Master."

"She didn't want usual or formal." And damn if the laughing bride and groom kicking up their heels in a dance on top of the cake didn't make her smile. "The artist really captured them."

"And we're going to be getting requests for personalized toppers like this the minute this one's unveiled."

"Which is relatively soon. I've got to—"

"Coffee." Malcolm handed her a cup.

"Oh. Thanks."

"He's handy," Laurel commented.

"My middle name. Got anything else?"

"Actually, we're right on . . . Crap." Parker tapped her earpiece. "She's just turned in. She's early. The woman's late for everything, but today she's early." As she spoke, Parker whipped off her apron, stepped out of the Uggs and into the heels she'd left beside Laurel's. She pulled lip gloss out of her pocket, applying it as she ran.

"How does she do that?" Malcolm asked.

"Multitask, that's Parker's middle name." Laurel stepped off the stool. "You two work out pretty well."

"You think?"

"She's happy, and she's confused. A lot of things make Parker happy. Spreadsheets, for instance, and for mysterious reasons. But very little confuses her."

Laurel paused to take a long sip from a bottle of water. "As her friend since always, I think, yeah, you two work out pretty well. I'm sure you've already heard this from Del, but if you mess her up, you will pay. We're like the Borg on this kind of thing."

"Resistance is futile?"

"I really do like you, Mal." She gave him a quick and brilliant smile. "So I hope I don't have to hurt you."

He hoped the same.

With Parker busy helping the bride, he was free to wander around. He'd been to a handful of events now, and it occurred to him that the four women and their army of assistants somehow managed to make each one unique. Parker's timetable might've been rigid, but under it, over it, around it, everything else reflected the personal. And from what he'd observed, the time and sweat that went into making it so.

He found Del, Jack, and Carter at the bar in the Solarium.

"Just what I was after."

Del reached down, put a beer on the bar. "We're keeping Carter sane."

"Yeah? What're you drinking there, Prof?"

"It's tea. It's a nice herbal tea."

"Jesus Christ, your sister's getting hitched and you're drinking pussy tea?"

"That's exactly right. I have to put on a tux, and I have to escort people, including my mother, down the aisle. I have to make a toast. I'm going to be sober."

"He's freaked," Jack commented.

"Shows. If you're freaked about your sister doing the I Do deal, how are you going to handle doing it yourself?"

"I'm not thinking about that yet. I'm going to get through today. I'd be better if I could be up there, helping Mac, but Sherry won't let me. I just need to—" He broke off, pulled out the beeper in his pocket. "Oh, well, that's me. I mean that's Nick. They're here. I have to go and be there."

He downed the tea like medicine. "I'll be fine," he said resolutely, then walked away.

"We'll get him drunk later," Del said.

"Looking forward to it." Mal lifted his beer, and the three men clinked bottles.

It WAS PERFECT, PARKER THOUGHT. SHERRY'S LAUGHTER FILLED THE Bride's Suite as she and her attendants dressed. The absolute joy proved infectious, and provided Mac with countless photos of happy faces, mugging faces, embraces—and the bride twirling exuberantly in front of the mirror.

Eyes watered up a bit as Pam Maguire helped her daughter adjust her headpiece, and when Michael stepped in for his first look at his baby girl.

"Sherry." He stopped to clear his throat. "You're a vision."

"Daddy." Still holding her mother's hand, she reached for her father's, pulled them together. Turned to the mirror again, her arms around her parents' waists, she beamed like the sun. "Get a load of us."

Get a load of you, Parker thought as Mac captured the moment. They were beautiful and happy and together. It made her ache, just a little, for what she'd never have. That moment would never be hers.

She took a breath, shook it off. "It's time."

The bride smiled her way down the aisle behind her pretty attendants. When she reached the groom, whose jaw had dropped satisfactorily at the sight of her before his grin burst out, she reached for his hand, laughed.

And Parker thought, yes, it's just exactly right.

"BEST PARTY EVER," MAC DECLARED. "AS ORDERED. HOW ARE WE going to top that?" She tipped her head to Carter's shoulder.

They hadn't managed to get him drunk—he'd held out and held up, and now slumped on the sofa in the family parlor, two fingers of whiskey in his hand.

"She sparkled," he replied.

"Yeah, she really did."

"Damn good cake." Malcolm shoveled in a bite. "It's my favorite part of these deals."

"A man of taste," Laurel said, and yawned. "Tomorrow's is chocolate ganache."

"Will I like it?"

"Yes, unless you go insane during the night. Haul me up, Del. I am so done."

"Go, team us." Emma, eyes closed, snuggled against Jack. "Can I just sleep here?"

Jack rose, gathered her up. She smiled sleepily as she wound her arms around his neck. "I love when you do that."

"You earned a ride. 'Night, all."

"I, on the other hand, am pumped. I'm going to take a look at some of the shots before I turn in." Mac elbowed Carter. "Come on, cutie, let's go so you can hail my genius."

He managed to unfold himself. "Parker, thanks for giving my sister a day none of us will ever forget."

"Oh, Carter." Touched, she rose to step over and kiss his cheek. "I promise you and Mac exactly the same."

She watched them go.

"I can see the wheels turning," Malcolm commented.

"I did get some ideas today. We'll see if I can make them happen."

"If anybody can." He paused. "Am I staying?"

"I'd like you to." She held out a hand.

ON A BRISK OCTOBER AFTERNOON WITH CLOUDS SCUTTLED ACROSS the sky, and tumbles of colored leaves scooting over the lawn ahead of the wind, Parker called a midday meeting.

To brighten the mood she lit a fire, as fires had always crackled or simmered in the library on chilly days in autumn. And as the flames caught, she wandered to one of the windows to look out on the roll of land, the shivering trees, the rippling gray water in the pond.

She didn't often wonder where her life was going. More often than not her focus centered on the details, plans, contingencies, needs, wants, fantasies of others. Maybe it was the contrasts of the day, that soft and gloomy sky against the still brilliant trees. The leaves shedding themselves to dance and whirl in the air while the mums and asters stubbornly bloomed.

Everything seemed paused for change, but was she? Change was as much about loss as gain, about giving something up even as you reached for something new or different. And, she admitted, she prized routine, tradition, even repetition.

Routine equaled security, safety, stability. While the unknown often grew on shaky ground.

And that, she realized, was a line of thinking as gloomy as the sky. The world was opening up, she reminded herself, not closing in. She'd never been a coward, never been afraid to take those steps onto unsettled ground.

Life changed, and it should. Her three closest friends were getting married, starting new phases of their lives. One day, she imagined, there would be children tumbling like those colorful leaves on the lawn. That's how it should be.

That's what home was for.

Their business was expanding. And if after the meeting they were in agreement, it would expand again, in new, uncharted areas.

Then there was Malcolm—and that, she had to admit, was the crux of this nervy, unsettled feeling. God knew he was a change. She couldn't decide if he'd just slid cagily, craftily into her life or kicked open doors she'd thought she'd cautiously bolted.

Most days, she thought, it seemed to be a combination of both.

However he'd gotten in, she still couldn't quite figure out what to expect from him. An attentive lover, then a wildly demanding one; an amusing companion, then one who peppered her with questions that pushed her to think both inside and outside the box. The risk-taker, the devoted son, the bad boy, the shrewd businessman.

He had all those facets, and she felt she'd barely touched the surface.

She appreciated his innate curiosity, and the skill he possessed in digging out information, histories, connections. He ended up, she'd come to realize, learning a great deal about other people.

And was frustratingly stingy with personal data.

Most of what she knew of his history came from other sources. He had a way of skirting around the edges whenever she asked a question about his childhood, his early time in California, even his recovery from the accident that had brought him home again.

If their relationship had stayed a surface one, the reticence wouldn't matter. But it hadn't, Parker thought, so it did. It mattered because she'd gone past interest, swung into attraction, burst through lust, tripped over affection, and was now skidding out of control into love.

And she wasn't altogether happy about it.

The rain began in thin, spitting drops as Laurel came in with a big tray.

"If we're going to have a meeting this time of day, we might as well eat." She cast Parker a look as she set the tray down. "Don't you look pensive and perturbed."

"Maybe I'm just hungry."

"That we can fix. We've got some very pretty, girlie sandwiches, seasonal fruit, celery and carrot straws, kettle chips, and petit fours."

"That ought to do it."

"It's nice." Laurel crunched on a chip. "A fire on a rainy afternoon. Nice, too, to get off my feet for a while." She opted for tea, then sat. "What's up?"

"A couple of things."

"A couple of things like here's what's up, or a couple of things like here's a deal, let's discuss it into many pieces?"

"I think the latter."

"Then I need a sandwich."

Mac and Emma walked in together as Laurel loaded a plate.

"So, we'd pick that up with the mini mango callas for the boutonnieres," Mac said, obviously continuing a conversation. "And you'd, like, pop them out in the bouquets and arrangements. All mixed in, but popped."

"Exactly."

"I think I like that the best. I'm consulting with my wedding florist," she told Parker and Laurel. "I believe she's brilliant."

"I completely am. Oh, pretty sandwiches."

"I'm also brilliant," Laurel reminded her. "If you're still in florist mode, Em, I've been thinking of going with cool colors. Sherberty."

"Don't make me wear raspberry." Mac tugged her bright red hair.

"I could, I could make you, but besides brilliant I'm also kind. I was thinking lemony. All three of you would look good in really pale lemon. Maybe chiffon. It's kind of clichéd maybe. Lemon chiffon, summer wedding, but—"

"It's good. And I can really work with a pale lemon," Emma speculated. "Using zaps of bold blues, trails of minty greens. Keeping it all soft, but saturated, with unexpected snaps of deeper colors."

"I want to get your engagement shots in the next week," Mac said to Laurel.

"We haven't decided exactly what we want there."

"I have." Mac bit down on a carrot straw. "In the kitchen."

Instantly Laurel moved to sulk mode. "Talk about clichés."

Mac just pointed with her carrot. "The counter heaped with gorgeous pastries, cakes, cookies, with you and Del in front of it. I want him sitting on a stool, and you wearing your baker's apron and cap."

And the sulk deepened. "Well, aren't I glamorous?"

"What you'll be when I'm done with you, ye of no faith whatsoever, will be sexy, adorable, cheeky, and unique."

"She was right about doing Jack's and mine in the garden," Emma pointed out. "We looked gorgeous, and hot."

"Also brilliant, but it did help that you're both already gorgeous and hot. So." Mac dropped into a seat. "What's the what for?" Her eyebrows lifted as she glanced at Parker, saw her friend grinning. "And what's that for?"

"It's fun, it's just fun to listen to all you talk about wedding plans. Your own wedding plans. Mac, I've asked Monica and Susan from the bridal shop to stand in for me—pinch running, we'll say—on your day. They're smart, experienced, capable. And if there's anything that needs to be dealt with during the ceremony, I won't have to excuse myself and bolt."

"That's really good thinking."

"Which makes us four for four in brilliance. They'll also help with guests while we're up in the Bride's Suite. Emma, I know you have a team, but—"

"Right there with you," Emma interrupted. "I won't be as available for the setup, and we won't be able to draft Carter or Del or Jack. I've got two florists I'm going to work with on a couple of the upcoming events. And if they're as good as I think, they'll work with my regular team for Mac's. We're going to need extra and experienced hands for the Seaman wedding in April—and for mine, for Laurel's."

"Good. And Laurel."

"Also on the same page. I've asked Charles, the pastry chef at the Willows, if he can take time to work with me on Mac's wedding. I told you how good he is. He's thrilled. I have to wheedle the time off for him, but I know how to handle Julio," she added, speaking of the restaurant's temperamental head chef.

"I think we've got that covered," Parker told her. "We'll need to have some strategy meetings, and all of these extra hands will need a tour of the event spaces, a tutorial on how we work. Mac, I've started the timetable for your wedding."

"My timetable," Mac said, and grinned. "Parker made me a timetable."

"It's varied from our usual, because it's you, and it's us. We'll work out any time constraints during rehearsal, which I also wanted to talk to you about. The rehearsal dinner . . ."

"We'll probably book the Willows, but . . ."

Parker met Mac's eyes, read them, smiled. "I was hoping you would."

"Oh yes!" Understanding the looks, Emma clapped her hands together. "Have it here. It's perfect."

"It is perfect," Laurel agreed. "Even with the added work, the cleanup, it's just right."

"Settled?"

Mac reached across the table, squeezed Parker's hand. "Settled."

"New business. It would be oddly new business. I got a call from Katrina Stevens. Memory refresher. She was one of our first brides. Towering, pencil-thin blonde, big laugh. I believe one of her attendants was the first to have sex with a groomsman in the Bride's Suite."

"Oh yeah!" Mac held up a hand. "She was easily six feet tall, wore spikes that added another four inches. The groom was about six-eight. They looked like Nordic gods."

"Silver Palace cake, six layers," Laurel recalled.

"White roses, eggplant callas," Emma confirmed.

"She and Mica are getting a divorce."

"Can't win them all. Too bad though," Laurel added. "They made an impressive couple."

"Apparently, at least according to Katrina, he didn't mind impressing others, and when she caught him doing so with one of his clients, she kicked him out. There was some back and forth, separation, reconciliation, separation, and now she's done. The divorce will be final in late February. She wants a divorce party. Here."

"A divorce party?" Emma's lips moved into a pout. "That doesn't seem nice."

"I don't think she's feeling particularly nice toward Mica, but she did sound as though she's feeling energized and happy. She's gotten the idea in her head that she wants to celebrate what she's calling the new start of her life, and she wants to do it here—in style."

Parker lifted the water bottle that was never far from her hand. "It's not what we do, which I explained to her, but she's got the bit between her teeth. She's set on it, willing to book a full day in one of our slowest months, not counting the Valentine's Day madness. I felt I had to put it out there for discussion."

"Just how do we list that kind of event on the website?" Mac muttered.

"I think divorce should make you sad, or mad." Emma frowned over her tea. "I can see going out, getting toasted with some friends, but this seems mean."

"Cheating on your wife's meaner," Laurel pointed out.

"No question, but it's . . ." Emma moved her shoulders to mime discomfort. "And here, where they got married."

"It's probably small of me, but I like the way she's thinking." Laurel shrugged and bit into a carrot straw. "Like she's closing a circle, and instead of bitching or mourning—and maybe, probably she's already done both—she's marking it with food, drink, flowers, music, friends. I wouldn't like to see us do this sort of thing regularly, but I can sort of see it for a returning customer."

"Maybe we should have a package deal." Mac snagged a sandwich. "We planned your wedding, now we'll plan your divorce. Celebrate at ten percent off."

"Did they have kids?" Emma wondered.

"No."

She nodded at Parker. "Well, that's something, I guess. You haven't said what you think about it."

"I had all the same reactions the three of you've had, in various degrees." She lifted her hands, let them fall. "My initial instinct was just no. Then, the more she talked, the more I saw where she was coming from, and why she wanted it. Then I stacked all those instincts and reactions up and took a hard look. It's business, and it's really none of our business if a client wants to hire us to celebrate the end of a bad marriage."

"You're voting yes?" Mac asked.

"I'm voting yes because she told me she wanted to have this party, this new beginning, here especially because it would remind her that the other beginning had started out beautifully, and full of love and hope. That it would help remind her she hadn't made a mistake. Things changed, and now she was going to start again, and by God, she was going to keep right on believing in love and hope. She sold me."

"You have to admire her—what is it?—chutzpa," Mac commented.

"I'm voting with Parker, and further vote that if anything like this comes up again, we take it on a case-by-case basis." Laurel looked around the table. "It's business, but if the client's just looking to take swipes at an ex, even deservedly, I don't think this is the place."

"Agreed," Parker said instantly. "And if I'd gotten that sense, I would have steered her away."

"Okay." Mac nodded. "Case by case."

"I'll go along," Emma decided, "because it sounds like she's just closing a door, and wants to see what's behind others. But it still makes me sad."

"With that, I have other new business that I hope cheers you up. I've finished fine-tuning the book proposal."

"Seriously?" Emma gaped. "I don't know if I'm cheered up or just scared."

"I'm going to e-mail you all the file. I want you to edit, adjust, suggest, bitch, moan, scoff. And in the portions that apply to the work you'd do on the project, double all of those. Like this event, this project has to be something we're all agreed on, happy with. We all have to want it."

"I have to say we all want it." Again, Laurel looked around the table for confirmation. "It's just such new ground. Sometimes you sink in new ground."

"I've been thinking a lot about new ground myself." Parker frowned at her water bottle. "New steps, new risks. I like to think we're tough enough and smart enough to risk taking those steps onto new ground."

"Well, when you put it that way." Laurel blew out a breath. "What've we got to lose but ego if we suck at this?"

"I choose optimism and not sucking," Emma decided. "I can't wait to see what you've already put together, Parker."

"I think it's got real potential. Mac, I inserted some of the photos from our files that show your skill set, and with the shots of Emma's and Laurel's work, theirs. It gives the flavor, in visuals, of what we do."

"I'm somewhere between Laurel's ego suck and Emma's optimism. And from that position I really want to see the platform."

"Good. When everybody's gone over it, when you're ready, we'll hash it out. Then when, and if, we'll send it to the agent. If, again, we're all agreed."

She let out a big breath. "And that's that."

"I'd like Carter to look at it. English professor," Mac added. "Aspiring novelist."

"Absolutely. He can also edit, adjust, and so on. That's all I have. Anyone else have anything to discuss since we're all here?"

Emma shot up a hand. "I do. I want to know what's going on with you and Malcolm. *Really* going on, with details."

"Seconded," Laurel said.

"And once again, unanimous." Mac leaned over the table. "Come on, Parks, spill."

CHAPTER FOURTEEN

$\mathcal{P}$ARKER SCANNED THE THREE FACES SURROUNDING HER. FRIENDS, she thought. Can't live without them. Can't tell them to mind their own business.

At least not these friends.

"What do you mean what's going on? You know what's going on. Malcolm and I are seeing each other, and when schedules and mood mesh, sleeping with each other. Would you like me to detail our sexual adventures?"

"I would, but hold that for Girl Night," Laurel advised. "One that includes lots of wine and Mrs. G's pizza."

"Question A." Mac held up a finger. "Is it mutual banging, an affair, or a relationship?"

Knowing she was stalling, Parker rose to pour another cup of tea. "Why can't it be all three?"

"Okay, mutual banging is for fun and gratification. An affair is more in-depth, and something you may or may not think may lead to something else. But it's generally what you have until the juice runs out or you move on." Emma paused, glanced around the table for general agreement. "And a relationship is something you put effort into, it's making and maintaining a connection. You can have elements of the first two in a relationship, but it's more than the sum of those parts."

"She should do a talk show." Laurel raised her cup in toast. "So, going by our resident expert, are you just having fun, are you considering there may be more, or are you making a connection?"

Parker decided she wanted a petit four. "The problem with the three of you is you're all *in* relationships, and more, you're madly in love and about to get married. So you're looking at me through that prism."

"Which not only avoids the question, but turns it so it's invalid. And it's not," Mac insisted. "We tell each other how we feel. It's what we do. Not telling us says to me that you're still chewing on it, and maybe a little bit worried. Just not ready. That's okay. We'll wait until you are."

"That's such a low blow." Scowling, Parker bit into the pretty little cake. "We'll wait—subtext—because we're the good and true and loyal friends."

Mac took a cake for herself. "Did it work?"

"Bitch."

"It worked." Laurel smiled. "And only Emma feels any sense of guilt. She'll get over it."

"It's only a tiny bit of guilt, but I don't think we should push Parker if she's not ready to talk to us."

"You, too?"

Emma lowered her gaze at Parker's deadly stare. "They're a bad influence."

"Fine. The simple answer is I don't know what it is, exactly. I guess I am still chewing on it. It's only been a few weeks. I like him. I'm enjoying him. He's interesting and smart without any of those pompous or overpolished or self-satisfied aspects that, well, either irritate or bore me. He understands what it takes to run a business, and respects what I do, how I do it. I respect what he does, even if I don't really know too many of the details of how he does it. You almost have to pry him open with a crowbar to get him to talk about himself."

"You have a whole toolbox of crowbars in various shapes, sizes, and colors," Mac pointed out. "And you know how to use them so well people tell you everything."

"Apparently Malcolm's not people. Under-the-surface details, I mean, which is frustrating because I want to say if it was a long time ago and no big deal—two of his default positions—then why not just *tell* me about it when it's obvious I'd like to know? Instead, I back off because I think it probably *is* a big deal, and that's why he won't talk about it. Then he redirects the conversation, something he excels at, or makes me laugh, or we have sex, and I really don't know much more than I did in the first place.

"Plus, he's cocky." She swallowed a bite of petit four, gestured with the rest. "He's got that attitude that shouldn't be appealing, it just shouldn't appeal to me at all, but at the same time he can be charming and just . . . just easy. And he looks at you—me—people, I don't know. A lot of men don't really look at you, but he does, so it's like he's not just taking in what you're saying, but taking you in. And that's powerful."

She grabbed another cake. "How was I supposed to know how much that combination of powerful and easy would get to me? Really, I couldn't be expected to know."

"Hmm," Laurel said, cutting her gaze to her two friends, hiking up her eyebrows.

"Exactly." Parker bit into the cake. "Conversely, he'll interrupt me a half dozen times when I'm trying to make a point or argue a position, which makes it hard to stay on target. So, obviously I don't know exactly what this is because he's slippery. He's slippery," she repeated, and reached for another cake. "What?" she demanded as her friends stared at her.

"You ate five petit fours," Mac told her. "You're going for six."

"I did not." Shock hit when Parker looked at the plate. "Five? Well . . . they're petite."

"Okay. Back away from the pastries." Gently, Laurel took the cake out of Parker's hand, set it on the plate, pushed the plate out of reach. "The problem is you've bottled that up, and once you popped the cork you instinctively fed the spew with sugar."

"Apparently."

"You're in love with him," Emma stated.

"What? No." Parker shook her head, said it dismissively. "No." More firmly. Then just shut her eyes. "God. I think I probably am, but if I am, where's the lift, the tingle, the glow? Why do I feel just a little bit sick."

"That's probably the petit fours." Mac glanced at Laurel. "No offense."

"None taken. They're meant to be savored, not popped like candy corn."

"It's not the petit fours." Parker pressed a hand to her stomach. "Or maybe just a little. I don't have my footing with him, not really."

"Which is harder on you than most," Laurel commented. "Love can kick your ass."

"I always imagined it would be a kind of lifting, that everything got just a little better, and more . . . And more."

"It does," Emma insisted. "It can. It will."

"But first it kicks your ass." Mac smiled as she lifted her shoulders. "At least in my experience."

"I don't like it. I like doing the ass kicking."

"Maybe you are, and don't know it," Emma suggested. "He might be feeling the same way you are. If you told him—"

"Absolutely no way in any circle of hell." Parker swiped a hand through the air as if to banish the very idea from the face of the planet. "Things are fine, they're just fine. Besides, let him tell me something for a change. I feel better," Parker insisted. "I should have vented or spewed or whatever I did before. We're both enjoying ourselves, and I started overthinking it. It is whatever it is, and that's just fine. I've got a client coming in."

As Mac started to speak, Emma squeezed her knee under the table. "Me, too. Hey, it's poker night. Why don't we have our version. Wine, pizza, movie?"

"I'm in," Laurel said.

"Sounds good. Why don't we—" Mac broke off as Parker's phone rang.

"Somebody run it by Mrs. G. If it's okay with her, I'm all for it. I have to take this." Rising, Parker clicked on the phone as she left the room. "Hi, Roni, what can I do for you?"

She had to be grateful the call, the meeting with a client, two more calls, and an emergency consult with the caterer regarding last-minute menu changes took up her time and attention. She couldn't overthink and obsess about Malcolm or her own feelings when she focused on the details, mini crises, and demands generated by clients.

In any case, she told herself as she finally walked downstairs, she probably wasn't in love with Malcolm. It was more likely a kind of infatuation blurred by an undeniable sexual haze.

Infatuations were harmless and fun, and could be looked back on when the vision cleared with fondness, even amusement.

Yes, she much preferred the infatuation theory.

Lighter, steadier, she swung into the kitchen to confirm the proposed Girl Night with Mrs. Grady.

"Mrs. G, did you . . ." She trailed off when she saw Malcolm at the breakfast nook.

An old cloth protected the surface of the table, and on it were scattered various tools, various unidentifiable parts of what she assumed was the vacuum cleaner lying gutted on the floor.

"On the phone," he said, and jerked a thumb toward Mrs. Grady's rooms.

"I didn't know you were here." And that was another thing, wasn't it? she thought. He so often gave her no time to plan, to prepare, to strategize. "What are you doing?"

"I had a Porsche to baby out this way, so I dropped by. Mrs. G was about to haul this to the household appliance graveyard." He shook his hair out of his eyes as he loosened a screw, or a bolt, or something that connected a thing to another thing.

"I can fix it."

Parker walked a little closer. "You can?"

"Probably. Worth a shot." He tipped his head to smile at her. "It's not as complicated as a Porsche."

"I suppose not, but how do you know where everything goes when—if—you put it back together?"

"Because I took it apart."

She'd have made a list, Parker thought. Drawn a diagram. She watched him fiddle with what might've been a motor or part of one. "What's wrong with it?"

"According to Mrs. G, it started clunking."

"Clunking?"

"Some clattering, too. You want a lesson in appliance re-pair, Legs? I can give you some basics, buy you some nice, pretty tools."

She looked, very deliberately, down her nose at him. "I have tools, thank you very much."

"Are they pink?"

She flicked the side of his head, made him grin. "Those *are* my tools."

"Yeah? They're good ones. Are you done for the day?"

"Hopefully." Look at his hands, she thought. Naturally she was infatuated. They were so competent, so sure. Just as they were when he put them on her. She took a step back, decided she'd go ahead and have a glass of wine now.

"I thought it was poker night."

"It is. I'm heading over to Del's later."

He hadn't shaved, she noted, and there were tears and grease stains on his jeans. She supposed the dress code for poker was very, very casual.

"Do you want a drink?"

"No, I'm good."

He worked in relative silence while she poured herself some wine. Just a muttered curse, a hum of satisfaction now and then. His foot tapped as if to some inner tune, and his hair fell in a dark, disordered mass that made her fingers itch to get into it.

Maybe she was a little in love with him, but that was as harmless as infatuation. Wasn't it? It wasn't as if she was planning the rest of her life around him, or with him.

God, why couldn't she just relax and keep it simple?

"How's that coming for you, Malcolm?" Mrs. Grady walked back in, winked at Parker.

"I think I've got it."

"Well, once you've got that thing back together, you wash up. You can have some cookies and milk."

He glanced back at her, grinned. "Okay."

"It's nice having a handyman around the house. We've been a household of women for some time now. Not that we don't muddle through, but the next time one of the washers gives me grief, I know who to call."

"*One* of the washers?"

"We've a utility room with a set on every floor."

"Convenient." He cocked a brow at Parker. "And efficient."

"It is that. I'm going out with some of the girls tonight. I'll see to your pizza before I leave," she said to Parker.

"We can just throw something together," Parker began. "Just go have fun."

"I plan to, but I can do both. I'll be seeing your mother tonight, Mal."

"Yeah? She's going?"

"A bite to eat, plenty of gossip. Then who knows what trouble we'll get into."

"I'll make your bail."

Mrs. Grady laughed in delight. "I'll hold you to it." Lips pursed she walked to the table. "Look how you've shined up those innards."

"Needed some adjusting, some cleaning, and the indispensable WD-40. How many of these do you have?"

"Only one like that. It's an old one, but it's handy for my rooms. Otherwise Parker's brought in a fleet of new, spiffy ones so I don't have to haul a machine up and down the steps if I want to do the floors between cleaning crews. Oh, I ran into Margie Winston. She told me you breathed new life into that rattletrap she drives."

"That old girl's got a hundred and eighty-five thousand miles on her. The Pontiac, not Mrs. Winston."

Parker listened to them talk, easy conversation, as he put the machine back together. That was another point in his favor, she mused, the easy conversation, the way he knew and obviously interacted with his client base.

And the way, when he plugged in the vacuum, tested the suction, he grinned. "She sucks."

"Would you look at that! And it doesn't sound likes it's grinding metal while it's at it."

"She should be good for a few more miles."

"Thank you, Malcolm. You've earned the milk and cookies. Just let me put this away."

"I'll do it." He crouched to wrap the cord. "Where do you want it?"

"Just in the utility room there, first closet on the left."

Mrs. Grady shook her head as he carried the vacuum out. "If I were thirty years younger, I wouldn't let that one slip away. Hell, I'd settle for twenty and try my hand at being a cougar."

Parker nearly choked on her wine. "I didn't hear that."

"I can say it louder."

Shaking her head, Parker caught her breath. "You're smitten."

"Something's wrong with you if you're not."

"Nothing's wrong with me."

"I'm glad to hear it," Mrs. Grady said as she started putting tools back in the trim silver toolbox.

"I'll get those. You promised your sweetheart cookies and milk."

"I'll see to that, then, and top off your wine. You keep him company awhile."

She set out a plate piled with cookies, a tall, cold glass of milk while Malcolm came back to wash his hands. "Drink that milk, and I'll tell your mother you've been a good boy."

"She won't believe you."

After Parker stowed the toolbox, she found him alone in the kitchen.

"She said she had some things to do, and you're supposed to keep me company. So what does the Quartet do after pizza when the guys are away?"

She sat across from him, took a sip of wine. "Oh, we have slow-motion pillow fights in our underwear."

"Another fantasy come true. Want a cookie?"

"Definitely not," she said, thinking of the petit fours.

"You're missing out. We've been here before."

She smiled. "Yes. But this time I'm not annoyed with you. Yet. Are you feeling lucky? Poker," she said in mock scold when his grin flashed.

"Feeling lucky can make you sloppy. It's better to be lucky."

"All right. Here's to being lucky." She tapped her glass to his.

"While you have homemade pizza and sexy pillow fights. What's a guy have to do to get invited to one of those events?"

"Not be a guy would be requirement one. Though we can arrange for the homemade pizza at some point."

"I could settle. Listen, speaking of invites, my mother wants you to come to dinner Sunday."

She'd lifted her glass halfway to her mouth, and now set it down again. "Dinner at your mother's. Sunday? This Sunday?" It was odd to feel the tickle of panic, however slight, in her throat. "Oh, but we have an event, and—"

"She'll work around it. I told her you had a work deal, but she knows it's a day thing." He shifted a bit, studied his cookie. "I think she and Mrs. Grady have started talking a lot, or hanging out or something."

"Hmm," Parker said, watching him.

"Anyway, Ma's dug in on it. I think she's got the idea that I . . . I've been spending a lot of time here, scrounging meals, and she should, you know, reciprocate."

"Uh-huh." Not what you were going to say, she reflected. And if she had felt a little tickle, she'd have to say Malcolm felt a deep scraping.

Wasn't that interesting?

"So, she's dug in, and believe me, there's no budging her. I can tell her you can't make it, but she'll just keep at it until you do."

Not just panicked, she decided. Considerably worried. He'd been maneuvered into bringing a woman home to his mother's for dinner. And she had a feeling he hadn't quite figured out how that worked.

"I'd love to come to dinner on Sunday."

His gaze zinged back to hers—wary. "You would?"

"Sure. We should have everything wrapped here by five thirty. If there's no holdup, I could be there by around six. I'll just drive over when I'm done here, and call if I'm going to be any later than six. Will that work?"

"Yeah. Sure. That'll work."

The more discomfort she sensed in him, the more enthusiastic she became. It was, she admitted, small of her, but what the hell. "Ask her if I can bring dessert, or maybe a bottle of wine. Or, never mind, I'll just call her."

"You'll call my mother."

She smiled, eyes wide and calm. "Is that a problem?"

"No. That's fine. You two figure it out." He waved it off. "It takes me out of the middle."

"I'll get in touch with her." She lifted her wine again, at ease now. "Is she seeing anyone?"

"What?" Pure, undiluted shock swept over his face. "My mother? No. Jesus."

She didn't manage to swallow the laugh, but softened it by reaching out, laying a hand over his. "She's a vital, interesting woman."

"Don't go there. Seriously."

"I only did because I wondered if she might have a friend there, or if it would just be the three of us."

"Us. Three. That's it."

"That'll be nice."

"Okay. Okay, I've got to get going."

"Have fun tonight." She rose as he did.

"Yeah, you, too."

"And be lucky." She moved into him. "Maybe this'll help."

And kept moving, slowly, deliberately, until her body molded to his, until her arms twined like ropes around his neck. Until her lips brushed, retreated, brushed, then sank soft and warm against his.

She let a sound of pleasure—escape, seduction, surrender, a shimmer of promises to come. And felt her body yearn with that promise when his hand gripped a fistful of her shirt at the small of her back.

He forgot, nearly forgot, where he was. Forgot, nearly forgot, everything but Parker. Her scent, that subtle, unforgettable hint of fragrance that was woman and secrets and cool breezes all at once. It stirred him, tangled in his senses with the hot, velvet punch of the kiss, swamped him with a staggering flood of need against the firm, lithe lines of her body.

Then she sighed again, skimmed her fingers through his hair, and started to ease away.

"No."

He yanked her back and took them both on a dangerous fall.

"Malcolm." She'd opened the cage door, and now however much she wanted to fling it yet wider, she knew she needed to gentle them both. "We can't."

"Wanna bet?" He pulled her across the kitchen, his strides long and fast enough to have her scrambling to keep up.

"Wait. Where are you going?"

Her breath stuck somewhere between her lungs and her throat when he dragged her into the utility room, shoved her back to the door. Flipped the lock.

"We're not going to—"

He smothered her protest with a ravenous kiss while his hands began to take and take.

He forced himself to flip open the buttons of her shirt rather than simply tear it off her, then tugged the cups of her bra down to rub calloused palms over her nipples.

She moaned. She trembled.

"God. Malcolm. Wait."

"No." He yanked up her skirt, then slid that calloused palm between her legs. "I'm going to have you here, right here. I'm going to watch you come first." He skimmed a finger under lace, into her. "Then I'm going to make you come again, and again, taking you right here, against this door, until I'm finished."

She had to grip his shoulders or fall as her knees trembled, as they buckled. As the vicious, battering heat assaulted her. His eyes, wildly green, captured hers, and she saw something flash in them—triumph, no less than triumph—when her body erupted.

She heard the swatch of lace rip, and could only moan again.

"Tell me you want me." He had to hear it. Had to hear her voice, throaty with passion, tell him she was as crazed as he. "Tell me you want this. For me to take you like this."

"Yes. God. Yes."

He gripped her thigh as she lifted her leg to hook around his waist. Opening, offering. His mouth muffled her cry of release when he thrust into her. Hard and deep.

She let him ravage her—no other word came close—and she thrilled to it, rushed with him, beat by mad beat, to the final, breathless fall.

Even then she shuddered. Even when her head dropped to his shoulder, when his hand stroked down her hair, she couldn't quite find her breath. When he tipped her face up, cupping it in his hands as his lips moved gently, gently over her cheeks, her temples, she thought: Who are you? Who are you that you can do this to me, take my body, take my heart?

Then she opened dazed eyes, stared into his, and she knew. Not all, maybe not enough, but she knew she loved.

When she smiled, he smiled. "You started it."

She would've laughed if she'd had enough breath. "That'll teach me."

He dropped his forehead to hers, began to button her shirt. "You got a little wrinkled."

He smoothed her skirt, her hair, tilted her head. "It's no good. You look like a woman who just had sex in the utility room."

"I guess I earned it."

"I'll say." He bent down. "And I earned these. I'm keeping them."

Her mouth dropped open when he pushed her torn panties into his pocket. "Like a trophy?"

"Spoils of war."

She sputtered out a laugh, then just shook her head. "I don't suppose you have a comb?"

"Why would I have a comb?"

She sighed, tried a little more smoothing and brushing with her hands. "That'll just have to do." She laid her finger on her lips, got that quick, cocky grin in response. "I mean it," she hissed.

As quietly as possible, she unlocked the door, opened it a crack. Listened. "You're going straight out, through the kitchen, out the door. And I'm—"

He grabbed her, giving her ribs a tickle as he pressed his mouth to hers. "Stop! Malcolm!"

"Just wanted to muss you up again." He took her hand, pulled her out.

Relieved to find the kitchen empty, she nudged, pushed, shoved him at the door.

"I feel so used," he said, and made her laugh even as she gave him a last push.

"Go play poker. Be lucky."

"Got my lucky charm right here." He patted the pocket holding her panties.

When her mouth dropped open again, his laughter rolled through the damp autumn air. "See you, Legs."

She made a dash for her room, then couldn't resist detouring to the window, looking out. She saw him change direction, walk to Mac's to speak with a man—a boy?—who'd just come out.

They talked for a moment, exchanged fist bumps. Then the boy climbed into a compact, gunned the engine, and drove off as Malcolm backtracked to his truck.

She jolted when she heard the step behind her, and turned to see Mrs. Grady. "Oh." And mortified to feel heat rise to her cheeks, Parker cleared her throat.

"Hmm," was all the housekeeper said. "You certainly kept him company."

"Ha. Well . . . Um, do you know who that boy was, over at Mac's? Malcolm seemed to know him."

"Well, he should as the boy works for Malcolm. Can't read," she added, "or only enough to skim by. Mal asked Carter to tutor the boy."

"I see." She stood there, looking out through the thin rain. Just when she thought she had a grip on the man, she found yet another angle, another layer.

CHAPTER FIFTEEN

"In the utility room." In her pajamas, sprawled on the sofa of the family room, Mac stared up at the ceiling. "Parker Brown of the Connecticut Browns doing the wild thing in the utility room."

"We were animals."

"Now she's bragging," Laurel commented and bit into a slice of pizza.

"And I like it."

"Let me say congratulations, but really, I'm just in love with him taking you to his mom's for dinner." Emma topped off wineglasses. "And being so obviously weirded out by it."

"It should be interesting."

"What I want to know is, can he fix small appliances? One of my stand mixers is acting hinky."

Parker glanced at Laurel. "Ask him. He seems to like fixing things. Which brings me to him asking Carter to tutor that boy. When did that start?"

"Last month," Mac told her. "Carter says Glen's really coming along. He's got him reading *Carrie*."

Emma swallowed hard. "You mean pig-blood-at-the-prom *Carrie*?"

"Carter found out Glen likes horror flicks, and he's seen the movie a bunch of times, so Carter thought he'd like reading the book. And it's working."

"That's smart," Parker commented. "A really good way to show someone how to read for fun, that it's not just work, not just studying or a chore, but fun."

"Yeah. Carter . . . he's just good, you know?" Mac's face went soft with a smile. "So patient and insightful and innately kind without being sticky about it. I think some people, like him, are lucky to end up doing what they were born to do. And the rest of us benefit from that."

"Like us. I really believe we're doing what we were born to do," Emma added. "That's what makes it more than a business— like teaching is more than a job to Carter. We make a lot of people happy, but one of the reasons—beyond, 'hey we're just that good'—is because what we're doing makes *us* happy."

"Here's to us." Laurel lifted her glass. "Happy, hot, sexually satisfied, and just that damn good."

"I'll drink a whole lot to that," Mac said.

Parker acknowledged the toast, started to drink. And her phone rang. "Oh well, I'll just step out and be happy. Be right back."

"Okay," Mac said the minute Parker was out of the room. "What do we think?"

"I think their chemistry is off the charts," Laurel answered. "And that they've each got an emotional hook deep in the other. A man with Mal's kind of edge and 'tude doesn't fumble his way through a dinner at his mother's unless it matters."

"Because when Mom's important—and Mal's is to him—it's a

step. It takes it up a level." Mac nodded. "If he didn't want it to go up a level, he'd have found a way to back his mother off."

"It's sweet it makes him nervous," Emma added, "because yes, it matters. Both these women matter. You know, my sense is he faces things head-on. The way he told Del straight off he was interested in Parker. The way he brought up the money-status deal to Parker when they first got physical. It's lay it out there and deal. Kind of his default. So I don't think much makes him nervous."

"What I see?" Mac contemplated another slice of pizza. "I see two strong, confident, I-can-fix-it personalities not only trying to figure out the vulnerabilities of being in love, but the risks and the potential outcomes. Basically? I think they're perfect for each other."

"Yes! So do I." Emma glanced toward the doorway. "But it's not the time to tell her that. She's not there yet."

"Neither's he," Laurel commented. "I wonder which one of them will get there first."

MAL RAKED IN THE POT. THE FINAL CARD TURNED HAD GIFTED HIM with a very pretty full house—queens over eights—which left Jack's ace-high straight in the dust.

"You're awful damn lucky tonight, Kavanaugh."

Mal stacked his chips and got a flash of Parker, the utility room, and the tattered white lace in the back pocket of his jeans.

Pal, he thought, if you only knew.

"Brought it in with me," he said, and smiled as he took a pull of his beer.

"How about passing some around." Rod, one of the poker night regulars, scowled as he tossed in his next ante. "I've had crap all night."

"Don't worry. This next hand'll clean you out. Then you can just watch the rest of us."

"You're a cold bastard, Brown."

"No heartstrings to pluck in poker."

Mal tossed in his own ante. The thing about Del, he thought, was the man was merciless at the table. Probably much the same in court, though Mal had never seen him work. But under it? A whole different engine hummed.

Poker night had been going on since Del and Jack had been at Yale together, and Del was the foundation of the continued tradition. Most of the men who came had been playing together for years. He and Carter were the newest members. Carter's entre had been through Mac primarily, though he and Del had known each other back in the day, too.

And his own? He wasn't quite sure, except that he and Del had simply clicked.

So the engine driving the man—other than poker and law— was a traditionalist, generous, loyal, fiercely protective of the people who mattered to him.

Parker mattered. He wasn't sure how Del, or Parker, would react to the fact she'd come to matter more to him than he'd ever imagined she would, or could. How could he speculate on their take when he didn't know how the hell he felt about it himself?

He studied the flop, his cards, calculated possibilities, and rolled with the next bet while conversation flowed around him. Trash talk, a little business, bad jokes.

When Carter turned up the next card, Mal recalculated, saw possibilities narrow. Then Del bumped the bet, and he folded.

The way he saw it, poker and life had a lot in common. You played the cards you were dealt, figured the odds, took the gamble or not. And when your cards were shit, you bluffed if the pot was worth it, and if you had the balls.

Otherwise? Wait for the next hand.

He figured the way he'd played the game had worked out for

him pretty well, life-wise. Now he needed to take a good look at the cards, figure the odds with Parker. She was worth the gamble.

Frank, another regular, tossed in his cards. "So, Del, when is your new male palace going to be ready?"

"Talk to the architect."

Jack saw Del's next raise. "Working on the permits. Things go smooth? We should be taking your money in the new place by March, April latest." Jack glanced around Del's game room. "I'm going to miss this place."

"It's going to be weird," Rod added. "Poker night with women right . . ." He pointed his thumb at the ceiling.

"Not just women," Frank pointed out. "Wives, once you and these three take the plunge. Jesus, this time next year we'll all have taken the dive. Except you," he said to Mal.

"Somebody has to hold the rope."

"Skirting pretty close to the edge yourself." Rod grinned at him around a cigar. "Dating Parker. The last holdout of Del's Quartet."

Mal flicked a glance at Del, but his friend's poker face stayed intact, and the return look was very cool. "I've got good balance."

Frank snorted. "Keep thinking that, buddy, right until you find yourself over the edge with your hands slipping off that rope."

"Good thing he used to be a stuntman," Jack added. "He ought to know how to fall."

Mal just took another pull on his beer. Yeah, he knew how to fall. But he also knew just what could happen if the landing didn't go the way you'd planned.

*H*IS MOTHER KEPT A TIDY HOUSE, MAL THOUGHT. THAT WAS PRIDE, habit, and basic disposition. But for Sunday dinner—this Sunday dinner—she'd gone on a cleaning binge equivalent to a drunk's binge with a bottle of Wild Turkey.

It was a nice house. He'd been careful when he'd started the hunt for one that would work for her, one he'd feel confident about her living in. He'd wanted a good neighborhood, the sort where people actually talked to each other, looked out for each other a little. He hadn't wanted anything so big she'd be overwhelmed or rattle around, or anything so small she'd feel closed in.

He'd found it in the modified ranch with its traditional brick face, the plot of lawn they could easily maintain between them. The attached garage with second-story apartment had been the big bonus.

They loved each other, even liked each other quite a bit, but neither of them had wanted to actually live together. This way they each had their space, their privacy, their routine. But he was close enough to keep an eye on her. And, he knew very well, vice versa.

He could, and did, forage in her kitchen if the mood struck, grab a cup of her coffee in the morning—or not. And she could call on him to see to some household repair or haul out the trash.

The system worked for them.

Except for the times she drove him crazy.

"Ma, it's just dinner. It's food."

"Don't tell me what it is." Kay wagged a finger at him as she stirred the sauce—again—for the lasagna that was, he knew, her signature dish. "When's the last time you brought a woman home to dinner?"

"It's been about never, give or take."

"Exactly." She stopped wagging her finger to jab it at him.

"I'm not bringing her anyway." The idea made his shoulder blades itch. "She's bringing herself."

"And shame on you for that."

"But she—"

"Eh!"

It was another signature, the sound that said "don't even try to argue with me."

He took a breath, changed strategy. "It smells good."

"Tastes better." She took a spoon, dipped, offered.

"Yeah it does," he agreed after the sample.

"It better. It's important to me. The girl's got class."

"So do you, Ma."

"Damn right, but you know what I'm talking about. It was class that had her calling me to thank me for inviting her. I'm going to give her a good meal." She winked. "With a little class. I made fancy hors d'oeuvres."

"Pigs in a blanket?" When she laughed, tossing back her head the way she did, he poked her. "I like pigs in a blanket."

"You're not getting them tonight. You're sure that's a good wine?" She pointed to the two bottles on the counter, one opened to breathe.

"I'm sure."

"You know more about that than me, with your Hollywood debauchery."

"Yeah, but back then I only drank it out of women's navels."

"Sure can't get a good drunk on that way," she said, and this time he laughed.

She stepped back from the stove, took yet another survey of the kitchen.

She had a pretty bowl of fruit on the little drop-leaf table under the window where she liked to sit and have her coffee in the morning. The cute little shamrock plant Mal had given her shot up white blooms from its perch on the sill above the sink.

Her collection of salt and pepper shakers filled the shelf on the wall over a bench he'd made in high school wood shop.

You could eat off her floor, and every surface gleamed.

She gave a satisfied nod, then opened her arms. "How do I look?"

"As good as your lasagna."

"Red and spicy?"

He tugged one of her mass of wild orange curls. "That's right."

"I'm going to put this lasagna together and get it in to bake. I want you to go on and light the candles I've got sitting around. And don't make a mess of anything."

"What am I going to make a mess of?"

She shot him a green-eyed stare. "Nothing if you know what's good for you."

Resigned, he took the lighter, walked around—dining room, living room, even the half bath. She had groupings of candles every-fricking-where. Probably arranged the way she'd seen in a magazine, or on the HGTV she was addicted to.

She'd put out fancy little towels and soaps in the half bath, and he knew from experience she'd skin his hide if he actually used them.

He poked into her little office, her bedroom, the master bath, mostly to keep out of her way so she couldn't nag him again.

She'd made a home here, he mused. A good one, a comfortable one. And in a very real way it was the first home they'd had. Everything else had been quarters, or rentals. Transitory.

So if she wanted to paint the walls—as she had, a different color in every room—if she wanted to play with candles and set out fancy soap no one could use but the guest, she was entitled.

When he figured he'd stalled long enough, he started back. The knock on the door stopped him.

"You take her coat," his mother called out. "And hang it in the closet."

"What am I, a moron?" he muttered.

He opened the door to see Parker, wearing a light trench open over a dark green dress, holding a bunch of baby irises in blues and white.

"Hi. I guess you didn't have trouble finding the place."

"Not a bit."

"I'll get your coat."

"What a nice house." She scanned the living room as he took her trench. "It looks like your mother."

"How?"

"It's colorful."

"You've got that right. Come on back. She's in the kitchen. How'd the event go?"

"It was . . . Oh, look at these!" With obvious pleasure she stopped to study a wall of framed postcards. "These are wonderful."

"She collected them on tour—different places my father was stationed or where she met up with him for R and R."

"It's a wonderful way to remember. You must've been to some of these places. Do you remember?"

"Not especially." He took her free hand, led her back to the kitchen.

They walked in just as Kay closed the oven door.

"Kay, it's so good to see you. Thanks so much for having me."

"You're welcome. Irises." Pleasure warmed her face. "They're my favorite."

"Someone mentioned that. It's Emma's work."

"Doesn't she have a way." Sniffing at them, Kay set the arrangement on the counter. "I'll have them here for now, but tonight I'm going to be selfish and put them in my bedroom. Mal, get the girl some wine. She's been working all day."

"I'd love some. You have such a pretty home. It feels happy."

Exactly right, Mal thought as he poured the wine. "Here you go. Ma."

Kay sampled, pursed her lips. "Not bad. You two go on out in the living room and sit. I'll bring out some hors d'oeuvres."

"Can I help? I'm not much of a cook, but I'm a very good assistant."

"Not much left to do now. We'll just have a seat for a while. I guess you can go ahead and take the tray in with you, Mal, and I'll be right along." She opened the refrigerator, took out her best platter and the cold appetizers.

"Oh, I love these." Carrying her wine, Parker stepped to the salt and pepper shakers.

She meant it, Malcolm concluded with considerable surprise. He'd gotten good at detecting her polite tone and her genuine pleasure.

There were fancy ones, funny ones, and, he guessed the most polite term would be, risqué ones.

"I started collecting them right after I got married. Something small I could pack up whenever we moved. Then I got a little carried away."

"They're wonderful. Charming and fun. Batman and Robin?"

Kay strolled over. "Mal gave me those for Mother's Day back when he was about twelve. Gave me those humping dogs, too—didn't think I'd put them out. He was sixteen then, I think, and trying to get my goat. I got his." She glanced back, grinned at him and the memory. "Embarrassed the hell out of him when I put them on the shelf."

Mal shifted. "What do you want me to do with this tray?"

Parker glanced at him, smiled. "Oh, thanks." She chose a pretty round of bread topped with brie and a raspberry. "And these?" Parker continued, bonding with his mother over salt and pepper shakers while he held a tray of canapes.

He wasn't sure, as the evening progressed, whether to be pleased, relieved, or worried about just how well his mother and Parker got on.

He knew very well Parker could and did adjust her manner and conversation to any sort of social situation. But it was more than that here. He knew, just as he'd known when they'd shared that first pizza, that she was relaxed and enjoying herself.

They talked about places they'd both been, places his parents had traveled before he'd been born, when he'd been too young to remember, others he barely remembered.

They talked about her business, and his mother's laugh bolted out time and again when Parker relayed some weird or funny anecdote about an event.

"I'd never have the patience for it. All those people calling day and night, whining, bitching, demanding. Hell, I want to pop one of Mal's customers at least twice a day."

"Parker doesn't pop them," Malcolm put in. "She crushes them like bugs."

"Only when absolutely necessary."

"What are you going to do about Linda Elliot, or whatever her last name is now?" When Parker hesitated, Kay shrugged. "None of my business."

"No, it's not that. I'm not sure, really. It's going to be tricky. I have crushed her like a bug, which gave me tremendous satisfaction. But she's Mac's mother."

"She's a slut who thinks she's better than everybody else."

"Jesus, Ma."

"No, you're absolutely right," Parker said to Kay. "She is a slut who not only thinks she's better than everybody else, but has a persecution complex on top of it. I've despised her all of my life, so there's nothing you could say about her that would offend me." Parker sampled another bite of lasagna and lifted her eyebrows at Malcolm. "What? I'm not allowed to despise anyone?"

"Just doesn't seem your style."

"She used and emotionally abused one of my closest friends as long as I can remember. She deserved a lot more than what I was finally able to give her. But . . ." Parker moved her shoulders, drank some wine. "She'll come to the wedding. She'll want to show off the new husband, flaunt it. She's currently barred from the estate, but I'll have to rescind the directive for that."

"You, what, banished her?"

Parker smiled at Malcolm. "Yes. Very satisfying. And believe me, she'll be handled at the wedding. I'm not sure how yet, but I'll lock her in the basement before I let her spoil one minute of that day for Mac and Carter."

Kay pursed her lips, nodded. "I bet you would. If you need any help on that, let me know. I've never had any use for her."

"I didn't realize you and Linda knew each other."

"Oh, she wouldn't know me from a naked Eve, but our paths crossed here and there. Used to come in for dinner when I worked at the restaurant. And she went to plenty of the parties where I helped out."

Kay moved her shoulders as Malcolm often did to signal "no big deal."

"She's the type who looks right through you when she's snapping her fingers for another drink or faster service, and doesn't quibble to complain about the help when you're standing right there."

Parker smiled, and there was something fierce in her eyes. "Kay, would you like to come to Mac's wedding?"

Kay blinked. "Well, I barely know the girl, or Carter either."

"I'd very much like if you'd come, if you'd be a guest in my home for my friend's wedding."

"To help bury the body?"

"Let's hope it doesn't come to that. But if it does . . ."

"I'll bring the shovel." Kay clanked her glass enthusiastically to Parker's.

"You two are a little scary," Malcolm observed.

At the end of the evening, after the meal was cleared, after dessert and coffee—and when his mother made apple pie from scratch she was *serious*—she waved him and Parker off. "I'll deal with the dishes in my own good time."

"Everything was wonderful. Really wonderful. Thank you."

Kay gave Malcolm a smug smile over Parker's shoulder when Parker kissed her cheek.

"See that he brings you back. Take her up and show her your place, Mal."

"Sure. 'Night, Ma. Thanks for dinner."

He walked Parker around to the steps leading up to his apartment. "You gave her a really good time."

"It was mutual."

"She likes you, and she's careful about who she lets in."

"Then I'm flattered."

He paused outside his door. "Why did you invite her to the wedding?"

"I think she'll enjoy it. Is that a problem?"

"No, and she will. But something else was going on in there." He tapped a finger to her temple. "Something else when you asked her to come."

"All right, yes. Linda hurts people. It's what she does, whether deliberately or carelessly. Your mother strikes me as a woman who doesn't bruise easily, but Linda managed to. So she should come to Mac's wedding as a welcomed guest while Linda will be there only out of duty, and will never be welcomed in my home again."

"That manages to be calculated and kind at the same time."

"Multitasking is my specialty."

"No question." He ran a hand down her arm, lightly. "You're careful about who you let in."

"Yes."

He studied her a moment longer. "I don't bring women here. It's . . . weird," he added, gesturing toward the house.

"I guess it could be."

He unlocked the door. "Come on in."

It wasn't colorful like his mother's, and came very close to spartan. And it showed an efficiency that spoke directly to Parker's sensibilities.

"Isn't this clever? I imagined a couple of small rooms, and instead it's like one open space. A kind of great room, with a kitchen tucked in the corner, and your living space angled off by the furniture."

She shook her head at the enormous flat-screen dominating the wall. "What is it with men and the size of their TVs?"

"What is it with women and shoes?"

"Touché."

She wandered over, saw the small, and again efficient and streamlined, bedroom through the open pocket door, wandered back again.

"I like the pencil sketches." The black-framed grouping on the wall held wonderfully detailed street scenes.

"Yeah, they're okay."

She took a step closer, peered at the signature in the bottom corner. "Kavanaugh."

"My father did them."

"They're wonderful, Malcolm. It's a good piece of him to have with you. Can you draw?"

"No."

"Neither can I." She turned, smiled at him.

"Stay."

"I have an overnight bag in the trunk of my car." She opened her purse, took out her keys. "Would you mind?"

He took the keys, jingling them as he studied her. "Where's your phone?"

"In my purse. I turned it off before dinner."

He leaned in to kiss her. "Answer your calls, then turn it back off. I'll get your bag."

She pulled out her phone when he went out, but took another moment to look at his space.

Ordered, efficient, she thought again, and very spare. The space, she thought, of a man used to moving on, and doing so with little fuss.

Shallow roots, she mused, and hers were so very, very deep.

She wasn't sure, not at all sure, just what that meant.

Pushing it away, she turned on her phone and began to work her way through texts and voice mail.

CHAPTER SIXTEEN

*M*ALCOLM ARRIVED AT THE CRASH SITE WELL AFTER THE COPS, THE fire department, the paramedics. As a concession to the cold, light rain, he yanked up the hood of his sweatshirt as he walked to the yellow tape and flares.

They'd removed the bodies—he had no doubt there had been bodies when he saw the crushed and twisted mass that had once been a BMW.

The second car had taken an ugly hit, but could probably be salvaged.

With some luck, whoever had been in the Lexus should have walked, limped, or been carried away still breathing.

His job was to tow away what was left.

Over a road slick from an incessant drizzle, the cop lights shone through the shifting mist onto broken and glittering safety glass, skid marks, bent and blackened chrome, blood, and, more horribly, a single shoe not yet recovered from the shoulder of the road. It etched a picture in his mind, one of fear and pain and shocking loss.

The accident reconstruction team was already at work, but he could put it together for himself.

Wet road, a thin haze of fog. BMW, driving too fast, swerves, skids, loses control, crosses the center line, clips Lexus. Goes airborne, flips, slams, rolls twice, maybe three times.

Yeah, given the weight, the velocity, the angles, figure three times.

Somebody goes through the windshield, probably a passenger in the backseat of the mangled M6 who hadn't been wearing a seat belt. If there'd been a front-seat passenger, he or she would've been crushed. The driver wouldn't have been any luckier.

He could see the fire department had sliced through the BMW, using the Jaws of Life like a can opener, but the odds they'd pulled anyone alive out of that violent wreck were next to nil.

He'd seen pictures of the car he'd been driving after his wreck, and got a flash of it now. It hadn't looked much better than the M6. But then stunt cars were built to wreck, built to protect the driver when they did, unless somebody up the chain decided to cut a few corners, save a few bucks.

He hoped the passengers had been unconscious or dead before that slam and roll.

He hadn't been. And he'd felt it all, the shocking pain, the brutal tearing and snapping. Felt it all before he'd gone to black. If he let himself, he could feel it all still, so the smart thing to do was not let himself.

He stood, hands in his pockets, waiting for the cops to clear him to tow away the destruction.

WHILE MALCOLM STOOD ON THE SIDE OF THE ROAD, BLOOD AND pain in his mind, Parker smiled at the roomful of women chattering and laughing their way through the final stages of Mac's bridal shower.

"We done good." Emma slipped an arm around Parker's waist.

"We done really good. She looks so happy."

"I didn't want to say it before in case it tempted fate, but I worried right up until the last minute that Linda would hear about this and crash."

"You weren't alone there. The advantage of having her living in New York now is she doesn't hear everything, and having a new, rich husband keeps her busy."

"May it last," Emma prayed aloud. "This whole evening's been great—and Linda-less. Everyone's had such a good time."

"I know. Look at Sherry. She still has that new bride glow, and the way she's talking to your sister—"

"Pregnancy really agrees with Cecelia, doesn't it?"

"It does, and the way they have their heads together, I think Sherry's already wondering how it would agree with her. I think I should take over as photographer for Laurel. She's—"

"No."

"I don't see why she should—"

"Parker, we talked about this." Emma turned. "Laurel got voted in because I get too distracted and end up talking to everybody, and you . . . Well, you take too damn long trying to make the perfect composition or whatever so you end up getting next to nothing."

"But they're very good next-to-nothings."

"Exceptional, but we'll take less exceptional bunches."

Parker sighed in defeat. She really *liked* taking pictures. "If we must. I guess we should mingle again. People are going to start leaving soon." She slipped her phone out of her pocket when it vibrated. "It's a text from Del."

"Probably wants to know if it's clear for him and Jack and Carter to come home."

"No. He says there's a bad accident on North, south of the parkway. Traffic's diverted and backed up. We should let anyone planning to use that route know, and that they'd be back in a couple hours."

"I hope no one was hurt," Emma replied, then smiled as her mother beckoned her from across the room. "I'll help pass the word."

Like a good party, it tipped over its scheduled time, involved numerous stragglers, and left its hostesses limp with happy exhaustion.

"Now I want champagne." Parker grabbed a bottle and poured. "You sit, Mrs. G."

"I believe I will." Mrs. Grady plopped down, slipped off her party shoes, stretched out her legs. "Fill that up."

Obediently, Parker filled glasses to the rim while Laurel cut slices from what was left of the triple-tiered buttercream cake she'd covered with free-form chocolate petals.

"Golly. Look at those fabulous prizes!" Mac beamed blurrily at the gift table, where Parker had carefully arranged gifts as Mac had opened them. "It's like I won a small, tasteful department store. Did I thank everybody?"

"Numerous times. Just how much champagne have you already consumed there, pal?" Laurel asked her.

"Bunches because I'm allowed to get a little blitzed at my own bridal shower. We had my bridal shower!" She took the cake from Laurel, plucked one of the chocolate petals. "Oh, *mmmm*. Did I tell you I love my cake?"

"Yeah, baby." Laurel leaned over, kissed the top of Mac's head.

"And that I loved absolutely everything? I'm so glad we did this in here, in family rooms. It just felt more home, you know? And everything looked so pretty. Em, the flowers. Just wow. You were so right to go with lots and lots of little arrangements and use that orange—what are they?"

"Cannas, and some zinnias."

"Yeah, those, with the purple stuff to play off Laurel's chocolate and the shiny green ribbons and all that."

"Trust your florist. And it was really sweet of you to give Carter's mom and his sisters flowers when they left."

"They're going to be my family now." She beamed at everyone again. "I have such an amazing family. You guys, you're the best ever, and I'm so lucky to have you. All of you, so damn lucky. And I'm so fucking glad my mother didn't come."

She took a breath. "Oops. Maybe I have had too much champagne."

"You're entitled." Emma moved over to sit beside Mac, rubbed her arm. "It's a happy time, and it was a really happy party. That's all you need to think about."

"You're right. I'm just getting all the sappy stuff and the bitchy stuff out before the wedding. I don't want to get all weepy and nervous on the day. So. Mrs. G, you're all the mother I need, and you've always been right there."

"I've had a good share of this bubbly, too. Don't get me watered up." Then she sighed. "Oh well. You're a skinny, smart-mouthed redhead. And I've loved you since the day you first toddled in the door."

"Aw." Rising, Mac dashed over to grab Mrs. Grady in a rib-crusher. "Okay, Laurel."

"Uh-uh."

Mac snorted at Laurel's reaction. "You're a hardass when I need one, a friend through thick and thin. When I'm stupid, you tell me, but you never hold it against me."

"That's a good summing up." Laurel laughed her way through Mac's hug.

"Emma. Always a hand to hold, a shoulder to lean on. You find a way to see the rainbow in the storm, and that's gotten me through a lot of storms."

"Lots more rainbows for you, sweetie." Emma hugged Mac hard.

"And Parker." Mac scrubbed her hands over her damp cheeks. "Never once in my life have you let me down. Let any of us down. You're the one who gave us family, gave us home, the one who opened us up to what we could do, who we can be."

"Mac." Parker got to her feet, laid her hands on Mac's teary cheeks. "We gave each other family, and home."

"We did. But it started with you." On a sigh, Mac wrapped her arms around Parker, laid her head on Parker's shoulder. "I know I'm buzzed, but I wish everybody everywhere could feel as happy, as loved, as *right* as I do this minute."

"After that, I think we do at least. So that's a start."

It was nearly midnight when everyone was tucked into bed, and the party debris cleared. Still revved from success, feeling sentimental about Mac's sweet, half-drunken speech, Parker wandered through the house, doing a final check.

Home, she thought. Their home, as Mac had said. Not just what had been passed down for generations—though that was the base—but what they'd made it. Just as her parents had made it their own, adding touches, living lives.

People would always call it the Brown Estate, she reflected, but those who lived there knew it was so much more.

Maybe one day she'd be able to share it, build on it, with the man she loved.

That, she knew, remained the underpinning of all her dreams, her goals, her ambitions. To love, be loved, to share, to build on that love and partnership something strong and lasting.

She could be successful without it. She could be content without it. But she understood herself well enough to know she'd never feel complete, never feel fully happy, without that loving partnership.

She believed, absolutely, in the power and the strength of love, the promises made, the endurance of commitment. Weddings were a celebration of that, a kind of show full of symbols and traditions. But, at the core it was the vows, the promises, the emotional knot tied between two people believing it would hold for a lifetime that mattered.

And she'd come to understand, was well on her way to accepting, that Malcolm was the partner she wanted for those promises, for that lifetime.

Still, she mused, partnership required that sharing, a depth of trust, a *knowing*. There were still so many places and pieces in him he shaded, or even closed off from her.

How could that underpinning hold, for either of them, if parts of him remained locked down?

Restless, she adjusted a pillow on the sofa. Maybe she asked for, maybe she expected, too much too soon. But Malcolm wasn't the only one who wanted to know how things worked, and why.

She caught the flash of headlights against the window glass, frowned. Moving closer, she recognized Malcolm's car and, delighted—it was as if she'd conjured him—went to open the front door.

"It's late," he said as he stepped into the portico, skimmed his fingers through rain-dampened hair.

"That's all right. Come in. It's cold and wet out there."

"I saw some lights on, so I figured you might be up."

"You figured right." Something's wrong, she realized as she scanned his face, saw the tension in it. "We just finished cleaning up."

"Right. Right. How did it go? The thing?"

"It was great." He didn't move to touch her, to kiss her. She leaned in, brushed her lips over his in as much comfort as greeting. "Start to finish."

"Good."

He wandered the foyer, obviously restless.

Tell me what's wrong, she thought. She could all but see the barrier between them, hated pushing at it. "Malcolm—"

"Got a beer?"

"Sure." Give him a little time, she told herself as she led the way back toward the kitchen. "I guess you had a long night. Did you get everything done you'd wanted to?"

"No. I made a dent in it, but something else came up."

She got out a beer, started to get out a glass.

"Bottle's fine." He popped the top, but didn't drink.

How could she not know how to handle this—him—she wondered, when she always knew? "Do you want something to eat? We have leftovers from the party, or Mrs. G's—"

"No. I'm good."

No, she thought as he wandered the kitchen, he wasn't.

Enough, she decided. Just enough. "Tell me what's wrong."

"I had things to do. After I did them, I didn't feel like going home so I took a chance you'd still be up. You were." He lifted the beer now, but after a single sip set it down. "Since you are, maybe I can talk you into bed."

Frustration and disappointment mixed uneasily with resentment. "If I thought you'd come by for a beer and sex, I might be amenable. Since I don't, no, you can't talk me into bed."

"It was worth a shot. I'll get going."

And now anger sifted into the mix. Her eyes flashed as he started out. "Do you think you can come here, knock on the door, then turn around and go when you don't get what you want on your terms?"

His face remained calm—neutral, she thought—and she imagined he'd wear that same expression playing poker.

"I don't remember laying out any terms. The mood's wrong, so I'm going home. We can both catch a few hours' sleep."

"Oh yes, that'll work now that you've annoyed and upset me."

He stopped, dragged a hand through his hair. "Sorry. That wasn't the plan. I should've gone home in the first place."

"Maybe you should have, since you seem to feel our relationship shouldn't involve any sort of confidences on your side, or expression of actual feelings."

Neutral shifted, lightning speed, to annoyance. "That's bullshit."

"Don't tell me what bullshit is when I'm looking at it. You know the way out," she added, and started by him.

When he grabbed her arm, frostbite burned his fingers.

"Look, bad night, that's all. Bad night, shitty mood. I shouldn't have brought them over here."

"You're absolutely right." She shoved his hand away. "Take them home with you."

She stalked over, poured the beer down the sink.

When she glanced back, she was alone. She felt the jab right under the heart.

"Well," she mumbled, and carefully rinsed out the bottle. "Okay then. All right. This isn't going to work for me."

She imagined heaving the bottle against the wall, hearing the glass shatter. But, she admitted, that didn't work for her either, so she took it to the recycle bin.

Switching off lights, checking locks, she made her way back through the house, walked upstairs to her wing.

In the bedroom, she undressed, put her shoes away, placed the clothes in the proper hampers before slipping into her oldest and most comforting pajamas.

She completed her bedtime routine, every step.

Then lay angry, miserable, and awake through the night.

"WE DIDN'T HAVE A FIGHT." PARKER PUSHED THROUGH HER SECOND mile in the gym. "What we have is an impasse."

"It sounds like a fight to me," Laurel said.

"A fight is where you argue, or shout, or say inappropriate things. This wasn't a fight."

"He left. You're mad. Those are also elements of a fight."

"Fine, have it your way," Parker snapped. "We fought our way to the impasse."

"He was stupid."

"At last, we fully agree."

"He was stupid," Laurel continued, "to come over here at midnight when something was bothering him if he didn't intend to tell you *what* was bothering him. And stupider to leave when you told him to leave because anyone who knows you understands you expected him to argue with you until you broke him down and he told you what was bothering him."

With a nod, Parker grabbed her water bottle and chugged.

"Then again, he hasn't known you as long as I have, so it's possible he took 'go home' as just 'go home.'"

A wet fist of tears clogged her chest. Parker pushed through them as she pushed through the next mile. "I can't be with someone who won't talk to me, who can't be intimate with me except physically."

"No, you can't. But intimacy, the real kind, is harder for some than others. I'm not defending him," Laurel added. "I'm assessing and extrapolating. I'm being you, since you're too upset to be you."

"Then I must be annoying. I'm sorry," she said instantly, and stepped off the machine. "I'm sorry. I didn't get any sleep, and I'm feeling mean."

"It's okay. Sometimes you are annoying."

With a miserable half laugh, Parker grabbed a towel. "Yeah, I am. I'm annoying myself right now." Burying her face in the towel, she scrubbed hard. Then just held it there when Laurel's arms came around her.

"I don't want to cry because it's stupid to cry about this. I'd rather be annoying than stupid."

"You're not being either, and you know I'd tell you if you were."

"I can count on you," Parker said, and taking a steadying breath, lowered the towel.

"You're pissed off, frustrated, sad, and really tired. So, take a few hours, get some rest. I can take anything that comes in. If I can't, I'll tap Emma and Mac."

"Maybe I'll take an hour. Go outside, take a walk, clear my head."

"Whatever works. Give me the phone."

"Oh, but—"

"I mean it, Parker, give me the phone." Eyes narrowed, Laurel held out a finger, crooked it. "Otherwise, I'll be forced to assume Malcolm's not the only one with trust issues."

"Unfair," Parker muttered, but unhooked the phone from her waistband.

She didn't bother to change, just tossed on a hoodie, zipped it. The brisk, cool air, so fresh from the evening's rain, felt good. Denuded trees raised their dark arms up into a sky so blue and sharp and bright she regretted not grabbing sunglasses. The grass, hardened from the night's frost, crunched under her feet.

Autumn, she thought, with its color and shimmer and smoky scents was nearly done and winter creeping up to take its place.

Mac's wedding was only a month away. Still so much to do, so many details, so many check marks. It was probably for the best she and Malcolm had taken this step back from each other. She needed to focus on the most important wedding Vows had ever planned.

God knew there was plenty to deal with on all the other events, and that didn't touch on the Seaman extravaganza in the spring, which needed constant attention.

She still had countless arrangements and plans to finalize for Emma's wedding, and for Laurel's.

Then there was the book proposal. With the changes and additions her partners had put in, it was as solid and ready as it could be. Time to send it to the agent, she thought.

Really, the simple truth was she didn't have time for a relationship.

At some point, down the road, maybe. But not now. And she would certainly expect and demand a full partnership, a real meeting of minds, absolute trust.

As her parents had.

She couldn't be—wouldn't allow herself to be—in love with a man who didn't want the same. However much it hurt now to realize that, to accept that, it would hurt more later if she denied it.

"Hey, Parker."

She jerked out of the internal debate, and stared at Carter as he veered toward her, briefcase in hand.

"Carter. I've lost track of the time. You're leaving for work."

"Yeah. Is everything okay?"

"Sure. I just . . . I'd better get inside, get to work."

He took her hand. "What's wrong?"

"Nothing. Really. I didn't get much sleep last night, so I'm . . ."
Doing exactly what Malcolm had done. Closing down, closing in.

"I think Malcolm and I ended things last night."

"I'll be sorry if that's true. Can you tell me why?"

"I guess we don't have enough common ground, or look at things the same way. Or want the same things."

That wet fist tried to flex again.

"Carter, I'm not really sure. I don't understand him."

"Do you want to?"

"I always want to understand, and I'd say that's why things aren't going to work."

He set his briefcase down where they stood, then draped an arm around her shoulders and began to walk.

"You have to get to work."

"I've got some time. When Mac and I were having problems, when I felt I didn't understand her, you helped me. You gave me some insight into her that I needed. Maybe I can do the same for you."

"He won't let me in, Carter. There are all these locked doors. Whenever I ask him about the hard things—and the hard things are a factor in making us who we are—he says it's no big deal, it was a long time ago, or just shifts the subject."

"He doesn't talk about himself much. I think you're right about the locked doors. And I think there are some people who lock them so they can open others. That they think they won't be able to walk through the others if they don't shut out what came before."

"I understand that, I do. To a point. But how can you be with someone, hope you might stay with someone, who isn't willing to let you see what they locked away, who won't share the problems, the bad times? Who won't let you help?"

"From the little he's said, and more from what my mother related, he took some pretty hard knocks as a kid. Emotionally when he lost his father, physically from his uncle and aunt. You can't be a teacher without dealing with kids who've been through something like that, or are going through it. In a lot of cases, trust takes time, and a lot of work."

"So I should give it more time, be patient, and work harder."

"Some of that's up to you." He rubbed her arm as they walked. "On his part, I'd have to say he's crazy about you and hasn't quite figured out how to handle it. You want, need, and deserve the whole picture, and he's thinking you should look at what he is now, that it should be enough."

"That's a good analysis." She sighed and, grateful, leaned on him a little. "I don't know if it makes me want to move forward or away, but it's a good analysis."

"I bet he didn't get much sleep last night either."

"I hope not." It helped to smile, and she did as she turned to hug him. "Thank you, Carter. Whatever happens, this helped."

She drew back. "Go to school."

"Maybe you could take a nap."

"Carter, who are you talking to?"

"I had to try." He gave her a kiss on the cheek, started toward his car again. Nearly tripped over his own briefcase before he remembered it.

"Mac." Parker breathed it as she turned to go inside. "You're so damn lucky."

She paused a moment, just to study the house, the soft blue of it against the brilliant sky. All those lovely lines, she thought, the pretty touches of gingerbread, the gleam of windows. Like a wedding, she decided, those were details. At the core it was more than house, even more than a home, which was so vital to her. It was a symbol; it was a statement. It stood as it had for generations, a testament to her name, to her family. By standing it proved it was in her blood to build to last.

How could she build with Malcolm without understanding his foundation?

She went in through the kitchen. Coffee, she thought, a decent breakfast to boost some energy into her system. Maybe the answers would come, one way or the other, once she made herself fall back into routine.

But when she walked into the kitchen, Mrs. Grady sat at the counter, her eyes wet.

"What is it, what's wrong?" Her own troubles forgotten, Parker rushed around the counter.

"There was a terrible accident last night. A car accident."

"I know. Del said something about it. Oh God. Someone was killed? Someone you knew?"

"Worse than that. There were three girls—teenagers. There'd been four, but they'd just dropped the other off at home. They're all dead, all of them."

"Oh, no. Oh God."

"I know the mother of one of them, from the book club I'm in."

"Mrs. G, Mrs. G." Parker wrapped her arms around her, rocked. "I'm sorry. I'm so sorry."

"There were two people in the other car. One's stable now, they say, the other still critical."

"I'm going to make you some tea." She brushed Mrs. Grady's hair back from her face. "You lie down awhile, and I'll bring it to you. I'll sit with you."

"No, I'm all right here. We know, you and I, how death—sudden and cruel like this—how it devastates you."

"Yes." Parker squeezed her hand, then walked over to make the tea.

"Dana, the woman I know from the book club? I never liked

her." Mrs. Grady pulled a tissue out of her apron pocket, dabbed at her eyes, her cheeks. "Disagreeable sort of person, know-it-all, that kind of thing. And now I think she's lost a child, and none of that matters anymore. Someone took pictures of the terrible wreck of the car, and they had it on the local news. I hope she doesn't see it, that she never has to see that, that they towed it away and locked it away before she ever saw it."

"I want you to . . ." Towed it away, Parker thought.

Malcolm.

She squeezed her eyes shut, took a breath. First things first.

"I want you to drink your tea while I make you some breakfast."

"Darling girl." Mrs. Grady blew her nose, almost managed a smile. "Bless your heart, you can't cook worth spit."

"I can scramble eggs and make toast." She set the tea in front of Mrs. Grady. "And if you don't trust me that far, I'll get Laurel to make it. But you're going to have some breakfast and some tea. Then you're going to call Hilly Babcock, because you're going to want your good friend."

"Bossy."

"That's right."

She grabbed Parker's hand as tears swirled again. "I've been sitting here, my heart broken for those lost children, for their families, even for the child who fate spared. And a part of me thanked God, couldn't help but thank God, that I still have mine."

"You've got a right to be grateful for that. We all do. It doesn't take away the sorrow and the sympathy for the loss."

She wrapped her arms around Mrs. Grady again because she remembered, too well remembered, when they'd lost theirs. The way the world had simply fallen away, and the air had closed off. When there was nothing but terrible, ripping grief.

"Drink your tea." Parker gave her a last, hard squeeze. "I'm calling Laurel and Emma and Mac, and we'll take some time to be grateful, and time to be sorry."

She kissed Mrs. Grady's cheek. "But I'm making breakfast."

$\mathcal{T}$HE FOUR OF THEM SWITCHED OFF KEEPING AN EYE ON MRS. GRADY, trying not to be obvious about it. With all of them juggling appointments, a rehearsal that evening, and a weekend with back-to-back events, Parker barely had time to think.

But she made a point of looking the story up online.

This, she thought as her throat clutched at the photograph, was what Malcolm had seen the night before. How much more horrible would it be to have seen it in reality?

This is what had put that look in his eyes, that tone in his voice.

He'd come to her, she thought. Closed in, yes, but he'd come to her.

So, as soon as she could, she'd go to him.

CHAPTER SEVENTEEN

*M*ALCOLM BLED THE NEW, LONGER BRAKE LINES FOR THE JEEP THE customer ordered lifted. He suspected the kid wanted the modification more for looks and peer status than any serious off-roading.

Whatever the reason, Malcolm figured he got paid the same.

Working methodically with his iPod blasting out his playlist from its port on a workbench, he replaced the front shock absorbers and the coil springs with their taller counterparts. The customer's requirement meant modifying the control arms, the track bars, and lengthening the brake lines.

The kid would end up right this side of legal—barely.

It wasn't a rush job, nothing he had to dig into after closing. But then neither was the oil change he'd slated to take care of next instead of passing the basic job to Glen.

Busywork, he admitted as the Killers rocked out. Well, he wanted to keep busy.

The time he spent jacking up the kid's ride, doing an oil change, then a brake job, meant he wouldn't spend that time thinking.

Mostly.

Thinking about what was screwed up in the world, and currently his life, wouldn't fix it. The world would continue to screw up no matter how long and hard he thought about it.

And his life? A little time and space was probably in order. The Parker thing had gotten pretty intense, and maybe a little crowded—and that was on him, no question.

He'd pushed, he'd pursued, he'd plotted the course. Somehow he—she—they, he wasn't entirely sure—had navigated that course a lot speedier and into much deeper territory than he'd expected.

They'd been spending nearly every free moment together, and plenty of moments that weren't exactly free. Then *boom*, he's thinking about next week with her, and the next months—and okay, beyond even that. It just wasn't what he'd banked on.

Plus, before he knows what's happening, he's taking her to dinner at his mother's, asking her to stay the night in his bed.

Both of those particular events broke precedent. Not that he had hard-and-fast rules about it. It was more a cautionary avoidance to keep things at a comfortable level.

Then again, Parker wasn't comfortable, he thought as he installed a skid plate for the oil pan. He'd known that going in.

She was complicated and nowhere near as predictable as she looked on the outside. He'd wanted to know how she worked, he couldn't deny it. And the more he'd examined the parts, the more caught up he'd become.

He knew those parts now, and how she worked. She was a detail-oriented, somewhat—hell, extremely—anal, goal-focused woman. Mixed in there she had a talent and a need to arrange those details into a perfect package and tie them with a bow.

If that, plus the money and pedigree, had been it, she'd have probably been a beautiful pain in the ass. But inside her was a deep-seated need for family, for stability, for home—and God knew he understood that one—and an appreciation for what she'd been given. She was unflinchingly loyal, generous, and, being hardwired to be productive and useful, had a work ethic that kicked ass.

She was complicated and real, and like the image he had of her mother on the side of the road in a pretty spring dress, he thought she defined what beauty was. In and out.

So he'd ended up breaking those not-exactly rules because the more he'd learned, the more caught up he'd become, the more he'd known she was exactly what he wanted.

He could deal with wants. He'd wanted plenty. Some he'd gotten, some he hadn't. And he'd always figured things averaged out in the end. But he'd realized the night before, when he'd gone to her because he'd been edgy and unsettled and just fucking sad, that want had merged with need.

He'd needed to be with her, just *be* there, with her, in that ordered space she created where somehow everything just made sense.

Needing something—someone—that was jumping off a building without a safety harness. He'd learned the hard way he was better off taking care of himself, dealing with himself and what was his. Period.

Except he'd started thinking of her as *his*. He'd already told her bits and pieces of things he'd never told anyone else, and didn't much see the point in thinking about.

So . . .

Better he'd pissed her off, he decided. Better she'd tossed him out. They'd both take a couple of breaths, simmer down. Reevaluate.

He checked the modifications, moving from the front end to the rear.

And over the music of the Foo Fighters he heard the distinctive sound of high heels on concrete.

He only had to angle his head, and there she was, wearing one of her sexy business suits, that arresting face unframed, a bag the size of a Buick on her shoulder.

"The door wasn't locked."

"No." He pulled the rag out of his back pocket to wipe his hands.

She shouldn't be here, he thought. The place smelled of oil and engine and sweat. And so, he imagined, did he.

"I thought you had a thing tonight."

"I did. It's finished." She gave him that cool-eyed stare. "But we're not, so would you mind turning that down?"

"I've got to get the wheels and tires on this thing."

"Fine. I'll wait."

She would, he concluded. She was good at that.

So he figured the Foo Fighters would have to learn to fly without him. He put down his tools, shut down the iPod, then opened the cooler he'd put on the bench beside it. He took out one of the two beers he'd packed. "Want one?"

"No."

He opened it, took a long pull while he eyed her. "Something on your mind, Legs?"

"Quite a bit, actually. I heard about the accident, about those three girls. Why didn't you tell me about it last night?"

"I didn't want to talk about it." The image—shattered glass, blood, blackened metal on a rain-slicked road—flashed back into his mind. "Still don't."

"You'd rather let it eat at you."

"It's not eating at me."

"I think, I really think, that's the first lie you've told me."

It infuriated him, unreasonably, that she was right.

"I know what's going on inside my gut, Parker. And talking about it doesn't change squat. It doesn't make those girls any less dead, or keep the couple in the other car from a fucking world of hurt. Life goes on, until it doesn't."

The heat he spewed did nothing to ruffle her cool.

"If I really believed you were that fatalistic and callous, I'd feel sorry for you. But I don't. You came to me last night because you were upset, but you couldn't or wouldn't tell me why. Maybe getting mad at me helped, maybe you could displace the upset with anger. But I don't deserve that, Malcolm, and neither do you."

Chalk up another in the *She's Right* column. The score, Brown: 2; Kavanaugh: 0, just pissed him off. "I shouldn't have come by last night when I was in a crappy mood. You want an apology? I'm sorry."

"Don't you know me at all, Malcolm?"

"Christ." He muttered it and took another swig of the beer he didn't really have the taste for.

"And don't take that dismissive *male* attitude with me."

"I *am* a male," he shot back, pleased he'd scraped away a layer of that calm, revved to scrape away more. "I have a male attitude."

"Then you can stuff this in your attitude. If I'm with you, I'm with you when you're doing flips and handsprings, and I'm with you when you're in a crappy mood."

"Yeah?" Something choked him, twisted in throat, in gut. "Couldn't prove that by last night."

"You didn't give me—"

"What part of 'I don't want to talk about it' don't you get? And how the hell does this get turned around into being about you and me? Three kids are dead, and if they were lucky, they died fast.

But it wouldn't have been fast enough. Five, ten seconds of knowing what's coming is forever. That and never getting to grow up, never getting to push the rewind button and say 'let me do that different this time' is a hell of a price for some girl who barely had her license a year and two of her friends to pay for being stupid."

She didn't jolt when the bottle he heaved smashed against the wall, but let out a sound somewhere between a laugh and a hum of sympathy. "I nearly did that same thing last night after you left. Then I thought what good would it do, and I'd just have to clean it up. Did it help?" she wondered.

"God, you're a piece of work. Not everything has a neat, practical answer. Everything doesn't always add the fuck up. If it did, three girls wouldn't be dead because they were driving too damn fast and texting friends."

Her heart hurt at the waste of it all. "Is that what happened? How do you know?"

"I know people." Damn it, he thought, and shoved at his hair as he struggled to box in the rage that had blindsided him. "Listen, they're keeping that under wraps until they finish the investigation."

"I won't say anything. Mrs. Grady knows the driver's mother, and it's hit her pretty hard. Maybe listening to her, making her tea, holding her hand didn't help all that much. Maybe it wasn't a neat, practical answer, and maybe it doesn't all add the fuck up. But I had to do something. When someone I care about is hurting or upset or just sad, I have to do something."

"Whether they want you to or not."

"Yes, I suppose so. To my mind, reaching out, reaching for one another doesn't make what happened to those girls less of a tragedy, or make anyone less heartsick for them and their families. But point taken. You don't want me to listen. You don't want me to hold your hand. So that makes the need to do those things about me, not you."

She took a long breath, and he heard the unsteadiness of it. That, more than anything she'd said or done, cut at him.

"You throw the glass against the wall, then you clean it up and throw it away. That's your practicality, Malcolm."

"Sometimes a smashed bottle's just a smashed bottle. Look, I've got to get the wheels back on this Jeep."

It wasn't anger he saw on her face, and her anger had been the goal. It was hurt. It was that single, unsteady breath.

She nodded once. "Good luck with that."

For a moment, just as she turned to walk away, he wished he still had the beer bottle in his hand. Just so he could smash it again.

"I thought I was dead."

She stopped, turned. She waited.

"When it went wrong, when I knew it was going south, I thought I could pull out of it. But the whole thing was fucked. Technical glitch, miscalculation, and some budget cuts that didn't get passed down to those of us on the line. Several people up the chain made a bad decision, doesn't really matter why. The why's the reason I ended up getting a big fat check at the end of the day."

"The why's the reason you got hurt."

"Put it down to a clusterfuck." That's what he'd done. That's what he'd had to do to get past it. "Anyway, I had that initial moment—gag's gone south; then the next—I can deal. Then . . . then the next when I knew I couldn't and thought I was dead. We're talking seconds from one point to the next, but it all slows down. There's noise—snatches and bursts—and outside this tunnel you're in, it's just a blur. But inside, everything's slowed down so that few seconds is endless. And it's goddamn terrifying. That's before the pain."

He had to take a breath, had to calm a little. While he did, she walked to the workbench and took out the bottle of water he'd tossed in with the beer.

She opened it, and with her eyes steady on his, handed it to him.

Jesus, he thought. Jesus, she *was* a piece of work. An amazing piece of work.

"Okay." He cooled his throat. "After the pain, you know you're not dead. You just want to be. Inside you're screaming, and that sound's barely human. You can't get even that sound out when you're choking on your own blood. When you can't breathe because your lungs have started to collapse. It's more than you can stand, those seconds, trapped in the pain, waiting to die. Wanting to so it'll just end.

"What good does it do for you to know this?" he demanded.

"It's part of you. We're not blank slates, Malcolm. What we've done, what we've survived, all go into us. What happened to those girls, your reaction to it—"

"I don't know why it hit me the way it did. Maybe because it had been a long day, maybe because it was close to home. I don't flash back to my own crash every time I deal with a wreck. It's not like that."

"What is it like?"

"It's over, or I wouldn't be standing here. It started being over when I woke up in the hospital. Not dead. It's a pretty big deal, not being dead, and I wanted to stay that way."

He put the water down to get the broom and dustpan, and started sweeping up the broken glass.

"If it had to hurt like ten levels of hell, okay. I'd lived through the crash, I'd live through that. Need to put me back together with pins? Go right ahead, as long as I walked out of there. I started making plans to do that; it was a way to get through. No more living day to day."

"You pushed the rewind button."

He glanced back at her. "Yeah, in a way. Or maybe I switched to forward. But I knew when I woke up, and my mother was sitting there, when I saw her face, I knew I wasn't going back. I'm not going to say I'm all she had, or has, because she's more than that. But I could stop living the kind of life that put the rest of her family at risk that way. I got the chance to do something for her, and to move forward for myself."

He sighed now, dumped the glass with a clatter into the trash. "She wouldn't go home. Even when I got strong enough to yell at her, to piss her off, I couldn't make her go."

"Is that what you wanted?" she asked quietly. "Did you want her to go?"

"I . . . No. God, no. But I didn't want her to stay the way things were either. She quit her job, picked up work waiting tables out there. I walked out on her when I was eighteen, that's basically what I did. Sure I sent her money, but I could count on one hand the number of times I came back to see her. But she wouldn't leave me alone. I got a chance to change things, and I took it. That's all."

"You're very lucky to have your mother."

"I know it."

"And she's fortunate to have you."

"We do okay."

"Malcolm, how would you define you and me? What we have going on?"

"How would you?"

"No, no, you get away with that too often. The question is on the table. Pick it up."

"Jesus, Parker, sometimes it's hard to follow you. I apologized for last night, and I gave you reasons. More than I like getting into."

"Do I take that to mean you can't define what we have?"

"I wasn't looking to define it." He picked the water back up, put it back down. "If I had to, I'd say we have a situation."

"A situation." Her breath came out on a laugh. "All right. Do you think I want to be in a situation with you and not know how you dealt with a trauma, how it affected you, how it—or you because of it—changed the direction of your life?"

"Clearly you don't."

"It's important to you to know how things work. Well, I can't know how you work, or how we might work, if I don't have all the pieces."

That hit home with him. "I get that, but I didn't like all the pieces, so—like I'm doing with this Jeep—I modified them. I don't run the same way I did before the crash. I don't think we'd be in this situation if I did."

"We'll never know, but I like who you are, Malcolm, and that includes where you came from. I don't want to feel like I'm intruding anytime I ask you a question about where you came from."

"That's not how I want you to feel. I just don't like digging through the past. It's gone."

"I just don't agree. Don't you remember the first time you rode a two-wheeler or kissed a girl or drove a car?"

"I remember the first time I kissed you, except you made the move. Fourth of July."

All right, she thought, enough for tonight. Let it go. "That was to kick at Del."

"I still got the benefits." He glanced at his hands. "I'm not in any shape to touch you without messing you up. And that's a nice suit."

"Then hold still and keep your hands to yourself." She moved to him, leaned in, laid her lips on his.

"I hope you don't consider that make-up sex."

"It's the best you're going to get under the circumstances."

"Maybe you could hang out awhile. Guys love it when women hang out and watch them work on cars."

"We do that to placate you."

He lowered the Jeep a couple feet. "When did you ever date anybody who got under a car?"

"I haven't—previously—but Mac did, so I have it on good authority."

Relaxed, with whatever had been balled in his throat, in his gut, loosened, he grinned at her. "That's sexist. I've known plenty of female motorheads."

"That sort wouldn't be expected to 'hang out and watch.'"

"Fine. Can you reach the steering wheel?"

"I suppose, but—"

"Do me a favor. Go on up there, turn it all the way to the right. Then all the way to the left."

"Why?"

"Because lifting the suspension like this involves a lot of mods, and I want to make sure there's no interference before I put the wheels on."

"What would you have done if I hadn't come by?"

"Stayed mildly pissed off. All the way right," he added, then got down on a creeper and scooted under the Jeep.

"I meant about the Jeep, but I actually prefer that answer." She leaned inside, turned the wheel. "Like that?"

"Yeah, looks good. Really good view from down here."

"You're supposed to be looking at whatever's under this Jeep, not under my skirt."

"I can do both. To the left, Legs."

"Do you think your mother would like to come to Thanksgiving dinner?" When he said nothing for a moment, she cast her eyes at the ceiling. "Or would Thanksgiving dinner be out of place in our situation?"

"Give me a minute." He rolled out, grabbed a tool, rolled under again.

She heard some light clanging. "Turn it again. There we are."

He rolled out, rose, then stepped over to pick up an enormous tire. Why did he call it a wheel? Maybe the wheel was what she thought of as the inside the tire holder—and fit it on . . . would that be the axle?

Why the hell did she care?

"I've never been in this particular situation."

"I see."

"No, you don't." He used some sort of air tool that made a loud hiss, a thump. "I've been in situations, but this particular one's different."

"I do see, Malcolm. It's a different situation for me, too. And I understand, really, if a traditional family holiday doesn't fit."

"I guess we can find out. I know she'd like it, but she's going to ask me all kinds of questions, like the dress code or—"

"It's black tie."

She kept her face bland for about five seconds while he made an obvious struggle not to swear. "Oh, for God's sake, Malcolm." She had to laugh. "There's no code. And for a good chunk of the day, like the majority of households in America, at least the male portion of the group will be in front of the TV watching football."

"I bet the cranberry sauce won't come out of a can, like in the majority of households in America."

"There you've got me. I'll talk to your mother, and spare you the inquisition."

"You'd think. Appreciate it, but she'll still grill me, and she'll stay on my ass so I end up wearing a suit."

"You look good in a suit. Why are those tires so big?"

"Because the kid who owns the Jeep is a show-off." He pressed the lift button until the tires were on the ground. "I need to check the steering again, like this, then with each side jacked up to max. Need to do the front-end alignment."

He studied the Jeep, then the woman. "I can do that in the morning. Why don't I wash up, lock up, then take you out to dinner?"

"It's a little late for dinner."

Since he wasn't wearing a watch, he gestured toward her wrist, angled his head to read hers. "Yeah, I guess it is, unless you haven't had dinner."

"Tell you what. Why don't you wash up, lock up, then follow me home. I'll scramble you some eggs. It's today's special."

"That'll work. Parker? I'm glad you came by."

$\mathscr{P}$ARKER GRABBED THE PHONE AND ROLLED OUT OF BED AT THE same time. Her quick glance at the time told her it was barely five, and Friday evening's bride was already up.

"Good morning, Leah. How—"

She broke off, slipping into the adjoining sitting room as the bride relayed the crisis.

"Oh, I'm so sorry. No, listen, don't worry about the time. I'm yours all day. I don't want you to worry about anything to do with the wedding. If you talk to Justin, tell him we're all keeping his mother in our thoughts. We'll work out the rest, Leah. Leave it to me. Let me ask you this: Can one of the other groomsmen stand as best man?"

Parker listened, grateful her bride kept her cool despite having the best man on his way to Seattle on her wedding day.

"That's good. Yes, that still leaves you short a groomsman. Is it possible either you or Channing knows someone who could fill in? Yes, I understand it's very last minute, and there's the matter of fit with the vests and the shirts you decided on."

Pursing her lip, she eased the door open, narrowed her eyes at Malcolm, who'd taken advantage of her absence to sprawl diagonally over the bed.

"I might have someone who'd fit. I understand neither you nor Channing know him, but . . . No, don't think about it. Let me see what I can do, and I'll get back to you. I promise you, we'll take care of everything. Give me about an hour."

Parker slipped back into the bedroom, considered strategy.

It never hurt to soften up the quarry.

She eased back into bed, snuggled up against his back. It was hard work, she thought as she stroked a hand down his flank, brushed her lips over his bare shoulder. But somebody had to do it.

And he was warm, firm. When she glided her hand over his hip, over his belly, down, she smiled and thought, very firm.

She danced her fingers down his thigh, up again. Then got serious about the task at hand. Using hands and lips, she stirred him awake, shifted him onto his back where she saw his sleepy eyes glint in the dark.

"Good morning," she murmured, laying a line of kisses down his chest.

"It's looking that way."

She nibbled at his throat, gentle, teasing bites. "Since I was up, and so were you . . ." She worked her way up to his ear as his hands moved over her. "I hope you don't mind if I just help myself."

"Do what you gotta do."

She laughed and straddled him. She slid up, offering her breasts to his mouth, and let herself fall into the lazy pleasure. There was still so much of him she didn't really know, so much about him she might never fully understand.

But here, in the dark, they knew each other.

She rose up, took him in.

She surrounded him, body, scent, the sound of her breathing sighing out, the taste of her lingering on his tongue. She moved over him, pale shadow, soft fantasy, warm woman. Before morning broke she took him over, ruled him, owned him.

When she bowed back, taking that reckless fall, she pulled him with her.

She made a sound he equated with a cat licking up the last drop of milk, then stretched out on him, full-length.

"Now that . . ." She repeated the sound. "That's a perfect way to start the day."

"Breakfast of champions."

"Mmm. When do you have to go into work?"

"Seven, maybe seven thirty. With this kind of jump-start I might grab a half hour in the gym. What the hell time is it?"

"You've got a couple hours. You'll be back later?"

"Yeah, I'll come back." His fingers trailed lazily up and down her spine. "I should be able to get away about four if you're looking for some help tonight."

"That would be great." She smiled, turned her head to kiss the side of his neck. "Since the call that gave us this lovely early start was from this evening's bride, and there's a complication."

"I'll make sure I get back. I figure I owe her."

It was, Parker thought, almost too easy. "Actually, you're just the one to solve the complication."

"What? The limo needs a tune-up? Or some Cinderella carriage needs a wheel changed?"

"You'd be the one to call. But no." She kissed his stubble-roughened cheek. "The groom's best friend, and best man, had to fly to Seattle this morning." Then the other. "His mother's having emergency surgery."

"That's rough. Serious?"

"Peritonitis. They're worried about sepsis, and other complications. More, she was out there taking care of *her* mother, who just had a hip replacement, so it's doubly difficult for everyone. Leah and Channing are worried about their friend, their friend's mother, and are missing a best man. They'll upgrade one of the groomsman for that, but that leaves them one short."

"Mmm-hmm."

"So, we'll need a substitute, and one who's about the same build as Justin, the best man, so the tux fits."

"Right."

"You're about a thirty-eight long, right? Thirty-two waist? I'd say a thirty-five sleeve."

"I guess. I haven't . . . Whoa. Wait." When he pushed at her shoulders, she just burrowed in.

"You'd be doing me a huge favor. You'll like Channing. He's a sweetheart. He and Leah actually grew up together, so to speak. They were an item for a while in high school, then lost touch for a bit during the college years until—"

"You've got to be kidding." This time he put a little more into the shove and rolled her off. "You don't seriously expect me to put on some guy's tux and—"

"I really think it'll fit. Del needs a forty, and Jack's a regular. And they wouldn't be able to wear their own, as the wedding party's coordinated."

"There's no way I'm—"

"Consider it pinch hitting. That's really all it is." She rolled back, sliding over his chest. "You've been in a wedding before, haven't you?"

"Yeah, but—"

"All you have to do is show guests to their seats, stand up there with the groomsmen, and then escort a very attractive attendant in the recession. It would really take a huge burden off Leah and Channing."

"Maybe I'd care about that if I knew Leah and Channing."

"You know me. You'd really be helping me out, Malcolm." She brushed a kiss along his jaw. "And I'd really appreciate it."

"I've got to work."

"But you'll be here in plenty of time. Really, if you're back by five forty-five, I can make it work. I'll take care of all the details. All you have to do is wear the tux—oh, and the shoes you wore for Sherry's wedding would be fine—"

"Thank God."

"Sarcasm noted, and ignored. You just show up, look gorgeous, and direct a few people to their seats. It's going to be a beautiful wedding. The cake's amazing. Chocolate marble with a marbleized fondant over buttercream. Laurel's serving it in pools of caramel sauce."

"You think I can be bribed with cake?"

"It's exceptional cake." Now she nipped, ever so lightly, at his jaw. "And I bet I can confiscate some extra caramel sauce for . . . later."

"Now you're bribing me with caramel-sauce sex?"

"I am."

"You're freaking diabolical, Legs."

"Thanks."

"And the wake-up call? That was to prime me for all this?"

"Absolutely."

"It was good thinking."

"You'll do it?"

"I'd like to meet the man who can hold out against caramel sauce."

"Thank you." She planted a hard, noisy kiss on his mouth. "Seriously, thank you. I've got to call Leah, let her know." She jumped out of bed, grabbed the phone. "Don't worry about a thing. All you have to do is be here, and I'll coach you through the rest."

"Yeah, yeah."

And as she called the bride, Malcolm pulled a pillow over his face.

CHAPTER EIGHTEEN

$\mathscr{H}$E THOUGHT ABOUT INVENTING AN EMERGENCY, BUT THAT WOULD be cowardly. And it wouldn't result in caramel sauce.

Plus, he had to admit she'd outmaneuvered him, and couldn't help but admire her strategy. And he'd revved on the execution most of the day.

He finished the work on the Jeep, rebuilt a carburetor, ran a few diagnostics for routine service checks, and took a couple of road calls, as he'd be passing the night shift to Bill.

He skimmed through some paperwork—most of which he intended to dump on his mother—and completed a list of replacement parts he needed her to hunt up for a rehab on a '67 Mustang.

He took a glance at his balance sheet. It always gave him an odd little jolt to realize he was flush.

Flush enough to pump some back into the business, give his

mother and the rest of the crew decent raises, and maybe take a little winter vacation after the holidays.

A week somewhere with a beach and blue water. Things slowed down some at Vows in January, according to Parker. She could probably figure out how to skip out for a week,. Nobody figured like Parker.

He'd teach her to surf.

Maybe she knew how to surf. He should ask her.

And it occurred to him he was planning a vacation around Parker. When had that happened?

He sat for a moment listening to the sounds from the garage, let himself absorb the notion. When it didn't give him the jitters, he let out a *huh*.

So it didn't matter when or how it happened, it just was. And he was okay with it.

Better than okay, he admitted, because he could see her with him on that beach with blue water, drinking some local rum deal, and just letting work go for a few days.

Or . . . maybe a break at her place in the Hamptons. Something to be said for winter beaches—solitude, sex by the fire.

So, he'd toss the idea at her, see where it went.

He gathered up the files, moved through the garage and into the office.

"Got some stuff," he began, and went over the lists and invoices while his mother peered at the paperwork through her green-framed glasses.

"You're taking off now?"

"I was going to. I sort of have a thing I have to do. Whatever you don't get to, I'll finish up by Monday."

"I didn't say I couldn't get it done. Come here."

He leaned over the counter. And she cuffed the side of his head.

"Hey."

"Why didn't you tell me we were getting an invite to Thanksgiving dinner at the Brown Estate?"

"It just came up." Aggrieved as only his mother could make him, he rubbed the side of his head. "And Parker said she'd call you about it, which I guess she did. What's the problem?"

"If you'd told me, I wouldn't have been taken by surprise. And if she hadn't called, I'd've bought a damn turkey on my way home from work today. Then I'd have a turkey I don't need."

"Well, she did so you didn't, and you don't."

"You're lucky I didn't." She gave him that smirk that made him want to hunch his shoulders. "You're wearing a suit."

He *knew* it. "She said it didn't matter."

"I don't care what she said. I'm saying you're wearing a suit. You should buy a new suit. When's the last time you bought a new suit?"

He nearly did hunch his shoulders, and thanked God all his men were out of earshot. "I don't know. Jesus."

"Don't take that tone with me." Her finger jabbed out at him like a switchblade. "You buy a new suit. And a tie. And some decent shoes."

"Good God."

"You're seeing someone like Parker Brown, you have more need for a suit than for a wedding or when somebody drops dead. And you're a successful businessman, don't you forget it. A successful businessman has more than one suit in his closet. And you could use a haircut."

"Anything else? Maybe I should learn French."

She wagged a finger, but her lips twitched. "You could parlay voo if you wanted. You're bright enough. You get that from my side of the family. You get your build from your daddy. That's why you look so sharp in a suit. Go on and get out of here so I can deal with this work you've tossed at me."

"If I'd known I was going to get bushwhacked, I'd have found more." He walked to the door, glanced back—and felt the smirk they shared move onto his face. "Since I have to spend all this dough on clothes, I guess I can't give you the raise I was planning on. Too bad."

It took some of the sting out of the idea of shopping when she scowled after him.

$\mathcal{B}$Y THE TIME HE GOT TO PARKER'S, THE PLACE WAS IN FULL-EVENT mode. Emma and her flower people had already decked out the entrance with a lot of big straw-colored things holding acres of flowers. She'd mixed in some pumpkins, and what might've been gourds.

He didn't think he'd ever seen gourds at a wedding, but he had to admit they looked good.

Inside they'd draped the staircase with miles of that filmy white stuff they used, more flowers, little lights. Still more flowers stood in pots and baskets and vases.

It was like walking through a fall dreamscape. Which, he supposed, was the goal.

He could hear more work going on in the Parlor, and in what they called the Grand Hall, but resisted the urge to poke his head in. He might get volunteered.

He considered easing through, hitting Mrs. Grady up for a sandwich before he dealt with whatever he was going to have to deal with upstairs, but even as he turned in that direction, Parker moved into view at the top of the stairs.

The woman, he thought, had better radar than NASA.

"Perfect timing." She shot out a killer smile as she came down. "The groom's party is just getting started. I can't tell you how much you've taken off their minds, and mine." She locked on to him like a tractor beam and began to lead him up.

"Everything's right on schedule."

"I worried about that all day."

She gave him a gentle elbow poke. "I know this is a lot to ask, but it does make you a hero. Justin's mother came through the surgery very well, so we're in complete celebration mode."

"That's good, about the mother."

"It really is. I'll introduce you to Channing and his men, help you get set up. Then I'll come back in about an hour, just to give you a run-through since you weren't at rehearsal."

She gave the door of the Groom's Suite a brisk knock. "It's Parker," she called out. "Is it safe to come in?"

The man who opened the door wore tuxedo pants and had a beer in his hand. "I can't say we're decent, but we're covered."

"Good enough. Malcolm, this is Darrin, recently promoted to best man."

"I told Channing I've always been the best man. You'd be today's pinch hitter. Nice to meet you."

They shook hands before Parker nudged Malcolm inside where beer poked their frosty heads out of iced buckets, and a bottle of champagne stood in another. Platters held sandwiches and finger food, and men hung around half dressed. Five of them. Six counting the newly appointed best man.

One—tall, golden, gym-ripped—broke away. "Malcolm? I'm Channing, and I'll be your groom today."

"Good luck with that."

"I really can't begin to thank you for doing this. It probably seems bizarre, but . . . I know you from somewhere."

"I've been somewhere, but you don't look familiar."

"I could swear—"

"Hey." One of the men paused as he poured a glass of champagne. "It's Kavanaugh, right?"

"Yeah." Malcolm narrowed his eyes at champagne guy. "Mercedes SL600. Tire rotation and detailing."

"That's exactly right. Best detail job I've ever had."

"That's it." Channing ticked the air with his finger. "I knew I'd seen you. You rehabbed my father's T-Bird. I was there when you delivered it. I dried his tears of joy."

"Hell of a car. So you're Channing Colbert."

"Yeah. I thought my father was crazy when he bought that car. Then I saw it after you'd finished with it and thought, why don't I have one? Want some champagne, a beer?"

"Beer."

"I'll leave you in good hands." Parker patted his arm. "Your tux is right over there. Our photographer will be here in about fifteen minutes."

It wasn't so bad, Malcolm decided. There was food, there was beer, and the other men were in such a damn good mood it was hard to feel put-upon.

At least he felt that way until Mac swung in and pointed her camera at him.

"Hey, I'm just subbing."

"And they'll want that documented. Don't pay any attention to me." She waved at him, and moved around the room like a redheaded snake—slithery and silent.

He felt a profound sense of relief when she cut Channing out of the herd for formal shots.

He changed into the tuxedo pants and shirt while she was gone. Parker had been dead-on, again. They fit, as did the dark red vest.

Half the guys had questions about cars, but he was used to that.

A mechanic was a car doctor, and everybody wanted free medical advice. Since advice could lead to new customers, he didn't mind handing it out.

When Parker came back, he was struggling with his tie.

"Here, let me do it."

"When I rent a tux, you just hook this bastard on."

She smiled up at him. "I think half the reason men wear ties is so women have to get in close to tie them. How're you doing?"

"It's okay." He glanced over her shoulder to his fellow grooms-men. "They're all pretty easy."

"Your attendant's name is Astoria."

His gaze shifted back to hers. "Seriously?"

She cleared a chuckle out of her throat. "They call her Asti. She's beautiful, a little bit shy—and married, so don't get any ideas."

"And here I was thinking about a quickie in the cloak room."

"They all do. She works with special needs children in Chicago. She and Leah met in college. There." She stepped back, angled her head. "You're fulfilling your part of the deal. You're having a good time and you look gorgeous."

Mac stepped back in. "Okay, boys, let's move out to the terrace for the formals. It's a risk. I don't know if my camera can handle this much handsome."

Parker helped Malcolm into his jacket, brushed at the sleeve. "I'll be back to do that run-through as soon as Mac's done with you."

"With me? I'm not doing the group shots. I'm not part of the group. I'm the sub."

"Channing really wants you in them. It'll only take a few minutes."

"Listen, Parker—"

"Oh, sorry." She tapped her headset. "I have to run."

Sneaky, Malcolm thought as she slid away like butter on a griddle. He was going to want a *lot* of caramel sauce.

He did his part, escorting people to seats in the shimmering lights of the Grand Hall. Candlelight and firelight added to the glow.

Laurel swung through for an on-scene check, sent him a wink. "How's it going?"

"Is the cake as good as advertised?"

"Better."

"Then it's all worth it."

"And there's plenty of caramel sauce."

He caught her smirk—they seemed to be going around—as she glided away.

Jesus, did those women tell each other everything?

Fine, he'd make sure they had plenty to talk about over breakfast. Maybe he'd just cop a bottle of the champagne to go with the—

"Well, well, moonlighting as an usher these days?"

His back went tight even before he turned to his uncle.

Not aging well, are you, Artie? Malcolm thought, and there was some satisfaction in that. The man still had all his hair—which had always been his pride and joy—but he'd put on weight, gone thick in the face, in the middle. His eyes, a deceptively mild blue, seemed shrunken in the wide plate of that face.

She'd fared better, he decided, glancing at his uncle's wife. Kept her figure, maybe had a couple nips and tucks. But the look of distaste didn't do anything attractive to her face.

"You can find your own seats."

"Courteous as ever. I'd heard you were chasing after the Brown girl and her money."

"You never knew your place." Marge Frank sniffed. "Now it looks like Parker Brown's forgotten hers. Her grandmother must be rolling over in her grave."

"Sit down or leave."

"It doesn't look like her breeding's rubbed off on you," Artie commented. "It shouldn't take long for Parker to see you for what you are. Just how do you know the bride and groom? Changed a few tires for them?"

Fuck it, he thought. Just fuck it. "That's right."

"You can scrub the grime from under your nails, Malcolm, but you're still a grease monkey. And people like the Browns always end up with their own kind. Come on, Marge."

He needed five minutes, Malcolm thought. Five minutes to get some air, to settle himself. But even as he backed out, started toward the foyer, Laurel came back.

"Less than a dozen guests left to seat. We're going to want you and the rest of the boys to take positions in two minutes. Are you— Is something wrong?"

"No."

"Okay. If you'd nudge the last stragglers into seats, then go around . . . Parker showed you how it works, right?"

"Yeah. I got it."

"I'll be there to cue you. Don't worry. It'll be painless."

He didn't feel pain. He felt a rage that wanted to claw out of his throat. He didn't want to be there, wearing someone else's tux, standing in front of a crowd of people in a room filled with flowers and candles watching people he didn't even know get married.

And feeling—helpless not to feel—the utter contempt from his uncle, coiling its way across the room to clamp onto his throat and trap that rage.

Once he'd escaped it, had traveled three thousand miles to

shed it. He'd come back a man, but there was still a piece inside him, he hated knowing it, that burned with that raw and bitter anger.

And struggled, even now struggled, with the echoes of humiliation.

He went along for photos after the ceremony, primarily as an escape route. He listened as Channing's father rhapsodized about the T-Bird, and did his best to keep up his end.

Then he broke away to find a place in the side garden, to sit in the frosted night and breathe.

She found him there. She was out of breath, coatless, her usual composure shattered.

"Malcolm."

"Look, they don't need me for the dinner deal. I'm taking a goddamn break."

"Malcolm." She dropped down beside him, took his hand. "I didn't know. I didn't know the Franks were coming. I didn't spot them until I did a walk-through at dinner. I'm sorry. I'm so sorry."

"You could be sorry if you'd invited them. Since you didn't, it's not your thing."

"I got you into this. I wish I'd—"

"It's no big deal."

"I'll fix it. I'll make an excuse to Channing and Leah so you can—"

"And let them have the satisfaction of running me off, again? I don't fucking think so. I'm just taking a goddamn break, Parker. Give me some space."

She released his hand, rose.

"Not everybody wants you to handle the details, to fix every damn thing."

"You're right."

"And don't be so damn agreeable. I know when I'm out of line, and I'm out of line."

"You're upset. I understand—"

"I don't want you to understand. You *don't* understand. How could you? This doesn't have anything to do with you. Did anyone every knock you around when you weren't able to fight back?"

"No."

"Tell you, over and over until you started to believe it, that you're useless, you're stupid, worthless. That if you didn't fall in line, you'd be out on the street?"

"No." But that didn't mean her heart couldn't break, her blood couldn't boil for the child who'd lived through it.

"So you don't understand. Hell, I don't understand why my way of coping with it was to do my level best to make it worse, to look for trouble, and to blame my mother, who didn't know what was going on because I was too afraid or proud or both to tell her."

She said nothing. She understood now, or hoped she did, that to push meant he'd simply close up. So she said nothing. She just listened.

"I made it as hard on her as I could for as long as I could. And if I wasn't giving her grief, he was, or his bitch of a wife was. She took it because she was trying to keep a roof over my head, give me a family, because she was trying to get through the grief of losing my father. And I blamed her for that, too. Let's just pile it on her. Why should she have a life? Artie's working her like a dog because he could. Her own goddamn brother. And we were supposed to be grateful.

"More than two years of that, every day a misery. I'm just waiting, just waiting until I'm old enough, strong enough, to kick his ass and get the hell out. Then she does it for me. After all that, she does it for me. She comes home early from work one night. Sick.

He'd had her pulling doubles and just wore her out. And he's got me up against the wall, his hand around my throat, slapping me. He liked to slap because it's more humiliating than a fist and doesn't leave a mark."

Someone had stepped out on one of the terraces, and a trill of female laughter floated out on the frosted air.

Malcolm stared toward the house, the lights, the laughter, but she doubted he saw the glow or heard the joy.

"I saw her come in. She was white as a sheet. Until she saw us, and then everything about her went on fire. I'd never seen her move that fast. I don't know if I've ever seen anybody move that fast. She yanked him off me. She was bone-thin. He had to have sixty pounds on her, but she yanked him right off his fucking feet, and he landed halfway across the room. She dared him to get up, dared him to try to lay hands on me again, and to see how fast she snapped them off and fed them to him."

He stopped, shook his head. "There, that's what I come from, and don't tell me you understand."

"I'm not going to argue with you now, but I will say if you think I'd blame a boy and his grieving mother in any way for the situation you were caught in, you must think very little of me."

His tone went as frosty as the air. "I told you, Parker, it's not about you."

"Of course it's about me, you idiot. You idiot, I love you."

She caught a glimpse of the utter stupefaction on his face before she stormed away.

She caught another glimpse of him during the reception, talking to the newlyweds, and again a bit later, seated at the bar with the FOG in some intense conversation.

She kept her eye on the Franks, prepared to move in if they headed in Malcolm's direction. Maybe he thought it was none of her business, maybe he thought she didn't understand, maybe he was just *stupid*. But she wouldn't allow anything or anyone to cause trouble at one of her weddings.

She was almost disappointed when it didn't happen.

"Did you and Mal have a fight?" Mac eased up beside her when the crowd began to thin.

"Why?"

Mac tapped her camera. "I know faces. I know you."

"I wouldn't say we had a fight. I'd say we appear to define relationship differently, except he doesn't acknowledge we're in a relationship. We're in a situation."

"Men can be dumbasses."

"They really can."

"Women should all move to Amazonia, or at least vacation there four times a year."

"Amazonia?"

"It's the girl world in my head, where I go when I'm annoyed with Carter, or just men in general. There are five shoe stores per capita, nothing has any calories, and all the books and movies end happy ever after."

"I like Amazonia. When do we leave?"

Mac draped an arm around Parker's shoulders. "Amazonia, my friend, is always there, inside every woman's head. Just close your eyes, think: Manolo Blahnik. And you're there. I've got to go get some more shots, then I'll be right behind you."

Amused, Parker let herself imagine a calm, soothing, shoe-ladened female world, but had to admit, she wouldn't want to live there. An occasional short vacation? It sounded very good.

She watched as the bride and groom took the floor again for the last dance of the evening.

So in love, she thought. So in tune. So ready to start their life together, as partners, as lovers, as companions and mates.

On their way to their happy ever after.

And that, she admitted, was what she'd always wanted.

To make her mark, yes, to do good work, to be a good friend, a good sister, to build something and share something. And with all that, to love and be loved, to promise and accept the promise. To find someone and take hands with him in their own happy ever after.

She couldn't try for less.

She didn't see Malcolm again until she'd stepped outside to wave the newlyweds off.

He'd changed into his own clothes, she noted, and looked considerably calmer and more himself.

"Got a minute?" he asked her.

"Yes, a couple of them now."

"I took a bad reaction out on you, something that's getting to be a habit. I don't like the habit."

"All right."

"I thought I'd moved on from having that kind of a reaction to Artie. Apparently not." He dipped his hands into his pockets. "I don't like going back there, so I don't. There's no point. I understand you were trying to help."

"But you don't want any help."

"I don't want to need any. I think that's a little different. That's no excuse for lashing out at you."

"I'm not asking for excuses, Malcolm. I don't need excuses when I know the reason."

"I guess I'm still working on the reason. So . . . I'm going to take off. Give us both a little time to smooth out."

"While you're smoothing, ask yourself this. Ask yourself if you actually believe I think less of a boy, one grieving for his father, for striking back, for looking for an escape from an abusive bully who held every control. Or if I think less of the man he made himself into because of it. When you're sure of the answer, let me know."

She opened the door. "Good night, Malcolm."

"Parker? Whatever the answer, I still want you."

"You know where to find me," she said, and closed the door behind her.

CHAPTER NINETEEN

HE LIKED TO THINK HE'D SMOOTHED IT OUT. HE COULDN'T RE-
member ever making that kind of a misstep—much less two in a
row—with a woman before.

Then again, Parker was a first on pretty much every level.

He understood a couple of major screw-ups required a reach
into the wallet for a token, a symbol—generally for something
smelly or shiny. Even the girl who had everything or could easily
get it for herself liked a basic I Was an Idiot gift.

He considered flowers, but her house was already loaded with
them. Flowers probably hit the low end of the idiot scale anyway.

He mulled the idea of jewelry, but it seemed over the top.

Then he thought of her weakness.

What the hell, since his mother would gnaw on his neck until
he got a new suit, he had to go shopping anyway.

He hated shopping, so that part of it felt like a kind of penance.
Worse, he had to shell out money for clothes that made him feel

like he'd decked himself out in some kind of package. It all took too long, included way too many annoying or baffling decisions, and came perilously close to giving him a headache behind his eyes.

But when he was done he had the suit and a nicely gift-wrapped box—and promised himself he would never, not in this lifetime or any other, go through that experience again.

He texted her twice, and he never texted anyone. He hated texting. His fingers were too damn big for the keys and made him feel clumsy and stupid. Still, he figured his strategy to stay out of her way for a few days had to include basic contact.

By Monday, he calculated he'd stayed out of her way long enough, and called her. He got her voice mail, another technology he hated, even when it included her cool voice.

"Hey, Legs. Just wanted to see if you were up for a drive tonight. We could grab a pizza. I miss your face," he added before he thought it through. "So, let me know."

He lay back down on the creeper, slid under the rattletrap he kept patching together for a customer, and got to work removing the useless muffler.

He'd nearly completed installing the new one when his phone signaled. He banged his knuckles, swore at the welling blood on the scrape, then fought his phone back out of his pocket.

He swore again when he realized it was a text.

It sounds nice, but I can't get away tonight. We're jammed right up to Thanksgiving. It'll be nice to see your face, and your mother, then. PB

"*P*B? WHAT KIND OF BULLSHIT IS THAT?"

"You brushed him off in a text? That's cold." Laurel sat back. "Kudos."

"I didn't brush him off. We had a full consult scheduled." Which, she thought, was finished now and very well. So she could relax and have a glass of wine with her friends.

"From what you told us, he was just trying to deal with a difficult situation." Sympathy shimmered in Emma's big brown eyes. "Some people need to go inside awhile when they're dealing."

"Yes, they do. So I'm giving him time, and the space he so clearly demanded, to do that."

"And just because he's finished doesn't mean he's finished. Besides," Mac pointed out, "you're pissed."

"Not really. Or only slightly," Parker amended. "I'd rather he— or anyone—vent and spew, even if I get hit by some shrapnel, than shut down and close in. But he doesn't want to accept sincere support, honest understanding. And that pisses me off. Slightly."

"Okay, here's what I have to say." Mac drew a deep breath. "My mother rarely laid a hand on me, so I don't have that sort of abuse to lay on her. But she used, belittled, and slapped at me emotionally." Mac gave Emma a grateful smile when her friend rubbed her leg in comfort. "I had the three of you to talk to, but even with you, sometimes I went under—or in. And sometimes, even with you, with Mrs. G, with Carter right there with me, I need to go inside, or I'm just used to going, so I do."

"I wish you wouldn't," Emma put in.

"I know you do, and because I know it, I add a little guilt to the brood. I've got a pretty good sense of what Mal's dealing with. My father didn't die, but he left, and since, he's never been there when I really wanted or needed him. And *I* was left with someone who, a lot less violently than Asshole Artie, made me feel diminished."

She picked up water to soothe her throat. "And sometimes, even knowing better, this shit comes down on me, and I look at Em, with her incredible family; at Laurel, who can just say 'fuck

them' and mean it; at Parker, who's so damn together, and just feel
you don't know. How the hell can you know? And that adds de-
fensiveness to the guilt and the brood. So sometimes I don't want
to talk about the shit that came down because, well, it's my shit."

"Such a way with words." Laurel toasted her. "We, however,
have ways of making you talk."

"Yeah, and I'm always better after. You all not only know which
buttons to push to open me up again, but I end up opening because I know you love me, and you'll accept all the shit that comes
with me because you love me."

"Not me." Laurel smiled. "I just feel sorry for you due to my
bottomless well of compassion."

Mac nodded. "Mother Teresa was a stone bitch compared to
you."

"I told him I loved him," Parker muttered, and Laurel's head
snapped around.

"What? Talk about burying the lead. When?"

"When I was more than slightly pissed. When he told me I
didn't understand and it had nothing to do with me. I told him he
was an idiot, and it did have to do with me because I loved him.
Then I came back in to work the event, which I should've been
doing all along."

"What did he say?" Emma demanded, a hand already pressed
to her heart. "What did he do?"

"He didn't say or do anything. He was too busy staring at me
as if I'd kicked him in the balls. Which would've been the better
option."

"On Friday? You told him on Friday." Emma waved her hands
in the air. "We've been working together all weekend, and you
didn't tell us?"

"She didn't tell us because it's her shit."

Parker shifted her gaze to Mac. "If we have to continue in that theme, yes, I guess that's true enough. I needed to think about it for a while. And because none of this, just none of it is going the way I always thought it would, always planned it should. I'm supposed to fall in love with a sensible yet brilliant man with a droll sense of humor and a keen appreciation of art. And I know you're rolling your eyes at me, Laurel, so just knock it off."

"It was the droll sense of humor."

"Whatever. This is my long-term plan, carefully constructed over more than a decade."

"Seriously?"

"Shut up, Mac." But Parker's lips curved, just a little. "This sensible yet brilliant man and I would date casually for some months, getting to know each other, to appreciate each other before we go on a short, romantic trip—location optional. It could be a wonderful suite in a hotel in New York, a cottage at the beach, a B and B in the country. We'd have a long candlelight dinner, or maybe a picnic. After, the sex would be lovely."

"Would it include banging in the utility room?" Laurel wondered.

"You shut up, too, or you don't get to hear the rest of the plan."

Looking a bit pained, Laurel mimed zipping her lips.

"So." Satisfied, Parker slipped off her shoes, tucked her legs up. "We'd be lovers, and we'd travel now and then as our schedules allowed. We'd argue occasionally, of course, but we'd always talk it out—reasonably, rationally."

Her gaze snapped to Emma. "You're keeping quiet, but I can hear you're thinking *boring*. However, you'll like this next part. He'd tell me he loved me. Take my hands, look in my eyes, and tell me. And one day, we'd go back to that wonderful suite or that cottage or B and B, and during our candlelight dinner, he'd tell me again that he loved me, that I was everything he'd ever wanted. And he'd ask me to marry him. I'd say yes, and that's how you build a happy ever after."

"He'd better have a square-cut diamond ring in his pocket," Laurel said. "Five-carat minimum."

"Trust you," Mac commented, but gamely swallowed a laugh.

"I think it's lovely." Emma shot Laurel a warning look.

"It is lovely, and it may be ridiculous, but it's *my* plan." Firm now, Parker tapped a finger to her own chest. "I'm capable of adjusting plans to fit the circumstances and requirements."

"None better," Mac agreed.

"But what's happening with Malcolm is completely off script. It's not even close, and I fell for him anyway. Now *I've* told *him*, which crumbles one more page in the script."

"I know that you know, and we all know, that love doesn't run according to any script. If it did," Laurel added, "I'd be canoodling with a hot, buff *artiste* named Luc in our pied-à-terre in Paris instead of marrying your brother, the hot, buff lawyer named Delaney."

"Of course I know, but that doesn't mean I have to be thrilled about it."

"You're not just giving Mal time and space," Mac concluded. "You're taking some yourself."

"I need it. Because there's one element to the script that can't be edited out or rewritten. Whoever you fall in love with has to love you back, or the ending just sucks."

"If he doesn't love you, he *is* an idiot."

"Thanks, Em."

"I mean it. You're perfect—in a good way, not the I-hate-that-perfect-bitch way."

"Sometimes we hate her," Laurel said, then smiled at Parker. "But it's a hate based on love."

Understanding, Parker raised her glass to her friends. "I hate you, too."

"All my favorite women." Del walked in, scanned, shook his head. "And if this is one of those girls-only discussions, you'll just have to break it up. I charmed Mrs. G into making her rosemary lamb chops, and she just gave me the two-minute warning. Jack and Carter are on their way."

"We're eating here?" Mac jumped up, pumped a fist in the air. "Woo! We have the best system in the history of systems."

"I'll go give her a hand." Laurel rose, gave Del a look. He cocked his eyebrows, then nodded. "Come on, Em."

As they left, Del sat on the edge of the coffee table, blocking Parker's exit. "So. What's the deal with you and Mal? Do I have to go tune him up?" Watching her face, he gave her knee a pat. "I think I can take him, but I'd bring Jack and Carter along just in case."

"That's so sweet, but unnecessary."

"Something's up. He passed on going in to catch the Giants play on Sunday, and hasn't been around here for days."

"We're . . . assessing the situation."

"Is the translation you had a fight?"

"No, we didn't have a fight. And if we had, I think you know I can hold my own."

"No question, but if some guy hurts you, even if he's a friend of mine, maybe even especially if he's a friend of mine, I have to take him down. Those are the Big Brother Rules."

"Yeah, but you're always changing the Big Brother Rules."

"Those are amendments, addendum, the occasional codicil."

"We didn't fight. And if I got my feelings hurt, it's because— and you'll have to deal with this—I'm in love with him."

"Oh." He sat back, hands on his thighs. "I'm going to need a minute."

"Take your time. I'm taking mine. Because we're all going to have to deal with it, Del. You, me. And Malcolm." She nudged his knees aside, got up. "Let's go eat before Mrs. G sends out a search party."

"I want you happy, Parker."

"Del." She took his hand. "I want me happy, too."

As arranged, Malcolm detoured to Emma's to pick up the flowers he'd asked her to put together for Mrs. Grady.

"Be right back," he told his mother.

"Make sure you are. It's rude to be late."

"She said to come around four, didn't she? It's around four."

To spare himself any more nagging, he climbed out and jogged to Emma's door. He found, as she'd told him he would, the sunflowers in a copper pitcher on the table in the front room. He snatched them up.

When he got back into the car, he pushed them at his mother. "Hold on to these, okay?"

"They're nice. You're a good boy at least half the time, Malcolm."

"I'm wearing the suit, aren't I? That should count."

"You look sharp, too. That's some house," she added as he three-pointed the car to drive to the main house. "Boy, I remember the first time I saw it up close, driving up wearing my starched uniform, scared to pieces."

She smoothed a hand over the skirt of the dress she'd bought special for today in her favorite bright green. Nothing starched about it, she thought happily.

"Then I got here," she continued, "and saw it, and I thought it was so beautiful, and it doesn't look scary. Old Miz Brown, she was scary, that's for damn sure. But it was worth it to see the inside, to walk around serving fancy food to fancy people. And the house-keeper back then, what was her name? Oh well, doesn't matter. She and the cook let us have a meal in the kitchen."

When he parked, she turned to grin at him. "I guess I've come up in the world. How's my hair?"

He grinned back at her. "Like nobody else's."

"Just the way I like it."

He got her mincemeat pie out of the back, and the wrapped box. Before they reached the door, it swung open.

"Happy Thanksgiving." Del kissed Kay on the cheek, eyed the box under Mal's arm. "Ah, you shouldn't have."

"Then it's a good thing I didn't."

"The pie looks great. Did you make it, Ma K?"

"I did. If Maureen's in the kitchen, I'll take it back to her."

"We've got the women in the kitchen where they belong." He winked. "The men are in the media room watching the game as per Brown family tradition. Let me take you back, get you a drink."

"This is the nicest house in Greenwich," Kay stated. "I thought so the first time I saw it, and I haven't changed my mind."

"Thank you. It means a lot to us."

"It ought to. It's got history. I worked some parties here in your grandmother's day, and later on when your mother had them. I liked your mother's better."

Del laughed as he laid a hand on the small of Kay's back to guide her through. "Our Grandmother Brown was a tyrant."

The scents streamed out of the kitchen, along with female voices. Malcolm picked Parker's out, and a knot he hadn't known was tied in his belly loosened.

She sat at the work bar, snapping beans. He tried to think of the last time he'd seen anyone snapping beans—then lost the thought as she glanced over, met his eyes.

Jesus, he'd missed her, to the point of pain. He wanted to

resent it, wanted to step back from it. But she smiled, slid off the stool.

"Happy Thanksgiving." She greeted his mother first, kissing her cheek as Del had. Then she brushed her lips lightly over his. The knot loosened again.

Everyone started talking at once, but he barely heard them. Just static. Movement and color—somebody took the pie out of his hand. And he was caught, just trapped in the look of her, the shape, the sound.

Del replaced the pie with a beer. "Let's go be men before they put us to work. Because, believe me, they can and they will."

"Yeah. I just need a minute."

"Hesitate at your own risk. Still, you'd look so pretty in an apron."

"Blow me," he said, and earned a quick cuff from his mother.

"Mind your manners. I wouldn't mind that apron. Half the fun of Thanksgiving is putting it together."

As Parker started to sit again, Malcolm took her arm. "Take five."

"I have an assignment," she told him as he pulled her out of the kitchen.

"The beans aren't going anywhere." He turned into the music room. "I got you something."

"Oh. That's a nice surprise."

He handed her the box. "When a guy screws up, he's gotta pay."

"I won't argue, since I like presents. I see your mother won the suit battle."

"My mother always wins."

"It's a nice suit." She set the box on a small table, pulled the bow. "How's business?"

"Steady. I picked up a recondition job on a '62 Caddy on a referral from Channing."

"That's terrific."

He watched, unsurprised, as she carefully unfastened the paper. No ripping and shredding, not for Parker Brown. He imagined, as oddly enough his own mother did, she'd save the paper for some future mysterious purpose.

"How about yours?"

"We're always busy around the holidays. Party events on top of weddings. And Mac's wedding's in two weeks. I can't believe it. We'll be jammed until after New Year's, then . . ."

She trailed off when she saw the shoe box, then thoughtfully opened the lid.

Her mouth dropped open. He doubted any other reaction could have been as satisfying.

"Shoes? You bought me shoes? Oh, really fabulous shoes." She took out one of the high, skinny-heeled pumps, holding it like a woman might hold a fragile gem.

"You like shoes."

"*Like* is a soft, weak word for my feelings regarding shoes. Oh, these are *gorgeous*. Look at the way all those deep jewel tones flow together. And the texture."

She slipped off the heels she wore, slipped on the new ones. Then sat there admiring them. "How did you know my size?"

"I've been in your closet."

She continued to sit, studying him. "I have to say, Malcolm, you astonish me. You bought me shoes."

"Don't expect me to ever do it again. It was . . . grueling. I thought, I should just go get her some sexy underwear, but that seemed self-serving. It would've been a lot easier and less weird. You women are vicious in the shoe department."

"Well, I love them." She rose, did what he thought of as a little runway walk. Pivoted. Smiled. "How do they look?"

"I can't take my eyes off your face. I really missed your face."

"Okay." She breathed it out, then stepped to him. "You just flatten me," she murmured, and moved into his arms. "I really missed yours, too."

"We need to be okay. It would really piss me off if my deal with Artie screwed us up."

"Asshole Artie isn't going to screw anything up."

He drew back. "Asshole Artie?"

"That's what we call him around here."

He let out a half laugh. "I like it. I want to be with you, Parker."

"That's good, because you are with me."

He rested his forehead on hers. "Listen I . . ." He didn't have the words, wasn't sure of his moves. "Hell. Let's just say you're the first woman I've bought shoes for." Again, he drew back, met her eyes. "And the last."

"It means a lot." She laid her hands on his cheeks, kissed him. "So, we'll take today to be grateful we're okay."

$\mathcal{T}$HE WEEK BEFORE MAC'S WEDDING MEANT SALON APPOINTMENTS. Manicures, pedicures, facials. It meant logging those last-minute acceptances and regrets and adjusting the seating chart.

It meant final fittings, opening gifts, updating the spreadsheet Parker had created for keeping track of the gift, the sender, the relationship of the sender to the bride or groom, and the mailing address for thank-you notes.

It meant errands and phone calls, confirmations, final consults.

When added to the business of planning and prepping for other events, it meant insanity.

"Why did we think December was a good idea for this?" Mac demanded with a wild look in her eye. "We're swamped, we're crazed. We're not going on the honeymoon until next month anyway, so why didn't I take advantage of the slow time to get married? God, I'm getting married. Tomorrow."

"And it's going to be perfect." Parker said it with grim determination as she worked at her laptop. "Hah! The weather's going to be perfect. Cold, light snow in the morning, one to two inches, and clear in the afternoon. Light winds and low thirties for the evening. Just what I wanted."

"Sometimes they say light snow, and we get dumped on. What if—"

"We're not going to get dumped on." As if daring the weather gods, Parker bared her teeth. "We're going to get a couple pretty, fluffy inches in the morning for a gorgeous December evening wedding. Go get ready for rehearsal."

"I'm afraid of rehearsal. My voice is going to squeak. I think I'm getting a zit right in the middle of my chin. I'm going to trip coming down the aisle. It's okay if Carter trips. People expect it. But—"

"Your voice is not going to squeak, you're not going to get a zit, and you're certainly not going to trip." Parker thumbed out Tums. For herself, and for Mac. "Do I know what I'm doing?"

"Yes, you do, but I'm—"

"Trust me. It's going to be perfect and beautiful and the happiest day of your life."

"I'm being a pain in the ass."

"No, honey, you're being a bride. Now go take a nice, warm bath. You've got an hour."

"Carter isn't nervous." Mac narrowed her eyes in a scowl. "I could hate him for that."

"Mackensie." Parker turned from the computer. "I was in the kitchen this morning when Mrs. G made him sit down and eat some breakfast. He put maple syrup in his coffee."

"He did?" She threw up her arms in a cheer. "He *is* nervous. I feel better. I want him to be nervous, too, and I want his ears to blush the way they do, and I want . . . Since I'm the bride it can be all about what I want, right?"

"Absolutely."

"Okay. So, I want to thank you for temporarily lifting my mother's banishment."

"Mac—"

"No, I mean it. Let me just vent this out, and it'll be over."

"Okay. Vent away."

"It's important she be here tomorrow, even though she's a massive pain in my ass, and everyone else's."

"She's still your mother."

"Yeah, and that's for better or worse, too. Anyhow, I know you've talked to her about it, and the rules of the road."

"It took one brief phone call. It's nothing."

"One brief, unpleasant phone call."

Now Parker smiled. "Not for me. Did she give you grief over it?"

"She tried. She failed. Her power is diminished in that area, which pisses her off." Mac's dimples fluttered. "I'm small enough to enjoy that."

"I'd say you'd be stupid if you didn't."

"Good. So I'm not stupid." On a breath, Mac folded her hands in her lap. "But I want her here because we've been through this enough to know you don't want to look back on the biggest day of your life and have a single regret. And hell, since my father apparently can't work the wedding into his busy schedule of parties and cruising the Ionian Sea, I should have one parent here."

"We know, even though it's our job to supply them, a wedding isn't just about the lights and the music and the show. It's about the feelings. Your family's going to be there, Mac."

"Yeah." Mac reached out, gripped hands with Parker. "The one that counts."

"And more, Carter is going to be there, waiting for you, looking at you, promising you."

"Oh God, yeah. I'm so ready. Nervous, but so ready."

"Go take that bath, soak out the nerves."

"On it." Mac got up, started out. "Parks? I love him so much it feels like there's more inside me, a better me in there than there used to be. I'm not nervous about being married to him. I'm just nervous about, well, the show. Forgetting my lines or not hitting my cue."

"Leave all that to me. Just think about being married to Carter."

"That I can do." She dashed back, caught Parker in a hug. "I love you so much, too."

As she hugged, Parker reached over for a tissue, put it in Mac's hand. "Thanks. I'm not going to cry tomorrow, so I'm planning to cry a lot tonight."

"That's a very good plan. Make sure to seal your mascara so it doesn't run."

Twenty minutes later, Parker dashed downstairs to check with Laurel.

And stopped as her breath caught.

"Oh, Laurel."

"She's demanding to be called Super-Laurel," Del told Parker as he sat at the kitchen counter munching a cookie.

"And who could blame her? She *is* Super-Laurel. It's the most beautiful cake ever created."

"Not done yet," Laurel mumbled, and continued to place sugar-paste flowers.

"Carter's is." Del jerked a thumb toward the remodeled mud-room that now served as Laurel's auxiliary kitchen.

Parker went in, opened the cooler. "I love it! It's even better than the sketch. The open book, the scene from *As You Like It*. I swear it looks like you could turn the page."

"Try it and die." Laurel rolled her aching shoulders and glanced over as Parker came back. "Oh God, don't cry."

"I'm following Mac's plan." She pulled tissues out of her pocket. "Cry tonight, stay dry tomorrow. I have gel masks for all of us chilling in the main fridge so we won't be puffy tomorrow."

"Thank God," Del said, "I was really worried I'd have puffy eyes."

"Take your cookie and go check on Carter," Parker ordered. "And you can call or run over to Emma's, tell her she's not allowed to be late. Have Jack carry her over if necessary."

"Fine. I know when I'm not wanted."

"I thought about letting you sneak into my room tonight," Laurel said. "But you didn't buy me a fabulous new pair of shoes."

"Mal's going to pay for that, for screwing the curve for the rest of us."

When they were alone, Laurel glanced down at Parker's feet. "They really are fabulous. Everything else okay?"

"It's fine. I got tomorrow's forecast, and—"

"I'm not talking about Mac's wedding, which is a change from most conversations this week. I'm talking about you and Malcolm."

"That's fine, too." She opened the refrigerator for a bottle of water, then sighed when she turned back to see Laurel staring at her. "No, he hasn't mentioned the fact that I told him I loved him, and neither have I. And no, he hasn't reciprocated. I'm fine with that."

"Liar."

"I'm trying to be fine with that, and mostly succeeding. Plus there's too much to do to think about it." She smoothed at the hair she'd coiled into a sleek twist for the rehearsal party. "We're in a good place, and that's . . . fine. Don't make me say fine again. Let's just focus on Mac and Carter."

"Okay. Where is the blushing bride?"

"Taking a bath to soothe her nerves. She needs to start getting dressed," Parker realized as she checked her watch. "We're going to start in—"

"Parker, relax. We're having the rehearsal dinner here. You can ease up on the timetable, at least a little. Does she know Linda's not coming tonight?"

"Yes. And I think she's relieved. We talked about tomorrow, and she's glad her mother's coming to the wedding. So, tomorrow's soon enough for Linda."

"What about—" Laurel broke off as Malcolm came in. "I wear a seven medium, just like Parker. Just in case."

"I only buy shoes for women I'm sleeping with." He grabbed a cookie from the plate on the counter. "If I slept with you, Del would get pissed off."

"He's so narrow-minded."

"Did you—"

"Picked up and delivered to Carter's, as instructed."

The weight on Parker's shoulder slipped off. "Okay. Thank you. *Thank* you." She took his face, kissed him.

"He's here." Laurel stepped away from the cake. "You pulled it off."

With a hand on her hip, Parker angled into a pose. "You doubted me?"

"I'm so ashamed. You can be Super-Parker. I need to go change my shoes, which unfortunately aren't those," she said with another envious glance at Parker's feet. "Freshen my makeup, and so on. I'll

get Mac moving if she's not. You did good, Parker." She grabbed
Parker, kissed her hard on the mouth.

"Could you do that again?" Mal asked. "In slow motion?"

"Perv." But tears sparkled in Laurel's eyes as she turned and laid
one on him. "She said again and again it didn't matter, but it did."
She sniffled, smiled at Parker. "We know it did. Back in fifteen."

"Everyone's getting the crying out of the way tonight."

"Thank God. I'm having a hard time holding it in."

"Funny guy." She drilled a finger in his belly. "I need to check
on the caterers, and the Parlor, and the Grand Hall, and—"

He grabbed another cookie and went with her.

THERE WAS ALWAYS A BUZZ IN THE AIR BEFORE AN EVENT, MAL
thought, but not like this buzz. This one almost shocked the skin.
The photographer Mac had trusted for her wedding already
worked with her assistant, getting candids as Carter's family came
in and the noise level rose.

He watched Parker move among them, offering drinks, crouch-
ing down to talk to the kids. In short order the big foyer, the Parlor vibrated with people and movement. Flowers—he imagined
they were a mild prelude to tomorrow's—perfumed the air.

He tried the champagne and glanced over as Parker talked
with his airport pickup. As he started toward them, Mac came racing down the staircase.

"I'm not late!" She laughed, searched Carter out of the crowd.
Her smile only beamed brighter. "I just wanted to—"

Malcolm saw her face change, and for a moment the utter
shock on it made him wonder if Parker had made a mistake.

Then her eyes welled. "Dad?"

Geoffrey Elliot, handsome, charming, and absent for most of
his daughter's life, stepped forward, opened his arms. "Baby."

She ran into them, pressed her face to his shoulder. "I thought you couldn't make it."

"As if I'd miss my baby girl's wedding." He drew her back, kissed her on both damp cheeks. "Aren't you a pretty picture?"

"Dad." She laid her head on his shoulder, found Parker, blinked her eyes clear. She mouthed *thank you*.

No mistake, Malcolm thought, and snagging a second glass of champagne, took it to her. "Nice work, Legs."

She took the champagne and pulled a tissue out of her pocket to dry her own eyes. "It's what I do."

CHAPTER TWENTY

$\mathcal{I}$T SNOWED. AND IT WAS FLUFFY AND BEAUTIFUL. BY NOON PARKER had the parking lot and walkways cleared, and the bride was stretched out upstairs, enjoying the hot stone massage her friends had given her as a wedding-day gift.

The entrance and the staircase both glittered and gleamed with the work Emma and her team had completed. Massive pillar candles flanked the wide doorway of the Grand Hall in groups of three, with masses and masses of richly hued flowers at their creamy white bases.

At dusk, miles of lights strung on the exterior of the house and on the small forest of miniature pines lining the walk in their silver pots would flicker and glow. Candles would shine in every window where wreaths of flowers hung, trailing long white ribbons.

The house, Parker thought as she circled it and checked every detail, was a celebration that would sparkle and shimmer through the night.

Emma had outdone herself, and with the added bonus of snow, guests would wander through that winter wonderland, then step through the garland-draped portico where bride-white poinsettias stacked into fanciful trees to flank the staircase.

She ran the morning schedule like a seasoned general preparing for the most important campaign of her career, zipping from room to room, floor to floor, in running shoes, praising, pep-talking, issuing orders.

"You're going to wear yourself out before this gets started." Del stopped her forward motion with his hands on her shoulders. "Take a breath. I thought Monica from the bridal shop was subbing for you today."

"She and Susan will be here in a half hour. What's Carter's status?"

"A-okay, Captain."

"Seriously, Del, does he need anything? If you guys stayed up half the night boozing and playing poker—"

"We had him tucked into bed by twelve thirty, as instructed. The rest of us stayed up boozing and playing poker."

She narrowed her eyes, noted his were clear and rested.

"Go check on him. I don't want him over here until three thirty."

"His best man has it under control. Bob's as bad as you with lists and time clocks. He'll go by the studio, pick up our groom at three fifteen."

"Then go be useful. Emma's team is working on the Solarium, with the second unit setting up for dinner."

"Jack's on Emma's detail."

"Jack's here? What about Malcolm?"

"He's hanging with Carter. We figured somebody should, in case he makes a run for it."

"Very funny. But it's good somebody's keeping Carter company. I was going to run over and check on him myself, but if Malcolm's with him, I'll go check on Mac instead. You can go tell Laurel she's got an hour and twenty minutes, then she needs to be up in the Bride's Suite."

"If she's in the middle of something, she could come at me with a pastry cutter."

"Those are the chances we take."

$\mathcal{M}$ALCOLM SPRAWLED IN A CHAIR WITH A COKE AND A BAG OF CHIPS and caught a motocross race on ESPN.

Carter paced.

He'd gotten used to the pattern. Carter paced, sat and stared at the TV, checked his watch. Got up and paced.

"Having second thoughts, Professor? I've got orders to get a rope if you try to run."

"What? No. Ha-ha. No. Is it really only one thirty? Maybe the battery's dead." He frowned at his watch, tapped the face. "What time do you have?"

Malcolm held up his naked wrist. "Time for you to relax. Want a shot of something?"

"No. No. No. Maybe. No. It's just . . . It feels like I've entered another dimension where five minutes is equivalent to an hour and a half. We should've gone for an afternoon wedding. We'd be getting married right now if we'd gone for an afternoon wedding."

"In a hurry?"

"I guess I am." He stared blindly. "Some days I don't know how all this happened, and others it's like it's always been. I'm just— it's—we're—"

"Spit it out."

"When you find somebody you love, all the way through, and

she loves you—even with your weaknesses, your flaws, everything starts to click into place. And if you can talk to her, and she listens, if she makes you laugh, and makes you think, makes you want, makes you see who you really are, and who you are is better, just better with her, you'd be crazy not to want to spend the rest of your life with her."

He stopped with a sheepish smile. "I'm rambling."

"No." As the words had something turning around inside him, Malcolm shook his head. "It's nice for you, Carter. You're a lucky bastard."

"Today, I'm the luckiest bastard on the planet."

Malcolm switched off the TV. "Get some cards. We'll play some gin, see if that luck translates."

"Sure." He looked at his watch again. "Is it really only one thirty-five?"

MAC STEPPED INTO THE BRIDE'S SUITE, STOPPED, DID A HAPPY DANCE. "Look, look, it's mine. Today, it's mine. Champagne, and the pretty fruit, the flowers, the candles. Oh, Em, the flowers."

"Nothing but the best for our brides. It is Vows, after all."

"Champagne first." Laurel crossed over to pour.

"Half a glass for me," Parker said. "I still have a few things to—"

"Parker, no." Mac grabbed her hands. "From right now until the last dance, you're my friend, one of my wonderful, beautiful, very-much-needed maids of honor. Monica's got the rest. I need you with me—and the bride rules at Vows."

"All right. Fill me up, Laurel."

"Karen, maybe you could get a wide shot of—"

"Uh-uh." Parker wagged a finger. "If I'm one of your MOH, you are strictly the bride, not the photographer."

"We've got you covered, Mac." Karen winked at her, changed lenses.

"I know, sorry." She took a deep breath, and a glass of champagne. "Okay. To Wedding Day. This time it's real."

After the first sip, Mac held up a hand. "And one more because I might forget later. Emma, thank you for making it all so beautiful, and Laurel, thank you for a truly spectacular cake. And Parks, for all the details, the little and the big, thanks so much. But mostly, just thanks for being mine."

"Okay, stop. Drink." Laurel blinked. "There's no crying today."

"Maybe just a little. We haven't had makeup yet."

As Emma slipped an arm around Mac, Parker passed out tissues.

Then the door opened, and Mrs. Grady stood grinning. "Hair and makeup's coming up."

"All right, tears off," Parker ordered. "Let's get to work."

She'd always enjoyed this part, even though she'd only come in and gone out as needed. Now Parker sat under the hairdresser's hands, a glass of champagne in hers, watching the makeup artist work on Mac.

A new perspective, she mused, enjoying the way Carter's mother hurried in to chat, to laugh, to cry a little, and pleased with how efficiently Monica or Susan checked in. She had to order herself not to get up when Monica reported the groom and his party were in the house, but settled back, assured herself everything would go according to plan.

And it did.

On schedule, she, Emma, and Laurel changed into their gowns. Mac had been right on the colors, the tones, she thought. The deep pumpkin added a glow to Laurel's skin while the russet highlighted Emma's dusky beauty. And the dark gold suited her, she decided.

Together, they looked like shimmering fall flowers.

"We rock," Laurel declared.

"You guys look amazing." In her corset and garters, Mac circled her finger so they'd do a turn. "Oh yeah, just amazing. And oh, Mrs. G, look at you."

"Not bad for an old broad." Mrs. Grady did a turn on her own in her midnight blue gown.

"Your turn," Parker announced.

"Oh boy, oh boy."

They helped her into her wedding dress, smoothing and fluffing the tissue organza overlay, hooking the flirty back with its ruffle train. Parker watched Mac transform as she stood in front of the cheval glass.

"I'm a bride," she murmured, eyes dazed with wonder. "And I'm beautiful."

"Here you are." Mrs. Grady stepped up to hand Mac the diamond earrings Carter had given her. "Little Mackensie— skinny-assed redhead—as beautiful a bride as ever stood in this room."

"Mrs. G." Mac lowered her brow to Mrs. Grady's. "Would you help me with the headband?"

It was a mother's pleasure, Parker thought, to crown the bride. And touching to watch as Mrs. Grady slipped the glittering band into Mac's bright hair.

"It suits you. You were right, Emma, it suits her." Stepping back, Mrs. Grady dabbed at her eyes. "You'll do."

"Not quite yet." Parker opened a drawer in the little bureau, took out a box. "I know you had something else in mind for something borrowed, but I'd like it if you'd wear this."

Opening the box, she took out a delicate diamond necklace, three thin, sparkling strands.

"Parker." Mac barely breathed the word. "It's your mother's."

"My father gave it to her for their anniversary. I know they'd like it if you wore it today, and for me, it's like having them here. A part of them here. They loved you."

"Oh God."

"No crying," Parker ordered.

"Well, you make it damn near impossible not to. I'd love to wear it. I'd love—" Her voice simply broke as she shook her head. "I can't say anything else or I won't make it."

"Here." Parker slipped the strands on, fastened them. "It's perfect."

Lifting her hand, Mac touched the necklace. "I like having them with me today, with all of us."

Monica stepped in. "Oh, Mac, you're just stunning. Carter's going to need oxygen when he sees you. You might need some yourself. He looks incredibly handsome. I wanted to let you know, Karen, you should start the formals. Is there anything I can do for any of you?"

"Is my mother here?" Mac asked her.

"Not yet."

"Probably just as well. Okay, Karen, I'm all yours."

"I want some in here, then out on the terrace, then some with the bouquet before we add your attendants."

"The flowers will be here when you're ready," Emma told her.

"I'm going to check on the guys," Parker told Laurel. "And don't start on me."

"I'm amazed you've held out this long. Go for it."

She slipped out, picked up her skirts, and made a dash to the Groom's Suite. After a quick knock she eased open the door. "Female alert."

"You're cleared," Del called out.

She stepped in. "Monica was right. Carter, you are incredibly handsome." And adorable when the tips of his ears blushed. "All of you look wonderful. I just wanted—"

As Jack moved over to adjust his tie in the mirror, she saw Malcolm, in jeans and a sweatshirt, sipping a beer. "I didn't know you were here. Hanging out with the boys?"

"What? Oh . . . ah. Right."

He looked a little glassy-eyed, she thought, and she started to suggest he go easy on the beer when he set it down.

"Karen's starting on the formals on our side, so she should be ready to start yours in about fifteen minutes. Carter, you're going to want your father. I'll send your mother over when it's time. Oh, and—"

"Out." Del steered her toward the door. "You're MOH not wedding planner today."

"I keep hearing that. Then I guess I'll see you when the clock strikes. Malcolm, I hope you've got a suit with you."

"What am I, an idiot? I've got plenty of time."

"We'll kick him out," Jack told her. "Looking good, Parker. Damn good."

She laughed, did a red-carpet turn. "Yes, I am."

"And don't worry." Bob, Carter's best man and colleague, held up a notebook computer. "I've got it handled on this end. And I memorized the vows just in case he needs me to throw him a line."

"You're a treasure, Bob."

She waited until she was out of earshot to laugh.

"Just in time," Emma said.

"That wasn't long enough for—"

"For the bouquet. I wanted all of us here. Mac." Emma lifted it from its box. "The final touch."

"Oh, Emma, oh wow. I even saw it in progress, but—just wow."

Mac took the waterfall of roses and lilies, deep colors, bold colors given subtle sparkle with tiny glass beads and pearls. It cascaded from waist to knee.

"It's just . . ." She stared down at it, then up at Emma. "The blue butterfly. There's a blue butterfly in the bouquet."

"It's for luck, and love."

"You didn't tell us you were doing that." Laurel moved closer to look. "Emma, you sentimental slob. It's absolutely great."

"Carter has one, too—just a tiny one on his boutonniere."

"I might as well tell you, I put one on the cake—sort of a Where's Waldo? deal."

"Laurel," Mac said with a watery laugh, "you sentimental slob."

"With the butterfly Parker had put on Mac's blue garter, that makes three of us." Emma reached in to take out the other bouquets.

"Just when I thought today couldn't get any more fabulous, it—"

Mac broke off as the door all but blew open and her mother made her entrance in murderous, low-cut red. "Well, don't you all look . . . sweet. Such interesting colors. I left Ari downstairs. I just had to dash up and . . ."

The smirk faded as her eyes tracked over, landed on Mac. Parker had the intense pleasure of seeing the stupefied shock land on Linda's face.

Yeah, that's right, you selfish, self-serving bitch. She's spectacular. And nothing you can say or do will spoil one moment of her day.

"Mackensie, you're lovely. You really are. Oh, my baby's getting married!" She threw up her hands and hurried across the room to embrace Mac. "I never thought I'd see this day come."

Over Linda's head, Mac rolled her eyes and grinned.

No, not a moment spoiled, Parker thought, and grinned back.

★ ★ ★

*M*ALCOLM PACED OUTSIDE THE BRIDE'S SUITE.

How the hell had this happened? Well, he didn't know, but it had happened. So . . . That was that. Or he'd make sure that was that. If she'd ever come out of that damn room.

If he'd worn a watch, he'd be tapping its face to see if the battery was dead.

What could possibly take so long in there? What exactly went on behind that damn locked door?

Finally, it opened, and women came out, all color and scent and sparkle. He stayed out of the way, ready to pounce the minute he saw Parker.

When he did, she—naturally—had her head together with the woman who was running things today.

"Hey."

She glanced back, tilting her head in surprise, then took another minute to recheck whatever she'd probably already checked five times with her stand-in, before walking toward him in that filmy, floaty dress the color of candlelight.

"Why aren't you downstairs? You should be seated. We're about to—"

"I need to talk to you for a minute. For a couple minutes."

"Malcolm, wedding. Now. I can't— Oh God, is there a problem? I knew I should've gone down to check on—"

"There's no problem. Everything's fine. It looks like the freaking wedding of the century. It can wait. Sure, no problem."

"Get down there." She leaned forward, kissed him lightly on the cheek. And turned when Mac stepped out.

"Okay, I'm so ready. Malcolm? Why aren't you downstairs?"

"I'm going. But let me say wow. A really big wow. Nice job. Carter's going to swallow his own tongue."

Her smile shone brighter than her diamonds. "I'm getting married."

"I got the memo. I'll see you later, Mrs. Maguire."

"Mrs. Maguire. Oh boy, hot damn." In her sparkly-heeled wedding shoes, she did a quick jumping dance. "Let's go, Parker."

Parker shot Malcolm one last smile, then led Mac down the hall. "Remember, head up, smile. Take your time, it's your moment. We'll go down in alpha order as we decided, after Carter's niece and nephew."

"Don't they look cute?"

"They do. And when the music hits your cue, remember to hold it there, count to five so everybody stands and gets a load of you. Then—"

"Parker, don't worry. My father's down at the bottom of the stairs, and he'll walk me down the aisle."

Mac's green eyes were calm now, and dry, but shining with joy.

"You're probably never going to tell me what you had to do to get him here, and that's fine. He's here, and it matters to me more than I knew—or would admit. But just like you said yesterday, more important than anything, Carter's down there. My knees are wobbly, but it's not nerves. It's excitement—it's, gosh, it's frigging bliss. I won't miss my cue."

At the top of the staircase, she and Emma and Laurel adjusted the train, gave Mac the bouquet, and stood for a moment as they had as children, smiling down at a blue butterfly.

"MOG being escorted," Parker murmured.

"Have you got an earbud in there?" Laurel demanded.

"No. I just know. Carter and Bob are in front of the fireplace, and the MOG, FOG are taking their seats. Linda's being escorted. I know you're good, Mac, but do a little yoga breathing now. MOB escorted," she said of Mrs. Grady, and Mac squeezed her hand.

"And music change. RB, then FG, both looking adorable." She peered around to watch them start down the steps at Monica's signal. "Seriously adorable."

"Karen's getting the shots, right?"

"Shh. You stop that. Okay. Emma."

"Here we go."

"Five, four, three, two. And Laurel."

"Rolling."

Parker gave Mac's hand a final squeeze. "It's your wedding day," she said, and started down the stairs.

She stopped worrying when she saw the room full of guests, of flowers, of candle- and firelight. When she saw Carter looking like the happiest man ever born. She glanced at Malcolm, puzzled for a moment at the intense look in his eye, then took her place by her friends.

Music change, she thought, and everyone got to their feet.

There was Mac, radiant, on her father's arm, all but floating as she came forward. And Parker's mother's diamonds caught the light and flashed.

Mac kissed her father's cheek. Carter already held out both hands for her. She stepped up, took them. "Hi, cutie." She pulled him in, kissed him lavishly.

"I couldn't wait," she said, loud enough for everyone to hear.

And they got married in the echo of laughter.

*H*E COULDN'T GET HER ALONE, AT LEAST NOT ALONE ENOUGH. There were pictures, and dinner, and crowds of people. Everybody wanted to talk to everybody.

"What's wrong with you?" His mother kicked him under the table. "You're fidgety."

"Nothing's wrong. I just want to get out of this stupid suit."

"Eat your dinner," she ordered, then turned to talk to Emma's father—thank God—and got off his back.

He tried to get to her when the meal was over, but the entire wedding party was herded in one direction, and the guests went in another.

In the Ballroom, Mac and Carter took the floor for their first dance. Watching them, he realized his timing was off. Way off. This day was about them, the rest could wait.

He got himself a beer, told himself to relax.

"Hell of a party, huh?" Jack dropped down beside him.

"They do it right, and apparently they do it righter than right when it's one of their own." He tapped his glass to Jack's. "You're next, partner."

"Can't wait."

Malcolm angled his head, studied Jack's face. "You mean that."

"More every day. Who knew? The big party? That'll be a kick, but it's the rest, the rest of my life I'm waiting for. Emma's. . . She's Emma. That's all she needs to be. Now I'm going to go find her and dance. You ought to grab Parker."

"Yeah, I ought to."

He sat another moment, then rose to start to wind his way through the tables and people. Music pumped out hot, drawing a crowd onto the dance floor.

He paused to watch a moment, and Del stopped on his way by. "Getting some champagne for my future bride. Did you catch Bob out there? He's a wild man on the dance floor."

"You can't miss him."

"It's a damn good day." He laid a hand on Mal's shoulder as they both grinned at Bob. "I know they've already started a life together—Mac and Carter—but this changes it."

"Changes it?"

"It makes it more solid, more real, more important. I've been to countless weddings, but I don't think I really got that until Laurel, until I wanted to make it more solid and real and important. Anyway, if you're looking for Parker, she's that way."

"Thanks."

Screw timing, he decided, and went on the hunt for her.

He spotted her—and Laurel—dancing together. When the music changed, they walked toward him, arm-in-arm.

"How come women can dance together, but when guys do it they look stupid?"

"You don't. You just think you do," Laurel told him. "Seen Del?"

"He's getting your—" He mimed drinking.

"I'll go find him, cut down on the wait. You want?" she asked Parker.

"I do, thanks."

When he had her alone, in a manner of speaking, he took her arm. "Listen, can we go out for a minute? I want—"

"Parker." Linda, a flute in her hand, glided up. "You put on a lovely event. You must have worked day and night for weeks to pull this off. It's no wonder you look tired."

"Do I?" Parker said, icily sweet. "It must be the lighting in here. I was just thinking how that shade of red, in this light, makes you look shallow. I mean sallow. Malcolm, you've met Mac's mother, haven't you?"

"Yeah. How's it going?"

Linda tossed her luxurious mane of blond hair, aimed her hot baby blues at him. "It's going very well, thanks. We've met? I can't believe that, as I never forget a gorgeous man." She gave him her hand, angled her body in. "When did we meet?"

"When you offered me a blow job."

Beside him, Parker made a choking sound. Linda reared back, shot Parker a vicious look. "You should take more care in who you invite into your home."

"I've already done that. This is your one free pass. Enjoy it. Let's dance, Malcolm. I really want to dance with you at my friend's wedding."

She drew him onto the floor, then just dropped her head on his shoulder, shaking with laughter. "Oh. Oh. You are going to be rewarded so very well at the first opportunity. That was—" She lifted her head, put her hands on the sides of his face and kissed him until his head swam.

"Come on." He dragged her away from the music.

"But I want to—"

"Five minutes, damn it."

People were every-fucking-where, he realized. He pulled her out of the Ballroom, down the stairs, ignoring her objections. He evaluated, then headed for her wing until he jerked her into the gym.

Nobody was going to come in there during a wedding reception.

"What in the world is this about?"

"Listen. You just listen to me."

"I am listening to you."

He took a breath. "Yeah, you listen to me, and that's why I end up telling you things I've never told anybody, never intended to tell anybody. You get inside, that's what you do, get inside and see what's in there, and it's okay with you."

"Why wouldn't it be? Malcolm, how much have you had to drink?"

"Probably not enough for this. I was never going here, not

with anyone. It just didn't seem like I'd be any good at it—and, well, damn it, it's important for me to be good at what I do."

He turned away from her and walked away, looking for his breath and his balance. "I spent the first decade of my life moving around, and that was okay, it's the way it was. I spent most of the second mad at the fucking world and raising hell. Then I tried to do better, in my own way."

He dragged a hand through his hair. "I did better, then I got my ass kicked. Fate, bad luck, whatever. I took the second chance, and made some changes. Through all of that, there was one person who stuck with me."

"Your mother is an amazing woman."

"Damn right. I've got a good business. I know how to run it, how to build it. I like what I do. No, I love what I do."

"That's why you're good at it. I wish you'd tell me what's wrong."

"I didn't say anything was wrong. I'm just . . ." He stood for a moment, just staring at her. "It was never supposed to be you, that's for damn sure."

"What are you talking about?"

"You said you loved me."

"So, you did hear me." She turned away now, walked over to open the minifridge for water.

"Of course I heard you. There's nothing wrong with my hearing."

"You just chose to ignore me."

"I didn't. You blindsided me, Parker. You knocked me flat. I never figured you'd feel about me the way I feel about you."

She lowered the water, and her gaze came back slowly to his. "How do you feel about me?"

"Like . . . How the hell did Carter put it? He's got the words."

"I don't want Carter's words. I'm not in love with Carter."

"I feel like you must be the reason I got through all the moving around, the raising hell. The reason I didn't die. The reason I'm here. I feel—"

He broke off, cursed under his breath as she simply stood there, beautiful, perfect, glowing.

"Listen I've got to grab some of Carter's words. It's when you love somebody and they love you, even where you're screwed up, everything clicks.

"Everything's clicked, Parker. So there it is."

She set the water down on a weight bench. "I always imagined, when this moment happened to me, it would be very different from this."

Irritation moved over his face. "So there's no poetry and moonbeams. I'm wearing a damn suit."

She laughed. "I'm so glad that this moment happened exactly this way, with you, right here, right now." She started toward him.

"I'm not finished."

And stopped. "Oh. Sorry."

"Okay. We need to do it."

Her eyes widened. "Excuse me?"

Everything in him relaxed. He just *loved* how she said those two words. "Jesus, Legs, get your mind off sex. I mean we need to . . ." He circled his finger toward the ceiling.

"I'm afraid I can't crack your ingenious code."

"We need to get married."

"We . . ." She stepped back, and joined the water on the weight bench. "Well. God."

"Look, if you know me and love me anyway, you get that I'm not going to get down on one knee and recite something some dead guy wrote a couple centuries ago. Damn it." He walked over, pulled her to her feet. "I could probably do better. I know how you work now. I know it's not just the details, but what the details make. What's going on up there—it's a great party, but it's what comes after that counts. You want what counts."

"You're right," she said quietly. "That's how I work. But it's not just about what I want."

"If you're looking for the full deal, the till-death deal, then look at me. No one's ever going to love you, stick by you, understand how you work the way I do. No one, Parker."

Her hands wanted to tremble, so she laid them on his face for a moment, looked in his eyes. "Tell me what you want."

He took her wrists, then linked fingers with hers. "I want a life with you, and I'm stealing from Jack and Del now—sort of. I want to start that life because you're Parker. You're it, you're all. I want to make what we have solid. I want—and this is all me this time—I want to make promises to you, and I want to keep them. I love you, and I want to promise to love you for the rest of my life."

He blew out a breath. "What do you say?"

"What do I say? I say yes." Giddy with joy, she laughed, squeezed his hands hard. "Yes, Malcolm, we need to do it." She threw her arms around him. "Oh, you're perfect. I don't know why, but you're absolutely perfect."

"I thought Carter was the luckiest man alive today. He just got bumped into second position." He pulled her back, took her mouth with his, swaying with the kiss. "I don't have a ring or anything on me."

"You damn well better get one soon."

"Check." He lifted both her hands to his lips, made her eyes shine when he pressed kisses to them. "I owe you a dance."

"Yes, you do, and I really want to dance with you. We've got to get back. It's Mac's night."

"We'll tell them tomorrow, so we don't take any of the shine off."

Yes, she thought, he knew how she worked. She framed his face again, and again kissed the man she loved. The man she would marry. "Tomorrow's soon enough."

She walked back with him, hand-in-hand, toward the music, the flowers, the sparkling lights. Tonight, she thought, was Mac's night. And it was the start of her own happy ever after.

EPILOGUE

$\mathscr{N}$EW YEAR'S DAY, PARKER THOUGHT AS SHE SETTLED DOWN AT HER desk to catch up with paperwork. The holidays, the parties, the events, Mac's wedding, had all combined to put her a little behind.

Add her own engagement, she mused, and held up her hand so her pretty diamond ring caught the wispy winter sunlight, and there was no wonder she'd slipped a bit off schedule.

She had all afternoon to take care of it, to reset the clock, so to speak. And to turn the calendar on a very eventful year.

What a difference twelve months could make.

Four engagements and a wedding.

A year ago, she hadn't known Malcolm Kavanaugh existed, and now in ten months they'd be married. God, she had a *ton* of planning and work and research to do.

She was going to marry the man she loved, and the wedding was damn well going to kick some serious ass. She studied her ring again until her eyes went dreamy. She'd ended and begun her first year with Malcolm. It was just the beginning.

And this, she reminded herself, was why she wasn't getting any work done. She already had Bride Brain Syndrome.

She booted up her computer.

She'd work in a quiet house, she thought, uninterrupted.

Mrs. Grady should be finishing up her packing for her annual winter vacation. Mac and Carter would be doing the same for their honeymoon. She imagined Del and Laurel, Emma and Jack, would all be cozied up in their own spaces, lazing the day away.

And Malcolm—*her* Malcolm—had already left for the garage where he planned to catch up on some work.

Tonight, they'd have a farewell dinner to send the three travelers off in style.

Then she and her Malcolm could take a few days—Vows always slowed down after the first of the year—for a quick winter break at the beach house. Just the two of them.

"So buckle down, Parker," she muttered. "You're not the only bride who needs attention."

She managed nearly an hour before the invasion.

"Why are you working?" Laurel asked as she walked into Parker's office with Emma and Mac.

"Because it's what I do. Why aren't you packing?"

"Packed." Mac made a check mark in the air. "Florence, here we come. But right now . . ." The three of them moved forward, pulled her right out of her chair. "You're coming with us."

"Do you know how far behind I am—"

"Five minutes, if that," was Emma's estimate.

"We may not have an event for two weeks, but—"

"Last night's went great, and I know damn well you're already packed even though you're not leaving for two days. You probably packed for Mal," Laurel said.

"I did not. I simply gave him a list of suggestions. Really, I just need another hour. We're all having dinner later anyway."

"We have more important things to do now than work." Mac kept a firm grip on Parker's arm as they steered her toward the stairs.

"You may, but I . . ." The light dawned as she realized the direction. "You picked out a wedding dress for me."

"It's a women of Vows tradition." Emma patted Parker's butt. "We ordered the men to make themselves scarce this afternoon. We're going to have a Parker's wedding dress party."

"With the qualification, as always, if it doesn't suit you, no harm, no foul." At the door of the Bride's Suite, Laurel turned, blocked the door. "Are you ready?"

"Of course I am. Wait." Parker laughed, laid a hand on her heart. "Wow. I'm having a moment, a really good moment. I've helped pick out so many of them, and now I'm going to try one on."

"And you're going to look beautiful. Open the door, Laurel, I'm dying here," Emma ordered.

"Here we go."

With her hand still on her heart, Parker stepped in. And her hand simply slid down to her side.

The bride-white silk flowed from the strapless, sweetheart bodice, down the narrow torso to a full skirt. The classic ballgown style shimmered with intricate beadwork and embroidery, sparkling on the bodice, trailing down the side, circling the sweeping hem and train.

Its lines, its style, would, unquestionably, suit her. But that wasn't what blurred her vision.

"It's my mother's wedding gown. It's Mom's."

"Mrs. G got it out of storage." As she spoke, Emma rubbed her hand up and down Parker's back.

"She was slim like you, and she was nearly as tall." Mrs. Grady dabbed at her eyes. "You may want to pick out your own, something new, but we thought—"

Parker shook her head, unable to speak, and simply turned to wrap her arms around Mrs. Grady.

"I can't take pictures if I'm crying." Mac grabbed at the tissues always on hand in the room.

"Here, everybody, drink some champagne, and suck it up." Laurel swiped a hand over her damp cheek before she poured.

"Thank you." Parker kissed both Mrs. Grady's cheeks. "Thanks, all of you. Yes, God, give me that." Parker took a flute of champagne from Laurel, a tissue from Emma.

"It's beautiful," she managed. "Absolutely beautiful. I've only seen it in pictures, only seen how wonderful she looked in it, how happy she and Dad looked. She married my father in that dress, and now I'll have both of them with me when I marry Malcolm. It's the best gift you could give me. The best."

"Well, for God's sake, try it on. Strip down, Brown," Laurel ordered.

"Okay. Here goes."

"Back to the mirror," Emma reminded her. "No looking until you're done."

They helped her into the gown, as she had helped each of them.

"Turn around, but close your eyes. I want to fuss with the skirt and train." Already thinking bouquets, Emma spread out the hem, swept the train. She glanced at Mac, got the nod as Mac positioned herself and her camera. "Okay, take a look."

In the mirror Parker saw on her face what she'd seen on so many other brides'. The thrill, the wonder, the glow.

"This was my mother's wedding gown," she murmured. "And now it's mine."

"Parks." Mac repositioned, pressed the shutter again. "You look spectacular."

"Happy's what you look." Mrs. Grady beamed at her. "Happy and in love. Nothing fits a bride more truly."

"I'm a bride. I'm happy and in love, and I look spectacular."

"Put that camera down, Mackensie." Mrs. Grady lifted her own. "I want my shot of the four of you. Don't step on the train! There. Now, think Wedding Day."

When they laughed, she snapped.

"Let's have a toast. Everybody get their glasses. Emma, you lush," Laurel accused. "Yours is empty."

"It helped me stop crying."

Refilled, Emma lifted her glass with the others.

"To a monumental year," Laurel began.

"Oh boy, howdy," Mac put in.

"To our men," she continued, "who are lucky to have us. To our mom."

Mrs. Grady teared up again. "Don't start."

"To friendship."

"And to Vows," Parker added. "And the women who run it. We marry you with love, with style, and with exquisite attention to detail. Especially when we marry us."

They laughed, clinked. As they drank, Mrs. Grady stepped back and took another picture. They began to talk of headpieces, of flowers, colors for the gowns the other girls would wear.

Her girls, she thought, all happy and in love, and all spectacular.

To my girls, she thought, lifting her glass in a solo toast. To the Brides of Vows, and their happy ever afters.

GO BACK TO WHERE IT ALL BEGAN, WITH

VISION *in* WHITE

THE FIRST NOVEL IN THE BRIDE QUARTET.

TURN THE PAGE FOR A SPECIAL EXCERPT . . .

PROLOGUE

*B*Y THE TIME SHE WAS EIGHT, MACKENSIE ELLIOT HAD BEEN MAR-
ried fourteen times. She'd married each of her three best friends—
as both bride and groom—her best friend's brother (under his
protest), two dogs, three cats, and a rabbit.

She'd served at countless other weddings as maid of honor,
bridesmaid, groomsman, best man, and officiant.

Though the dissolutions were invariably amicable, none of the
marriages lasted beyond an afternoon. The transitory aspect of
marriage came as no surprise to Mac, as her own parents boasted
two each—so far.

Wedding Day wasn't her favorite game, but she kind of liked
being the priest or the reverend or the justice of the peace. Or,
after attending her father's second wife's nephew's bar mitzvah, the
rabbi.

Plus, she enjoyed the cupcakes or fancy cookies and fizzy lemonade always served at the reception.

It was Parker's favorite game, and Wedding Day always took place on the Brown Estate, with its expansive gardens, pretty groves, and silvery pond. In the cold Connecticut winters, the ceremony might take place in front of one of the roaring fires inside the big house.

They had simple weddings and elaborate affairs. Royal weddings, star-crossed elopements, circus themes, and pirate ships. All ideas were seriously considered and voted upon, and no theme or costume too outrageous.

Still, with fourteen marriages under her belt, Mac grew a bit weary of Wedding Day.

Until she experienced her seminal moment.

For her eighth birthday Mackensie's charming and mostly absent father sent her a Nikon camera. She'd never expressed any interest in photography, and initially pushed it away with the other odd gifts he'd given or sent since the divorce. But Mac's mother told her mother, and Grandma muttered and complained about "feckless, useless Geoffrey Elliot" and the inappropriate gift of an adult camera for a young girl who'd be better off with a Barbie doll.

As she habitually disagreed with her grandmother on principle, Mac's interest in the camera piqued. To annoy Grandma—who was visiting for the summer instead of being in her retirement community in Scottsdale, where Mac strongly believed she belonged—Mac hauled the Nikon around with her. She toyed with it, experimented. She took pictures of her room, of her feet, of her friends. Shots that were blurry and dark, or fuzzy and washed out. With her lack of success, and her mother's impending divorce from her stepfather, Mac's interest in the Nikon began to wane. Even years later she couldn't say what prompted her to bring it along to Parker's that pretty summer afternoon for Wedding Day.

Every detail of the traditional garden wedding had been

planned. Emmaline as the bride and Laurel as groom would exchange their vows beneath the rose arbor. Emma would wear the lace veil and train Parker's mother had made out of an old tablecloth, while Harold, Parker's aging and affable golden retriever, walked her down the garden path to give her away.

A selection of Barbies, Kens, and Cabbage Patch Kids, along with a variety of stuffed animals lined the path as guests.

"It's a very private ceremony," Parker relayed as she fussed with Emma's veil. "With a small patio reception to follow. Now, where's the best man?"

Laurel, her knee recently skinned, shoved through a trio of hydrangeas. "He ran away, and went up a tree after a squirrel. I can't get him to come down."

Parker rolled her eyes. "I'll get him. You're not supposed to see the bride before the wedding. It's bad luck. Mac, you need to fix Emma's veil and get her bouquet. Laurel and I'll get Mr. Fish out of the tree."

"I'd rather go swimming," Mac said as she gave Emma's veil an absent tug.

"We can go after I get married."

"I guess. Aren't you tired of getting married?"

"Oh, I don't mind. And it smells so good out here. Everything's so pretty."

Mac gave Emma the clutch of dandelions and wild violets they were allowed to pick. "You look pretty."

It was invariably true. Emma's dark, shiny hair tumbled under the white lace. Her eyes sparkled a deep, deep brown as she sniffed the weed bouquet. She was tanned, sort of all golden, Mac thought, and scowled at her own milk white skin.

The curse of a redhead, her mother said, as she got her carroty hair from her father. At eight, Mac was tall for her age and skinny as a stick, with teeth already trapped in hated braces.

She thought that, beside her, Emmaline looked like a gypsy princess.

Parker and Laurel came back, giggling with the feline best man clutched in Parker's arms. "Everybody has to take their places." Parker poured the cat into Laurel's arms. "Mac, you need to get dressed! Emma—"

"I don't want to be maid of honor." Mac looked at the poofy Cinderella dress draped over a garden bench. "That thing's scratchy, and it's hot. Why can't Mr. Fish be maid of honor, and I'll be best man?"

"Because it's already planned. Everybody's nervous before a wedding." Parker flipped back her long brown pigtails, then picked up the dress to inspect it for tears or stains. Satisfied, she pushed it at Mac. "It's okay. It's going to be a beautiful ceremony, with true love and happy ever after."

"My mother says happy ever after's a bunch of bull."

There was a moment of silence after Mac's statement. The unspoken word *divorce* seemed to hang in the air.

"I don't think it has to be." Her eyes full of sympathy, Parker reached out, ran her hand along Mac's bare arm.

"I don't want to wear the dress. I don't want to be a bridesmaid. I—"

"Okay. That's okay. We can have a pretend maid of honor. Maybe you could take pictures."

Mac looked down at the camera she'd forgotten hung around her neck. "They never come out right."

"Maybe they will this time. It'll be fun. You can be the official wedding photographer."

"Take one of me and Mr. Fish," Laurel insisted, and pushed her face and the cat's together. "Take one, Mac!"

With little enthusiasm, Mac lifted the camera, pressed the shutter.

"We should've thought of this before! You can take formal portraits of the bride and groom, and more pictures during the ceremony." Busy with the new idea, Parker hung the Cinderella costume on the hydrangea bush. "It'll be good, it'll be fun. You need to go down the path with the bride and Harold. Try to take some good ones. I'll wait, then start the music. Let's go!"

There would be cupcakes and lemonade, Mac reminded herself. And swimming later, and fun. It didn't matter if the pictures were stupid, didn't matter that her grandmother was right and she was too young for the camera.

It didn't matter that her mother was getting divorced again, or that her stepfather, who'd been okay, had already moved out.

It didn't matter that happy ever after was bull, because it was all pretend anyway.

She tried to take pictures of Emma and the obliging Harold, imagined getting the film back and seeing the blurry figures and smudges of her thumb, like always.

When the music started she felt bad that she hadn't put on the scratchy dress and given Emma a maid of honor, just because her mother and grandmother had put her in a bad mood. So she circled around to stand to the side and tried harder to take a nice picture of Harold walking Emma down the garden path.

It looked different through the lens, she thought, the way she could focus on Emma's face—the way the veil lay over her hair. And the way the sun shined through the lace was pretty.

She took more pictures as Parker began the "Dearly Beloved" as the Reverend Whistledown, as Emma and Laurel took hands and Harold curled up to sleep and snore at their feet.

She noticed how bright Laurel's hair was, how the sun caught the edges of it beneath the tall black hat she wore as groom. How Mr. Fish's whiskers twitched as he yawned.

When it happened, it happened as much inside Mac as out.

Her three friends were grouped under the lush white curve of the arbor, a triangle of pretty young girls. Some instinct had Mac shifting her position, just slightly, tilting the camera just a bit. She didn't know it as composition, only that it looked nicer through the lens.

And the blue butterfly fluttered across her range of vision to land on the head of a butter yellow dandelion in Emma's bouquet. The surprise and pleasure struck the three faces in that triangle under the white roses almost as one.

Mac pressed the shutter.

She knew, *knew*, the photograph wouldn't be blurry and dark or fuzzy and washed out. Her thumb wouldn't be blocking the lens. She knew exactly what the picture would look like, knew her grandmother had been wrong after all.

Maybe happy ever after was bull, but she knew she wanted to take more pictures of moments that *were* happy. Because then they were ever after.

CHAPTER ONE

𝒪N JANUARY FIRST, MAC ROLLED OVER TO SMACK HER ALARM CLOCK, and ended up facedown on the floor of her studio.

"Shit. Happy New Year."

She lay, groggy and baffled, until she remembered she'd never made it upstairs into bed—and the alarm was from her computer, set to wake her at noon.

She pushed herself up to stagger to the kitchen and the coffeemaker.

Why did people want to get married on New Year's Eve? Why would they make a formal ritual out of a holiday designed for marathon drinking and probably inappropriate sex? And they just had to drag family and friends into it, not to mention wedding photographers.

Of course, when the reception had finally ended at two A.M., she could've gone to bed like a sane person instead of uploading the shots, reviewing them—spending nearly three more hours on the Hines-Myers wedding photos.

But, boy, she'd gotten some good ones. A few great ones.

Or they were all crap and she'd judged them in a euphoric blur.

No, they were good shots.

She added three spoons of sugar to the black coffee and drank it while standing at the window, looking out at the snow blanketing the gardens and lawns of the Brown Estate.

They'd done a good job on the wedding, she thought. And maybe Bob Hines and Vicky Myers would take a clue from that and do a good job on the marriage.

Either way, the memories of the day wouldn't fade. The moments, big and small, were captured. She'd refine them, finesse them, print them. Bob and Vicky could revisit the day through those images next week or sixty years from next week.

That, she thought, was as potent as sweet, black coffee on a cold winter day.

Opening a cupboard, she pulled out a box of Pop-Tarts and, eating one where she stood, went over her schedule for the day.

Clay-McFearson (Rod and Alison) wedding at six. Which meant the bride and her party would arrive by three, groom and his by four. That gave her until two for the pre-event summit meeting at the main house.

Time enough to shower, dress, go over her notes, check and recheck her equipment. Her last check of the day's weather called for sunny skies, high of thirty-two. She should be able to get some nice preparation shots using natural light and maybe talk Alison— if she was game—into a bridal portrait on the balcony with the snow in the background.

Mother of the bride, Mac remembered—Dorothy (call me Dottie)—was on the pushy and demanding side, but she'd be dealt with. If Mac couldn't handle her personally, God knew Parker would. Parker could and did handle anyone and anything.

Parker's drive and determination had turned Vows into one of the top wedding and event planning companies in the state in a five-year period. It had turned the tragedy of her parents' deaths into hope, and the gorgeous Victorian home and the stunning grounds of the Brown Estate into a thriving and unique business.

And, Mac thought as she swallowed the last of the Pop-Tart, she herself was one of the reasons.

She moved through the studio toward the stairs to her upstairs bed and bath, stopped at one of her favorite photos. The glowing, ecstatic bride with her face lifted, her arms stretched, palms up, caught in a shower of pink rose petals.

Cover of *Today's Bride*, Mac thought. Because I'm just that good.

In her thick socks, flannel pants, and sweatshirt she climbed the stairs to transform herself from tired, pj-clad, Pop-Tart addict into sophisticated wedding photojournalist.

She ignored her unmade bed—why make it when you were just going to mess it up again?—and the bedroom clutter. The hot shower worked with the sugar and caffeine to clear out any remaining cobwebs so she could put her mind seriously to today's job.

She had a bride who was interested in trying the creative, a passive-aggressive MOB who thought she knew best, a groom so dazzling in love he'd do anything to make his bride happy. And both her B and G were seriously photogenic.

The last fact made the job both pleasure and challenge. Just how could she give her clients a photo journey of their day that was spectacular, and uniquely theirs?

Bride's colors, she thought, flipping through her mental files as she washed her short, shaggy crop of red hair. Silver and gold. Elegant, glamorous.

She'd had a look at the flowers and the cake—both getting their finishing touches today—the favors and linens, attendants' wardrobes, headdresses. She had a copy of the playlist from the band with the first dance, mother-son, father-daughter dances highlighted.

So, she thought, for the next several hours, her world would revolve around Rod and Alison.

She chose her suit, her jewelry, her makeup with nearly the same care as she chose her equipment. Loaded, she went out to make the short trek from the pool house that held her studio and little apartment to the main house.

The snow sparkled, crushed diamonds over ermine, and the air was cold and clean as mountain ice. She definitely had to get some outside shots, daylight and evening. Winter wedding, white wedding, snow on the ground, ice glistening on the trees, just dripping from the denuded willows over the pond. And there the fanciful old Victorian with its myriad rooflines, the arched and porthole windows, rising and spreading, soft blue against the hard shell of sky. Its terraces and generous portico heralded the season with their festoons of lights and greenery.

She studied it as she often did as she walked the shoveled paths. She loved the lines of it, the angles of it, with its subtle touches of pale yellow, creamy white picked out in that soft, subtle blue.

It had been as much home to her as her own growing up. Often more so, she admitted, as her own had run on her mother's capricious whims. Parker's parents had been warm, welcoming, loving and—Mac thought now—steady. They'd given her a calm port in the storm of her own childhood.

She'd grieved as much as her friend at their loss nearly seven years before.

Now the Brown Estate was her home. Her business. Her life. And a good one on every level. What could be better than doing something you loved, and doing it with the best friends you'd ever had?

She went in through the mudroom to hang up her outdoor gear, then circled around to peek into Laurel's domain.

Her friend and partner stood on a step stool, meticulously adding silver calla lilies to the five tiers of a wedding cake. Each flower bloomed at the base of a gold acanthus leaf to glimmering, elegant effect.

"That's a winner, McBane."

Laurel's hand was steady as a surgeon's as she added the next lily. Her sunny hair was twisted at the back of her head into a messy knot that somehow suited the angular triangle of her face. As she worked, her eyes, bright as bluebells, held narrowed concentration.

"I'm so glad she went for the lily centerpiece instead of the bride and groom topper. It makes this design. Wait until we get to the ballroom and add it."

Mac pulled out a camera. "It's a good shot for the website. Okay?"

"Sure. Get any sleep?"

"Didn't hit until about five, but I stayed down till noon. You?"

"Down by two thirty. Up at seven to finish the groom's cake, the desserts—and this. I'm so damn glad we have two weeks before the next wedding." She glanced over. "Don't tell Parker I said that."

"She's up, I assume."

"She's been in here twice. She's probably been everywhere twice. I think I heard Emma come in. They may be up in the office by now."

"I'm heading up. Are you coming?"

"Ten minutes. I'll be on time."

"On time is late in Parker's world." Mac grinned. "I'll try to distract her."

"Just tell her some things can't be rushed. And that the MOB's going to get so many compliments on this cake she'll stay off our backs."

"That one could work."

Mac started out, winding through to check the entrance foyer and the massive drawing room where the ceremony itself would take place. Emmaline and her elves had already been at work, she noted, undressing from the last wedding, redressing for the new. Every bride had her own vision, and this one wanted lots of gold and silver ribbon and swag as opposed to the lavender and cream voile of New Year's Eve.

The fire was set in the drawing room and would be lit before the guests began to arrive. White-draped chairs sparkling with silver bows formed row after row. Emma had already dressed the mantel with gold candles in silver holders, and the bride's favorite white calla lilies massed in tall, thin glass vases.

Mac circled the room, considered angles, lighting, composition— and made more notes as she walked out and took the stairs to the third floor.

As she expected, she found Parker in the conference room of their office, surrounded by her laptop, BlackBerry, folders, cell phone, and headset. Her dense brown hair hung in a long tail— sleek and simple. It worked with the suit—a quiet dove gray—that would blend in and complement the bride's colors.

Parker missed no tricks.

She didn't look up but circled a finger in the air as she continued to work on the laptop. Knowing the signal, Mac crossed to the coffee counter and filled mugs for both of them. She sat, laid down her own file, opened her own notebook.

Parker sat back, smiled, and picked up her mug. "It's going to be a good one."

"No doubt."

"Roads are clear, weather's good. The bride's up, had breakfast and a massage. The groom's had a workout and a swim. Caterers are on schedule. All attendants are accounted for." She checked her watch. "Where are Emma and Laurel?"

"Laurel's putting the finishing touches on the cake, which is stupendous. I haven't seen Emma, but she's started dressing the event areas. Pretty. I want some outdoor shots. Before and after."

"Don't keep the bride outside for too long before. We don't want her red-nosed and sniffling."

"You may have to keep the MOB off my back."

"Already noted."

Emma rushed in, a Diet Coke in one hand, a file in the other. "Tink's hungover and a no-show, so I'm one short. Let's keep this brief, okay?" She dropped down at the table. Her curling black hair bounced over the shoulders of her sweatshirt. "The Bride's Suite and the Drawing Room are dressed. Foyer and stairway, nearly finished. The bouquets, corsages, and boutonnieres checked. We've started on the Grand Hall and the Ballroom. I need to get back to that."

"Flower girl?"

"White rose pomander, silver and gold ribbon. I have her halo—roses and baby's breath—ready for the hairdresser. It's adorable. Mac, I need some pictures of the arrangements if you can fit it in. If not, I'll get them."

"I'll take care of it."

"Thanks. The MOB—"

"I'm on it," Parker said.

"I need to—" Emma broke off as Laurel walked in.

"I'm not late," Laurel announced.

"Tink's a no-show," Parker told her. "Emma's short."

"I can fill in. I'll need to set the centerpiece of the cake and arrange the desserts, but I've got time now."

"Let's go over the timetable."

"Wait." Emma lifted her can of Diet Coke. "Toast first. Happy New Year to us, to four amazing, stupendous, and very hot women. Best pals ever."

"Also smart and kick-ass." Laurel raised her bottle of water. "To pals and partners."

"To us. Friendship and brains in four parts," Mac added, "and the sheer coolness of the whole we've made with Vows."

"And to 2009." Parker lifted her coffee mug. "The amazing, stupendous, hot, smart, kick-ass best pals are going to have their best year ever."

"Damn right." Mac clinked her mug to the rest. "To Wedding Day, then, now, and always."

"Then, now, and always," Parker repeated. "And now. Time-table?"

"I'm on the bride," Mac began, "from her arrival, switch to groom at his. Candids during dressing event, posed as applies. For-mal portraits in and out. I'll get the shots of the cake, the arrange-ments now, do my setup. All family and wedding party shots separate prior to the ceremony. Post-ceremony I should only need forty-five minutes for the family shots, full wedding party, and the bride and groom."

"Floral dressing in bride and groom suites complete by three. Floral dressing in foyer, Parlor, staircase, Grand Hall, and Ballroom by five." Parker glanced at Emma.

"We'll be done."

"Videographer arrives at five thirty. Guest arrivals from five thirty to six. Wedding musicians—string quartet—to begin at five forty. The band will be set up in the Ballroom by six thirty. MOG, at-tended by son, escorted at five fifty, MOB, escorted by son-in-law, directly after. Groom and groomsmen in place at six." Parker read off the schedule. "FOB, bride, and party in place at six. Descent and procession. Ceremony duration twenty-three minutes, recession, family moments. Guests escorted to Grand Hall at six twenty-five."

"Bar opens," Laurel said, "music, passed food."

"Six twenty-five to seven ten, photographs. Announcement of family, wedding party, and the new Mr. and Mrs. seven fifteen."

"Dinner, toasts," Emma continued. "We've got it, Parks."

"I want to make sure we move to the Ballroom and have the first dance by eight fifteen," Parker continued. "The bride especially wants her grandmother there for the first dance, and after the father-daughter, mother-son dance, for her father and his mother to dance. She's ninety, and may fade early. If we can have the cake cutting at nine thirty, the grandmother should make that, too."

"She's a sweetheart," Mac put in. "I got some nice shots of her and Alison at the rehearsal. I've got it in my notes to get some of them today. Personally, I think she'll stay for the whole deal."

"I hope she does. Cake and desserts served while dancing continues. Bouquet toss at ten fifteen."

"Tossing bouquet is set," Emma added.

"Garter toss, dancing continues. Last dance at ten fifty, bubble blowing, bride and groom depart. Event end, eleven." Parker checked her watch again. "Let's get it done. Emma and Laurel need to change. Everyone remember their headsets."

Parker's phone vibrated, and she glanced at the readout. "MOB. Again. Fourth call this morning."

"Have fun with that," Mac said, and escaped.

She scouted room by room, staying out of the way of Emma and her crew as they swarmed over the house with flowers, ribbons, voile. She took shots of Laurel's cake, Emma's arrangements, framed others in her head.

It was a routine she never allowed to become routine. She knew once it became rote, she'd miss shots, opportunities, bog down on fresh angles and ideas. And whenever she felt herself dulling, she thought of a blue butterfly landing on a dandelion.

The air smelled of roses and lilies and rang with voices and footfalls. Light streamed through the tall windows in lovely beams and shafts, and glittered on the gold and silver ribbons.

"Headset, Mac!" Parker rushed down the main staircase. "The bride's arriving."

As Parker hurried down to meet the bride, Mac jogged up. She swung out on the front terrace, ignoring the cold as the white limo sailed down the drive. As it eased to a stop she shifted her angle, set, and waited.

Maid of honor, mother of the bride. "Move, move, just a little," she muttered. Alison stepped out. The bride wore jeans, Uggs, a battered suede jacket, and a bright red scarf. Mac zoomed in, changed stops. "Hey! Alison!"

The bride looked up. Surprise turned to amused delight, and to Mac's pleasure, Alison threw up both arms, tossed back her head, and laughed.

And there, Mac thought as she caught the moment, was the beginning of the journey.

Within ten minutes, the Bride's Suite—once Parker's own bedroom—bustled with people and confusion. Two hairdressers plied their tools and talents, curling, straightening, styling, while others wielded paints and pots.

Utterly female, Mac thought as she moved through the room unobtrusively, the scents, the motions, the sounds. The bride remained the focus—no nerves on this one, Mac determined. Alison was confident, beaming, and currently chattering like a magpie.

The MOB, however, was a different story.

"But you have such beautiful hair! Don't you think you should leave it down? At least some of it. Maybe—"

"An updo suits the headdress better. Relax, Mom."

"It's too warm in here. I think it's too warm in here. And Mandy should take a quick nap. She's going to act up, I just know it."

"She'll be fine." Alison glanced toward the flower girl.

"I really think—"

"Ladies!" Parker wheeled in a cart of champagne, with a pretty fruit and cheese tray. "The men are on their way. Alison, your hair's gorgeous. Absolutely regal." She poured a flute, offered it to the bride.

"I really don't think she should drink before the ceremony. She barely ate today, and—"

"Oh, Mrs. McFearson, I'm so glad you're dressed and ready. You look fabulous. If I could just steal you for a few minutes? I'd love for you to take a look at the Drawing Room before the ceremony. We want to make sure it's perfect, don't we? I'll have her back in no time." Parker pushed champagne into the MOB's hand, and steered her out of the room.

Alison said, "Whew!" and laughed.

For the next hour, Mac split herself between the Bride's and Groom's suites. Between perfume and tulle, cuff links and cummerbunds. She eased back into the bride's domain, circled around the attendants as they dressed and helped one another dress. And found Alison alone, standing in front of her wedding dress.

It was all there, Mac thought as she quietly framed the shot. The wonder, the joy—with just that tiny tug of sorrow. She snapped the image as Alison reached out to brush her fingers over the sparkle of the bodice.

Decisive moment, Mac knew, when everything the woman felt reflected on her face.

Then it passed, and Alison glanced over.

"I didn't expect to feel this way. I'm so happy. I'm so in love with Rod, so ready to marry him. But there's this little clutch right here." She rubbed her fingers just above her heart. "It's not nerves."

"Sadness. Just a touch. One phase of your life ends today. You're allowed to be sad to say good-bye. I know what you need. Wait here."

A moment later, Mac led Alison's grandmother over. And once again stepped back.

Youth and age, she thought. Beginnings and endings, connections and constancy. And, love.

She snapped the embrace, but that wasn't it. She snapped the glitter of tears, and still, no. Then Alison lowered her forehead to her grandmother's, and even as her lips curved, a single tear slid down her cheek while the dress glowed and glittered behind them.

Perfect. The blue butterfly.

She took candids of the ritual while the bride dressed, then the formal portraits with exquisite natural light. As she'd expected, Alison was game to brave the cold on the terrace.

And Mac ignored Parker's voice through her headset as she rushed to the Groom's Suite to repeat the process with Rod.

She passed Parker in the hallway as she strode back to the bride. "I need the groom and party downstairs, Mac. We're running two minutes behind."

"Oh my God!" Mac said in mock horror and ducked into the Bride's Suite.

"Guests are seated," Parker announced in her ear moments later. "Groom and groomsmen taking position. Emma, gather the bridal party."

"On it."

Mac slipped out to take her stand at the bottom of the stairs as Emma organized the bridesmaids.

"Party ready. Cue the music."

"Cuing music," Parker said, "start the procession."

The flower girl would clearly be fine without the nap, Mac decided as the child nearly danced her way down the staircase. She paused like a vet at Laurel's signal, then continued at a dignified pace in her fairy dress across the foyer, into the enormous Parlor, and down the aisle formed by the chairs.

The attendants followed, shimmering silver, and at last, the maid of honor in gold.

Mac crouched to aim up as the bride and her father stood at the top of the stairs, holding hands. As the bride's music swelled, he lifted his daughter's hand to his lips, then to his cheek.

Even as she took the shot, Mac's eyes stung.

Where was her own father? she wondered. Jamaica? Switzerland? Cairo?

She pushed the thought and the ache that came with it aside, and did her job.

Using Emma's candlelight, she captured joy and tears. The memories. And stayed invisible and separate.